THE
BLOOD
OF
BROTHERS

A SYCAMORE MOON NOVEL

DOMINO FINN

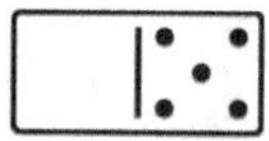

Published by Blood & Treasure, Los Angeles
First Edition

Cover by James T. Egan of Bookfly Design LLC.

Print ISBN: 978-0-692-32955-9

DominoFinn.com

★★★★★

"***Supernatural* meets *Sons of Anarchy.* Detective Maxim Dwyer is a man on a mission and nothing is going to stop him from finding his missing wife—not shape-shifting hard cases, outlaw bikers, or government cover-ups. Finn's *Seventh Sons* is a story you're not going to want to put down."

- James A. Hunter, Author of Strange Magic (Yancy Lazarus Series)

THE BLOOD OF BROTHERS

Day One

Chapter 1

A 6 a.m. phone call was never a good thing. Whether a family member in trouble, a friend who needed a favor, or a telemarketing recording from another time zone, it didn't matter—the call was a recipe for immediate anxiety. An overbearing ring that demanded attention, right at that moment. It was a jarring, imbalanced way to wake up, creating an edgy tension that wouldn't dissolve until the day ended with a beer in hand.

In short, early phone calls were unwelcome.

As the sole homicide detective in Sanctuary, Arizona, Maxim Dwyer knew these calls heralded an entirely different kind of pain. To a lot of people. And he was the lucky one.

The darkness of the morning was foreboding. In the peak of the summer, the bedroom should've been bright by now. Some days it was a struggle just for the sun to come up. But it always did, in the end. As did Maxim.

Sanctuary was a small town. The police force was nine men strong, including the marshal, and Maxim was the only assigned detective. That meant he handled all sorts of calls: robberies, violent crimes, and cases that required tact. The uniforms managed the day-to-day stuff: domestic violence, drunk and disorderlies at the biker roadhouse, accidents, theft, and vandalism. Most of the work this season involved keeping ornery groups of campers in line. But the officers on duty were trained to handle light investigative work if needed. For Maxim to be summoned this early, there was only one explanation.

No time to shower or shave. No brushing or flossing. A slap of cold water to the face was an amazing stimulant when it needed to be. And breakfast was overrated.

Maxim threw on an old suit and headed to the crime scene. An unnatural fog hung in the air, blocking out the sky. On the way, his sleep-filled eyes squinted as the sun gained ground in the sky. It pierced the glaze of weather and seemed to burn it away. By the time he pulled his silver Audi TT into Sanctuary High, daytime was official.

The detective idled past the large building of gray and brown brick. Wide paths of concrete and asphalt with newly painted lines covered the lot all the way into the parking area in the back. It was summer break, so the only two cars present were the brand-new cruisers driven by Hitchens and Cole, the department's oldest veterans. The cars were pretty slick for Caprices, making it look like the Sanctuary Marshal's Office had better resources than it did.

Maxim parked his coupe between the squad cars and

scratched his prickly chin. He gazed across the large green field before him. Surrounded by a chain-link fence, it shared the school's back grounds with the parking lot. The asphalt section didn't need an outer fence, however. The curb was enough.

Besides the current police presence, nothing appeared amiss. An empty school, an off-season, and a whole lot of quiet. Immediately, Maxim decided the serenity of the location played a part in the crime.

He exited his car and spied the police tape across the field, where the metal fence kept out a thick cluster of trees. The forests in the greater Sycamore area were dense. The tree line had only been cut back as much as the school needed, and even that encroachment seemed unwelcome. Sanctuary was a beautiful town precisely because it hovered on the edge of civilization. Its inhabitants appreciated being reminded of the wild. As the detective watched Hitchens and Cole work outside the fence, he realized nature had inched a little too close to society once again.

Maxim strode through the open gate and made his way across the field. The lawn was freshly cut and still wet with dew. The expanse was mostly wild grass, natural in this climate and easy to maintain. The football field, along the street beside the school building, was laid with sod and more meticulously cared for. Closer, there was a cement court for basketball and other activities. The larger area here, where it was more natural, was mostly used for pick-up games of soccer and other general activities, like running.

Large swaths of grass were cut, but other sections grew

long and appeared ignored. Maxim noticed the ride-on mower on his side of the fence, right next to the scene, and immediately ran the events through his head. The groundskeeper was mowing the lawn as he probably did once a week, judging by the grass length. He had only managed to do about a third of the field before he made the grisly discovery and called the police. As Maxim approached the officers standing on the other side of the fence, he noticed a Mexican man in his late forties hunched next to them. He wondered why he hadn't seen his car in the parking lot, and made a mental note to check on that.

As Maxim reached the fence, the other two officers shared a smile.

"How's it going, rock star?" asked Cole through the chain-link. The tallest of the three, and the most built, he was an imposing figure, but his demeanor alternated between bouts of sobriety and jest in a way that was unexpected. He wore black nitrile gloves and held a small camera—standard investigative procedure for crime scenes.

"I told you not to call me that," said Maxim tiredly. Ever since he'd closed out a federal case the year before, things had been different. To the media, he had captured a serial killer. To the Centers for Disease Control, he had saved their reputation. It was a huge win for the marshal's office and for the detective, but the unwanted attention made his job more difficult. And that was without the added torment of his fellow officers.

"Sorry, just trying to make you feel good after we rousted you from your beauty sleep."

Maxim clenched his jaw. Hitchens and Cole weren't like most veterans who punched in and out of work watching the clock. They were in prime physical condition. Even Hitchens, who didn't look it because of the extra weight. They liked action and they liked the midnight shift. Maxim knew they were as reliable as any on the force, and they knew the same of him. The banter was just how they passed the time. "I work nights when I need to."

"Yeah?" asked Cole. "I'll remember that next time a drunken camper stabs his buddy with a s'mores stake."

Maxim grimaced. It was Cole's favorite story. Only two weeks old, he repeated it loudly and often. Two best friends had gotten into an argument. One had stabbed the other straight through his forearm with the metal wire. The hot end of the pole had gone in and out cleanly, but the melted marshmallow and chocolate burned his skin pretty badly. Cole had handled the call without involving Maxim.

"If I hear that goddamned story one more time..." grumbled Hitchens. He had less patience in this early hour than the others. Unlike Cole, he hadn't been on shift, but as acting sergeant, Hitchens had been awakened alongside Maxim. He appeared especially irritable today. "I don't wanna hear about s'mores or rock stars. I don't wanna hear about how the media attention got extra funds for the department and that's the reason we have our new cruisers. I don't wanna hear that the CDC gave us a wide berth as thanks. And I especially don't want to hear anymore goddamned Spanish today."

Maxim and Cole shared a look of warning. Within the

span of seconds, Barney Hitchens had simultaneously predicted and headed off the direction of their banter. They knew not to press him.

Allowing the rant to simmer, Maxim again looked to the groundskeeper. The man sat in the grass on the other side of the fence. "He doesn't speak a word of English, does he?"

Hitchens scowled and turned his back to them. Cole shook his head. "Negative."

"And none of us can translate." Maxim chuckled to himself. Arizona was a good place to know Spanish. He'd been meaning to learn. But who had the free time? "I assume you have Gutierrez en route?"

Hitchens turned around. "I called his ass three times. Imparted to him a sense of urgency." Then he stormed off again. Maxim smiled. Poor guy. As the rookie, Gutierrez would be feeling the brunt of the sergeant's ire today.

The detective could see part of the body from where he was standing, as the groundskeeper first did, but he preferred to walk through the crime scene systematically, examining the stage before he watched the play. "Any vague translation of the 911 call?"

"Didn't call it in," answered Cole. "Doesn't have a phone. He flagged me down in the street as I happened to be driving by."

"Any sign of anyone else? Any other vehicles?"

"Negative. Just him. I've seen him cutting the grass here before. He works alone in the summer."

"So what do you know?"

"Well, it's pretty clear the man was working and

stumbled on the vic. He ran around with a wild look in his eyes for a while until he calmed down. I think he's worn out from the shock. What do you think? Can you use your famed 'stubborn grit' to understand Spanish?"

Maxim flashed a fake smile. The veterans liked to quote media reports to comedic effect. Maxim was just happy none of them had picked up the line comparing him to a pit bull. It was just part of the extra shit he had to deal with for being on TV. Apparently, the joke still wasn't old nine months later. "I'll wait for the translator. And you shouldn't believe everything you hear, Cole. All I am is an observer of life. I know what people do and why they do it."

Cole nodded, only half listening. "Yeah, well, not this time."

Something in the man's voice, a sense of surrender, said he didn't even want to make jokes about this. Maxim peeked past the tall man again. He could already tell this was a morbid scene. Refocusing on the officer, he decided to cut to the chase. "What about the vic?"

Cole stepped away from the chain-link toward Hitchens. "Well, I think you'd better come to the other side and take a look."

Maxim considered the high fence that separated them, then checked down its length to the left and right. "Where the fuck is the gate?"

Cole chuckled. "Tell me something. If you're such a great observer of life, then how'd you manage to wind up on the wrong side of the fence?"

Maxim's face turned red as his eyes traced the path to the

street, past the school. There was probably a gate there but it might be locked. Better to go around the back way, where the cars were, and circle the outside fence from the parking lot, through the wild ground. "Well, why the fuck didn't you drive your cruisers around?"

"The groundskeeper jumped into my car and I drove in before I knew where to look."

"What about Hitchens?"

Cole shrugged. "I guess he just parked where I parked."

Maxim cursed and considered climbing the obstacle but figured that would only give the officers a better story. He turned and made his way back to his car.

"For the record," called out Cole, "the sergeant didn't fall for it."

Maxim Dwyer smiled, careful not to let the others see. It was a funny joke. He would need to repay the favor.

When the detective got back to his car, he considered driving it over the curb and into the hilly grass, but only for a moment. Sports cars weren't built for that abuse. Looking at the shiny new police cruisers, Maxim realized that Hitchens had the same thought. Maxim hiked up and around, carefully examining the ground for any clues that might have been left by the events earlier in the morning. He reached the others without seeing anything amiss.

There were two lines of crime scene tape, each tied to the fence on one end and a tree on the other. Cole hadn't bothered closing off the border in the trees. The officer held the tape up as Maxim ducked underneath.

"I didn't touch a single thing," said Cole. "You might not

want to either until the doc shows up."

"You have the ME on the way? I thought Medina was on vacation?"

"Nope. ME-dina just came back yesterday. You believe that luck?"

Maxim whistled. He'd assumed they would tap the morgue in Flagstaff. That would have been slow going because County had a larger caseload. Sanctuary didn't have a backlog of autopsies to deal with. Having the doc back meant they could expedite things locally.

Maxim approached Hitchens, who silently contemplated the body. Maxim stepped in line with him and caught the whiff of a butcher's shop. "Hell of a way to go," said the sergeant.

A large sycamore towered above its neighbors. Its stout trunk split into two main branches. Hanging on the heaviest outcropping, upside down, was a mutilated man. There was no skin on the body.

Maxim grabbed a pair of black nitrile gloves from a cardboard box and snapped them up to his wrists. "I don't suppose anyone checked vital signs."

"Oh shit," said Cole. "Did I forget that?"

A thick rope tied to the overhanging branch held up both legs by the ankles, which were bound together. The victim's hands hung loose, barely brushing the ground, leaving his head at waist height. Empty, dark eyes stared from a meaty skull. Bone was visible in some places, but most of the surface area was exposed muscle and fat. The naked man had been strung up and skinned like a deer.

The grass on this side of the fence was unkempt. Deeper beneath the canopy, the shade prevented too much from growing, but the growth along the tree line fared better. It was thick enough to prohibit footprints.

"How close did either of you get?"

"This is it," answered Hitchens. "Cole figured there might be all kinds of evidence that fell around here."

Maxim nodded and stepped forward carefully. He circled the body, giving it a wide berth. As he passed the tree trunk, he carefully examined it. Even though there was plenty of sunlight, he took out a flashlight and ran the beam up and down the bark. Not finding anything, the detective finished his circuit around the body.

"Well, he wasn't killed and skinned here," he said.

Hitchens shook his head slowly. "Not enough blood."

"Not enough is right. The vic was drained dry. Time of death is gonna need to wait for the lab, I think. Lividity and body temp are gonna be thrown off by the drainage. Probably rigor, too."

Hitchens let out a heavy sigh that seemed to empty his wide frame. "Have you ever seen anything like this?"

Maxim shook his head. "It's cold blooded. Calculated. Meant to incite emotion."

"Or vomit," said Cole.

Maxim ignored the remark and carefully inched closer to the body. He noticed a blackened section of muscle over the rib cage. The flashlight revealed some yellow-white puss. He would need to wait for the ME to figure that one out. Moving down the body, it was clear that the flesh of the left arm was torn. The bones in the forearm were more exposed, and the thumb was missing entirely.

"These look like animal bites," said the detective.

Maxim knew the three of them were thinking the same thing. Sanctuary wasn't like other American towns. This one had a large population of wolves, present company included.

The older men scoffed. "New moon's not for another two days," said Hitchens. "Besides, you don't think the Seventh Sons would be this stupid, do you?"

Maxim didn't answer. The Seventh Sons were an outlaw club affiliated with criminal activities. They were brash, tough guys who frequented town and had a clubhouse in the woods. They were werewolves, but they weren't stupid, and they knew it was in their best interests to keep a low profile.

As far as the moon was concerned, not a month went by when Maxim wasn't aware of it. Not in Sycamore. Not anymore. The wolves came out every fourteen days. As Hitchens had said, it was too early, and there was no way this body was twelve days old.

"I don't know," said the detective, finally. "This looks ceremonial. Supernatural, maybe. I don't take the motorcycle club that way. But we will need to rule them out. Let's assume the time of death was early this morning until the ME tells us otherwise."

A double chime interrupted Maxim's next thought. Hitchens checked his phone and read a message. "It's Gutierrez... I don't believe this."

The rookie was the best option to translate and it

appeared he would be late. "What's he say?"

Hitchens grunted. "Verbatim: 'Shit my pants. Going to Starbucks.'"

Cole let out a bellow. Maxim rolled his eyes. He was past joke-telling time and was getting impatient. The longer it took the rookie and the medical examiner to show up, the later he would be up tonight. The longer before he could settle down with a beer. He stomped over to Hitchens and grabbed the phone from him.

Maxim was stunned to see that Hitchens had not lied about the contents of the message.

"What the fuck?" Maxim exclaimed, tossing the phone back to the sergeant. "What sense does that kid make? Those two sentences don't go together. You can say, 'I shit my pants. Going home.' Or you can say, 'I want coffee. Going to Starbucks.'" Hitchens and Cole started giggling like kids, and Maxim slipped into a smile in the middle of his rant. "What you cannot fucking say is, 'Shit my pants. Going to Starbucks.' That's a non sequitur."

The officers laughed some more, and Maxim imagined Gutierrez walking into the Starbucks bathroom with a load in his pants and couldn't hold back anymore. He joined them. It felt good to release some tension, and they would surely call on this laughter in the future just as often as Cole brought up the s'mores story. The rookie wouldn't live this one down.

"Fuck it," said Maxim, wiping his eyes with the sleeve of his jacket. "Tell him to meet you at the station. You mind taking our wit down there until I meet you?"

Hitchens strutted away. "Was waiting for you to ask. I don't want to smell this meat market anymore. You all have a good one."

"Wait," said Cole. "Tell him to pick me up a vanilla Frappuccino."

Hitchens and Maxim both stopped what they were doing and turned to the officer.

"What?" Cole asked. "It's getting hot out."

Hitchens shook his head and continued on his way. "You better hope that boy washes his hands."

Maxim turned to the body and felt his smile leave him. Hitchens was right. This vic was a piece of meat. Chewed on as an animal might do, but drained and skinned as only a person could. Of course he had to consider the werewolves. But until he had an ID, ruling anybody out would be difficult.

Maxim kneeled next to the body. He turned the flashlight on again and searched for clues in the grass. Some blood was below the body, of course, so it hadn't been left out to drain for days. The smell was still fresh. This morning was still looking good for time of death.

"Did you get pictures of this blood down here?"

Cole carefully inched closer. "I was afraid of disturbing the evidence." The officer leaned over and took a few shots. Then he turned the digital display to face the detective and scrolled through his pictures. "I got all angles of the body, wide shots with the tree, the rope, the knots, the trunk."

Maxim nodded. "Get close-ups of the wounds. The tearing in the arm and shoulder. The missing thumb. The puss on the torso." As he spoke, the body spun slightly on the rope, and a flash of the skull caught Maxim's eye. He shined his flashlight at the right side of the suspended head and saw a small indentation between the ear and the temple. "And get a picture of this gunshot wound too."

It was difficult to detect on the massacred body, but there was a tiny hole. A single, long strand of black hair stuck out, glued to the head by matted blood. Maxim leaned around the body to check the other side. The skull had no other anomalies.

"Probably a small round that bounced around in the brain and never came out. I bet it's still stuck in there. Hopefully the slug's in good enough shape for ballistics." Cole silently nodded as he snapped several pictures.

Maxim stood up and shined the flashlight along the rope. It was rough hemp, possibly littered with fibers or DNA, but nothing visible to the naked eye. Maxim allowed his gaze to travel up to the tree and just stared, as if the new perspective would help him. He thought of the common crime scene adage: never forget to look up. Evidence could end up anywhere. It almost made the detective laugh. This was one crime scene where nobody would need to be reminded to check the tree. Almost dizzy, Maxim shook his head and backed away.

The detective peered up and down the corridor between the high school fence and the tree line. To his right, through the football field, was the street. The left was the back of the grounds, where he had come from. Somebody could have skirted the property from either direction to get here. Then Maxim considered the trees. He looked straight into the forested lot and saw how quickly everything turned to piles of leaves and brush. Maxim hated outdoor crime scenes. There was too much to rule out. Some early guesses at this stage, if incorrect, could tank the investigation.

Maxim moved towards the football field, seeing what this path offered in the way of criminal harbor. The field was set off from the school building but directly adjacent. There was no entrance to it from this outside lot. However, a gate at the corner led into the basketball court. Maxim noticed a rusted chain and lock holding it closed. A quick inspection left him confident that it hadn't been opened in a long time.

Maxim turned away from the school, walking along the football field now, parallel to the front street. This was no stadium; it was an open-air arena with bleachers. While it didn't provide full cover from the street, the combination of size and seating afforded a large amount of privacy. Maxim walked the entire length, searching the grass for anything out of the ordinary. At the far corner he made his way to the street. Dirt sat flush with the asphalt, impressed with tire tracks.

Immediately, Maxim imagined the crime as it occurred. The vic was strung up at another location. Skinned. Drained. Shot in the head either before or after. Then he was brought here in a vehicle, likely a truck or van of some sort. The killer pulled to the side of the road, unseen in the early morning hours, and lugged the body along the fence in relative privacy. He strung the dead man up and disappeared, waiting for its inevitable discovery.

But why here? Why Sanctuary High?

Maxim shook his head as he made his way back to Cole. He would tell the officer to rope off the area by the street and take pictures of the tracks. It wouldn't likely lead to anything, but it was worth a shot. Along the way, every twenty feet or so, the detective kneeled, turned on his flashlight, and shone it across the grass. He could barely see the light he cast against the daylight, but he was confident in the technique.

When he was almost back to the body, he made one last sweep with his flashlight and saw a glint reflected back his way. Maxim cocked his head and tried to make out the object in the tall grass. He pushed up against his tired knees and advanced on it, smiling when he stood over a skinning knife. It had a small, stubby blade that was shorter than the handle. Three colors of wood were glued together to decorate the length, but the bottom half of the handle was a carved deer antler. The blade was covered in blood.

"Cole. You'd better get a picture of this."

This wasn't the murder weapon, Maxim guessed, but it was damning all the same. The detective knew the biker it belonged to.

Chapter 2

Diego de la Torre watched as the eight ball bounced between both edges of the corner pocket without sinking. He hovered over the missed shot, but his eyes were on Omar. The kid was a quick study, but he was only nineteen and impetuous.

"That would have been a great shot," assured Diego, lining up his cue down the rail in explanation. "You kept your eye on the eight ball, kissed it with the cue ball nicely, and had enough touch to make it down the table." Diego pulled his cue back and grabbed a square of blue chalk.

Omar butted his cue on the floor impatiently. He wiped his slicked-back hair and regarded the lesson. "I told you I should have hit it harder. *Más fuerte*, man."

Diego glanced around the clubhouse. They were alone by the pool table but some of the other Seventh Sons were in the attached living room. They sometimes gave the kid shit when he spoke Spanish because they didn't understand him. The MC wasn't overtly white—being a werewolf was more of a requirement than race was—but Omar was still the lone Mexican.

Diego de la Torre shook his head. Since the kid had a tough enough time being the youngest member, and with Diego being South American, he was a natural fit to watch over him. "Omar, you can do everything else right, but your shot will only ever be as steady as your bridge hand. If the stick is resting on a shaky surface, all that aiming and planning is useless."

The kid swiped his hand in the air as the mistake occurred to him. Diego smoothly strode around the table and leaned in. "You didn't leave me with a great angle, though, precisely because you didn't bang the cue ball to the other side of the table. Speed is about strategy, not flash."

An unexcited breath left Omar's lips. "Now you're just trying to make me feel better. I know you can make that shot."

Diego let himself crack a smile as he tilted his head confidently. The clubhouse bustled with more activity so it was time to end the game anyway. His left hand was a rock. The cue slid over it back and forth in a practiced motion. Then Diego knocked the cue ball, firmly slicing the eight, which headed straight for the pocket. Before it could sink, a large Indian man scooped the ball from the table.

"You ladies done chatting?"

West Wind was an Apache. He was the newest member of the Seventh Sons, having heard of them in the wake of Sanctuary's recent media coverage. The serial killings had been blamed on their ousted leader almost a year earlier. The MC was nearly obliterated. A few of their members were killed. Diego and Maxim had saved them from a CDC crackdown that could have shut the Seventh Sons down for good. Afterwards, only six men strong, all wolves, they welcomed Diego as one of their own even though he could never succumb to lycanthropy because of his vaccination. West Wind came knocking later, reading between the lines, seeing the club for what it was, but annoyed that Diego wasn't one of them.

"Fuck, West," whined Omar. "You can't block shots like that. What if there was money on the game?"

The brown eyes of the large man showed disappointment. "You mean there wasn't? I was hoping I'd messed up someone's payday."

Diego smiled, turned his back on them, and sat against the edge of the table.

"Don't worry, West. If you mess up one of my paydays, you'll know about it."

The Apache ambled around the table slowly, stomping his boots on the floor. He was an imposing figure. Taller than both other men, a little older than Diego at thirty, and in good shape. Although his frame wasn't as wide as his height might've allowed, his lean mass was all muscle. The Indian had long arms and legs that gave him superior reach in a fistfight, a prowess which Diego had personally witnessed.

"What does that mean?" challenged West.

Diego met his eyes, already bored with the man's tough-guy act. "You're just gonna have to find out when it happens."

West exploded into laughter, a little too closely to Diego's face. "I've gotta admit," he said, "for someone who knows he's surrounded by wolves, you've got balls."

"Come on," appealed Omar, "you know he's one of us, West."

"Yeah, that's what the good president says. But ask him this," he said, talking to the kid while staring at Diego. "If he's one of us, why doesn't he ride with us when there's work to be done?"

Diego remained quiet. He knew West was hitting a sore point with the club. When Diego had joined, the president, Gaston, welcomed him with open arms. But Diego didn't want anything to do with the drug running and other illegal activities. He just wanted brotherhood. A sense of camaraderie. And yes, some adventure. But he didn't want to fall into a life of crime. His friendship with Maxim, Sanctuary's only police detective, reinforced that. But as the months passed, the understanding he had garnered with the club slowly waned. Everybody knew Diego was half in and half out—even him.

"Just because I choose not to be a criminal doesn't mean I can't be a brother. Just because I'm not a wolf doesn't mean I can't hold my own."

"That's right," said West mockingly. "You used to be a CDC assassin. You hunted our kind with silver, bullets and blade. It's just a shame you lost your little knife."

"It was a pretty big knife actually. But I can be a help

without it. You're ignoring the fact that it was me who found the Mexi van of cash."

West grunted.

A week earlier, while Diego had been riding alone on Interstate 40, he noticed a suspicious black van being escorted by two bikers flying California colors. After following them for a while, the bikers fell off, hoping to lure Diego away from the vehicle. Instead, he'd gotten the attention of his fellow Sons, and they intercepted the van. The contents were... enriching. It had been a drug run, except in reverse—it was cash to pay for the drug run.

The Seventh Sons were a small motorcycle club. They didn't have the kind of reach that the cartels or international outfits had. But they were a small core of men with a powerful secret: they were wolves, nearly unkillable without specialized means. Whether people believed the rumors or were ignorant of them, the Seventh Sons owned the Interstate in Arizona and everybody knew it. They commanded their toll for safe passage and someone had tried to skirt that arrangement. Now, the entire MC was gearing up to meet with the Cali gang. That was why Diego was playing pool. Omar was still a kid, no matter his affiliation, no matter his condition, and he was nervous. Diego had just wanted to put him at ease.

West didn't budge. "I know what you lucked into. I also know that you're not coming with us. If you want to help the club, then prove it and back us up. Ride with us."

Diego averted his eyes and saw Gaston standing in the living room. The president heeded them with interest.

Gaston had allowed Diego to keep away from the illicit activities thus far, but he was no doubt hoping that West made a convincing case.

Diego was afraid to check if other club members were watching as well. He returned West's stare and removed any trace of joviality from his voice. "You're asking me to be involved in a drug deal."

"I'm asking you to shit or get off the pot," said West, raising his voice.

Clint stormed over as the bickering came to a head. "Shoot me in my hairy ass! How many times have I asked you to keep it down in the mornings? You thick-headed sasquatch."

Clint was a mess. He was the oldest club member in age and tenure. His brown beard was thick and mangy and always had pieces of dirt or slobber in it. His large belly was a record of his excesses, but his breath was a more overpowering indicator. He had a hangover. An especially bad one, Diego thought, because he looked much worse than usual. He was scratched up and had a welt under his left eye.

"What the hell happened to you last night, bro?" asked Omar.

"You know I was over at the Lodge. More of the same. But my head feels like a firecracker, and you all are lightin' the fuse."

Diego smiled. Clint was a bit of a hillbilly, a perfect example of the type who would have sassed Omar for speaking Spanish, but he was mostly harmless. He disappeared for days, visited his family in New Mexico, and drank at every available opportunity. But he was steadfast and mostly reliable, and had come into town last night for this very meet.

The heavy man trudged to the beer fridge next to the pool table and grabbed himself a bottle. "Don't worry, Pres. A little hair of the dog will straighten me up. And you three should come over and take a seat, too." With that, he chugged the beer and passed through the archway that led to the living room.

Diego slid his cue onto the table and followed. The whole club was in attendance. Clint sat down on a couch next to Curtis and Trent. Omar did the same. Diego flipped the recliner around and made himself comfortable. West Wind chose to lean in the corner, towering over everybody except Gaston, the only other club member who could match his height. He was also standing.

Gaston was an imposing figure himself. A big man with a wide frame, his stocky features were considered handsome by many. His spiked fauxhawk, blond highlights, and abundance of earrings showed that he took great pride in his appearance, but it had surprised Diego to discover that the man cared more about the MC. Despite his hotheadedness and other faults, he was willing to sacrifice himself for his brothers, and none of them could ask for a better leader.

"West is right," started the president, addressing the entire MC. "This is an important meet. Business hasn't been too rough since I was voted in but we were bound to be tested. Maybe some other gang gets new leadership too.

Wants to make an impression with their bosses and gets big ideas to cut us out as middlemen. We need to meet them in force and show them we're not backing down."

"Damn straight!" said Clint. "They need to go through us or don't go through Arizona."

Gaston nodded. "That's right. And you know how it is with these new gangbangers. They won't stop charging ahead until they slam straight into a wall. Well, they've never dealt with us. We need to show them that we *are* the wall around this state." Gaston hesitated and glanced at Diego as he spoke. "Now, our numbers are still a little low after last year. We need all hands on deck."

"You said this wasn't going to be a firefight," said Diego. From Gaston's tone, he was expecting things to go bad.

"It won't be—if we don't look weak. And act like pros."

"How many of them will show?" asked West from his corner.

"If they bring too many it will make them look scared."

"How many?" demanded West.

Gaston bit his lip. He didn't know the answer, but his message was clear: Diego was letting his brothers down by not going.

Chapter 3

Maxim observed the clubhouse door swing open as he stepped out of his car. The wooden structure was in a clearing of white grass in the wild forest. Technically outside Sanctuary's jurisdictional limits, the area was sprawling and unincorporated. Known as Sycamore to the locals, it didn't have any actual borders. It was more like a neighborhood, but one that spanned two counties and stretched into the desert, away from its namesake.

However, because of Sanctuary's proximity, Coconino County deputies ceded the handling of the motorcycle club to the marshal's office. It was a practical agreement for both departments, even when it proved impractical.

Gaston sauntered onto the deck. He wasn't ecstatic to see the detective. Maxim placed his white panama hat on his head and just shrugged as he approached. He brushed his suit jacket to make sure his gun was comfortably in place as he reached the step.

"This isn't the best time, Detective."

"That's what I said when I got a phone call at six in the morning." Maxim turned and examined the line of Harleys parked in the dirt. He noticed Diego's Triumph Scrambler in line as well, mostly because it was cleaner than the Harleys. "It looks like you have a full house." Maxim hopped up the two steps and peeked in the open door. There was a bustle of movement, as if the club was gearing up for something.

Gaston gritted his teeth. "That's exactly why this isn't a fucking good time."

Maxim feigned shock at the rude welcome. "I guess I'll show myself in then." The detective pushed past the big man, into the small foyer. A hallway stretched to the back alongside a staircase. To the right was the dining room, and to the left was the living room and den. Maxim had been inside this clubhouse once before, when he'd needed Gaston's help locating the previous president. Deborah had become a fugitive, complete with hostages and the threat to kill Diego's sister. Gaston had helped both men, and his cooperation had afforded him and the club a long leash. Now Maxim was hoping that his trust had not been misplaced.

"Clint Dailey James," he announced as he saw the man in a red leather jacket walk by.

The brown beard spun around as he noticed the detective for the first time. "And what's the police doin' here?"

"I was looking for you, actually."

Clint puffed out his chest, as much as he could over his belly, and sidled up to Maxim. His breath reeked of alcohol and vomit, and his eyes were bloodshot. "And how can I help you, Ociffer?" He mispronounced the last word on purpose, with a condescending slant.

"First I'm gonna ask you to put the beer bottle down."

Clint raised it quickly, forcing Maxim to take a step back and put a hand on the gun at his belt, then the man overturned the bottle to his lips. Clint had done it just to make him flinch.

"Settle down," said Gaston, speaking to both of them.

"Sure thing," said Clint. "And as for this here bottle, I don't make a habit of holding on to them once they're empty." Clint flipped the glass over his shoulder and it smashed on the floor behind him. The other club members took note of the drama playing out and surrounded them, except for West, who stayed in the other room.

"Hey Maxim," said Diego, as if this were a friendly visit.

The detective nodded and relaxed his arms again. He was in a room with dangerous people, but they knew better than to attack him. Besides the agreement he had with the Seventh Sons, the last president's mistake had been attacking the police. Gaston wouldn't let that happen again.

"Clint Dailey James," Maxim repeated, reminding everybody he was on official business. "Where were you last night?"

The man chuckled and looked to his brothers. "Well hell if I remember!"

Gaston cut in. "He rode in last night and kicked it at

Sycamore Lodge. What's this about?"

"And overnight?"

"He slept here. We all did. Why?"

Gaston was getting more demanding, but the detective didn't want to jump ahead just yet. Even though he knew he wasn't in danger, he suddenly wished he had brought Hitchens with him as backup. The two veterans were wolves affiliated to the blue team.

"I have some business I need to ask about," replied Maxim calmly. "We can be civil around each other. Remember we went hunting for mule deer together last November?"

"Sure do," answered Clint. "Bagged a big one." He stuck his chin out proudly, more at ease. Maxim could tell that Gaston and Diego were still wary.

"Hey," said the detective offhandedly. "You remember that skinning knife you used on the carcass? The one your daddy gave you?"

The beard rose and fell. "Sure do. It never leaves my side."

Maxim smiled. "That's why I'm here. It's come up in an investigation. You mind showing it to me?"

Clint's eyebrows creased and he peered at Gaston. The president nodded and the rotund man started outside to his bike. "Fine then. Them's were good times, but don't think we're friends again. Not after that business with the laundromat."

Maxim smiled and followed the man outdoors. The incident he was referring to was entirely Clint's fault. He'd gotten drunk and methed up and crashed his bike through the glass storefront of Lucky's Laundry. Not so lucky for the store owner, but perhaps so because no one inside had gotten hurt. Hitchens had still arrested him, and Clint added a DUI charge to his jacket. The old biker had treated Maxim as an outsider ever since.

"You didn't get drawn this year, did you?" asked Clint, forgetting about their differences as he thought about hunting again. Gaston and Diego kicked up gravel and dust as they followed. It must have been over eighty degrees already. With the town's high elevation, that was the summer showing its heat.

"No," said Maxim, shaking his head. "Just wondering what your daddy's knife has been up to."

Clint paused when he reached his bike. The man checked the other side, then realization replaced confusion. "Actually, Officer, now that I think about it, I don't own that knife anymore."

"It's Detective. What happened to it?" Maxim checked Clint's Harley himself to see if there were any compartments or bags with a knife. All the other motorcycles in the line were prepped and ready to go, loaded with saddlebags. Clint's Harley didn't have the extra gear. It was clean.

"Uh, sorry," he said. "I just remembered. I was proper sloshed last night—not that I rode my bike in that state. No, Officer, believe me—Detective. I was good and sober when I came back to the clubhouse."

"What happened to the knife, Clint?"

"Pawned it."

Maxim blinked patiently. "You pawned your daddy's custom skinning knife?"

"Had to. Back in New Mexico. For covering legal fees and whatnot." Clint nodded confidently when he added the last part.

"So there'll be a record at the shop you sold it to?"

Clint stuttered. "I don't know. I don't really remember which shop it was, specifically, you see. But I swear I don't have it. You can search me."

"I will." Maxim spun Clint around and patted at his pockets. He checked the legs and arms under the leathers. Keys and a wallet were all he found. But Maxim already knew he didn't have the knife anymore. "Where were you last night, Clint?"

"Sycamore Lodge."

Maxim appealed to the others. "Can anyone else account for the time you spent there?"

Diego and Gaston shook their heads. Clint threw up his hands. "No one knew I was in town yet. I came in from New Mexico last night. Stopped at the Lodge first."

"What time did you leave?"

"I don't quite recall. But you can ask Deborah's girl. She stopped in for a bit and said hi."

Melody Holton. She owned Sycamore Lodge now. She was a club member, once, but it was just an honorary status now. Her mother had been the ousted president. Once Deborah went, Melody decided to focus on the roadhouse. She wouldn't be a useful witness. She was still a Seventh Son in spirit and would back any club member's alibi.

"Clint," said Maxim, "if you don't have the knife, I'm gonna need you to come with me."

"Why?" protested Clint. "That knife's none of my business anymore."

"Hold on," said Gaston. "None of my guys are going anywhere."

"I'm investigating a murder," said the detective plainly. "I'm not trying to get in the middle of your business." Maxim turned back to the suspect and studied his bruises. "How'd you get those?"

Clint turned to Gaston and stuttered. "A fight back home."

"What happened?" asked Diego. "Who got killed?"

"I don't know yet."

"I don't think he did it, Maxim."

The detective put a stern note in his voice. "I didn't say he did one way or the other, but he can help my investigation."

Gaston put his arm around Maxim's shoulder and nodded him aside. Maxim almost brushed it off but decided to go along with it. They walked to the side of the clubhouse, onto a patch of grass. "Listen," said Gaston discreetly, "I really need Clint today. Can he go into the station tomorrow?"

Maxim was firm. "Sorry. His knife was found with the body. It looks bad."

"Fuck, man," blurted out Gaston. "Work with me, here."

"Why?" demanded Maxim. "What are your guys gearing

up for?" The detective pointed inside. The club preparation was obvious. "Because if it's anything like what happened last night, I might as well just arrest you now."

"Just normal club stuff," said the big man, shaking off the accusation. "Clint is important to me. He didn't do what you think."

Maxim shook his head. "I can't help you. Our deal protects your club only as long as shit like this doesn't happen. Whether Clint's guilty or not, I would need to answer for not bringing him in. He's coming with me, and you're going to tell him to come peacefully. If you refuse, I'll send out Patrol to keep an eye on the club's activities today. See how well you can manage 'regular club stuff' then."

Gaston sneered. He would cooperate, Maxim knew, but the uneasy peace between the two men was becoming more uneasy.

Chapter 4

Besides City Hall across the street, the Sanctuary Marshal's Office was the oldest building in the town square. It was a brick fossil with cramped quarters that served various municipal functions. The main floor housed the police offices, the top floor was a hospital wing, and enough space was underground to double up as a morgue and a jail. The facilities were all fairly small and saw limited but regular use.

Maxim guided Clint past the desks in the main office. Nine desks were arranged, three-by-three, in the large room. One for every officer in the force. Of course, that was counting the marshal, but he had his own desk in his own private office. Since Sanctuary was a town of only 3,500, the eight men who served under him were enough, and the department was content to let the desk sit idle.

Maxim was surprised that Hitchens was the only officer in the station. He saw the disapproving look on the face of the sergeant as he walked by. He remembered the shitstorm he had created by dragging Seventh Sons into the station before, but the detective had instituted a new deal since then. The motorcycle club was no longer untouchable. They had to be accountable for their actions. And whatever connections they had with the marshal, or his father the mayor, didn't matter.

The detective led Clint into the hallway beside the marshal's office and into an interrogation room. He wasn't a prisoner, or handcuffed, because Gaston had told him to cooperate.

"I'm gonna need a few minutes," said the detective. "You want a soda or something?"

The man plopped down in the plastic chair and slapped his hands on his belly. "I could use some hot wings and a Bud Light."

Maxim rolled his eyes and shut the door behind him, then returned to the main office. He glanced around for the rookie, then noticed the vanilla Frappuccino sitting on Cole's desk. "Gutierrez made it back?"

The sergeant nodded as he approached. "He's in number two with the groundskeeper. Cole's still tied up at the scene."

"Did the ME show, yet?"

"Sure did. You mind me asking what Clint's doing in number one?"

"His hunting knife was found close to the vic. He says he sold it."

Hitchens raised his eyebrows in shock. "That redneck in there? He's a killer for sure, but he preys on the four-legged variety."

"It feels a little off to me too, but meth does some crazy things."

Hitchens sighed. "That boy using again?"

"I don't know yet. I'll see if he'll go for a drug test. Right now it's just a courtesy visit. I think I'll start with the groundskeeper. He's had a hell of a day." Maxim pulled his jacket off and placed it around the back of his chair. Then he tossed his hat on his desk. As he stepped away, Hitchens spoke up.

"Son, why do I feel like we got a whole new can of worms opening up on us?"

Maxim shook his head. "Because bodies like that don't just happen randomly."

The detective entered the second of the station's two interrogation rooms. Gutierrez was in there, wearing his blues, sitting across from the groundskeeper. With Maxim's entrance, the rookie surrendered his seat and leaned against the wall.

"Javier Gonzalez, sir," said the officer, pointing to the groundskeeper. "He's lived in Sanctuary his whole life. Worked the school for the last twenty-two years."

Maxim nodded thanks. "Did you really fucking shit your pants?"

Gutierrez only showed minimal embarrassment. "Yo, I had some *heavy* carnitas last night. Greasy as a mofo. The sergeant wanted me on the scene as fast as humanly possible and I slapped on my uni and left the house without taking my morning dump. Halfway there, I knew I was in trouble. I was running full lights and sirens to that Starbucks, but I didn't make it. I'm talking about serious leakage."

Maxim put his hand up, sorry he had asked. "I'm gonna cut you off right there." Maxim tried to put the strange events out of his mind. It was hard for him, as a detective, to not ask questions. The mind of the rookie was a strange one that Maxim was curious to understand, but he was taking Mr. Gonzalez away from his work. The man would likely take the rest of the day off, but that field would still need tending tomorrow or some other day in the future. He didn't look like the type of guy that got a lot of breaks.

The detective sat on the plastic chair and studied the man across from him. He was disheveled, hair a little too long, bushy mustache. His skin was cracked and darkened from long hours in the sun, and his eyes showed more wear than his probable age. He had strong, calloused hands that were evidence of honest work. Maxim guessed the man was usually stolid but would forever be haunted by what he had seen today.

Maxim shook the man's hand and identified himself. "Ask him how he found the body."

Gutierrez spoke in Spanish and Javier answered, then the rookie translated to English. "He says he was mowing the lawn. Just riding past and it was there."

"Did he see anyone else?"

Javier stared at the table as Gutierrez asked. The groundskeeper took a moment before answering, and when he did, he simply shook his head.

Maxim believed the man was being defensive, but he

couldn't pinpoint why. "What did he do then?"

"He didn't even turn off his mower. He just darted to the parking lot and out into the street. His family only has one cell phone, and he leaves it with his wife. He was lucky to flag down Mr. Clean." The rookie sometimes referred to Cole like that. Maxim started putting the pieces together.

"Ask him where his car is."

Gutierrez answered without checking with Javier. "His wife drops him off in the morning." The rookie must have already gotten the information earlier. It showed his knack for investigation.

"When he was dropped off, did he see any cars or people at all this morning?" In response to the rookie, Javier shook his head.

"Did he see a van or a truck parked by the football field?"

Again, a no. That fit Maxim's interpretation of the events, as the crime would have been complete before the groundskeeper ever arrived. Javier didn't know anything. Yet his eyes betrayed something ominous. Fear, maybe.

Maxim leaned back in his chair and yawned. The day had barely started but he'd been without his coffee. Like Gutierrez, the emergency had thrown him off his morning ritual.

The hanging corpse had been partially hidden in its position, obscured by a bushy branch. It was hit or miss whether someone focused on work within the fence would have noticed it, but it wasn't implausible. The detective decided to emphasize the unlikelihood to get Javier to open up.

"The man's cutting the grass," Maxim started, changing the tenor of his voice to imply dissatisfaction whether the words were understood or not, "driving along the fence, looking ahead and making sure not to veer off course, not hit the fence, keep a straight line, and he notices a body behind the trees?" Gutierrez spoke to the groundskeeper as the detective continued. "I find it hard to believe that he discovered the body so quickly without any foreknowledge of it being there."

The rookie paused, unsure if he should indict the groundskeeper with an exact translation of Maxim's words. The detective urged him to finish. When Javier heard the words, he panicked slightly and spouted off exclamations in Spanish.

"He says he had nothing to do with it," translated the rookie. "He's legal. He's worked hard for his family for twenty years." Every statement was hurried as Gutierrez attempted to keep up with the pleas of the man. "Uh, he's always kept his head down. He's never gotten in trouble. He swears. He didn't do anything wrong."

Maxim looked Javier in the eye. "Tell him if he's not telling me one hundred percent of what he knows then he is committing a crime."

The rookie did, and Javier lowered his gaze. Gutierrez spurred him on. Finally, just above a murmur, Javier said, "*Los hombres lobos.*"

The rookie let the words hang in the air as he slowly turned to Maxim. "He said, 'the werewolves.'"

Maxim's face darkened. "Did he see wolves or men?"

Some more Spanish before Gutierrez answered. "Wolves, sir. At first, it was only movement outside the fence. He saw it from across the field and didn't think much of it. When it came time for him to pass by, he looked."

"And he saw wolves by the body?"

"Well, not anymore. He says the animals were spooked by the mower. But then he saw the body. They were eating him." Javier spoke to the rookie in a pleading tone, unsolicited. Gutierrez translated. "He says he didn't say anything because he thought we wouldn't believe him."

The detective nodded. "Tell him it's okay. As long as he explains everything he saw, he'll be fine. Ask him if he specifically saw the wolves chewing on the corpse."

"No," answered the rookie, "he didn't. But he saw the bite marks."

"Did he get a good look at any of the wolves?"

"He thinks there were two or three of them, but they scattered before he got there. Afterward, he only got a close look at one. The baby, he says."

Maxim smiled. "The baby werewolf."

Javier threw his hands up and complained to Gutierrez. "He says he knew you wouldn't believe him."

Maxim patted the man's arm. It wasn't that he didn't believe the groundskeeper. It was simply a matter of interpretation. Sanctuary was a small town, naturally prone to superstition. Especially so with the Seventh Sons in their backyard. When Maxim had first learned that werewolves did in fact exist, he wondered if he'd given enough credit to other supernatural claims in the past. But he called himself an open-minded skeptic. People exaggerated in the face of the unknown, no matter the truth. Just because one thing existed, it didn't mean everything did.

There couldn't have been any werewolves around—it wasn't even a full or new moon. Javier's sighting of a "baby wolf" suggested to Maxim a coyote more than anything else. The common animals were smaller and weaker than wolves. It might take several of them to pull a body down, or rip it in half. The bite marks on the vic ran up the arm to the shoulder, but no higher. That meant the animal wasn't as tall as a wolf.

What made the most sense was that the groundskeeper had witnessed wild animals feeding on a dead body. That somewhat eased Maxim's concerns about the Seventh Sons being involved, but he still had the knife to deal with. And, even worse, that meant he had no other leads. The real murderer was out there without suspicion.

As the detective asked more questions, it became clear that Javier Gonzalez couldn't help the case. Maxim told him to stay away from the school the rest of the day while the crime scene was processed and asked Gutierrez to take him home. Then he decided to get to the real crux of the problem, and stepped into interrogation room one.

Whereas Javier Gonzalez was withdrawn and afraid, Clint James was the opposite. He sat forward aggressively. He was loud and demanding, still drunk from the night before, and had a chip on his shoulder. Which meant that whether or not he had something to hide, he would make the interview miserable. Immediately, he did not disappoint.

"Well here I am," he said, "as a service to you and the marshal's office, and you leave me locked in here like a criminal."

"Still have a penchant for the dramatic, I see," rebuked the detective. "The door wasn't locked and you're not detained. You're just doing your civic duty."

"And fucking glad of it. I'm a pillar of society, I am." Clint attempted to tame his bushy beard back to make himself more respectable. It didn't suit him.

Maxim studied Clint James. He appeared both wild and tired, an aging man who'd found that partying wasn't as fun as it used to be. He had a black welt under his eye. Some scratches on his forearms. He was even missing a patch of hair. "Mind telling me where you got those injuries?"

The biker pressed his lips together and shook his head dismissively. "It was just a little incident in New Mexico."

"And the PD over there could confirm that?"

"I don't see how. I never called them."

"What about the other guy you tussled with? What would he have to say?"

Clint smiled. "That he got his ass whooped."

Maxim nodded and cleared his throat. "Well, I should check with him anyway."

"Good luck. I don't know the guy's name. Never seen him before."

"You expect me to believe that someone with your strength just got in a random fistfight?"

"Hey," said Clint, throwing his hands up. "I held back. I know the rules. Can't let the secret out or the CDC's on my ass. I kept it low profile. In fact, that's why I didn't go to the police." The man smiled at his clever rationalization.

"Just tell me where you were last night," said Maxim, still not bothering to sit down.

"Sycamore Lodge, Ociffer. I had just come from my aunt's house on the outskirts of Bernalillo. That's outside of Albuquerque, to you."

"Stay there a lot?"

"I live there, most times."

"And what prompted your momentous visit to Sanctuary?"

"You getting smart with me, Detective?"

Maxim grinned. "Of course not. I just mean that it looked like the club was gathering for a specific reason."

Clint's eyes wandered around the room, searching for an explanation. "I don't know what you mean. I figured it had been a few weeks since I'd seen my good brothers. I just happened to swing by for a visit, on account of saying hello. But what kind of asshole would I be if I didn't stop at the Lodge first for a pitcher? The MC gets a special discount, you know."

"So you have no specific knowledge of what the Seventh Sons are up to?"

"Didn't I just say that?"

Maxim twirled his hand to indicate that he wanted to move on. "Just get back to the part about the bar. Were you with any of your brothers there?"

"Good Lord," said Clint, rolling his eyes and looking to the heavens. "Are you hard of hearing or something? I went straightaway to handle my business before I checked in."

"And you don't remember when you left?"

"I do not, sir, on account of me being tired from the long ride. I don't want you thinking I was intoxicated or nothing." Clint laid his hands on the table and sat up straight. "You mind hurrying this up?"

"Settle down," ordered the detective. "Did you see anyone else at the bar?"

"Sure I did."

Maxim stared at Clint until the man realized he should elaborate.

"Well, the usual crowd, I suppose. Some Mexicans. Some Indians. Some tourists. You know, I was surprised I didn't see you there."

Maxim ignored the comment.

"I mean," said Clint, "seeing as to the frequency of your visits."

"I got your meaning," said the detective, doing his best to keep calm. "Did you see any fights or have any words with anyone? Was anybody messing with your bike?"

Clint shook his head. "Officer, I only saw the bottom of my glass. Now can I get going?"

Maxim shot the man a stupefied look. Clint was not worried about his situation. The detective decided to deliver a wake-up call to the suspect. He pulled out his phone and scrolled through the few pictures he had personally taken of the crime scene, then slid it in front of the biker.

"When was the last time you saw this knife?"

Clint stared hard. "I cannot recall, Officer."

"Detective."

"Right."

The fluorescent light hanging close to their heads began to buzz, and Maxim rapped against the housing to silence it. "But you carried it with you down from New Mexico?"

The suspect shrugged. "Now I don't think I said all that."

"But you did. Carry it, I mean. You always have your daddy's knife on you. You wouldn't part with it, wouldn't sell it. Unless you accidentally dropped it at a homicide scene."

The biker's eyes widened. "What?"

The detective leaned past Clint and swiped the image on his phone over to the next. It was a wide shot of the victim. "You do know a man was murdered? Hung upside down, drained, skinned. A bit like that mule deer you cleaned last winter."

The suspect was surprised but didn't grimace or show displeasure at the photo. "Now that's a common technique, there. Certainly not something that can be attributed only to myself."

"Can't say the same about the custom-made knife, Clint."

No one said anything for a minute. The evidence was damning and the picture of the victim convinced Clint he was in trouble. He was beginning to close up. Maxim wondered if he should lay off. He could ask about the gun. He could ask about the vic's identity. No matter what he came up with, however, he was positive the knife was the easiest link to establish. Starting there was best.

Maxim thought about how Clint had been so willing to show him the knife when he'd first asked. The biker had led him out to his Harley as if everything was normal. It wasn't until they were outside that the misdirection began. The detective recalled Clint's bike. Unlike the others, it was missing gear.

"What happened to your saddlebag, Clint?"

The man stammered before answering. "What saddlebag?"

"The one that hangs off the back seat of your bike. I've seen it many times before. Where is it? And don't tell me you pawned it."

Clint didn't answer.

"You don't have it stashed anywhere, do you? Because if Sanctuary officers find it and it's full of drugs—"

"I ain't touched that stuff since Lucky's. It's against my parole."

"You sure, Clint? Once you cross the line, it's easy to go back."

"Of course I'm sure. Listen, I wish I could help but I can't. This ain't got nothin' to do with drugs anyhow. One fuckup and I'm tagged for life. I ain't the only one who does things we ain't supposed to, you know."

Maxim didn't follow. "What are you talking about?"

"I'm talking 'bout your high and mighty superior fucking attitude. Like just 'cause a man breaks the law once, all of a sudden he's a shitbag. Don't you forget that I was in the clubhouse last year when Gaston gave you that briefcase full of money."

The detective's eyes darted to the one-way mirror, then he quickly turned away so as not to draw suspicion. He hoped nobody was outside watching. Maxim stormed around the table and leaned over Clint so that their faces were only inches away. "Listen to me, you fuck. That case of money was used to draw out the previous Seventh Sons president. To get her away from hostages. It wasn't a payoff."

"That's funny," retorted Clint, mildly unsettled but appearing resolute in his accusation. "Because, to my knowledge, that briefcase was never recovered."

Still keeping his voice low in case they had a spectator, Maxim whispered, "There were scores of officials on that scene. The money was lost. It could be anywhere."

The biker returned Maxim's fierce stare. "You think Gaston cares what you did with his money once it left his hands?"

Without thinking, Maxim grabbed Clint by his shoulder and lifted him from his seat. He tried to pin him against a wall, but felt the man's overwhelming strength kick in. Clint was, like the other Seventh Sons, a werewolf. An *hombre lobo*. And he didn't need his animal form to overpower the detective.

The biker shoved Maxim away. Clint sneered as the detective slammed his shoulder into the window. It sent a loud rap through the building. Maxim turned to grab his pistol but saw Clint raise his hands in the air. He backed into the wall and said, "Now, I wasn't trying to hurt you, but you need to be thinking twice before you manhandle me."

The detective stood still, not drawing his weapon. Within moments, the interrogation room door swung open. It was Hitchens. The sergeant. Another wolf, but one that wore blue.

The black man's eyes were bloodshot red. "Is something going on in here that I should know about?"

The biker quickly shook his head. He wasn't interested in starting a fight. Maxim contemplated the situation and relaxed his pose. "No. Sorry about the noise. It was my fault —just got a little excited."

The sergeant stood in place, still fuming. "Good," he replied to Maxim, but his aggressive tone was for Clint. "Because if I get even a whiff of a detective getting assaulted, you will not exit this building." Clint nodded.

"It's okay, Barney," said Maxim, using the sergeant's first name to emphasize their friendship. "I can take it from here."

Hitchens nodded. "Sit down, Clint." The suspect did as he was instructed. "I don't need to chain you up, do I?" Clint shook his head. "Okay then." With that, Hitchens left the room.

Maxim took a few moments. He realized antagonizing the wolf wasn't his best tactic. As they settled down, the detective recovered his cell phone and glanced at the picture. He got to thinking about the case again.

"This body is bad for Sanctuary, Clint. It's bad for the Sons."

The biker swallowed. The brief scuffle had sobered his expression. "Listen, Maxim. You're asking me to admit to carrying a knife near the scene of a murder where it was used."

Maxim nodded, agreeing on the heart of the matter. "Can we talk in hypotheticals, Clint?"

"I hypothetically don't give a shit." He said it quickly, like a built in part of his renegade nature, but no mirth was in the words.

"I'm inclined to believe that you had nothing to do with this man's murder, but if you lie to me you are backing yourself into a corner. At best, you're impeding an investigation. If there's some other charge you might be concerned about, the marshal's office doesn't need to look into that."

Clint pushed out his lips. "I would have believed that before you had that angry black man arrest me for DUI."

The detective nodded. He understood the bitterness, but that was Clint's mistake to live with. Sanctuary could forgive certain transgressions that might be punished in bigger cities, but endangering citizens was not acceptable.

"Hypothetically," repeated Maxim, "if you had that knife at Sycamore Lodge, then knowing what happened to it from there would be the best way to clear your name."

Clint took a deep breath. He was still unconvinced, but warming to the idea. Before either of them could speak, the door opened again.

"I need another minute," said Maxim.

"You won't get it," replied a female voice. Maxim turned

and saw a woman wearing a business suit pushing past him. She was blonde, a little younger than him, and from what he could tell, new in town. "Mr. James, do not say another word. I'm your legal representation."

"It's okay," said Maxim. "Clint is just about to tell me what he knows."

"No he isn't, Detective."

Maxim turned back to the biker and nodded. Clint glanced at the woman, then back at him, then shrugged and remained silent.

"What the fuck, Clint? I thought we understood each other."

"Detective Dwyer!" admonished the lawyer. "We'd love to assist the police, but I need time alone with my client beforehand. We can schedule a formal interview at a later time."

Maxim wanted to scream, but this was part of the job. "Assisting the police means answering my questions now, while the body's still warm."

The woman flashed a blank expression. She had nothing left to say. Maxim took another peek at Clint, but the interview was over.

"Fine then," said Maxim sternly. "Take your time. You're officially under arrest. Get comfortable."

Chapter 5

The Public Health Service Commissioned Corps, which Diego had long served, was a United States uniformed service, but not an armed service. As an ex-Ranger, Diego was an exception and received ancillary weapons training. In fact, he had a great fondness for firearms. He had just never used them illegally before.

Diego checked the payload in his Benelli M4 combat shotgun. It was modern and silver colored, a private joke since he used to hunt werewolves. Of course, there was nothing silver about his high-velocity buckshot. Weapons like this needed the right ammo. Autoloaders were prone to jamming, but that was user error. Not the gun's fault. Put a cheap shell in this shotty, get a cheap result.

West Wind exited the clubhouse supporting three heavy duffel bags over his shoulder. He chuckled when he saw the care Diego gave his weapon.

"We're not hunting pheasant today, little man," said the

Apache.

"We're not hunting anything."

"You know what I mean. I hope you've got more than birdshot in there, 'cause this trip's for real."

Diego knew what West was saying. He'd fired the shotgun at the range and when hunting, but that was the extent of its use. He ignored his uncertainty and held up the Benelli. Aside from its color and the lack of certain attachments, marines were outfitted with the same firearm. "This is large game buckshot. 12-gauge. It'll take anything down."

West Wind puffed out his chest and squared himself to Diego.

"Well, almost anything," admitted Diego.

"Nah," said Omar, walking away from his bike. "That's a badass shotgun. Don't let West get you down—some of us just have classier taste. Check this out, for instance." The kid pulled out a .44 Magnum. "A Colt Anaconda. Plenty of stopping power, even in a revolver."

West muttered something under his breath. Diego tried a smile, but seeing Omar so excited to get use out of his giant handgun was unsettling. "Whatever you say, Taxi Driver."

"Nah, that was a Smith & Wesson. But De Niro was a badass in that anyway."

"He got shot up."

"But he didn't die. Anyway, that's the life. They can pry this from my cold, dead hands if it comes to that."

Diego shuddered. There was no shaking the feeling that

he was making a big mistake by going along.

Sometimes the biker told himself he had no choice. He had a duty to help his brothers, just like when he was in the Corps. Then he would realize he was being an idiot. What was he thinking by getting involved? It was an unsettling kind of indecision that turned his stomach and made everything bitter.

Diego felt a hard slap on his back, Gaston's way of making a friendly gesture.

"You need to know how much I appreciate this. With Clint out of commission, you're really coming through for us."

Diego nodded and slipped the shotgun into a holster attached to his Scrambler.

The Seventh Sons all readied their bikes in the morning sun. None of the jovial mood from earlier remained. A determination was in their eyes, a burden in their thoughts. Each of them knew the stakes.

The bikers were all decked out in their riding gear. Gaston only wore thick cargo pants and a red workout shirt. West had a jean jacket on with cut-off arms. Most of the others had more traditional jackets. For Diego, that meant his black leathers. Except for the steel buckles on his boots, his entire body was covered with a worn, matte finish. The leather was thick and protective because it needed to be. While the rest of the MC members had their individual styles, none needed the protection as much as Diego. They were wolves. Their bones were stronger. While they could suffer damage and break, the next moon would see them completely healed. Without that advantage, Diego needed the interior armor plates and helmet. The stuff even came in handy in fights.

West watched them from the raised porch of the clubhouse. "He'll only come through if he does his job," he grumbled.

"You weren't here last year," said Omar, already sitting on his Harley. He wore a brown leather bomber jacket with the collar up. "He helped the club out when we were in a bind."

"I've heard the stories," said West. "But I haven't seen shit yet."

"And you're not gonna see any today either," cut in Gaston. "Things are gonna go smoothly today. We're just riding in a show of force, but nobody's gonna shoot anybody." The president walked away to ready his Harley.

Diego turned around as well. He was hoping if he ignored the Apache, he would go away. But the man was tenacious. Diego heard his boots hit the dirt and approach him.

"I'm not worried about things going smoothly. I'm worried about shit hitting the fan and relying on a weakling to watch my back." West stopped right behind Diego. "You haven't proven yourself to me. You haven't even been bit."

Diego turned around. Some of these guys, West included, liked to scuffle to settle differences. With their inhuman strength, that would never be a fair fight. He knew that. He had to accept that. But he didn't need to put up with the trash talk.

"I've been bitten before." Diego pulled a sleeve back and exposed the scar on his left forearm. During the club's conflict a year ago, Maxim and Diego had gotten into a shootout at the train yard. Carlos Doka, one of the Yavapai Indian werewolves, had almost killed him. Instead, Diego had stabbed him near the heart with his silver knife. That was how he'd lost the weapon. The wolf scampered away with it embedded in his chest. It was unlikely that he lived the night.

The biker pulled his jacket sleeve back down. It wasn't his only scar. It wasn't the only time he'd been bitten by a wolf. When he had worked for the Commissioned Corps, he hunted them. That was his job. That's why his training had allowed him to fight the stronger opponents. And that's why he wasn't scared of West. But there was a time and place for everything, and Diego didn't have his silver knife anymore. Besides, he told himself, the wolves weren't his enemies now.

West Wind snickered. "You let that mercenary live. He got away." West spat on the floor. He hadn't dealt with the Yavapai outfit before, but he hated them anyway. Diego wondered if it had something to do with his Apache blood. "But it's not the same, Diego. You got the shot. You didn't need to beat the disease. Not like everybody else here."

The other bikers were silent. They weren't even pretending not to be watching. Diego knew they liked him, but he also knew that West was right. They all shared a bond that he would never know. His vaccinations permanently protected him from their affliction. Beating the disease, surviving something with a near one hundred percent fatality rate, was something they were all proud of.

Diego decided not to suck it up this time. He knew he was being reckless, but it was a reckless kind of day. He was about to ride out to a meet with a rival gang. Who was West next to that?

"Let's get something straight, asshole," Diego said, stepping forward to the Apache. "You're the new guy here. You might have wolf blood, but you're a loose cannon. And if anybody hasn't proven themselves yet, it's you."

West glanced at the other bikers and let out a guffaw. To a normal human, Diego would have taken that moment to knee the man in the stomach, but wolves were too strong. The blow wouldn't do any damage and would just open him to retaliation. Instead, Diego leaned in and grabbed the duffel bags behind him. With a sharp tug down, West was pulled backwards by the neck and lost balance. Then Diego used that moment to ram his shoulder into the big man, knocking him to the floor.

The Apache fell to his side and rolled over the bags. With a mix of embarrassment and frustration, he threw the straps away and sprang up to meet his attacker. Immediately, Gaston and the other Sons grabbed hold of him.

"Lay off!" screamed Gaston. "Damn it! I need every one of you in the game."

There was a bit of a struggle, just enough for West to show that he wasn't backing down easily, but then they all relaxed. West clenched his jaw and fumed, never taking his eyes off Diego.

"It's easy to talk shit," said Diego, "when you're nearly invincible. You might not mind riding into enemy territory knowing that you'll be healed up in a few days. I don't have that fucking luxury. And on top of making sure things go smoothly, I don't need you breathing up my ass."

West didn't make a move. The others let him go and patted him on the back. Everybody knew Diego was right. Even West. Fighting amongst themselves now was the last thing they needed.

Gaston nodded and addressed the MC. "These guys are dangerous. The Pistolas used to be a small club. Local. But they've more than doubled their membership. They've made deals with San Diego and Los Angeles. It looks like they own the California desert now. Until we settle this dispute, our main line is at risk. And I don't want stupid grudges getting in the way."

The president turned to the newest club member. "He's coming along with us, isn't he?"

West didn't respond. Then Gaston turned to Diego.

"And I have no idea why you would pick now of all times to make a statement. Maybe it's 'cause you knew we would stop West 'cause we don't need this shit now. But you'd better watch yourself. I won't stop what you start again. You wanna rumble, that's on you."

Diego and West made sure to stare each other down during the speech.

"I'm not kidding," continued Gaston. "The Pistolas should not be taken lightly. They've made a lot of moves in a short time. As we found out when Diego discovered their money van, we were one of those moves. We know for a fact that they tried to cut us out. And for all we know, they still want to."

"They have to cut out my heart before they cut me out," said West.

Gaston nodded. "Don't think they won't. Word on the street is that their new top tier is ruthless. They've used clever tactics to one-up their competition. They play nice at first. One second, you think they're business partners. Then they shoot the shit out of you. Their MO is to shoot you in the back twice."

Omar chimed in. "I still don't know why we don't just take them out."

Gaston shook his head. "We can't shit on El Paso like that. In the end, we *are* middlemen. That means we'll always be sandwiched between supply and distribution. That's why we have the setup between California and Texas. It's perfect for us, but part of the job is dealing with scumbags who don't want us around."

"Not to mention we need to keep a low profile for the CDC," added Diego. If anyone was a constant reminder of the agency's oversight, it was him.

Diego had never liked the illicit activities of the club. He had no interest in the drug business. But there was something romantic about the way the Seventh Sons did business. It wasn't about drugs or guns or an empire—it was all territorial. The Sons owned Arizona, and if anybody wanted a piece, they had to go through them.

"One last thing," said Gaston. "Without Clint, it's six of us. We need to watch our backs. The Pistolas are big. They'll likely show up with more men than we have."

West recovered the duffel bags from the ground. "Yeah, well we have fewer bodies but better firepower." He gave two of the bags to Curtis and Trent and kept one for himself. He unzipped it to show it off. "Adaptive Combat Rifles."

Diego recognized the sleek black weapon. They were replacements for Army carbines. "Bushmaster ACRs?"

"Nah," said West Wind, grinning like a toddler up to no good. "Remington."

"That's the military model. They're illegal for civilian use."

"Damn right on both counts. Fully automatic selective fire, 6.8 mm Special Purpose Cartridge assembly—this is the perfect urban warfare weapon."

"They also look like the same assault rifles the Yavapai used to carry." Diego leered at Gaston. "Where'd we get these?"

West laughed. "I thought you didn't want to know about the club's extra-curricular activities?"

Diego tilted his head. "It's a little late for that."

"These rifles are contraband," instructed Gaston. "Keep them out of sight. Do not get caught with them. Everybody else's sidearms are fine. You know what kind of ship I run. I like legit guns. We don't wear colors, so we won't be breaking laws anywhere. Just in case, we'll have Omar scout ahead." Gaston turned to the kid. "Then you'll ride behind us, making sure we're not followed. I don't know what Maxim is up to but he can't trail us on this one. Understood?"

Omar nodded and zipped up his jacket. Everyone else straddled their bikes. Diego's black Triumph Scrambler had a shiny wax coat. He hoped it, and all of them, would come out in the same condition.

"Let's play it cool," Diego said. "I don't want shit to get ugly. I don't want to have to kill anyone."

West scoffed but didn't say anything. The others started their motorcycles. Gaston walked his hog beside Diego.

"Make no mistake. I know you're buddies with that cop, but the boys in blue ain't your brotherhood. No more one foot in and one foot out. You're riding with us now. You need to jump in."

His throttle roared and Gaston sped ahead. A cloud of dust swirled as the Seventh Sons rode out in force.

Chapter 6

Maxim Dwyer took the steps down two at a time on his way to the morgue. Waiting was a big part of the job. Sitting in a car, expecting a phone call, getting a hold of the judge—the wheels of investigation turned slowly but steadily. Maxim was accustomed to it. But for some reason, waiting on autopsies always got the better of him.

Working a body was an urgent affair. Fresh murders needed big breaks in the first day or two to show promise of being solved. Luckily, Sanctuary was a small town. The marshal's office was rarely overloaded. Maxim would have weeks to work the case before anybody batted an eye. It was an atmosphere that allowed the detective to really get involved with the background players and make sure all loose ends were tied off. But none of that meant that he didn't need that big break first.

Although the ME had only gotten the body a few hours ago, he was already finished with the preliminary examination.

That was another great thing about small towns. The facilities and funds were limited, but they didn't need a lot of manpower for immediate results. Large cities had morgues with waiting lists, pathologists that needed to examine several bodies a day. Not so in Sanctuary. They didn't even need a full-time medical examiner.

Dr. Medina was fairly young, not yet in his forties. A short man with a clean appearance and a strong hairline, he was well liked in town. Not strictly a pathologist, he primarily worked as a general practice physician. Out of necessity he had garnered a background in forensics, and now, whenever the marshal's office needed an autopsy, they contacted him.

The detective glanced at the sign above the doorway to the morgue: "*Hic locus est ubi mors gaudet succurrere vitae.*" Below the Latin inscription was the English translation: "This is the place where death rejoices to help life." Maxim entered the tiled room and pulled a paper mask from a dispenser box hanging on the wall. He nodded to the doctor as he approached his workstation. The skinned body rested on a stainless steel table that was slanted to allow blood to run into a drain. The ME had cabinets and a counter with a sink running alongside him, giving him easy access to his tools. Above the table was a large light in a metal housing that could be adjusted to ensure that every nook in the deceased could be carefully scrutinized. The white tile floor beneath them resembled a walk-in shower, with its own slope and drain, reminding Maxim that the entire workstation was meant to be sprayed down and sanitized between jobs.

Once he fit the mask to his face, Maxim spoke. "What do you have?"

Dr. Medina was wearing scrubs and a paper hat in addition to the same mask. It was obvious the examination was over, but his latex gloves were clean, indicating he had put on a fresh pair.

"The victim is a male. Thirty-five to forty-five. I'll know more after we send the DNA out. Since you are light on identifying factors, I tried examining the skull for any indicators of race."

"You can do that? Based on the shape of the skull?"

"Yes and no. Geography plays a much larger part in biological imprints than the familiar concepts of race. Various traits can be indicative but not conclusive. X-rays of the skull gave me some clues, but direct examination of the teeth was more valuable. They are well spaced. The incisors are scooped in the back. Additionally, they exhibit minor sclerosed dentition. I see some thinning of the root canal but nothing that would cause damage to the teeth. Combined with the long strand of black hair you found, I think it's fairly safe to say this man is of Native American ancestry."

Maxim nodded. He was more concerned with the "when" than the "who" right now. Identifying this body was going to take time. If his DNA was in the criminal database, it would be about a week before that came back to them. Maybe less if they could rush it.

"Have you narrowed down time of death?"

Dr. Medina nodded. "I'm getting to that. Lividity can be difficult when a body is skinned, but certainly not impossible. Blood vessels get congested either way. The draining of the blood, however, is trickier. Depending on how much has exited the body, the aftereffects can vary. Take a look at the shoulders."

Maxim examined the body more closely but it turned his stomach. The paper mask did nothing to soften the stench. The detective had seen plenty of corpses, bloated and discolored, in his career. What they had before them, however, was something out of a horror movie. The body's chest cavity was still open, its rib cage spread apart. Usually corpses were sewed up pretty quickly. It was surreal.

"That bluish color?" asked Maxim.

"Yes, it is very slight. This wouldn't often be the case with dead bodies suspended upside down. But then you have this," he said, pointing to the neck. "Both carotid arteries have been cleanly severed."

Maxim hadn't noticed before. Picking out details on a corpse of bloody muscle and fat was hard. "Sliced through the neck and drained."

"Exactly," affirmed the doctor. "Once the heart stops, the only pressure on the blood comes from gravity. Blood that would have settled in the shoulders found an outlet. Now look at this."

Dr. Medina motioned the detective over to his side of the table. Maxim stepped around and saw the man holding his finger to the hole in the skull, tilted upward. "This is a rough trajectory of the bullet. The shooter was below the head. Or, in the case of the body being suspended upside down, standing above him. The lack of skin has prevented any recovery of powder burns, but this angle suggests the gun was held close. This man was executed before the skinning happened."

Maxim nodded. "No sign of torture then?"

The doctor bit his lip and adjusted his wire glasses with his forearm. His gloves were no longer clean. "There's no hard evidence of torture. It's impossible to tell with the missing left thumb, for instance, but the muscle tearing indicates animal tampering more than anything else. The actual kill and postmortem skinning show a skillful hand. Nothing sloppy about it." Maxim wanted to ask about the chest wound, but he suspected he was drawing the ME off subject and annoying him. He let Dr. Medina finish.

"We got lucky with the gunshot wound. First, it was a . 22 caliber bullet. It bored through the skull and shattered, bouncing around the brain. Sudden death. No exit wound. That itself is not too uncommon. But the entry wound nearly sealed up as the skull caved in on itself." Maxim thought he knew where the medical examiner was headed. "Surprisingly, the skull fracture didn't result in massive blood loss."

"The blood didn't drain from the head," said the detective.

"Exactly. There's enough congealment in the capillaries of the head to gauge lividity. Judging from what I've seen, this man was killed between 12 and 1 a.m. this morning."

That was exactly what Maxim was looking for. If the body was discovered between 5 and 6 a.m. then the window for its drop-off was still wide.

"Last year I saw an elk drained in three hours. Is that about what we're looking at here?"

"Maybe four hours," said the doctor, "including skinning."

Maxim nodded. That meant that the man could have been murdered anywhere. An hour, maybe two, away. Not in Sanctuary. But, with the hunting background of the kill, likely somewhere in Sycamore.

"What about identifying markers? Are we lucky on that end?"

Dr. Medina quickly shook his head. "Not quite. DNA will be our best bet. There's no skin for tattoos or fingerprints. No sign of dental work. I can give you the X-rays but there's no guarantee a dentist has these on file. It's safe to say that John Doe never got braces. The teeth are crooked, but strong. The gums are healthy. In fact..." said the ME, moving back to the counter to check his notes, "the man was exceptionally healthy, discounting his murder. I sectioned his coronary arteries and saw no signs of heart disease. His lungs were pink. Usually, a man his age will show some signs of wear."

That last fact struck Maxim as strange. While an anomaly to the medical examiner, the detective knew of another reason this man may have been free from degenerative disease: it was possible he was a werewolf. If that were true, then maybe the Seventh Sons were involved with the murder after all.

"What material was the bullet?" he asked. The doctor gave Maxim a strange glance. "I mean, was there anything special about it?"

Dr. Medina took another step and pointed to a clear bag on his desk. Maxim picked it up and saw four bullet fragments inside. Lead.

"I'll have those sent for ballistics," said the doctor. "The largest fragment looks promising, considering."

Maxim nodded and put the bag down. Would a single bullet to the brain be enough to kill a wolf? He remembered needing to fire into Deborah's heart multiple times. The old Seventh Sons president had been especially powerful, though. She couldn't be put down without silver. For his theory about this man being a wolf to hold up, there needed to be additional explanation.

"Did you test against the blood on the skinning knife?"

Maxim had tried to dust the knife for prints but it was clean. He recalled how close it was to the body when he found it. Not immediately obvious, but it would have been sloppy to miss it. Almost as if the killer wanted the knife to be found.

"It's the same blood type as the John Doe. It looks to be a match, but we haven't confirmed that yet."

The detective nodded. The only clue they would garner from the knife was the one he already knew: the owner. Clint was still in the interrogation room. The lawyer had come and gone, but she was due for a formal interview soon. Maxim needed stronger leverage against the man than his father's knife.

"So what else do you have?"

"Unfortunately, Detective Dwyer, that completes my solid findings from the initial examination. We'll need to wait for Coconino for the lab results." The Sanctuary morgue was limited. It could only hold six bodies on ice. Autopsy one at a time. All DNA and fiber testing had to be outsourced. It was standard procedure and Maxim expected that, but he had hoped to get something more from the exam. "However," said the ME, interrupting Maxim's thoughts, "there is something else. I can't draw any conclusions from it. It's puzzling. I need to get in touch with some colleagues to identify it."

"What is it, Doctor?"

"The chest wound. There's a deep slice penetrating John Doe's lung. It was immediately obvious, but I haven't been able to conclude when it occurred. It's clear that it happened before this incident."

Maxim remembered the blackened area on the outside of the rib cage. Now, with the chest cavity opened up, the wound was not visible. "Why is that?"

"The infection. The abscess. The puss surrounding the area was not postmortem. The blackened muscle showed atrophy. Even the lung had some milky fluid around the wound."

"So our vic suffered a stab wound in the chest at some point."

"Yes. It was a serious wound, too. He would have needed immediate medical attention."

"What would that have involved?" asked Maxim.

"Well, the lung would have needed repair. The muscle and flesh stitched. I don't see any signs of that."

A picture was forming in Maxim's head. This man could have been a missing person. A prisoner. He may have survived his initial attack only to be killed some time later.

"How long could this man have survived in that condition?" he asked.

Dr. Medina shook his head. "A week, maybe. This man should have drowned in his own blood. But there's no sign of that. In fact, gauging from the deterioration and the advanced infection, I would conclude that the wound was much older than that."

Something tugged at Maxim. "How long?" Dr. Medina seemed averse to answer. "How long, Doctor?"

The man raised his eyebrows in exasperation. "It defies logic, Detective, but I would have to say months. At least. Only..."

"That's impossible," finished Maxim.

The ME nodded. "I've never seen anything like it. An exterior infection, a gangrene, sure. But a pierced lung like this would have been life threatening. Extremely painful. For this man to have been stabbed so near the heart and survived more than two weeks is a miracle."

The heart. The healthy heart. It clicked in Maxim then. This man *was* a werewolf. And he was struck with silver, which is why it hadn't healed. It just wasn't a bullet.

Nine months ago, Maxim and Diego had fought off Deborah and two Yavapai werewolves. Diego had stabbed one of the wolves between the ribs. It scampered off to a sure death. Except they never found the body. Diego never recovered his weapon. If the wolf had survived all that time in hiding, that would explain the lack of closure.

"Shit," said Maxim. "I have an ID."

The doctor regarded him expectantly.

"Carlos Doka. The Yavapai Indian."

Dr. Medina's eyes widened in recognition. "One of the Paradise Killers? The man that tried to kill you when you worked the case?"

Maxim couldn't tell if he nodded because he was fighting back a fierce rush of adrenaline. The Yavapai mercenaries had been working with the old Seventh Sons president. They were abducting and killing vagrants and dumping them in Paradise Tank. The case could have torn the motorcycle club apart, but Maxim had isolated the guilty parties and limited the blowback. The Seventh Sons were saved. And if anybody wouldn't want Doka to return and draw the spotlight, it was them.

Chapter 7

The Colorado River, to the north of Sanctuary, ran through the Grand Canyon. Following it west, past the vast mountain ranges and forests, the body of water persevered in the driest of climates. It cut south and formed the western border of Arizona, first lining Nevada, then California.

The river was a beautiful respite from the surrounding desert. The blues and greens were the lifeblood in the middle of sand. Many communities sprouted along the water. Where Interstate 40 met the border, the highway weaved past several trailer parks full of residents who would rather be somewhere serene than convenient. It was the type of area where people minded their own business, and the perfect spot for the Seventh Sons to meet the Pistolas.

Diego rode with the others into a clearing off the highway. They circled around an old, broken-down storage structure and saw the Mexican gang waiting by the river. Five guys sat on bikes next to a black van. West indicated others on the perimeter. Diego counted five of them standing at a distance. They each wore a black jacket with their colors on the back.

Diego wanted to slow down. To confer with Gaston quickly about the lay of the land. But it would have shown weakness to appear nervous. West and the others had already drawn their ACRs. They were ready, so Gaston and the Seventh Sons rode to the central group without hesitation.

The lower land was surrounded, thought Diego, but they weren't outnumbered by as many as he had expected. Maybe the Pistolas did mean to do business.

The bikes came to a stop at a figure with his back to them. The white patch on his back stood out against the black leather: a skull with two pistols as crossbones. The man slowly turned. His bare torso was exposed beneath the open jacket. He wasn't especially large, but his chest and arm muscles were oversized. To Diego, it was the look of a convict who had spent all his incarceration working out. Prison tattoos on his hands. He had faded words printed on his stomach and a handprint on his chest. Thick eyebrows and a mustache complemented his black hair, and he wore brown sunglasses that looked straight from the nineteen-eighties.

Despite never personally meeting any of the Sons before, the man immediately picked out Gaston and approached him.

"You the prez, huh?" he asked.

Gaston remained casually seated on his bike. He was a

big guy, but his muscles were not as well-defined as the Mexican's. The Seventh Sons all knew that his strength, however, was much greater. "Gaston," he announced, loud enough for the others to hear.

One of the Pistolas leaning on the van spoke up. "Hector. He's the one."

Diego recognized the speaker as the man who'd driven the money van they had intercepted. When Diego had notified the rest of the MC, Gaston had been front and center when pulling the vehicle over.

Hector, the shirtless man, nodded to his friend and turned back to Gaston. "I hear you put a gun on my homie." It wasn't a question. The man was a veteran, well into his forties, and had probably seen as much as there was to see on the street. He wasn't afraid of strangers.

Gaston dismounted his bike and approached Hector. He towered over the shorter man and smiled. "If your guys make moves without telling us, how are we supposed to know not to?"

The man smiled back, cold eyes barely visible behind the brown lenses. He pulled in a deep breath that sounding like a boat engine turning, as if he were about to spit.

"*Suave*, Hector." A skinny guy behind the convict neared and patted him on the back. "We're here to do business, not front."

Diego hadn't taken note of the kid before, but he now recognized he was important. He was young, maybe nineteen or twenty. He had a bald head and a thin mustache and goatee worn in a more modern style. He wore a loose, white wifebeater under his open jacket, and his entire torso was covered in tattoos that ran up to his neck and abruptly stopped at his chin. The only tattoo on his head was a small teardrop outside his left eye. And his eyes, they were deep and dark and striking. They showed intelligence. And something else. Ruthlessness.

"Sergio Lima," he said, extending his hand to Gaston. They did a quick shake and capped it off by bumping their fists together. Hector spat in the dirt and Sergio chuckled. "This is my Sergeant-at-Arms, Hector Cruz. He's a little rough around the edges. Spent more of his life in a cage than on the outside. He doesn't know how to act in social situations. Thinks everything is about fronting and showing strength. Isn't that right, Hector?"

The man looked to be a stone statue, menacing and determined.

"You see?" joked Sergio. "It cracks me up. *Calmate*," he said to Hector, grinning from ear to ear. As Sergio turned, Diego noticed the president patch on his jacket. This young kid was the gang's leader. No wonder they made reckless moves. "So you *éses* hijacked our money?"

Gaston's face showed annoyance already. "We finished the delivery for you. I hope you don't mind, but we took a small fee."

"I've heard. Had to explain myself to *La Eme*. You can't blame a brother for trying to save some scratch."

"You've got plenty of choices. You can run up in Vegas if you want—deal with Chicago—but they're greedy. Or you can roll south of Phoenix and take your chances with Border

Patrol. You know, they strip search Mexicans over there for not using turn signals. Now, if you want the easiest route, I'd suggest you run through the Sons."

Sergio Lima nodded. "I understand your position, holmes. We didn't know each other before. You can't blame me for moving money."

Gaston was firm. "You knew this was our highway."

Sergio's face tilted to the side and he pinched an eye closed, as if he considered it an open point. "Let's just say I know that now. But, I need you to understand something. I know El Paso puts up with you guys, but don't think they have love for you. We can work together, but I don't want you drawing on my boys again."

Hector Cruz stepped forward. "Or you might get some lead in your back, *ése*."

Next to Diego, West Wind laughed. "Better men have tried."

Sergio put his hand up to Hector and nodded at the Apache's assault rifle. A glimmer struck his eyes. "That's some serious hardware, holmes."

The sound of a bike approached them from behind. It was Omar, just arriving after watching their tail. Some of the Pistolas reached for their weapons.

"It's okay," said Diego as Omar pulled up. "It's one of our guys."

Sergio raised his eyebrows and signaled for his men to relax. "Look at this! You got a cholo riding with you! *Como te llamas?*"

The kid looked to Gaston, then Sergio. "Omar." He

tried to sound tough. Even though he was the same age as the Pistolas president, he didn't have any of the confidence or swagger.

"*Entonces*, Omar. *Tú eres Mexicano.* You should be riding with your blood."

Omar glanced at Gaston again, then shook his head.

Sergio laughed and turned to Diego. "*Y tú?* You really wanna ride with these white boys and Tonto?" Besides remarking on West, Sergio was ignoring that Curtis was black. It must have been shocking for the gang to see a club of mixed race. "Why don't you come over to *las Pistolas*?"

Diego reached down and patted the holster on his Scrambler. "I'm more of a shotgun guy, myself."

Sergio smiled, an insincere expression that attempted to express levity. But he knew the seriousness of the meet. He was just testing their members. Getting a feel for how they reacted.

"Oh, that's right," said the Pistolas president. "*Los hombres lobos.* That's your blood." The Seventh Sons didn't respond. "Well, I don't care what stories you have your hood believing about you. You bleed. Just like us."

"This is bullshit," exclaimed West. The Apache wasn't much on patience, and Diego was personally surprised he had behaved this long, especially after the Tonto slur. "We're not getting paid to trade war stories. Let's get the van and get out of here." The Indian hopped off his bike and brushed past the Mexicans, towards the vehicle. West didn't wait for anyone to follow. He just went off without concern for the danger.

That's when Diego's eyes shifted to the van parked by the river. He thought this was supposed to be a meet and greet. Apparently, more was going on.

Sergio raised his eyebrows and opened his mouth into a sideways smirk. "Homie's too tough for small talk, huh?"

Gaston stared down Hector. "Every club has one."

The men moved to the rear of the van. The Pistolas opened up the back. From his bike, Diego could only imagine the contraband within. The biker observed the area to make sure it was clear. Some of the Pistolas watching from the fringes had moved in a bit. Diego glanced across the river and saw an old trailer standing alone. It was run down and appeared unoccupied. Thinking this was Arizona and that was California was strange. No indication of a border existed.

"That's it?" asked Gaston.

Sergio put his arm around his fellow president. "Call it a get-to-know-you load. Manolo will drive again. This time he stays with you. He wants to see you all the way to the hand-off in Albuquerque. If he reports back that everything went smoothly, we'll be in business."

Diego grimaced. Gaston hadn't mentioned the run to him. He had known that Diego wanted no part of a drug deal. Now it was too late.

After some more words were exchanged, Gaston shook Sergio's hand again and headed back to his bike. West stared down Hector as he followed. Both men were muscle and knew it. Somehow, they had to outdo the other. Hector continued his stoic appearance, his eyes hidden behind his sunglasses.

"Let's roll out, brothers," said Gaston. "We've got a ride ahead of us."

Chapter 8

Maxim closed the interrogation room door behind him. Clint was seated, his hands fidgeting on the table. Next to him was his lawyer, the blonde woman who interrupted them earlier. Her hair was short and combed behind her ears. She had pinkish cheeks and a well-worn smile but looked more business than pleasure. She sat up straight with her legs crossed in pressed business pants. She was about Maxim's age. Attractive in a traditional way but a bit too plain for his tastes.

"Good afternoon, Detective. My name is Teresa Banks. I'm counsel for Mr. James." She looked over at Clint, who had a bored expression on his face.

Maxim held back a chuckle. The two looked ridiculous next to each other. Clint was a drunk with a beer belly, long hair, and a wild, bushy beard. An old-school outlaw biker to the core. His companion was a WASP, well-educated, and probably didn't even smoke cigarettes. The detective figured she was a married mother of two.

"Nice to properly meet you, Mrs. Banks."

"It's Ms., Detective Dwyer."

Maxim nodded, then saw the woman wore no wedding ring. He should have noticed that. "Fine," he said, then sat down. "I'm happy your client has finally chosen to cooperate with police."

Clint suddenly scowled. "I don't need—"

The detective shot his hand up to stop him and withdrew a paper and pen from his jacket. "I need you to read this form and sign it, Clint. It's a statement of your rights."

"I know my rights," he said in protest, brushing the form away.

"Ms. Banks?"

The lawyer slid the paper back to Clint.

"We take Miranda very seriously in this state, Clint," said Maxim. "The reason they're called Miranda Rights is because Ernesto Miranda challenged his Arizona conviction."

The older man paused as he considered that. "And what happened?"

"The Supreme Court overturned the ruling."

"So there is justice."

"Sure there is," answered the detective. "He was retried and convicted."

Clint flashed a dry smile. Teresa Banks had him sign the form and slid it back to Maxim.

"My client can't be charged with any wrongdoing," she stated as she pulled a paper from her briefcase. "Here is a statement from Melody Holton, the owner of Sycamore Lodge, stating that Mr. James was in her establishment between the hours of 10 p.m. and 1 a.m. last night."

Maxim took a look at the statement. He thought about the time of death, between twelve and one. It didn't rule Clint out definitively, but Ms. Banks would stress the inconsistency in court. It was enough for reasonable doubt.

Teresa Banks allowed herself a smug smile before returning her attention to the statement. "Ms. Holton goes on to say that there were no physical altercations in her bar last night involving my client."

Maxim thought about the wording. "In her bar." It was a weak attempt at walking the line. Melody used to be a Seventh Son herself. When her mother was ousted as president and she inherited the roadhouse, she'd decided she was done with the outlaw life. Gaston agreed, but they still had a good relationship. This statement was Melody's way of not lying to police but covering Clint's ass. Maxim tossed the paper back to the lawyer.

"I'm gonna cut you off right there before you go down the wrong path with me. I've looked into things between now and this morning. I've talked to a few Sycamore Lodge regulars." The detective turned his attention to Clint. "I know for a fact that you arranged a fight in the back lot." Maxim frequented the bar himself. He knew who to talk to. It was a popular enough location that nothing could be hidden from him there. Although the witness had only mentioned that the other brawler was Native American, Maxim had more information after the autopsy. "A

Yavapai."

Clint immediately stuttered. The detective had nailed it. Ms. Banks regarded the two of them.

"What is he..." she started to ask, then stopped and recovered herself. Maxim figured the woman didn't want to appear surprised in front of him.

"Listen to me, Clint. I'm not gonna arrest you for a punching match. Especially an organized one. But you know better than to tangle with the Yavapai. After the serial killings last year, you know damn well that the Seventh Sons have cut all ties."

Clint looked nervous. His eyes shifted between the detective and the lawyer. He didn't trust either of them.

Maxim pressed him. "It doesn't look good, Clint. Not when I have witnesses that put you in a fistfight hours before a Yavapai body turns up close by."

"Okay," said the biker, exasperated. His eyes were wide with what Maxim read as panic. Clint sat at attention and opened his hands in compliance. "Okay," he said more softly. "I..."

The biker didn't say anything for a moment. Maxim knew better than to interrupt. The man was coming clean.

"I was stupid," he finally said.

Ms. Banks cut in. "Mr. James. I'm going to request that you don't answer any more questions."

The detective didn't take his eyes off the man. He ignored the lawyer. "Clint, what did you do?"

"Look," the man said, facing his lawyer, "I didn't tell you because you work for Gaston. If he finds out that I scrapped with a Yavapai he'll have my head."

"Mr. James! Anything you tell me is privileged."

"Whatever."

She nodded and put her hand up to stop him. "Detective, I'm going to need a moment with my client."

"That's bullshit. You've had your time. There's a dead body downstairs that doesn't have any skin on it. I need to know how that happened. And right now, all clues are pointing to your client."

"It wasn't me!" he cried. "Lord! I didn't kill anyone. It was just a quick scuffle. We had a three-minute bell in the backyard. We roughed each other up and walked away. You know how it is," he said, pleading with Maxim. "We couldn't let loose."

He was talking about the fact that both of them were werewolves. A fight between them could have been savage if they hadn't held back. Exposing themselves wouldn't be in either of their interests.

"Three minutes?" he asked.

Clint shook his head, confused by the question. "Sure. It's a thing we do sometimes. Keeps the action civil. Contained."

"And others watched?" Maxim already knew the answer to that question, but he wanted to establish that Clint was telling the truth.

"Yeah. Must have been eight, ten people out there."

"Who was it? Why'd you fight?"

"I forget his name, but he's strong. A good fighter. He was alone. I didn't recognize him as one of the tribe immediately. The dude was drunk. Harassing the customers. I told Melody I'd take care of it as soon as I found out he was a—"

Clint stopped himself suddenly. He was going to say that he found out the Yavapai was a wolf. Maxim considered the lawyer. She worked for the MC but did she know their secret?

"An asshole," Clint finished.

"Was this what the man looked like?" Maxim slid an old picture of Carlos Doka, the victim in the morgue.

"Doka?" asked Clint? "What the fuck you have this picture for, man? I know who Doka is. Everybody does. But he disappeared last year. He wasn't the guy I fought."

"But he was Yavapai?"

"That's what I figured. I used to see him around more, before last year. Once I was already in his face, it was too late to back down."

Teresa Banks grabbed the picture. "Do you have an ID of the victim, Detective? Is this simply a matter of proving that my client did not have an altercation with the victim?"

Maxim tore the picture from her hands. "No ID yet." Technically, it was true. He didn't have confirmation of it and Carlos Doka was a bit of a stretch. But something about it felt right to Maxim's every instinct.

"This sounds like the fight is not linked to the crime," stated the lawyer plainly. "What is relevant, however, is that some time after the altercation, when Mr. James exited the bar at 1 a.m., his saddlebag was missing."

"Missing?"

"Stolen."

Maxim turned to the biker. "You suddenly remember that now?"

Ms. Banks answered for Clint. "He recalls having it before entering the bar. He knows it was missing this morning. I have a list of the full contents of the bag, none of which are illegal. His father's skinning knife was inside. Here's a copy." She pulled a printout from her briefcase and placed it on the table. It had a list of innocuous possessions. A pack of Marlboros. A Zippo with a skull on it. Leather gloves. Sunglasses.

"No pistols?" asked Maxim.

Ms. Banks shook her head. "Mr. James doesn't own any handguns."

Maxim nodded his head slowly as he pondered the new information. If Clint's saddlebag had been legitimately stolen, then it didn't matter much whether there had been a gun inside or not. The skinning knife was enough of a link to the crime.

That meant at least one Seventh Son and one Yavapai were involved. Two, if the man Clint had fought was not Doka. The Yavapai body was terrible for the motorcycle club, either way. Maxim would need to question Melody about her knowledge. If she had tipped off Gaston about a Yavapai in town causing trouble, things could have gone south quickly. He dearly hoped that wasn't the case.

The Indian reservation was about half an hour south. A small band of them, mercenaries and werewolves, used to do business with the old Seventh Sons president. Things went sour and both gangs took hits to their leadership. The Yavapai still hated the Sons, and Maxim was sure the feeling was mutual.

"So when can you get me out of here?" asked Clint.

Maxim shook his head. "You're in custody. You're gonna be held until I figure things out."

"What is my client charged with?" asked Ms. Banks.

"I don't know yet."

Clint slammed his hands on the table. "But what about my rights?"

Maxim stood up to go. "Read the form next time."

Chapter 9

Manolo exited the black van and swiped a credit card at the gas pump. He held the fuel nozzle in place as he leaned against the side of the vehicle, casually chewing gum and watching his escort. Curtis and Trent pulled their bikes up to the storefront and went inside. Diego figured they wanted the air conditioner more than anything else. It was ninety degrees outside. That was about the peak of the summer heat in Sanctuary, but as they continued east through Arizona, to lower elevation, it would quickly get worse.

Diego took the momentary break to get off his bike, unzip his jacket, and remove his helmet. He could feel sweat running down his arms, back, and ass. Riding in the desert was fun, but he much preferred it at night. The biker paced back and forth to get the air flowing, keeping an eye on the Mexican twenty yards away. Gaston and West were still straddling their Harleys. Ever stoic. But Diego didn't have the same confidence as they did in the events unfolding.

"You figure it out yet?" asked Diego, uneasy.

Gaston and West shot him puzzled looks. The president wiped the sweat through his spiked hair. "Figure what out?"

"What the hell is going on," answered Diego. "Since when does the drug pipeline flow east? The cartel comes through El Paso. Distributes out from there. Everything moving through us comes from them to California. The only thing we've ever moved east was money."

West scoffed. "So it's 'we' all of a sudden."

"I'm here, aren't I? You wanted me along, so you need to hear me out."

Gaston nodded. "I know. I didn't ask why the tar was going back east. Maybe they're having shortages. But they also have us moving SIGs."

Diego cursed and checked Manolo again. The man was observing them but was too far away to hear. Diego kept his voice down anyway. "They're fucking guns in that van?"

"Relax," said West. "It's a small load."

"Guns can bring terrorism charges against us. Shit, our ACRs can do that."

"Exactly," joked West. "So what's the worry?"

Gaston shook his head. "Diego, I know you're nervous. Trust me. I've done this before."

"No," said Diego. "You're not seeing something." The biker paced away a few steps as he heard Omar, who had lagged behind them on the road, roll up. Seeing the discussion, he stopped next to the group. Diego ignored him and kept talking through the problem. "Something's weird.

This kind of thing is too risky for a small load."

"It's a test," said the Apache. "The Pistolas don't trust us. They wanna see how we operate. See all the gears in motion to make sure the whole thing works."

The explanation didn't satisfy Diego. "This is no test. El Paso could vouch for us. This is a hit, man."

Now it was Gaston who scoffed. "If the Pistolas were gonna try to take us out, they would have done it when they had us outnumbered and surrounded."

"I'd like to see them try," said West, chuckling.

"We rode in to that meet with our weapons hot. They didn't want to take the chance. They outnumber us but we outgun them. They knew we'd be ready." Diego shook his head. "Think about it. A small load. Heroin going the wrong way. Guns. And only one Pistola driving instead of two. This is a test all right. A test to see if we can fight them off. We're not meant to get to Albuquerque intact."

Trouble crept into the faces of the other men, and for once they didn't immediately reject the idea.

"There's nobody behind us," said Omar. "I personally saw the Pistolas cross back into California. I waited a while. No one followed."

"It's not what's behind us that I'm worried about," said Diego.

The four of them sat silently, each considering the angles. When the lone California outlaw finished pumping, he approached them. Manolo had the sort of playful smirk that meant trouble.

"Everything cool, bros?"

Gaston nodded.

"Get off your bikes, at least," said the Mexican. "Get some water. Get out of the sun. We still got a long ride."

"We're fine," cut in Diego.

Gaston studied him. The possibilities dawned on him as well. "Let's hurry this up," he told Manolo. "I wanna get as much out of the daylight as possible."

The other man shrugged and tightened his bandanna. "Have it your way, *ése*. I'm gonna take a quick leak. Then we'll go." He ambled away grinning, enjoying a private joke that hadn't been told.

"Fuck me," said West, scanning the street. "I think de la Torre's right. He flipped the duffel bag around his shoulder so it hung on his chest and unzipped it, getting a grip on his assault rifle while it was still hidden within. As Curtis and Trent came out of the store, West whistled them over. They were laughing about something but noticed West's stance and quickly readied themselves.

Gaston's boot went up and down, stomping the dirt as he worked the problem. "I don't know. Attack us in Arizona? I don't think they have the balls."

Diego nodded. "They might, but they'd have more friends in New Mexico."

They all nodded absentmindedly, watching their surroundings for any signs of danger.

"Fuck it," said Gaston. "We can't ditch the escort. If we do that, then we might not have El Paso's backing anymore."

"Damned if we do, damned if we don't," said West.

Diego didn't like the expressions his brothers wore. "So we just ride with targets painted on our backs?"

"Look. Whether we like it or not, we're gonna be judged by this run." Gaston turned to Omar. "Hey, kid. How about you ride up ahead? As far as you can get. All the way to Albuquerque. Keep an eye out for anything waiting for us."

Omar turned the throttle. "Okay, but I think we're just being paranoid." He had never even turned off his hog. Without worrying about the rest of the details, he sped off, trying to get as much distance between them as possible.

Diego knew the kid worked hard to impress the other bikers. He just worried about the kind of life he would have in twenty years. The thought hit Diego that he should be worrying about his own life. He was in the same situation. He faced the same dangers.

Even worse, because he wasn't a wolf.

"As for everyone else," continued Gaston, "let's give the escort some extra leeway and spread out. Stay locked and loaded."

West clenched and released his jaw, a visual cue of the adrenaline in his veins. "Damn. I wish Clint was here. That redneck can shoot."

"You, Curtis, and Trent have the ACRs. That should equalize any odds. And we've got a ranch off the highway before the state line. I figure we'll make it at least that far safely. We can pick up some extra firepower there and continue on to New Mexico."

Curtis ran his hand over his bald head and lifted his duffel bag. "I don't like rolling into the city with this kind of weight." Because of their unusual resilience, the Seventh Sons were usually very careful about the hardware they carried. One traffic stop could lead to years in prison if they had anything illegal. Unless there was a real threat, it was better just to get shot and heal.

"It can't be helped," said West. "If the Pistolas are coming after us, we need to be ready."

Curtis just gritted his teeth and exchanged a look with Trent.

Chapter 10

Marshal Boyd held a finger in the air as he continued speaking into his cell phone. He was grinning from ear to ear like a politician even though whoever he was talking to couldn't see it. But the words could be clearly heard. They were strong words. Action words. "Mobilizing." "Command post." "Top priority." They were words meant to inspire confidence in the listener. Maxim wondered if Boyd was talking to his father, the mayor of Sanctuary.

The detective closed the door silently and sat across from his boss. He'd been in this office many times. It was the place where he talked through his cases. The first time he was required to vocalize his theories. It was also the first time that outside pressure crept into his investigation. The marshal wasn't a real police officer—he had been appointed to his position by his powerful family without ever having patrolled the streets—but it wasn't as bad as it could have been. For the most part, Boyd left the police work to the officers. Despite Maxim's initial fears when Boyd took over, the man hadn't overstepped his bounds. He supervised at a macro level, choosing to place more emphasis on his role as a civic leader and the public image of the marshal's office. It was an arrangement that worked well for Maxim—and Marshal Boyd was an expert at managing expectations—but judging from the phone call he was finishing up, it didn't look like this case could afford free rein.

"Did he do it?" asked the marshal, suddenly tossing the phone to his desk and shifting his full attention to Maxim. Boyd's cold blue eyes engaged the detective. They worked on many levels. Now all they were seeking was gratification.

Maxim almost winced under the glare. "It's not looking solid."

"I don't want to hear that, Detective Dwyer. Did Clint James string that man up next to Sanctuary High School or not?"

Maxim cleared his throat. "No, Marshal. It doesn't work for me so far."

The blue eyes searched the ceiling. "I've been on the phone all afternoon saying we had a suspect in custody."

"And that's true. I did put him in custody, and that's where he's gonna stay for now. But I don't think he was involved."

The marshal took a few moments to process the news. It was unwelcome. It meant that they were further behind than he had thought. He slowly leaned back into his leather chair and waved his fingers towards him, wordlessly asking for Maxim to continue.

"This is what I've got so far," said the detective. "The vic was killed early this morning, off site. He was suspended upside down and killed with a single gunshot wound to the head. Then he was skinned and bled dry. We have the knife but not the gun yet. Hitchens has his guys searching the school grounds as well as local dumpsters and drains, but I don't think we're going to find anything. Furthermore, we don't have a definite ID on the body. But I have a feeling. I think the vic is Carlos Doka."

Marshal Boyd immediately sat forward. A manhunt the year before hadn't been able to find the fugitive. Maxim could see the wheels turning on the man's face.

"You know this for sure?"

"Like I said, it's my theory. There are some indicators. An old wound matches up. He's a Native American. A single long hair that was embedded into the skull when it cracked survived the skinning, and it's long and black, like Doka's. There's enough there to make it my operating theory."

Boyd chewed his lip. The initial news was great for Sanctuary. It was a missing puzzle piece finally coming into place, and another win for the department. But the troubling implications began to crease into his face. "This sounds like the Seventh Sons beef with the Yavapai. Payback for last year."

"We don't know that for sure."

"They have the best motive," reasoned the marshal. "This was done on their turf."

"*Moved* to their turf. We don't know where it was done. Not yet. Could be anywhere in Sycamore."

"Close enough. The skinning knife is pretty damning. What's the biker have to say?"

"Not a whole lot. He's only making statements through his lawyer. A Ms. Teresa Banks. I looked her up. She made a name for herself in Los Angeles and recently started a practice in Flagstaff with an associate. She may be new here, but she's not small time. I think she's going to be the regular defense attorney for the club from now on."

"That's all we need."

"Anyway, we can't dick her around. The knife gives us a direct link but he's claiming his bag was stolen. I think I believe him."

Marshal Boyd folded his hands in front of his face and looked past them, paying attention to the potential reality one, two, seven days from now. The one where he would need to be accountable to the public. "There's going to be a public outcry, Detective. You've done a great job the last nine months ensuring that these two gangs didn't break out into open war, but that bottle may have just been uncorked."

"Maybe. I'm not discounting the motive. I just don't understand the method yet. The skinning doesn't make sense."

"Perhaps it was meant to muddle forensics."

"I mean the whole thing. The rope. The display."

"Some kind of warning?"

"Sure," said Maxim. "Yavapai stay away, right? I've considered that."

"And?"

Maxim shook his head. Vocalizing his gut feelings wasn't always easy. "I don't know. This is definitely a message. I don't know why the Seventh Sons would risk this."

The marshal rested back in his seat again. "Believe me, I would like nothing more than for them to be miles away from this. Their involvement would be... tricky."

The motorcycle club had connections that Maxim only suspected. If he had to guess, he would say they had an in with the mayor himself. The police had habitually ignored their infractions in the past, but that had all changed last year. Once national attention was put on their department, the Sanctuary Marshal's Office needed to shake any impression of impropriety. Maxim had pulled the department and the motorcycle club out of the mud and had become the star of the moment in the process. The rock star. Since, the detective had tended to set his own rules when it came to what could be enforced.

"Nevertheless," continued Boyd, "we can't appear to be shielding the motorcycle club. Everybody on the street thinks they were involved. Keeping Mr. James in-house while you investigate other angles seems most prudent. Notify Ms. Banks that he's being held overnight. That will give you ample time to balance the other end of this equation."

Maxim blinked. He was surprised at the marshal's even temper. But there was something else. He had missed something. "Sir?"

"Well, Detective, you said it yourself. This is a message of some sort. The victim's family is the most likely candidate. You need to test the air at the reservation."

Maxim nodded. "I'm heading there tomorrow. I want to compare the vic's X-rays to Carlos Doka's dental records, assuming they exist. With the tribal PD involved, I figured it would be faster in person." If the body sitting in the basement cooler was Carlos Doka, the dental records would be the quickest way to get an official ID.

"Tomorrow's not soon enough, Detective Dwyer. If this is a war, I need you to gauge tensions now. Because of the circumstantial evidence, Ms. Banks will tolerate us holding Clint James tonight, but tomorrow she's likely to raise a stink. We need to move quickly here. I want you to drive down immediately. Alone. I'll notify the tribal police."

"Uh, Marshal, I was planning to avoid them completely. I'm not effecting any official jurisdictional powers. They'll just hinder my progress."

"We're already under the microscope on this one," said the marshal sternly. "We can't conduct an investigation on the reservation without alerting them. It could land us in some serious shit."

Maxim released a heavy breath. Boyd didn't curse like that often. It got his point across. The detective knew it couldn't be helped. He didn't trust the police on the reservation. The Yavapai mercenary outfit that had been led by Carlos Doka had a lot of respect among the tribe. They brought in money and supported the community, and they offered protection that no outsiders had ever been able to guarantee. They would be tough to talk to without the police acting as buffers.

"Tell you what," conceded the marshal. "I'll tell them that you're heading down to notify the family. I'll leave you to confirm the ID with the dentist independently. But, if he doesn't cooperate, don't go so far as to threaten him with a warrant without notifying me. At that point I will have no choice but to alert their department."

Maxim nodded. "Fair enough."

The marshal leaned forward and placed a finger firmly on his desk. "Tread lightly, Detective. Use no official powers on that reservation without first contacting me. If I get any complaints that you did anything without my knowledge, it'll be your head."

"Yes, sir." Maxim stood up, seeing no problem with the terms.

Chapter 11

It was more beautiful than she remembered. The valley. The sweeping hills teeming with brush that rustled under vast sheets of wind. The rolling clouds over Watson Lake reflected off the black surface. Impressive rock formations towered high along the edges, hosting groups of spectators as kayakers paddled by. The residents hadn't mowed the land over as much as they had settled within it; they allowed it to live free, as they did. Absent were the manicured lawns, the man-made overpasses and other blights to nature. Here it was just a peaceful coexistence that felt quaint after coming from Manhattan.

Prescott was the center of Yavapai County. Its location afforded the Quad-City area room to stretch as far as the eye could see along the north-south valley corridor. To both sides it was sandwiched between national forests, walled off from the outside, away from the reaches of the Interstate that connected Phoenix to Flagstaff, away from the highways where cars passed on their trips to California.

In a very real sense, the Yavapai Indian reservation was also cast aside. It was the tribe's own area on the border of Prescott. Not as central, perhaps, but a lively destination in its own right. The opening of the brand new casino was why she was here, after all.

Kayda Garnett sat in the back seat of the taxi, turning her purse over in her hand as she hesitated to open the door. She had come this far already. It was too late to turn back.

She had grown up on the reservation. Lived there most of her life, only leaving when she was seventeen to go to school at Columbia. Now a young woman of twenty-two, a graduate, she had felt that she was ready to face her family again. Except the long trip had shaken her resolve. She wasn't so sure that returning home was right. She didn't know if she would still fit in.

She didn't know that she ever had.

Kayda's mother had been a beautiful Yavapai woman from a well-respected family. After her husband died and left her to raise two boys, she'd met a wonderful man. A white man. A business man. It was a more modern time. If people weren't as accepting of the union, they had at least tolerated it. But Kayda couldn't say that it made growing up in the tribe any easier. Even her two half brothers, much older than her, didn't protect her. At times, she thought they'd been harder on her than most.

It had shattered her self-confidence as a child. It wasn't that she didn't think she was pretty. Her face resembled her mother's. Big, brown eyes. A full smile. But she had broad shoulders, thick, ropy arms and legs, and always weighed more than she liked to admit. She'd inherited her large breasts from her mother, but she never could manage the same slenderness or sexy grace she saw in her mom's old photos.

Her mother had died when she was fifteen, and Kayda finished up school with the tribe, but her father wanted to give her a better foundation. He thought the outside world offered a better chance, and Kayda didn't complain. The last four years at Columbia University were an education in and out of the classroom. Her experiences with boys were not always the best, but it felt normal to have highs and lows. She was different from many of the students—she knew that —but it was her differences that made her stand out. Shine, even. She had become a confident woman. Better, she liked to think.

A sharp rapping at the window startled Kayda. She turned and saw a young girl in a ceremonial dress with swaths of yellow and red. She didn't recognize her. Kayda smiled, and the little girl smiled back, then quickly darted down the street.

The grand opening of the casino would see the attendance of the entire tribe. Almost two hundred people in a space that could fit thousands. A sort of soft-opening celebration before the floodgates were thrust away.

Kayda Garnett took a breath and opened the car door. The casino event was just an excuse for her homecoming. She wanted to see everybody one more time before she went out into the world and made her place in it. Prove to them that she'd become a woman. That she was stronger than they had thought.

Now, here she was. Back home. And the little girl inside her trembled.

104

Chapter 12

Maxim's silver Audi sped down the 89 as the last of the sun disappeared behind the mountains. He hated the drive through Chino Valley. The land was arid, flat, and boring. But the state road was in decent shape and the TT made quick work of it.

The detective had called ahead and spoken with the dentist. The man's workday was over but he had agreed to examine the X-rays at his home. It would be quick and simple. With any luck, the first twenty-four hours of the investigation would confirm the ID of the victim. Maxim would close the day with good headway and he would have time to relax with a beer.

Maxim sobered at the thought of having to notify Doka's family. It occurred to him that he wasn't familiar with any of them. He knew of a brother from word of mouth but that was it. He also knew of a man with priors, Hotah Shaw. Both of them were possibles for mixing it up with Clint the night before. They were also part of the Yavapai mercenary outfit. While Carlos Doka had been a biker who liked to associate with the Seventh Sons, the rest of the Indians didn't follow suit. Maxim would need to familiarize himself with them now.

Several billboards along the way broke up the drive. One showed a grand tower with a wide foundation of buildings, shining brightly like a beacon. It said, "The Jewel of Prescott." Another showed an Indian woman wearing a headdress. Face paint extended down her neck and led suggestively to her breasts, which were out of frame. "Overload Your Senses." It took until the third billboard before Maxim realized they were ads for a new casino on the same reservation he was headed to.

The detective played poker a bit. Especially a few years earlier when Texas Hold 'Em had been all the rage on TV. Maxim preferred to play the game with friends. As a detective, he liked to think that he could read people well, that he picked up on things that others didn't, but the math of the game was his weakness. He didn't have a head for quickly calculating the odds. For realizing if he should call or fold. Still, he enjoyed the games, the time spent drinking with friends. The games eventually broke up and discontinued. Maxim thought about trying to resurrect them sometimes, but he didn't have too many friends since his wife had died. There were the other officers, of course. And he'd started to get friendly with some of the Seventh Sons, but in light of recent events, maybe that wasn't such a good decision.

Maxim sighed. Maybe he could see if there was any action at the casino.

Almost immediately upon entering the Yavapai reservation, a police car pulled up behind him. Maxim hadn't been speeding and there was no checkpoint. Access to the land was free and open. For a minute he was hoping the officer was just doing a routine check, but as soon as he flipped on his reds-and-blues, Maxim knew he had been singled out.

The detective didn't drive a marked car. He should have blended in with the other luxury sports cars. There was no reason for him to be pulled over and the Yavapai-Prescott Tribal Police were likely not in the habit of hassling reservation visitors. It was clear the local PD already knew about him. Maxim wondered what they would do.

He pulled over to the dirt and waited as the patrolman recorded his plate. The detective rolled both windows down, turned on the overhead dome light, and readied his badge. It was departmental courtesy not to pull over other officers knowingly, but courtesy went both ways. If it happened, polite cooperation was expected. Maxim didn't have anything to hide, so he waited patiently.

A minute later, a man in a uniform approached his car on the right. He was about Maxim's age, but worse for wear. He looked like an overstuffed scarecrow, the seams of his pants and shirt pulled taut. At the same time, the man had a barrel chest and long legs, giving him an imposing height. While he wasn't exactly in shape, the man could serve as a good cop. Nobody would easily overpower him, anyway.

The officer leaned forward and stuck a sweaty face in the passenger window. His blond hair was slick and bristling in the wind. It was cooling down outside so Maxim guessed the officer's squad car needed AC work. From appearances, what he really needed was a new car. It made Maxim happy that he had finally splurged on the TT.

"You're the detective, right?" the man asked.

Maxim nodded and showed his badge. "Detective Dwyer. That's me."

The officer suddenly opened the door and fell onto the seat. "You don't need that," he said casually as he tried to squeeze his knees past the dashboard. The Audi was a small car that rode low. It wasn't built for large men with sasquatch legs. Maxim watched half-stunned, half-entertained as the man shifted his position several times. Finally, he just sat sideways with his legs outside the car and twisted around.

"I hear you're doing a death notification?"

Maxim contemplated him awkwardly. Entering the vehicle was presumptuous, but Maxim didn't feel threatened. Just uncomfortable. Maybe it was how they did things down here.

"Yeah," Maxim answered, "and maybe confirm something for myself."

The officer nodded. "I'm Officer Winston. But you can call me Chuck." He raised a fat hand in greeting.

The detective took it and suddenly felt bad about being so formal earlier. "Maxim," he said, trying to match the man's hospitality.

"Maxim," he repeated. "You're the one that was in the news some time back. The Paradise Killings, right?"

"In the flesh."

Chuck shook his head. "I don't really believe what the media reports."

Maxim didn't know how to respond. He wasn't even sure what the officer meant by that. Did he not believe that a bunch of bodies had been dumped in Paradise Tank? Did he not believe that Maxim had killed Deborah Holton, a woman instrumental in the killings? "Okay," was the best answer he could come up with.

"You're aware you need to give us a courtesy call before proceeding with any investigation on the reservation, right?"

"Did Marshal Boyd not do that?"

"He did," answered Chuck. "But we prefer more of an in-person visit."

"Ah," said the detective. "Well, thanks for saving me a trip to the station, Chuck. That was nice of you."

The officer's face tightened. He hadn't meant this as a sincere courtesy, but he had in fact made things easier on the detective. Still, Maxim didn't know if Chuck was going to let it go at that. After a moment passed, the officer relaxed and began chewing a piece of gum that Maxim hadn't noticed was already in his mouth.

"No problem," said Chuck. "It beats doing the rounds at an empty casino. I'm not just some security guard, you know."

Maxim nodded. Chuck obviously had some issues, but

who could blame him? The tribal department was small, like the marshal's office, but there was much less to do. Crime on the reservation was notoriously low. Maxim always figured it had to do with the mercenaries. They were the ones running the show, probably even running the police. But Chuck was a white guy. He didn't seem to have overflowing love for the Yavapai. Maxim wondered if he was even part of the tribe.

He considered asking about those details before something else Chuck had said stuck out to him. "Wait, what do you mean empty casino?"

"The new one," answered the officer with aplomb, as if the casino was the biggest thing in the news. In Prescott, it probably was. "There's an opening ceremony tonight."

"Oh," said Maxim. He knew there was another casino or two on the reservation, but they were old. Outdated. The new one was the casino of the future to replace them all. Maxim had no idea it was just opening. "Maybe I'll head over there after I talk to the family."

Chuck shook his head emphatically. "It's a soft opening only. You can't go without a personal invitation from somebody important."

The detective beheld the officer with obvious amusement. "Well it's a good thing I know you, Chuck."

Officer Winston worked his jaw hard on the gum in his mouth. Maxim figured it was a stress reliever or something. Finally, Chuck reached for the roof of the car, pulled his frame halfway out, then paused. "Maybe I can work it in after we do the rounds."

"Rounds?"

Chuck winked. "The notification to the family. I'm coming with you."

Maxim didn't want an escort. He still had to check for a match with the dentist. "Hey, Chuck. That's another nice gesture, but it's really not necessary."

"Yes, it is," he said, struggling to pull free from the bucket seat. When Chuck was finally on his feet, he slammed the car door and turned away. "You and me are gonna be real good friends."

Chapter 13

Kayda knocked on the warped front door. The house was older than she remembered, but already she was comforted. This was, after all, why she was here. She would work herself up to facing everybody else, but her grandfather would be the first and most enjoyable visit.

While waiting for the old man to answer, the wind chime hanging from the metal lattice caught her ear. It brought back a flood of memories as a child, stretching her arms high in an attempt to reach it. It was funny. She had so many memories of jumping up at it, but she couldn't remember the first time she was tall enough to grab it. It was one of those milestones that wasn't a big deal as soon as it could be done. There was always something better to reach for. She brushed her fingers across the clay and string, as if to prove she was taller now.

While pacing on the small porch, Kayda's thoughts turned to the old neighborhood. Her eyes eventually moved to the street. That's when she saw the red pickup. She thought her grandfather would be here alone. Now she knew she would have to say hi to her brother as well.

The door swung open and a man with wiry skin browned by the Arizona sun stood on the threshold. "Kayda."

Kelan was her half brother, really. The younger of two big brothers from another father, they were ten years apart. She had always looked up to him and Carlos. They were cool. Confident. Leaders of men. But their status had made them tough and distant.

At first Kayda feigned surprise, but she realized she was trying to feign excitement. "I didn't expect you here, Keekee."

"Don't call me that," said Kelan. He stepped away from the door to let her in.

Kayda stepped inside, already feeling awkward. "You shaved your hair?" she asked, although the answer was obvious. His short-clipped black hair was buzzed evenly around his long head. She had never seen him like that before. It made his features more statuesque. The two brothers had always had hair running down their backs. Then Kayda suddenly realized why Kelan's hair was short.

"I cut it when Carlos went missing," said the man. His eyes were smoldering.

Kayda had never gotten along with her eldest sibling. He was a cutthroat. Sure, Kelan wasn't the nicest of brothers either, but Carlos was downright cruel. When Kayda had seen the news reports about the Paradise Killings, it hadn't surprised her.

"I'm sorry," said Kayda. She wasn't, but she said it. The

truth was that she was always afraid of the influence of their older brother. If Kelan was a firecracker, Carlos was the lighter. With one gone, maybe the other had a chance.

"Don't be. You disappeared. Your healthcare degree was too important." Kelan said the last part with mockery on his face. He didn't respect her desire to get an education. To help others.

Kayda didn't know what to say. She wasn't sorry that she had left. That she hadn't even called on the phone when the media reports broke. Getting involved in the family's crime spree was the last thing she needed to worry about while she was working on her degree. Not to mention, it was Carlos and Kelan who drove her away in the first place.

Her half brother clenched his jaw and avoided looking her directly in the eye. "You should have stayed away."

"I came here to see *Pahmi*, you know. You weren't supposed to be here."

"You're not supposed to be here, half sister. He's not your father so stop calling him that."

Kayda shot her chin up, refusing to be baited by her brother into an argument just as she arrived.

After their mother had died, Kayda had gone back and forth between living with her real father, off the reservation, and living here with her grandfather. He'd always treated her as his own child, chiding her brothers for picking on her. She'd come to realize that continually moving away from the tribe to live with her real dad had made her more of an outcast, but she wouldn't change her past. Her father had instilled a sense of duty in her. A sense of gratitude.

Going to school in New York had opened her eyes to more than just her tribe and the casinos and the highways. After she was done here, she would join the Master's program in the Peace Corps and escape far, far away from the Yavapai. If they didn't want her, she wouldn't insist on staying.

It was only her *pahmi* that she needed to say goodbye to.

"What are you doing here?" asked Kayda.

Kelan progressed into the kitchen and slung a backpack over his shoulder. "Just dropping off food for the old man. Someone has to take care of him, you know." Her brother had finally looked her in the eye when he said that. "We'll all be at the casino tonight. Except for him. He's too frail to move that much. He mostly stays in bed. If you don't upset him, maybe you should stay with him tonight."

"You don't want me at the opening celebration?"

"What do you think?" Kelan strode out the front door and paused for a second. "This life was never for you."

He closed the door and left her standing there alone. It was rough. Kayda hadn't been prepared for seeing him yet. She thought she'd have more time to ready herself. Now, it was over and done with, and her brother had been colder than she imagined.

"*Pahmi*," she called out, moving to the bedroom. Her grandfather's name was Wicasa, but she used a term that meant simply "father." "*Pahmi*."

He was waiting for her, right there on the bed as Kelan had said. He was old, but he didn't look ancient or brittle. His brown skin and large nose were worn, but not strained by the effects of extreme age. If it wasn't for his long mane of white hair running down his shoulders, he wouldn't have appeared older than sixty. He certainly didn't look sick or decrepit.

"Wiha," said the old man lovingly. Kayda's full name was Wihakayda. It was more traditional. Her half brothers' father had wanted normal American names for his boys and overrode their mother's wishes. Strangely enough, her white father had let her choose whatever name she wanted. It was ironic, thought Kayda. She had the traditional name, yet she was the outsider.

Kayda gently hugged her grandfather. She hadn't realized how much she'd missed him until she saw his kind eyes and measured smile.

"Are you sick, *Pahmi?*" she asked. His eyes lit up at hearing the endearment once again.

"I'm fine, Wiha. My bones just don't have the patience for celebrations anymore. I see you received my letter."

She nodded. Although she hadn't spoken to him, he had tried to get in touch. He'd written that the tribe was going through changes and opening a new casino. It was a simple letter, but there was a subtext to his words. The family was changing, he meant. Things would never be the same. There was a sort of subtle urgency to the letter, the only one ever sent, including during the period of her brother's disappearance. Along with finally getting her bachelor degree, it was what had convinced Kayda to come home.

"Maybe you don't find that much to celebrate, lately?"

The man's smile grew taut. "You returning to me brings greater joy than any casino could."

Kayda almost felt a tear in her eye. "Stop." Her grandfather was a sap, but she fell for it every time. She rapped him on the shoulder and sat on the edge of the bed.

He took a moment to study her. He beamed proudly, but with a forlorn sentiment. "Your skin is so light," he said.

Kayda laughed. No it wasn't. She was much darker than all the white people in her class. "I didn't get as much sun in the city, I guess."

The old man nodded as if he understood. "How was school? Your graduation?"

"You wouldn't believe it, *Pahmi*. I met so many people. Saw so many things."

"And healthcare management? Have you decided where that will take you?"

The girl looked away from him. She didn't want to tell him that she would be leaving the country. All this time apart and then reunited, only to leave again. She didn't want to spoil the moment. "I'm not sure, yet." It was true enough. The Peace Corps couldn't promise to send her anywhere specific.

Wicasa's face grew serious. "Is Robert happy with you?"

That was her real father. Her grandfather didn't dislike him, but he had never agreed with the man's decision to leave the reservation after her mother died. It had meant taking Kayda from him for weeks at a time.

"He just wants what's best for me, *Pahmi*."

"It's best for you to be with your people. To reconnect with your roots. To be a member of this tribe once again."

Images of her brother flashed through her mind. "They

don't want me here."

"Of course they do."

"They don't respect me."

"You must work to gain that respect."

Kayda flailed her arms in the air. "What would you have me do? Go to the opening ceremony? Give a speech about the importance of family? Why should anybody listen?"

"The Doka family has great Yavapai heritage."

"I'm a Garnett, not a Doka," she asserted. "I've never been a Doka. Carlos made that clear."

The old man's eyes lost some of their tension, as if they were tired. "Carlos is no longer with us."

Kayda nodded. Nine months was a long time to remain missing. "I know, *Pahmi*. And I expect Kelan to fill his shoes well. You heard him out there. He doesn't want me at the casino. He doesn't want me on the reservation. Then you resent my father for trying to give me something better. Dad never had anything against the Yavapai ways. He just didn't want me to be limited."

Wicasa nodded as if the crux of the conversation had been reached. His granddaughter shot him a questioning look, and he appeased her with an answer. "The only limits, my daughter, are the ones you place in your own path. I never resented your father. I never begrudged you the chance to go to the big city. To study. To gain knowledge, not just from school, but from the world. No, sweet Wiha, I am proud of you. More than you can ever know. But now that you are home, now that you are a woman, you must find the strength not to run away."

Chapter 14

New Mexico was especially uninviting today. The sun had set but the asphalt still emanated heat like an idling engine, punishing the road warriors who dared expose themselves to the elements. Diego smiled. Exposure was the thrill. Snaking through the mountain passes at a heavy lean. Speeding along open highway, one with the rubber and the road. The Interstate was built for this onslaught.

This time, however, Diego de la Torre couldn't enjoy the ride. At this point, after Omar's phone call to Gaston, they knew they were riding into a trap. The biker did a head check behind him and saw West fifty yards at his tail. Ahead of him at the same distance was Trent. They were keeping themselves spread out, not easily contained, but that was about the extent of their plan.

The Seventh Sons had no way of knowing for sure if bullets would be flying their way. It was unlikely, they had decided, but large amounts of money had a way of bringing about the unexpected. They knew the risks, and they rode on ahead towards them.

For the others, all to a man except Diego, there was less cause for concern. They could take a bullet or three. Of course, nobody wanted that—the pain could be unbearable—but when it came down to living or dying, the werewolves had much less to worry about than Diego did.

The biker wanted to kick himself. He was scared but that wasn't the problem. Fear was good. It kept a person sharp. Diego certainly wasn't unfamiliar with danger. He used to hunt werewolves, back when he thought it was a just cause. He had been in a shootout with Maxim against the Yavapai mercenaries. Doka had nearly taken his head off. But all that was for a noble purpose. A driving instinct within him to protect his little sister.

Now? Diego was worried about taking two in the back because of the drug business. Cold hard cash. It cheapened the danger and made it pointless. Stupid, even.

Diego had wanted brothers. Now he was involved in the family business.

Everything was fine, he assured himself again. They had gotten Omar's call in time. The kid had raced ahead while the others slowed the transport down, making a long gas run and faking mechanical trouble. It had given them time to get to their ranch on the edge of Arizona and prepare. The rest of the ride? That was just waiting. And it was the hardest part.

The darkness had taken over along the way. The Interstate wasn't well lit in this stretch. Diego took comfort in the taillight ahead of him and the headlight behind. The winding road often stole from him even that ease, but eventually, the darkness proved a boon. Up ahead, Diego saw the glow of red lights strobing on and off.

It was beginning.

As planned, Trent didn't alter his speed and rode on past. Diego and West, taking up the rear, would do the same. As Diego approached, he saw the van pulled over to the side of the highway. Two black state police cruisers sat behind, the officers still inside their vehicles. Riding past, Diego saw Manolo waiting in the driver's seat of the van, watching them ride by. That same playful smirk contorted his face.

Step one was showing no association with the vehicle. If this was a random stop, the bikers would only call attention to it. Riding on by, drawing attention away, would have been the usual course of action anyway. And if the contents of the van were discovered, the MC would be far away by that point. But the Seventh Sons knew this stop was anything but random.

Omar had seen the unusual police presence when he scouted ahead earlier. It wasn't much, but he was a sharp kid. He'd come this way enough to know what was normal and what wasn't, and along with Diego's suspicions, it had been easy to put two and two together. Still, Gaston was taking a chance on what would happen next.

The bikers all continued ahead, pulling in to a tighter formation. Within minutes, Diego had accounted for everybody except Omar, who must have been in

Albuquerque by now. That's when a line of police Tahoes and motorcycles came screaming onto the Interstate from behind an overpass.

Lights flashed everywhere. The police yelled over loudspeakers. Two SUVs blocked off the street ahead and behind, and the motorcycles herded them towards the dirt. It was a well-executed stop, likely planned days in advance.

It's too bad, thought Diego, that the MC had pulled in close again. He would have liked to see how the police handled them if there was half a mile between the lead and the tail. But once the van was out of the picture, Gaston had figured that they were safer together. Diego had to agree.

His Triumph Scrambler came to a halt. Two police bikes skidded in the dirt and the officers immediately dismounted and charged him, guns in hand. Diego only had time to raise his visor before he raised his hands. He sat on his bike and waited.

"What were you doing with that van?" one of them barked at him, grabbing him and pulling him away from the Scrambler.

"What van?" Diego answered as they shoved him toward the road and sat him down, lining him up with the others. The trooper pulled Diego's hands behind his back and zip tied them at the wrists.

"What's this?" asked another.

Diego twisted in the dirt to see one of the officers slipping a silver-colored shotgun from its sheath on his bike. "That's a legal weapon, Officer."

Arizona and New Mexico had some of the most lenient

gun laws in the US. No permits were necessary to openly carry. Shotguns were especially common.

"Get your hands off me," yelled Gaston as he allowed them to sit him down. "What did we do?"

"Why don't you tell us?" one replied.

Now that the entire MC was properly detained, a man exited one of the parked Tahoes and approached them. He had the same black uniform as the others, but the three stripes on his arm signified he was the acting sergeant. As soon as Gaston noticed him, there was recognition in his face.

"Cortez. What's going on?"

The man turned his head in a single stiff shake in response. "Just doing what the chief tells me to, Gaston."

"Yeah, well this is bullshit. I'd like a word with him."

Cortez eyed the bikers on the floor. "You might just get your chance. You sure you boys aren't doing anything illegal out here?"

"Sure as shit," said Curtis. One of the officers shoved a boot into his back, but Curtis held strong. It didn't have the intended effect. When Cortez turned at the commotion, the officer backed off.

"You mind if we search you boys?" asked the sergeant.

"Do we have a choice?" asked Gaston.

Cortez nodded and the officers began rummaging through their pockets.

"We're just taking a ride," said Gaston. "Since when is that a crime?"

"It's a crime to transport illegal narcotics and firearms in this state. In all fifty of them, in fact."

Gaston shook his head. He played it off pretty well, but it didn't matter that much. Everyone knew he was lying. The important thing was not admitting guilt. Police officers, unfortunately, had to account for such details of the law.

"Firearm," called the officer looking in Curtis' jacket. He pulled out a pistol.

"That's mine," said the man.

"I got one too," said the officer searching West.

"Same here," for Trent.

"Yup," said the cop who pulled a pistol from Gaston's ankle holster.

The president shook his head. "It's not illegal to carry without a permit."

"In Arizona you don't need a permit to carry concealed, but you do in New Mexico," replied Cortez. He waited as the final officer checked the last of Diego's leather clothing.

"Nothing here, sir." Diego de la Torre smiled.

Cortez was unruffled. "Search the bikes."

It was no matter to Diego. They'd already found his shotgun.

As the state troopers executed the order, the sergeant continued. "Unlawfully carrying a concealed firearm is a petty misdemeanor, boys."

Gaston rolled his eyes. "Cortez, concealed carries are okay for vehicles."

"You got off your vehicle."

"I was dragged off by your boys."

Cortez nodded. It was a dismissive gesture. The police weren't concerned with pistols. They were legal, by any stretch of the law. Their lawyer would see that they weren't even fined.

One of the officers from an SUV slung the black duffel bag from West's Harley to the floor. The two other bags were dropped beside it in quick succession. The state trooper unzipped it. Sergeant Cortez stepped over and examined the contents.

"Firewood?" he asked.

Gaston shrugged. "We were gonna make some s'mores." The Seventh Sons tried to hide their smiles as the officers continued their search in vain.

When Trent and Curtis had taken a detour to the Arizona ranch, they replaced the contents of the duffel bags. They could have just dropped them off, but they wanted to see what kind of intelligence the police were working with. From what Diego could tell, the troopers didn't specifically look for the ACRs. The duffel bags were among the last of their possessions searched.

The mystery of the stop aside, the police didn't have anything on them. No drugs, no prohibited weapons, no criminal acts. The Seventh Sons hadn't even been speeding.

"Well," said Cortez, returning to the bikers, "here's what we're gonna do. We're going to look through your cell phones to see if you have any suspicious calls connecting you to that van. You boys are gonna come down to the station where we can straighten that out and settle these gun charges."

Gaston scoffed. "It's a misdemeanor. And a bullshit one at that."

"And if you don't do what I say it's resisting arrest which, I assure you, is a felony."

The MC president almost growled.

It didn't matter. Not really. They had been escorting the van to Albuquerque. That shipment would never make it now. Their time was no longer reserved. The officers slowly stood each of them up.

"Diego," intoned Gaston softly. He beckoned him over with a nod of his head. "Get back to the clubhouse ASAP. Contact our lawyer. She's gonna rip these charges apart and have these cops' badges."

Cortez stepped in between the two men. "I thought you said you wanted to speak to the chief, Gaston. Besides, this one's not going anywhere."

"You can't hold bullshit gun charges over me, Sergeant," said Diego. "My shotty's strapped to the bike."

Cortez extended his lower jaw as he mulled over his play. The difference between cops and gangsters wasn't always that great. Both could pretty much do whatever they wanted in isolated circumstances. The rub was that police officers were accountable for the legality of their actions after the fact. Every step of the way, however fabricated, required a legitimate trail.

"You'll need to stick around as we go through your cell phone, at least," he countered.

Diego flashed his teeth again. "That's not an issue, Sergeant. I never carry one with me."

Chapter 15

The crowd buzzed with anticipation. The night was getting cool and dry, and the shuffling of feet and murmuring of voices gathered electricity in the air. The new casino had opened to a celebration dinner and sample of table games. Now the attendees had all been escorted outside for the final unveiling.

The front entrance of the grand casino was a marbled terrace lined with exotic plants. Their lush greens, blues, and yellows were out of place in the middle of the desert. But then, that was the point. This place was an oasis, a break from the rest of the arid valley. During the day, a mist of cold water would rain from above. But it wasn't all relaxation.

A broad walkway shot straight out into the parking lot, splitting it in two. Solid pillars of stone dotted the path on both sides, large flames dancing on every one. It was a commanding presence. A rank and file beacon to both attract and guide. It was only after following this path that the patrons were welcomed to the lush terrace.

In attendance tonight was pretty much every single member of the Yavapai-Prescott Tribe. Kayda had been welcomed despite her brother's earlier unvitation. For the most part, everyone she had encountered had been excited to see her. She didn't get any of the jeers or looks she had expected.

Perhaps, she thought, her four years away had cooled the hate of her detractors. Or maybe setting aside differences was easier in the face of the night's excitement.

The large terrace was wide, easily accommodating the crowd. In its center, a large fountain drew the eye. It was the last component of the oasis metaphor. In addition to inlaid fixtures of bronze and detailed reliefs, jets of water sprang out at random intervals to make extra sure the fountain called attention to itself. But the grand presence was not yet fully realized—a large curtain hung on a ring around the statue in the center. It was to be the big reveal. The main event.

The Jewel of Prescott.

Although it was currently hidden, Kayda knew what was behind the veil. Her grandfather had explained it to her. A large strong fist, starting at the wrist, rose high from the water. In its clutches was the round moon, shining with a silvery iridescence. The moon was important to everything below it. It was a beacon for hunters, but it was also a weakness. It lit the hunter as well as the prey. Of course, her family had a deeper affinity for the full moon.

Kayda heeded the activities with fatigued attention. The terrace was packed. Conversation abounded all around her. The occasional laugh, especially, caught her ears. Everybody was happy. Together. Except her. Despite the politeness that had surprised her so much, Kayda wasn't much of an attraction. Old acquaintances said hello, friends she'd played with as a kid, but they smiled and moved on, settling in with their insular groups.

And then she thought about her grandfather. Why hadn't he come? He didn't appear as bedridden as Kelan had suggested. The man was well loved by the tribe. A sage. His absence was a hole in this community. A hole in Kayda, as he was the only reason she had come back.

Again, his words came to her. She was a woman. She needed to fight for her place. She needed to stop running away. How could she tell him about her plans to join the Peace Corps? If going to New York was running away, what would he say about going to the other side of the world?

Just when Kayda's thoughts threatened to take her away from the ceremony at hand, a fluttering of something light, like paper, brushed her hair. She threw her hands up and spun around, but nobody was there. Then she heard a soft flapping above her, like that of a flag snapping in the wind. Kayda spotted a large crow flying away from her.

The girl instinctively took a step backwards and ran her fingers through her long hair. She didn't know what she was feeling for. It was just a reaction, as if there had been ants in her hair. She shook her fear away and took a breath, then searched the sky again.

The bird was there, sitting on one of the cables that crossed over the terrace. The cables were in place to support the curtain drawn over the statue, and the crow landed near the center, as if it were the attraction that everybody waited to see. Except it was just a bird, and if anybody else had noticed what had happened, they didn't show it. As Kayda scanned the crowd, a pair of gray eyes locked with hers and she froze.

Hotah Shaw. He stood still, at a distance, with a look of wonder on his face. He wore a tight shirt that showed off his strong form. When he realized they were staring at each other, he quickly approached.

Kayda recovered herself and resumed her casual stance. Had Hotah seen the crow fly into her? She told herself it didn't matter and tried to act naturally. She liked to believe she was above simple embarrassment these days. But of all the people to have seen, why him?

Hotah was her brother Kelan's best friend. That made him off limits. Besides, he was one of them. A wolf. A mercenary. But although her older brothers were hard on her, Hotah had always held back. She never knew why. Then one day she had dreamt they kissed, which made everything awkward after that. Now, those long forgotten feelings were confusing.

Hotah smiled and hugged her. "You need me to get my hunting rifle?"

Kayda widened her eyes and laughed. She swatted at the man's shoulder. "Don't you dare!" Hotah peered at the bird, still lording it over the ceremony. It gave Kayda a chance to look at him up close. Hotah had a strong nose and chin. He was a bit short, but Kayda liked that. It matched her height perfectly. What she wasn't so sure about was the whole bad-boy thing he had going on. He wore his brown hair wild and messy, haphazardly cut at different lengths from his eyes to his chin. There were scratches on his face and she could swear his neck was bruised.

"I didn't know you were coming back home for this," he said.

She swallowed and wondered why she was nervous. "I'm not staying," she blurted out, thinking it would be best.

He cocked his head at her, almost defiantly. But then he nodded. "I always figured you'd move on to bigger and better things. There's not a whole lot going on in the middle of the desert."

"That's not what it looks like to me."

"Yeah, well, you know what I mean. How's your grandfather?"

"I just came from there," said Kayda, happy he had asked. "He's not as bad off as people have been making it sound. He's just tired, more than anything."

Hotah nodded knowingly. "We all are, Wihakayda. This casino means a lot to our outfit. But you shouldn't get involved in tribe business. Why don't you let me take you home?"

A flurry of excitement went through her. Was he being forward with her? "We can't leave before the grand unveiling," she countered, trying to buy time.

"Really, Kayda, this isn't meant for you."

She paused, not sure what he was getting at. For a moment, he almost sounded like her brother. A ribbon of tension fluttered between them, and Kayda shot him a frustrated look. A caw interrupted them. The bird still perched nearby. It broke the ice that had formed, and they both laughed again.

"Hotah!" came a call from the crowd. It was Yas. He was Kayda's age, in her class, and had always looked up to the mercenaries. Now he was old enough to be one of them. Hotah turned back to her with resignation.

"I've got to check on something, Kayda. You should be with your grandfather."

He left her there, with her fake smile hiding her befuddlement. She tried a casual stretch of her neck to appear aloof, whatever that looked like, but the more she tried to act naturally, the more she was sure she was failing. Luckily, Hotah disappeared into the crowd without glancing back.

It was a strange feeling. Kayda wasn't a virgin anymore. She had snuck around the dorms with a few boys in New York. She had learned about relationships, mostly that they weren't all they were made out to be. It wasn't that she loved Hotah or anything so stirring, but being so apprehensive around the older man surprised her. What had that been about?

Left with nothing else to attend to, the bird once again drew her eye.

Under inspection, she realized it wasn't just a crow. It was a raven. A huge bird with an impressive wingspan. A smart bird. It had been a long time since she had seen one so close. Kayda smiled as she remembered her grandfather's stories about ravens. They were tricksters, experts at deception. But her *pahmi* said that the opposite was also true, like the moon that both helped and hindered the hunt. To recognize and manipulate the truth, one needed to know it. The raven was not only a liar, but a truth-seer. Kayda's grandfather had always taught her to attune herself to the world, to discern the meaning behind the incongruous. She wondered what the raven was trying to tell her.

Kayda smiled and shrugged off the thought. As a kid, she had always pretended she was attuned to the totem spirits. She would catch squirrels, save injured deer, have conversations with the birds. It was all part of the game of loneliness. But that wasn't her anymore. It was a bit silly, if anything. Looking back, those must have been some pretty one-sided encounters.

But she did like to wonder. She had always respected the Yavapai half of her. Unlike most Americans, the tribe had always been more open to the inexplicable, accepting that there was still much that was unknown. It was arrogant to think otherwise, really. Perhaps the Yavapai bloodlines, and the prevalence of the wolf, had given her that intellectual advantage.

But that wasn't her. She was a Garnett, not a Doka. And not a Shaw either.

"I didn't know you were back in town," came a voice from behind her. She turned to see a familiar police officer smiling at her. She studied the face that had aged in her absence.

"Hello Chuck."

Officer Chuck Winston was on the list of people Kayda had wanted to avoid. Not as high on the list as her brother, and for completely different reasons, but on the list just the same.

"I can't believe how good you look," he said, his eyes wide. At first he was chewing gum slack-jawed, but then he shut his mouth. After a few seconds, he gave up on that and swallowed the gum altogether.

Kayda smiled politely. She had always felt uncomfortable around Chuck. It wasn't something she could explain. He was nice enough, but he was a strange guy.

"You decided to check in with the family for the big unveiling, huh?" he asked.

"I just graduated and came back to see my grandfather."

"Of course. You know, things have changed around here. I should show you around."

"It's okay, Chuck. I'm not staying."

"No?" He looked hurt. As though he had gotten a surprise gift, but opened the box to find it empty. "You should. You know, I'm gonna be a detective soon. I'm taking the exam again and, well, they have me working with a detective from out of town right now."

"That's great," said Kayda with detachment. Why was it that years could pass but nothing would change?

Officer Winston wasn't put off. In fact, he leaned closer and spoke in a hushed tone. "Check it out," he said, nodding towards the other side of the fountain. Kelan was there, talking to a man wearing a navy-blue business suit and a white hat. He looked a bit silly, like he wanted to be professional yet casual in the thin-cut jacket. Everything about him was like that. He was clean-shaven except for a day or two of scruff. His collar was unbuttoned yet his tie still hung loosely around his neck. Still, something about the man commanded attention. He stood with composure and purpose.

"Who is he?" she asked Chuck.

"That's what I'm trying to tell you," said the officer. "That's the detective from Sanctuary I'm paired up with."

Kayda nodded absently. She wasn't really listening as long as Chuck wasn't really saying anything. She watched the two men exchange words after the detective showed his badge, but it wasn't until she saw her brother puff his chest out and scowl that she knew something was wrong.

"What does he want with my brother?"

Chuck put his hand on Kayda's shoulder and tried to pull her away. "Don't worry about that, Kayda. You should stay out of it."

She was sick of hearing that. She flashed a dark look at the taller man. "Chucky."

The tribal police officer melted under the icy word. It was spoken as a warning. With a single word, she had told him not to touch her, not to treat her like a child, and to tell her what the fuck was going on.

"Okay," he acquiesced, "but you should leave it to Kelan. Maxim's here looking into the murder of a tribe member. We went to the dentist and got some records confirmed.

Now he's talking to the family."

Kayda stared at him, fuming. "*My* family?"

"Well, yeah, but—"

Kayda pushed past the cop and made her way to Kelan. She was appalled that Chuck had acted so casually with her during this crisis. Even more worrisome was what the detective might have been saying.

Judging by the state of her brother, she had gotten there just in time.

"And what's it to you, pig?" warned Kelan.

"Kelan!" chided Kayda in a voice bordering between scream and pleasant surprise. "Who's your friend?"

Her brother turned, unhappy at her intervention. "I told you to go home, Kayda. You're not welcome here."

"I'm part of the family too."

The detective arched an eyebrow as he studied her. "Maxim Dwyer, miss. Are you two related?"

Kayda flashed a political smile. "I'm Kayda Garnett. He's my brother."

"Half brother," he corrected.

He nodded. "Well, I'm sorry to be interrupting at a time like this. Believe me, I had no idea this thing was opening tonight. But this is important. I'd like to step aside for a moment and talk in private."

Kelan scoffed but Kayda jumped in. "About what, Detective?"

"Well, I'd really prefer to tell you somewhere else."

The man was unsure how to proceed. Her brother's animosity was normal. He hated cops. He hated outsiders. It was easy to imagine how any conversation between the two would work out. Still, she was puzzled by his entrance. Kayda turned her head toward the night sky and saw the raven, staring down at her. Deceit. Truth. Knowledge.

She put her arms around her brother. His shoulders tensed up. "I don't see why we can't go inside and hear him out."

Kelan didn't take his eyes off Maxim. "Do you know who this man is, Kayda?"

She tried to pull her brother back, to protect him from himself. He was a wolf, much stronger than an average person, and he had a bad temper. It was a bad combination in a world where survival meant keeping a low profile. "Calm down, Keekee."

"This is the man who arrested Carlos at Sycamore Lodge. He's the man who conspired with the CDC assassin to kill our brother."

Kayda blinked slowly. Or maybe the world slowed. Truth.

Maxim knew about her family. Suddenly she didn't know how she felt about the man. Maybe she should let her brother rip his head off.

"It's not like that," assured the detective. "I arrested your brother in connection to a crime. He attacked a police officer and escaped custody before he was ever charged. What happened to him later was on him."

"You mean when he was killed?" asked Kayda.

Maxim contemplated the two sternly. "He wasn't killed last year."

"This is horseshit!" said Kelan. "You want to talk to the family? Come to Wicasa's house tomorrow morning. We'll set up a meet and greet with everybody you've affected. You can see the results of your work firsthand!"

Maxim measured his breath. He had the look of a man who both understood and dreaded the position he was in. But he was resolute. "Is there any way we can do that tonight?"

Kelan scowled. "You know what? You're not welcome on this reservation. And you're not welcome in this casino. I want you off this property, Dwyer."

And then Kelan completely surprised his sister by storming away.

Four years must have changed him. Or maybe it was just the last year. Kelan would never have walked away from something like this before. His big brother was his idol. Continuing without him must have been hard. Suddenly, Kayda felt guilty that she hadn't been around.

"Look," said Maxim to her, "I'm sorry if I'm intruding. Believe it or not, I'm trying to help your family find answers."

In a million years Kayda wouldn't have expected to feel sympathy for her oldest brother, but a tear came to her eye. "Is Carlos okay?" she asked in a pleading voice.

The detective released a heavy sigh. "Can we step aside for a moment?"

She wordlessly nodded and followed him away from the roar of the crowd into the parking lot. It was open air and surprisingly cool away from the walkway flames.

"You said your name was Garnett?" The detective was just making small talk while they distanced themselves from the festivities.

"Yeah. We all shared the same mom."

He nodded and stopped, deciding that their location was private enough.

"And how well did you know Carlos Doka?"

He was torturing her, asking questions endlessly. No wonder her brother was furious. "Do you mind if we get to the point?"

Maxim nodded. They shared a wordless gaze, then his lips tightened. As he opened his mouth to speak, a roaring applause came from the audience. They both turned to see the crowd gathering closer to the fountain. Spectators pressed into each other tightly as they abandoned the outer areas. Four women clad in bejeweled bikinis stood atop the fountain walls and raised their hands in celebration. They each grabbed a corner knob of the curtain.

In unison, the spectators all began counting down. *Ten. Nine. Eight.* Kayda's heart still waited on the detective's words. *Seven. Six. Five.* She peered at Maxim. He was captivated by the excitement. *Four. Three.* She turned back to the fountain. The draw was magnetic. *Two.* The raven no longer sat on its perch above the statue. Something was wrong.

One.

The next few moments did not progress smoothly. The four women gave the curtain ill-timed tugs. The back opened as one of the front corners became tangled. Two of the showgirls pulled late. The perfectly executed countdown was ending in an anticlimactic bumble.

Then there was a scream. One of the girls fell into the crowd. The last side of the curtain finally fell away and the people staring below erupted in a frenzy.

More yelling. Suddenly a panicked rush to escape the terrace broke out. Spectators rammed into the locked doors of the casino. Others fled into the parking lot. The models remaining on the fountain turned around to examine their handiwork. One fainted. The others scrambled away.

As the riot of people rushed towards them, Maxim stepped forward to protect Kayda. His fingers went to the gun on his belt.

Kayda's breath stopped along with her heart.

On the bronze statue of a fist holding a silver full moon, a loose cloth hung, flapping in the wind. Only it wasn't a cloth. Its browned color was hardened and cracked. Thin in some places, black in others. A patch of dark brown hair hung from the top, and Kayda saw the deformed face of her older brother below it. The cloth *was* her older brother, Carlos. Only it wasn't him. It was just his skin, split along the back, all in one piece, strung up for display.

A piercing scream rose through Kayda. It started deep in her belly, reverberating in her diaphragm and lungs. At her neck, tonsils vibrated until they were sore, and her wide open mouth projected the ghastly sound, somehow louder than all the other horrified shrieks combined. Kayda yelled more vehemently than she had ever remembered being able. Then she felt lightheaded.

The world started to make sense again, as if she were waking from a dream. But she wasn't. She was nearly on the floor of the parking lot. The detective held her. She couldn't recall his name at the moment. He shook her shoulders and moved his mouth, saying something but not making much noise. Then she heard him ask if she was okay. Kayda weakly nodded. She stared past his face into the sky, but there were no birds to guide her.

Kayda remembered that she wasn't supposed to be weak. She brushed the cop away and took to her feet. Everything came into focus. Her heart pounded. She took a step towards the statue and saw her brother standing there.

Kelan. He ripped the skin down and threw it to the floor. He stood above it, tears streaming down his face. She needed to go to him. To be strong with him. But her steps were coming too slowly.

"This..." Kelan cried out to the small crowd who lingered. The men. The mercenaries. "This is what remains of my brother. This is what remains of a great tribesman!" Kelan's stance was bottled energy. His legs were bent at the knees, ready to pounce yet still standing tall. He held out his arms to either side, enclosed fists flexing, wiry muscles threatening to explode from under his skin. The short hairs on his head rose like the hackles of a dog.

"My brother was not a perfect man," he proclaimed. "He had his faults. He was no chief. But to his dying moments, he did what he did for the Yavapai people!"

The young men surrounding Kelan roared in agreement and patted him on the shoulders. Hotah and Yas were with him. The initial scatter of tribe members slowed. Some pulled closer.

Kelan hopped up onto the fountain wall and stood over his audience. He pointed to his brother's remains and spoke in a commanding voice. "This is what the Yavapai mean to the outside world! We are pushed away from the rivers and the highways. We are set aside as a nuisance. Then, when we build a casino, when we make it so that people want to come to *us*, they remind us of our place!"

An uproar rolled through the crowd like a wave crashing on a rocky shore. It was sharp, final, and deadly. Kayda stopped. She was relieved not to see her broken brother anymore, but she was worried about the other one.

Kelan Doka raised his hands into the air to silence the crowd. It took some time but a hushed whisper overtook the wind. The world itself quieted for what came next. Her half brother lowered his voice to a reverent tone.

"We all know what my brother was. We all know what I am. And some of you, as well." Kelan traded a look with Hotah and put his hand on the full moon statue behind him. All Kayda could think about were her grandfather's words. The moon was a beacon for hunters. And then she thought of her dead brother. The moon lit the hunters as well as the prey. "There's only one group of people who could have taken down the great Doka," Kelan said, even more softly.

"No," said Maxim. He strode forward with urgency, trying to put out the fuse before it was lit.

Kayda blinked slowly. The world was in slow motion again, but somehow, crystal clear. In the distance, she thought she heard the flapping of a bird's wings, miles away. Then her brother's voice broke the silence, hitting everybody's ears as nothing more than a whisper.

"The Seventh Sons."

Day Two

Chapter 16

Fast as the Triumph Scrambler was, it couldn't beat the sun. Diego had ridden through the night, but by the time he arrived back at Sanctuary, it was the next morning. During the entire trip, the scene from the night before replayed in his mind.

The New Mexico State Police had ended up detaining Diego. Even though there was no legal justification to do so, they had bent the rules to take him out of play along with the rest of the MC. The bikers had been separated. After his numerous requests to be released, Sergeant Cortez had complied. Not knowing how long his brothers would be detained, Diego sped west to familiar lands to carry out Gaston's wishes.

The troopers had nothing on the Sons. It was all posturing, no doubt a message to the club, but the takedown had been well executed. Planned. The million dollar question was, why now?

Diego parked his bike and ripped his helmet off. Heavy boots stomped towards Sycamore Lodge. He wasn't just upset at the turn of events, he was upset at himself. At what he had gotten himself into. It had never been his intention to be an outlaw. The Seventh Sons had entered his life through his sister's poor choice of company; she was the reason he was in Sanctuary at all.

Staying, however, was on him.

The biker scowled as he approached the front door. He slowed his steps; they mirrored the hesitation in his thoughts. The Seventh Sons didn't wear colors. They weren't a crime syndicate. Not really. But for Diego to remain convinced that they weren't a gang was a wild act of self-deception. It forced the biker to consider his true motivations for joining the Sons. After a stint as a CDC assassin, a hunter of wolves, was working with them penance?

This period was a turning point in his life, he admitted. A wild card. Only he didn't know if it was worth aces or deuces.

The biker flung the front door open. The roadhouse was empty at this time, as he expected. The single person in the front of the house was the bartender, owner, and the girl that Diego had come to see.

Melody was a hot piece of work: dyed maroon hair, dark eyeliner, bright lipstick. She was naturally busty and squeezed her waist into a studded corset to exaggerate the effect. Pretty and deadly, but much the same as Diego. Moral. Weighed down by a conscience.

"Hey cutie," said the biker, trying to draw her attention away from washing glasses behind the bar. She had seen him already, of course. The rumbling of his Triumph's engine had betrayed his arrival long before he stepped inside.

Melody didn't raise her head. "Those charms don't work on me anymore."

Diego eased onto a barstool. Collapsed might have been a better word. He was tired after the long night and the long ride. "Don't be so sure about that, Mel."

His fatigue almost made him sentimental about the girl and the few months they had dated. It had always been a good match on paper. When Diego had broken it off, he was sure there was good reason, but the logic wasn't coming to him now.

Melody's painted lips formed a crooked smile. "Don't overestimate yourself, hotshot. You're not as much fun as you think."

Diego was called a lot of things by a lot of girls, but boring wasn't one of them. "You trying to call me some kind of buzzkill?"

"Not if you're having a drink." Melody finally turned off the sink and grabbed two shot glasses and a flavored vodka. Diego stopped her before she poured the second.

"You know I don't drink."

"And you know I don't believe in straight-edge. Everybody needs a vice." She winked at him. She always did that.

"You know a New Mexico state trooper named Cortez?"

Melody pounded the shot and smacked her red lips

together. The sourness prevented her from answering, but Diego enjoyed watching her work her cheeks together. It accentuated her high cheekbones.

"He's friendly. Lets the boys run through his backyard. He gets a cut."

Melody's honorary MC status proved her history with the club, but she had always been on the fringes. Like Diego. Uninvolved with the dirty business. Nowadays she focused on running Sycamore Lodge, but she still knew a lot.

"Well something's up," said Diego, spinning around on his stool and facing the room. "He busted the whole club last night." Melody widened her eyes. "We were on to it so he didn't get shit on us. It's nothing—not yet. But I need to contact that new lawyer. You know her?"

"Sure do. After Clint was popped for trashing the laundromat, Gaston said we couldn't count on the police to watch our backs anymore. He hooked up with this woman out of Phoenix. He says she's a real cold bitch. She's like this soccer mom, you know? But she'll gut ya when you ain't looking."

Diego nodded. He'd heard Gaston make the same boast. It seemed overkill for what they needed. "You got her number? We need to make sure the clubhouse isn't raided or searched. We need her there in case the police show up with a warrant."

Melody paused and leaned over the bar in the way she did to show off her cleavage. "What about that cop friend of yours, Maxim? Why don't ya ask him?"

"I'm not worried about Sanctuary PD. This isn't them or I would have known about it."

She grabbed Diego's arm and spun him around to face her. "You sure you can trust that cop?"

Diego looked deep into her eyes. "With my life."

He could tell Melody was sizing him up. She was Deborah's daughter, and Maxim had killed her. It was an unfortunate connection in such a small town, but Melody had been strong. She'd hated her mother in the end, after she'd seen what the woman was capable of. She'd told Diego that blood wasn't thicker than water, that who she chose was more important than who fate dealt her. It was a grown-up way of looking at the world, and why not? At twenty-five, Melody wasn't a child anymore.

"Melody, do you ever regret leaving the club?"

Her eyes sized him up again, but this time with empathy. "Best decision I ever made in my life. Why? Now that things are heating up, you getting cold feet?"

Diego took a measured breath. "I just don't know if that's me," he said finally.

She pursed her lips but remained silent. Melody had never told Diego what to do one way or the other. She had never judged him. She probably figured that her life had been more than enough for one person to untangle.

After a moment the two shot glasses clacked together as she picked them up in one hand. She dropped them by the sink and wiped down the bar. "You go to the clubhouse. I'll make the phone call."

Diego nodded slowly. He wouldn't cut and run. The

Sons were relying on him and he wouldn't let them down. But the drugs, the guns—Diego didn't want any of that. When the guys returned, he would set things straight with them.

As Diego stood to leave, he remembered one last thing. "And can you call Omar? I don't know where he is and my phone's at the clubhouse."

Melody nodded, another smile playing over her lips. "Why do you do that anyway?"

Diego shrugged. "Maintains the drama."

Chapter 17

Marshal Boyd's crisp, blue eyes tracked Maxim as he made his way to his desk. The detective made it to work a bit late, still rough around the edges. Without a word of greeting, he slung his jacket over his chair, dropped his hat on his desk, and went for the coffeemaker.

It was a new machine, or rather, an old machine that had been newly donated by one of the officers. Since there were nine desks in the station and eight personnel, the extra workspace was treated as a communal area. The desk was often used by visiting investigators and auditors. It was stocked with a computer, an empty filing cabinet, and now, a single drip coffee machine.

Maxim poured himself some overcooked brew and sneered when he saw it was the last of the pot. Not only would he be forced to drink the sludge but office courtesy obliged him to prepare the next batch. As he set the filter in place, he considered dumping his cup out, but the anticipation of caffeine won out and he sipped it. It had a bit of a kick, and Maxim liked that.

Maxim heard footsteps approaching and turned, casually leaning on the desk. "Good morning, Marshal."

"Good morning, Detective. Since you were out at the reservation last night, I won't mention your tardiness."

"I thought you just did."

Boyd shook his head in a quick, spastic move. He jumped around too much. He was too eager. His sprite-like actions and boyish features were easy targets in the police station, but his last few years working the job had earned him some respect.

"Let's talk about the Seventh Sons," he said.

Maxim finally surveyed the room. The only other officer in the station was Kent. He sat at his desk typing a report, but his ears perked at the marshal's statement. The motorcycle club was the most notorious subject in town, and this new murder was the biggest event since the Paradise Killings.

"I know the Seventh Sons need to be treated as suspects, but it doesn't hold for me so far."

Boyd raised his eyebrows. "That would be great. The last thing we need is for the motorcycle club to be involved. I already have the FBI asking me questions."

"About what? Why?"

"Carlos Doka. The Civil Rights Program sees this as a possible hate crime."

"Fuck that," spouted Maxim between sips of coffee.

"A Native American skinned and strung up on a tree is not a simple act of passion. You said it yourself. There's a message here. After last night's development, it's clear the Yavapai are the target of that message."

"I don't dispute that, Marshal, but this has to do with more than just race." The detective wondered if Boyd knew that already. Maybe he was just allowing the angle to play with the feds to keep away different lines of inquiry. The only thing worse than a race war for Sanctuary was a gang war. The Seventh Sons could have been eviscerated last year. The whole point of the deal Maxim had made with Gaston was so things like this didn't happen again. If it turned out that the MC was involved, there would be an outcry. People would wonder why changes didn't happen the year before. There would be a lot of blame to go around. Heads would roll.

Maxim hoped he wasn't betting on the wrong people.

"Detective, the FBI calls, I listen. We don't need them invading Sanctuary as long as we have a handle on things. The key is to prevent a war between the Yavapai and the Seventh Sons. There are two fronts to fight here. The immediate need is security. We are stepping up patrols and maintaining an active presence across town. I don't know why that body turned up in city limits but we're not getting another one."

Maxim nodded. It was a good move, and it covered their asses if he was wrong about the Sons. Staying out of the limelight, especially hiding from federal eyes, was the driving motivation of a wolf pack. Killing Doka publicly, bringing the body into town—it didn't make sense for the club.

But perception was a hell of a beast. If the public believed the Sons were guilty, the hammer would swing. The marshal's father was the mayor, and if Maxim was a betting man, that was the link to the Seventh Sons. It would explain why the department had protected them in the past. Why it didn't want them in trouble now. The political angle was something Maxim had stayed away from. It wasn't a game he liked to be involved in. Now, he began to wonder if it was a key to the murder.

"What's the other front we need to fight?" asked the detective.

The marshal smiled. "That's where you come in. We need to catch this killer. If you really believe the motorcycle club isn't responsible, then someone else's crime is about to get them, and us, into hot water. Announcing that we caught the murderer is the quickest way to appease the public."

"You mean the Yavapai."

As far as perception went, the opinion of the tribe was paramount. Kelan and the mercenaries had been judge and jury last night. They screamed for blood. As wolves, they'd be able to get it too. Boyd was right to take the oxygen out of that fire.

"They're going to be trouble," admitted Maxim. "And the tribal police won't be any help. Have you talked to them about releasing the skin to us?"

"They won't do it, but they've allowed Dr. Medina to

examine it. The family has also demanded we return the body for cremation."

"Well they can't get it. It's part of an investigation."

"They won't, Detective. Not yet. But it might go a little way towards appeasing them."

Maxim understood the sentiment but placed little stock in it. Then again, he figured they had all they were going to get from the body. The DNA had been collected, the lab tests initiated. The body had told them all it could say. It wouldn't help them catch a killer at this point, only confirm the killer once they nailed him.

Maxim hesitated. He didn't want to ask but figured it was better to clear the air. "What about the CDC?" Boyd's eyes bore into him. The Centers for Disease Control and Prevention was tasked with containing werewolf outbreaks. They had not sent a replacement agent to the Flagstaff area since the Paradise Killings. It was only a matter of time.

"A sick person dying is not their concern." The marshal spoke lightly, as the subject required. Kent was probably listening, but he was already in on the secret. Not all officers were, but seeing a prisoner transform before his eyes and nearly kill him had allowed him entry into the exclusive club. When Marshal Boyd referred to a sick person, he meant someone infected with late-stage rabies, otherwise known as lycanthropy. "When a sick person kills a healthy person, then we need to notify them. That's why I want this stitched up fast."

Maxim understood. He wasn't so sure what to do next. The police had searched all day yesterday and had not found the pistol used in the murder. No witnesses had come forward. It was like the body had been dropped out of thin air.

Chapter 18

Wicasa sat at the kitchenette table. His tired eyes had the grim look of experience, as if the sad weight of truth was the inevitable burden of time. Kelan, representing the polar opposite, was too indignant to sit. His muscles were taut. Kayda wondered if he had gotten any rest the night before. She knew that she hadn't.

After the horrific reveal of her dead brother, a mob had built up. Maxim had taken her back to the house but returned to the scene to coordinate with local police. She hadn't seen him again.

She had cried in her grandfather's arms before retiring to the guest room, frightened and unsettled. Her dreams had brought her nothing but disturbing images. Her brother's skin lay on the floor, curled and grotesque. A susurrant voice beckoned her with words that were beyond comprehension. The body began filling with a ghostly spirit; it struggled to stand. Carlos was inside, yearning for answers. Kayda kept calling for Kelan but was ignored. She was alone with Carlos. Empty flaps of skin stared at her, eyeholes with the depths of hell behind them. And his crumpled, twisted arm reached for her.

Kayda shook the thought from her head. Kelan and Wicasa turned at her sudden motion. She wanted to explain but didn't know how. Instead, tears welled up in her eyes.

For the first time, the hard lines around her brother's face relaxed. He put his arms around her and made a calming noise with his voice.

"What happened to him?" she cried. "I saw him in my dream, begging for help, but no one was inside. I don't even know if it was him."

"There's nothing to worry about, Kay." Her brother spoke with a strong confidence that assured her. "I'll fix everything."

She stared blankly past him, past the guilt. In a way, she had always expected this outcome. Carlos was a wanted criminal. He had always acted precipitately, without remorse or caution. How could this *not* have happened? "How?" she asked.

Kelan simply shook his head. She could hear his words repeating in her head. *Stay out of it.* She knew he didn't want her involved. For now, she didn't argue. She just closed her eyes and yielded to her tears.

"He had the wolf's strength," said their grandfather softly, "but not its wisdom."

Kayda felt her brother tense up again. He turned away from her. "He asked for your wisdom, grandfather.

Remember? Where were your words of guidance then?"

"His ambition was louder than this old man before you. Do not let your anger drown me out as well."

"Or what?" demanded Kelan, leaning forward onto the table to give the old man a defiant look. "You'll turn your back on me as well?"

Wicasa smiled. It was an expression filled with more pain than Kayda thought possible. But love was in his eyes as well. It was as if he were scolding a young boy for his own good. "When you were young," started the old man, "you had wide eyes for the world. You used to look on it with hope. You once told me you would scale every mountain in Arizona. You used to try so hard with the other boys. But you were smaller than them. You couldn't run faster or climb higher or swim farther. You never had the physical gifts of your older brother, yet you remained so hopeful."

Kelan drew back, suddenly disarmed. Kayda had never heard about a young, hopeful Kelan before. He was ten years older than her. He and Carlos had always been cut from the same cloth, as far as she had known. But recognition was in her brother's eyes. A remembrance of something he once was. Of something lost.

Suddenly the mundane moment became overwhelming. Magical. The three family members understood each other unequivocally. No denials or accusations were spoken. Nobody stormed away or tried to change the subject. They paused in the kitchen as the bond between them became something tangible. Something real and hard and unbreakable.

Wicasa took a long breath and slowly shook his head. "I never blamed you, sweet Kelan, but I have never forgiven Carlos for what he did to you."

And just like that, the moment shattered. Kelan spun away, his defenses at full alert, his anger welling. "This again!" he exclaimed, moving to the other side of the room. His shoulder carelessly brushed Kayda as he passed. "The wolf is a part of me now. It could have killed me, but it didn't." Kelan turned to face his grandfather, scowling at having his childhood weakness revealed. "Don't you see, grandfather? I'm not that powerless little boy you remember. I proved strong. I lived. Carlos knew what was inside me. He knew his bite wouldn't kill me. He was the only one in this family who ever put that kind of faith in me. But ever since then, you thought us animals."

Wicasa shook his head again. "I do not blame the wolf for its nature. I blame the little boy."

Kelan shoved the first loose object he could reach on the counter. It was an old plastic toaster and it exploded against the wall in a rain of burnt crumbs. "And this is what comes of turning your back on your family," he said solemnly.

"Keekee," chided Kayda, seeing the wounded look on Wicasa's face. "He didn't mean for this to happen. None of us did."

"But it happened," returned Kelan. "We need to deal with it."

"First," cut in Wicasa, his voice sounding more authoritative, "we need to understand it."

The old man gestured for them to sit down. Kayda didn't

feel like it but she respected her *pahmi's* wishes. Kelan stood firm, attentive but willful.

"Many nights ago," said Wicasa with a reverent wistfulness, "during a period of long drought, Wolf searched desperately for water. Days passed. Wolf was dying. His bones began wilting from the inside out. But then he saw Crow in the sky above him, flapping his strong wings proudly. Wolf followed Crow as he flew across the plains until he landed by a small bank of water and drank. Wolf was hungry and thirsty and couldn't believe his good fortune. He ran at the water, guzzled greedily, and snapped at Crow any time he neared. 'Stand your ground, Wolf,' said Crow. 'There is more than enough water for the both of us.' Wolf laughed and said, 'But I am hungry as well, and it is my nature to devour the weak, just as it is yours to fly away from the strong.'"

Kayda and Kelan stood surprisingly silent. They had heard about the wolf and the crow before. Wicasa was a sage of the tribe, passing on the old stories, which he thought were more than trite lessons. It had been so long for Kayda that she smiled as she heard the words, both familiar and foreign, as if they were a homecoming.

The old man continued. "So Crow did what was in his nature and flew away. Wolf laughed and drank and filled his belly. But then the watering hole dried up, and Wolf went thirsty again. This time a great storm cloud came into the sky. It approached slowly and, just when Wolf could not take it anymore, thunder cracked, and it rained.

"But Crow flew under the cloud and spread his wings.

The rain never made it to the ground, and Wolf was never able to drink. 'I am of the sky,' said Crow. 'It is my nature to soar, and it is yours to scurry below. So go, Wolf. Scurry. Scrounge. And look to me no more.' And so it was that Crow taught Wolf a lesson."

Kayda smiled as her grandfather finished. It must have been ten years since she'd heard the parable. It made her reminisce about her childhood on the reservation. The folktale didn't have the same effect on Kelan.

"This is all we are now," he intoned. "Storytellers. All this talking and sitting. We're content to let our greatness slip away like it never was. Well, that's not good enough for me. You can talk of wisdom and animals and lessons. I'm going to teach the Seventh Sons that the Yavapai are strong."

"And so the wolf is destroyed by his own nature," said Wicasa.

Kelan scowled. "There's more to the story, grandfather. That's the short version—the one in the children's books. Carlos always told me that the wolf eats the crow in the end. That it gets the last laugh. And besides, I'm not gonna let words stop me from avenging my brother." Kelan stormed from the kitchen and Kayda followed.

"Where are you going?"

"Keep away from this, little sister. Keep away from me."

"I want to help."

"This is no place for schoolgirls."

"Carlos was my brother too. I won't just forget about this!" Kayda screamed the last part just as Kelan was about to leave the house. Her brother turned to her, hard lines etching out his scorn.

"That dream you had was a charade. You think Carlos would have turned to you for help? We don't need you." And he was gone, the door slammed in his wake.

Kayda stood at the edge of the kitchen, feeling brittle again. She leaned against the wall and pondered Kelan's words. "Maybe he's right. Carlos picked on me just as much as the others. In fact, everybody in the tribe wanted to be like him. They probably picked on me *because* of him. Carlos was the last person who would have sought my help."

She heard the metal leg of the chair scrape against the kitchen tile and turned to see her grandfather standing up. "Let me help you, *Pahmi*." She moved to support the man but he brushed her away.

"Wolves and wisdom," he said. "They are stories, but they are told for a reason. You are a woman. You don't have the strength." Kayda didn't say anything. For a moment, she thought her grandfather was taking Kelan's side. "You lack the wolf," he said. "To compete, you need to be wise."

The words hit the young woman like a rock. She thought about the crow and the wolf. She thought about her brother's crumpled skin, reaching out to her. Then she thought about the raven, flying high above the Jewel of Prescott. The hunter's moon.

"Who are the Seventh Sons?" she suddenly asked with razor focus.

Her *pahmi* glared at her. It was clear he didn't want to answer, but he surprised her by doing so. "Wolves.

Criminals. Associates of your eldest brother."

"The other Paradise Killer? She was one of them?"

"She was their leader. Like Carlos, she crumbled under the weight of her decisions. Shame has been brought to both our families. Now your brother is in the same danger. The blood of brothers is a vile stimulant. It incenses the body into action."

"I want to help, *Pahmi*."

He nodded slowly. "So you do not mean to leave us?"

Kayda bit her lip. She tried to hide her shock. How did her grandfather know she was just stopping by? But then she understood the deeper meaning of his question. If Kayda truly wanted to help the family, what else was she willing to put off for it?

"I... I don't know. I'd like to help. We both know that Kelan could use a level head."

He nodded. "And what would you do?"

Kayda ruminated on the question. It made her feel silly because she didn't have a strong answer. She bet her brother already had a plan. He was probably already working at it. "I need to understand first. Carlos was killed in Sanctuary. That police officer talked to me last night. He already knew Carlos was dead. I need to talk to him again. And maybe talk to the Seventh Sons."

It wasn't a good answer, but she knew her grandfather would approve. Information seeking was his way, not warfare. "Wiha, you must open your eyes. Attune yourself to the world." He led her to the garage door and opened it. "See what everybody else sees, but understand more. Then you will see more."

Kayda beheld the dusty garage as her grandfather flipped the light on. It was filled with tools and boxes and old keepsakes from her grandmother. The room was used as storage instead of housing cars and had a musty smell, as if the door hadn't been opened in a long while. But one thing didn't fit.

Kayda passed the boxes and lifted a tarp. Underneath it was a motorcycle, black and rusty and worn. The girl had grown up around the bike. She'd hitched a ride on it before but had never driven it. It belonged to Carlos. It was his hobby. Not many of the other Yavapai had followed suit.

"Your brother left it here when he got a new one," he said. "The police have that one now, I think."

Kayda turned back to the bike and ran her fingers along the metal handlebar. It was rough under her skin.

"I want you to have it, Wiha. If you need to go to Sanctuary, you have my blessing. If the Yavapai depended only on the wolf, then we would doom ourselves."

It was clear they shared the same worry: Kelan might do something rash. Kayda didn't see how her involvement could harm anything, but she also wasn't sure what she could do to stop her brother. He had a mind of his own, more than ever, now that Carlos was dead.

"Is it true what Kelan said?" she asked plainly. "About the wolf eating the crow at the end of the story?"

Her grandfather's lips stiffened. After a moment of hesitation, he finished the folktale.

"Wolf and Crow made a pact. They agreed to be friends

and help each other. But the next time Wolf was hungry, he pounced on Crow and ate him up. 'You should have known,' he said. 'It is my nature.' Then when the rains came he drank and drank and worried about Crow no more. But the rains didn't stop. The clouds kept coming. The rivers widened and the waters rose, overtaking the land. Mighty Wolf climbed the highest mountain, fighting off all the other animals who tried to stand with him and save themselves. And the tide kept climbing. 'Where are you, Crow,' he cried, 'that could pick me up and fly me to safety?' Even as the sea flooded over him, Wolf never saw his mistake."

Chapter 19

Omar's bike shouldn't have been knocked on the ground like that. It was immediate cause for concern. Either the kid was injured or in a hurry and let his bike fall over as he rushed into the clubhouse.

Diego cursed to himself. He parked his Scrambler next to the Harley, right off the building's porch. If anybody was inside that wasn't supposed to be, they would have heard him already. Diego cut the engine and slipped out his Benelli M4.

"Omar!" he called out, eyeing all the windows. "You in there?"

There was no answer. The biker threw his gold helmet to the dirt and sprang to the porch.

He hadn't heard from the kid since his call to Gaston that warned them of the state troopers. Diego had assumed that he was waiting for them in Albuquerque, but this was evidence to the contrary. Evidence that something wasn't right.

If Diego didn't know any better, the Seventh Sons were being played.

But that was just it. Diego *didn't* know any better. He wasn't familiar with the illicit relationships and pay-offs. He'd never talked to the leadership in El Paso before. He didn't know how well Gaston knew Cortez, or for how long. Pointing fingers in every direction was easy, but how many accusations were correct?

That was club business, reasoned Diego. How much longer would it be his?

The biker set the shotgun against his shoulder and headed for the front door. It was unlocked. Diego quickly swung it open and swept the long barrel of the M4 across the room as he scanned it. A single, bloodied body lay in the center of the room. The kid's leather bomber jacket was riddled with bullet holes.

Diego surveyed the immediate area, but he knew: whoever had done this was long gone. He didn't bother with an exhaustive search. It was reckless. He had been trained by the Commissioned Corps to secure an area completely, but something told him in his gut that this was over.

Diego bolted for Omar. The kid was on his back, eyes staring uselessly in a mixture of shock and fear. But he was a wolf. Maybe not as strong as Deborah had been, maybe not as tough as Gaston, but he could still live. The biker felt for a pulse on the kid's neck.

Nothing. Omar was dead. With a fractured sigh, Diego

slid the kid's eyes closed.

How could this have happened?

Diego set the shotgun aside and examined the carnage. Omar was lying in the middle of the foyer. The entryway was mostly barren but ransacked all the same. Pieces of a glass vase were scattered in the corner. Blood was on the floor and walls. Omar still gripped a revolver in his right hand that smelled of gunpowder. He had fought back, at least. But he was overcome.

His body was peppered with holes from his waist up. There were too many for Diego to count. Some shots had been wild, hitting the wall behind; others right on their mark, a cluster centered on the torso. There was even a hit on his forehead.

Was that what could have killed him?

No, thought Diego. Not unless it was silver.

But who had known to put stock in the werewolf rumors? Who would know how to take down a wolf, besides another wolf?

Besides the MC, and after Carlos Doka had disappeared, Diego only knew of two other werewolves in Sycamore. Kelan and Hotah, Yavapai mercenaries. No love was lost between the two outfits, but why would they wait nine months after losing their leader to strike?

Shit. Diego realized his boot and knee were in a pool of blood. He recoiled, knowing he was contaminating evidence. He needed to think about this carefully.

This couldn't have happened very long ago. The body would be more stiff, guessed Diego, right? Or there would be more of a smell.

Damn it. He didn't know what he was thinking. The Commissioned Corps hadn't trained him for this.

His mind went numb as he noticed just how many bullet holes studded the walls and front door. For a short window of time, this room had been a war zone.

And then the anger came. Diego's heavy boots kicked the wall as hard as he could. He knew this would happen. The drugs. The money. It was like asking someone to come take it from you. Omar had been a Seventh Son longer than Diego, but he had been the youngest of them all. He had always been treated like a rookie. Like a prospect. Diego had sometimes worried about him and now, when he gazed down at the destroyed body on the floor, Diego saw himself.

This was the end for Omar. Where would it be for the rest of the MC? For him?

One thing that was now firm in his mind was that he couldn't leave the club. Not like this. Not with Omar on the floor.

The biker paced back and forth, trying to sort his thoughts. Focus them. Then he set his jaw. Diego wasn't a wolf, but he had other resources. He had other strengths. And he had other friends.

He reached into the kid's jacket with a final moment of mourning, and then he pulled out Omar's cell phone and made a call.

"Detective Dwyer," answered the voice on the other end. "Who's this?"

"Diego."

"You really need to start carrying your own cell phone with you. You know that?"

"I got another body for you."

Chapter 20

Kayda Garnett had the sinking feeling that she wouldn't be able to get to Sanctuary in time. She had gotten a late start and it was already the afternoon. After Kelan had abruptly disappeared, she had spent more time with her grandfather, then found help getting the motorcycle running again. After that came the practice riding. Hotah and Kelan were long gone by then.

She rode the old Harley tentatively. Kayda was an inexperienced rider, but without a car this was the best she could do. Sanctuary was only an hour away. Even less. Plus, she thought it was befitting to use one brother's motorcycle to save the other.

Kelan Doka and Hotah Shaw were troublemakers. Overworked testosterone and angst. Even worse, their antics fed off each other. The two didn't like outsiders much and they tended to be bullheaded. It was all the influence of her older brother Carlos—not here anymore, but with them in spirit. And Kayda had to stop that spirit before it made them do anything that was irreversible.

How much trouble could they get into in one morning?

The heavy motorcycle she straddled was a coarse beast. Her brother's old half helmet was strapped tight to her chin. Kayda thought it made her look tough, but part of her knew she couldn't pull off the act. She didn't wear spiked leather boots or a heavy jacket. She didn't ride like she had a chip on her shoulder. Hell, she was too scared to push the machine past fifty miles per hour.

She rode the 89 north through Chino Valley. It was out of the way and not especially interesting, but it was the land of her people. Her family controlled it. Or at least, they did when Carlos was in charge. He had always stressed the importance of being the king of something, even if it was a little-used state road through a valley that no one cared about. She tilted her head, feeling the breeze. The opinions of the outside world made no difference to her. She thought the valley was beautiful all the same. The outsiders didn't know what they were missing.

Dust continually kicked into her face. It was unusually dusty today. She wished she had gotten a helmet with a visor, or at least a pair of sunglasses. What kind of biker got on the road without sunglasses? Kayda cursed and felt silly again. She decided she would pick up a pair in town.

Then she heard the rumbling. Bikers in the distance ahead. It was stupid, but it made her nervous. The highway was fairly empty. There wasn't a lot of traffic either way, but she had passed a single motorcyclist ten minutes earlier.

Kayda had tried to wave at him. She thought it was some kind of biker code or something. With one hand on the handlebars, she had rolled over a bump in the road and almost lost control. It had scared the life out of her and convinced her to slow down.

Now, with more bikers approaching, Kayda was determined not to appear an idiot again.

There looked to be several bikes ahead. Four of them. Seeing was difficult because they were shrouded in dust. The cloud was barely noticeable, but it slowly enveloped her as she pressed ahead. It wasn't something tangible that stood out from a distance; instead it was a gradual reduction in visibility. It wasn't until Kayda tried to make out the bikers ahead that she realized she was riding into the middle of a dust storm.

The wind kicked up. Grains of sand whipped against her eyes. Sunglasses, she thought. That was why she needed them.

The four bikers sped southbound in a roar of speed and practiced badassery. They moved fast in pairs, two and two. One of them hunched over, as if he was reaching for something. Their heads turned to her as they passed. For her part, Kayda kept both hands on the handlebars and stared straight ahead. She told herself it was for safety, because of the worsening weather conditions, but underneath it she was scared.

Act natural, she told herself. The girl managed a quick glance and a nod. She wasn't sure if the bikers had seen it.

She didn't see them all, but she noticed the two closer to

her had half helmets as well. Still, they wore large sunglasses and bandannas over their faces, like bandits. Smart. She would need to pick up one of those too.

In a heavy gust they were gone, now behind her. Something about the group was tough. Mean. They frightened her just by their proximity. They weren't the friendly, vacation sorts. Were they the Seventh Sons? If so, she couldn't confront them now. She didn't even dare to glance back at them. Kayda felt they had seen through her. They knew she was just faking it.

But what did she care? Kayda shook her head, and with that dismissed her silly childhood notions of belonging. She wasn't in grade school trying to get kids to think she was cool anymore. She had a college degree and planned to go overseas and earn her Masters. She wasn't here for reputation—she was here for family. At first, she had told herself it was only to see her grandfather, but Kayda realized it was more. Carlos was dead now. That changed things. She only had one brother left—she wasn't going to lose him as well.

The dust was heavier. She was already within it, a dry bath of texture, now enough to darken the sun. Ahead, she could barely see the road narrow as it straddled the sheer edge of a hillside. The shoulder on the side of the road all but disappeared; in its place a short cement barrier that was barely enough to keep her from going over it. On the other side was rocky terrain before a sharp drop-off, a hundred feet to the canyon below.

The terrain there was ragged and unforgiving. She knew

that men with their toys liked to go off-roading out there. They would take their trucks down the long way, jump on their all terrain vehicles, get drunk, and see who could get stuck. Kayda didn't really see the point. She figured the harsh environment was some kind of communal enemy, an adversary to bond against.

As Kayda slowed her bike, thoughts of the precipice making her nervous, she heard a noise behind her. It was a police siren, getting louder. Had the bikers gotten in trouble?

She realized the sound was past them, getting closer to her. She tried to look behind but the old bike had no rearview mirrors. Kayda's hands tightened on the handlebars and she risked a head check. She turned quickly and saw the outline of a police car, flashing lights in the storm, speeding closer.

Kayda spun around again and clutched the handlebars. She hated turning around on the bike. While it was moving, anyway. Should she stop? There was no space on the edge of the road until she cleared the hillside. No place to go but forward. Kayda tried to see through the barrage of sand. Where did this cliff face end?

She grew more tense as the siren grew louder. The cop was coming up fast. She would need to pull over. Even if he wasn't after her, he would need to speed by. Then she realized he might not even notice her in these conditions. What if he raced ahead, oblivious, and slammed into her?

Should she speed up to beat the cop to the wider stretch of road? Should she stop and hug the concrete barrier as closely as possible?

Her lights. She would turn on the motorcycle's lights, at least. That should make her stand out against the storm, ensure that the police car didn't run into her. But where was the switch?

Kayda didn't consider herself cool under pressure. Right now, in the dimming sun, in the middle of a dust storm that was getting more and more violent with each passing moment, dirt scraping her face and getting in her eyes, the police car closing in—it was too much. Her inexperience on the bike only heightened her indecision. As the car approached, her fear became palpable. She could taste it.

Something needed to be done, and she shook herself out of her reverie. That was it. She needed to stop.

Kayda slowed the bike and moved off the asphalt, the wheel skipping in the gravel next to the barrier. She glanced down, searching for the light switch but unable to keep her eyes off the road. There were no switches on the handles.

The siren was deafening, bearing down on her. Then her fear got the better of her. Kayda looked behind her.

She saw the police car. The wildly flashing lights. The breakneck speed that told her the driver had no idea she was in his path. And then she felt her motorcycle twist around.

The bike flipped.

Kayda didn't know what had happened. If she had to guess, she'd turned the front wheel into the barricade or hit a pothole. Either way, it knocked her clear off the motorcycle. Kayda slammed into the ground and rolled head over heels on the rocks. She heard the crunching of metal somewhere behind her. In that moment of unabated chaos, there was no pain, no up or down, no here or there; Kayda only tumbled and slid and prayed to anybody who would listen that the heavy machine would not land on top of her.

The battered girl skidded to a halt in the gravel, coarse sand in her mouth. She wasn't in pain. She felt fine, more confused about what had just happened than hurt. From her vantage, lying along the side of the road, she couldn't see her bike. She was facing backwards and stared in terror at the oncoming vehicle. It flew up the highway, loosely obeying the road boundaries in the low visibility. She was suddenly confident that the car would clip her.

Without thinking, without even looking over the side, Kayda Garnett pushed herself to her feet, leaned over the concrete barrier, and fell over it.

The ground on the other side was welcome. There was limited clearance before the deadly slide down into the canyon. But this collision was more painful than the initial crash. She heard the police siren loudly blaze by, then the skidding of tires against asphalt a little further up.

The police car stopped.

Kayda lay in the sand, unable to rise. She found that strange since she had stood just seconds before. Sure, her crossing of the concrete barrier was more of a tumble than a vault, but she had been able to rise to her feet.

Now was different.

The sand in her mouth threatened to choke her and dry her insides. A sharp pain burned in the side of her chest. She tried to twist to ease the pressure: it sent a jolt through her torso up to her neck. Lying on her side in the dirt, Kayda was suddenly acutely aware of all the razor blade cuts across her body. She wore no protective gear besides the helmet. Not even gloves. Her flesh was exposed. With this realization, her skin began to burn.

The siren quieted, but she could still see the lights as a vague presence in the air. Besides the wind whipping her hair around her face, it was silent now. She clearly heard the car door open and slam shut.

It was farther away than it should have been. By how much had the cop passed her?

Sudden panic set in. She had thought she was rescued. Now she wasn't so sure. She needed to move. To get up. With an intense effort, Kayda drew herself onto her elbows, grabbed the top of the concrete wall, and pulled.

She wasn't strong enough. Push-ups and pull-ups had always been her weakness. She chided herself. No matter how hurt she was, she only needed to do one. It took an eternity, but Kayda drew her head over the barricade.

The police car had passed her a ways. By the time it had stopped, it was fifty yards ahead. It sat on the edge of the road, halfway blocking the northbound lane, its emergency lights silently strobing. A single officer lumbered towards her, holding a raincoat over his head to shield himself from the heavy assault of dust.

Kayda tried to raise her hand but it was supporting her weight on the wall. She was only leaning on it, not fully on her feet, exhausted just to have gotten that far. She searched up and down the street. Her motorcycle was nowhere to be seen. She saw no evidence that it had ever been there.

"Is anyone here?" the officer called out. It was Chuck Winston. What was a reservation police officer doing in the Quad-City? Did it matter?

Kayda answered with a gurgled cough. Now, more than ever, she felt the sand in her mouth. It was more than that. It invaded deeper, into her lungs, into her spirit. It smothered her will just as easily as her breath.

She gawked desperately at Chuck, her old friend, or acquaintance anyway. Life was funny. The man was an annoyance the night before, but now he was the sweetest sight she could imagine. A wetness cooled her face and cleansed her eyes and Kayda realized she was crying.

"Chuck," she forced out in a low rumble, her voice hoarse and scratchy. It hurt to open her mouth, but she didn't care. Chuck strode towards her and shielded his face with his arms. The man spun around as he moved, scanning the highway. He was looking for something. The bike? Her?

"Is anybody here?" he repeated, continuing his slow approach. He hadn't seen her yet. With the motorcycle lights off, in the dust storm, he may not have ever had a clear sight of what happened. But he had stopped, so there was hope.

Chuck neared, but she was only a head peeping above a concrete barricade. If the bike had gone over the edge, there wasn't a whole lot that would attract his attention.

Then Chuck stopped.

No, thought Kayda. Keep walking. But the officer just stood there and inspected the barrier. His eyes crossed over her.

He saw her.

He was looking right at her.

Kayda smiled, keeping her hand on the concrete but wiggling her fingers in a meager wave. That was it. She would be okay. Embarrassed, but alive.

Chuck Winston turned around and marched away.

Kayda tried to yell, louder this time, but the effort broke something inside her. Nothing at all came out this time. She puffed heavily as she watched her friend getting farther away, the dust picking up in speed and intensity. She summoned every last ounce of strength left in her to scream.

The officer dove out of the harsh weather and back into his cruiser. The door shut, the siren resumed, and he drove away.

"Chuck," managed Kayda, little more than a whisper. Then her grip gave out and her jaw scraped against the cement as she fell back to the ground.

Chapter 21

The Coconino County deputy leaned against the wooden beam of the clubhouse porch. It was a disinterested pose, a guard at a post. He nodded as Maxim Dwyer identified himself.

"You guys got here fast," said Maxim.

Most of Greater Sycamore was unincorporated; the Seventh Sons weren't technically based in Sanctuary. It was wild land, both its appeal and its fault. While the clubhouse resided in the county's jurisdiction, because of Sanctuary's proximity and working relationship with the club (and Maxim thought because of the mayor's pull as well), Coconino often handed off Seventh Sons cases to the Sanctuary Marshal's Office. Boyd had already confirmed it with their sheriff.

For Coconino, it was an easy deal: no negative headlines and no crimes on their books. But for Maxim, he was now two murders in the hole.

"We were in the area," said the deputy. Then he nodded towards the other car of backup deputies. "They're from the Bellemont substation."

That was the closest town to Sanctuary. He was still surprised they had beaten him to the scene. Next time he would take longer to notify them.

"Who's the detective on site?" he asked.

The Coconino deputy shook his bald head. He wasn't an old guy. It looked more like he was beating the inevitable to the punch. "No one's en route. I was advised that you were heading this up. We're just here to secure the scene."

Maxim nodded and peeked through the open front door. The body was hard to miss. Besides the deputy at the door and the two standing by their SUV, another uniform was inside. Two motorcycles were outside. A Harley lying on its side, which Maxim assumed belonged to the victim, and Diego's shiny Scrambler, which was hard to miss. There was also another vehicle outside that Maxim hadn't seen before: a gold Lexus minivan.

"You have a tech inside?"

"Thought you boys did that yourself up here," said the patrolman. He started at the approach of another vehicle. His hand went from his hip and pointed to the dirt road. Maxim turned and saw a Coconino van pulling up behind his TT. "Looks like he didn't hear we were punting the call. I can send him back."

"Actually, I don't mind the help."

The Coconino County Sheriff's Office was a larger department: more personnel to cover a more expansive area.

They had civilian technicians on staff to assist with forensics. Maxim watched the young crime scene tech jump out of the van with a little too much enthusiasm. He was too bright-eyed to have been on the job for a long time, but the extra manpower wasn't unwelcome.

"What about me and Diaz? You need us too?"

"Diaz is your man inside?"

The deputy nodded.

"How about this? You can send the other car back but you two can stick around if you want."

"Sure. I could use the overtime. I'll go let them know."

Before the officer was able to take off, Maxim stopped him. "Who else is inside?" The detective nodded towards the minivan parked out front.

"Bitch from hell. But don't tell her I said that."

Maxim immediately knew who it was and let the deputy go. "Diaz!" he yelled. The clump of heavy boots came from deeper inside until the Coconino uniform appeared at the door.

"You the detective?" asked the patrolman.

"I sure am. You mind staying outside while the tech and I take a look?"

"I didn't touch anything."

"Good job, Diaz."

Each man waited for the other to say something. It was sort of a standoff until a light bulb went off in the deputy's head.

"Okay, sir. I'll be outside if you need me." Diaz stepped around the detective and out into the yard just in time for the young tech to arrive. He was an Asian kid who looked twelve. He wore a brand new T-shirt that read "I see dead people" across the front. Maxim introduced himself and explained to him that he would be assisting the marshal's office.

"I know you," said the kid. "You're the one who cracked the Paradise Killings. You know, when I was first hired, I just missed those bodies in the morgue by four weeks. I got to do some related follow-up analysis, but the big stuff was over."

"It's never really over, kid."

"Damian." Maxim nodded and the tech got right to work inside.

Maxim followed him in. He had stood in this room not twenty-four hours ago. It was a sparse entryway—the motorcycle club wasn't well known for its interior design sensibilities—but what little possibility for disarray the room afforded was actualized. An array of micro-clues spread out before the detective, lots of little hints that alone told only part of the story. Overall, there was a narrative to build. This little room may have only been a foyer, but for two to three minutes, it was the Wild West.

The Seventh Sons clubhouse was in the middle of the Sycamore forest. It sat in a large clearing of wild white grass, with a single dirt road leading to it. The Coconino deputies had been wise enough to park away from the house, but the Lexus had trampled over any possible track marks. Not that it mattered much; there wasn't anything outside, besides the downed Harley, that caught the detective's eye.

Starting, then, at the front door. Maxim pulled out his cell phone and opened a note-taking app. He noted the damage to the front door frame. The wood where the handle clicked into place was cracked as if the door had been forced in. Interestingly, the dead-bolt wasn't extended, and judging by the damage, it hadn't been when the door was breached.

Maxim sank to his knees. Without touching the handle, he took several pictures of the damage pattern.

"What's your name, Deputy?" asked Maxim, just as the bald officer returned to his post on the porch.

"Anderson," he replied.

"Detective Dwyer." Maxim stood up and offered his hand. Anderson shook it. "You and Diaz were first on the scene?"

"Yes, sir. The woman and the civ who called it in were already here."

"And who else went inside?"

"Just me and Diaz, sir. Jackson and Renteria didn't even peek in."

Maxim nodded. Anderson wasn't overly interested in the crime scene. The detective had a bead on the two partners immediately.

Some cops were like Diaz. He wanted to poke his nose into everything, maybe play detective, or just get the most out of what the job threw his way. Maybe he was excited to see dead bodies. Maybe he wanted to look around a motorcycle club's inner sanctum. Then there were the guys like Anderson. He came in, did what he was supposed to do, and didn't get in anybody's way. Faults could be found in both attitudes, of course, but in this instance, Anderson was what Maxim needed. He didn't want to have to keep his eye on Diaz, wonder what he was doing inside. Immediately, Maxim felt he could rely on Anderson.

"Was this door open like this when you arrived?"

"Yes it was, untouched by police. The two inside think they touched it, though."

Maxim twisted his mouth in disappointment. There probably wouldn't have been usable fingerprints on the doorknob anyway. It was likely whoever did this wore gloves.

The detective approached the body. It was Omar. Maxim had first met him when Gaston took over the club the year before. The kid had been playing pool with Clint, generally acting tough and backing up their new president. He was the first of the club to be so young, but not the first to die.

"Someone must have been packing silver," said Diego solemnly. Damian looked up from the body momentarily at the odd announcement. Maxim glanced over and saw Diego brooding in the connected living room. Maxim walked over to shake his hand.

"What happened here?"

"Omar was a good kid. He wasn't cutthroat like some of the others. This is the last thing I wanted to happen."

Maxim kept a harsh edge in his voice. "You're just realizing that club business isn't a vacation?" When Diego didn't answer, Maxim returned his gaze to the body. "Who did this?"

The biker shook his head. "Who could have?"

"Where is everybody?"

"Most of the MC is locked up with the New Mexico State Police."

Maxim raised an eyebrow. The fact would have been humorous under less trágic circumstances. Before he could ask a follow-up question, they were interrupted by a woman walking into the room from the back. It was Teresa Banks, the lawyer who represented Clint.

"Not another word, Mr. Torre. This incident had nothing to do with club business. The Seventh Sons were all out of state when this occurred."

"This isn't a deposition, Ms. Banks. I'm just questioning the first witness on the scene. He called us, remember?"

"Well, I'd like to be present when you do."

Maxim turned to Diego. "You believe this shit?"

The biker was resigned. He weakly shrugged. "This *is* club property."

"This is a crime scene."

Teresa Banks interjected herself between the two men. Her metal bracelets jingled as she pointed to the dead body. Maxim noticed her eyes avoided the gruesome scene. "As far as that goes, Detective, you are free to search this open area as part of your duties, but the rest of the house is off-limits."

The detective shot the lawyer a grave stare. She didn't notice.

"I just got off the phone with your marshal after speaking to the magistrate and you're going to need a search warrant to get any deeper into the house."

Maxim couldn't believe what he was hearing. The judge would never approve a search warrant for this clubhouse. They hadn't been able to do it for the Paradise Killings, and they wouldn't now. The motorcycle club must have had the judge on their payroll.

"Anderson!" yelled Maxim, not taking his eyes off the lawyer. In a moment, the deputy popped his head around the corner.

"Yes, sir?"

"Please escort Ms. Banks from the crime scene."

The woman stared at him defiantly.

"Certainly," said Anderson with a smirk on his face.

Teresa's face burned red until it looked as if it would explode. "This is preposterous!" she cried. Anderson took her by the arm but she tore free. "The Sanctuary Marshal's Office has already agreed to these terms."

"Anderson," said Maxim, turning to the deputy. "Which office do you work for?"

"Coconino County. Ma'am, I'm only gonna ask you one time to come outside." Anderson took a step back and put both hands on his belt. Teresa shifted her gaze back and forth between the two.

"You have no authority to remove me from the premises."

"Lady," said Maxim, "I am the authority."

With a gentle push from the deputy, Teresa Banks begrudgingly went outside. If the lawyer was as good at her job as he'd heard, then Maxim would hear about this again, but he could always explain that he was trying to preserve the evidence on the scene from being contaminated.

Maxim turned to Diego, hoping to get more cooperation from him without her present. "You know Doka's dead, right?"

"What?"

"The vic we found without skin at Sanctuary High. It was Carlos Doka." Maxim watched as Diego struggled to absorb the news. Diego was the one who had stabbed the man last year. When he didn't respond, Maxim said, "In any case, the Yavapai are out for revenge."

"The Sons didn't have anything to do with that."

Maxim raised his voice. "Would you listen to yourself? You used to be a military man, on the right side of the law."

Diego scoffed. "Killing—"

He stopped as Damian studied them again. Diego was going to say "killing werewolves." This wasn't something they could talk openly about.

The biker continued, in a lower voice. "It wasn't exactly as noble a calling as homicide detective." No sarcasm flavored his sentiment.

"Great. So you throw in with criminals?" The biker turned away, but Maxim caught his troubled eyes. They bared his conscience clearly. The detective wondered how far that guilt went. Was he responsible for Omar's death? "Why was the club arrested in New Mexico?"

"They're just being held for questioning. There was a thing. A delivery on the way to El Paso."

Maxim put his hand up. He didn't want to hear it. He had been told by the feds to keep out of interstate drug enforcement, that they were building a bigger case, except most of him thought that was just more cover. More club connections. One thing was sure: Maxim didn't need to hear about illegal activities, as long as they were outside his jurisdiction.

"It's bullshit," complained Diego. "The MC isn't on the hook for anything. They'll be back here before sundown."

The detective shook his head sadly.

"Look," said the biker. "I didn't want this, okay? It just happened. I was helping the MC out as a show of force because you took Clint away. We were meeting the Pistolas. All hands on deck."

"The who?"

Diego shook his head. "They're a Mexi outfit based in SoCal."

"So the Sons are warring with the Yavapai, fronting for the Pistolas, and in hot water with NMSP. Bang up position you've landed yourself in."

Maxim stormed away. He didn't understand how the man, his friend, had made such bad decisions. Having an understanding with the club was one thing. To use friendship as a means of enforcement. To keep them out of trouble and the citizens safe. Hell, Maxim had even had fun hanging out with some of the bikers at times. But to take part in illicit activity wasn't just crossing the line—it was also stupid.

Maxim Dwyer knelt beside Omar's corpse. This kid had learned that the hard way.

Chapter 22

Kayda didn't know how long she lay motionless by the side of the road. She figured her perception was warped—it seemed to be hours and hours, but the sun was still high in the sky. Huddled against the concrete barrier, the dust storm went through waves, sometimes fierce and then gentle. Several cars had passed her by, unable to see her behind the roadside wall.

She didn't call out to the cars. She didn't attempt to stand up. Kayda just lay still, wondering what to do, wondering how she could have possibly found herself back in Chino Valley, dying.

It was hot out and she was thirsty. The lack of lubrication in her throat was physically painful. It felt like her tongue had expanded and filled the space in her neck, making it difficult to so much as breathe.

A quick death, Kayda thought. That's what she deserved. Not to lie here baking in the sun, drying up like a dead leaf that had fallen away from its tree. Another vehicle, this one a large truck, blazed by in a spirited rage. How Kayda wished to have been in the middle of the road beneath that overbearing juggernaut. To have caught an end with finality. A quick death.

Heavy breaths slowed as she calmed her thoughts. Kayda wasn't going crazy. She wasn't truly thinking of death. At least she told herself that. She had been in shock. Adrenaline had pumped through her body until it was spent. Death wasn't what she needed. Only sleep. Peace.

All she required was a reprieve.

And then she heard a cat's meow. On the side of the road in the middle of nowhere, Kayda considered that maybe she actually was going crazy. The meow repeated itself, and after having not moved for what seemed like hours, the girl decided to turn her head.

A house cat stood next to her, a slight purr vibrating through his body. He had a beautiful black coat, but it was uneven and scratched up, and further marred by the red sand of the blowing storm. The cat watched her intently with wide green eyes that never blinked. Then it opened its mouth wide in a yawn, meowing before it finished, and turned its tail as if it was bored. The cat slinked into an open pipe under the road.

It was a drainage pipe. It carried water from the higher ground on the west side, under the road, and swept it off into the canyon below. The pipe was open at the end, only wide enough for the cat. As the wind spiked and whipped the grit more aggressively, Kayda dug her fingers into the dirt and heaved herself closer.

Dragging her body, she discovered, wasn't that difficult. Most of the trouble was the inertia, just getting started. Once she began, she moved quickly, and before she knew it she was at the pipe opening. The cat pressed deeper into the small tunnel, and Kayda stuck her head in.

Gentle air caressed her face. It was cool inside. Dark. Lying in the dirt below the barricade with only her head inside, Kayda closed her eyes and allowed the breeze to work its magic. It was damp. Although stagnant, the humidity excited the girl beyond description. Kayda opened her eyes and adjusted to the dim light, looking for water.

It was bone-dry, unfortunately. An illusion created by the breeze. Kayda had only been in town for a day and she had no idea when the last rain had been, but it couldn't have been very recent. She still managed a smile. The lack of water wasn't a setback. She had found shelter at least. She had found a chance.

Kayda wanted to be home. In bed. She wanted to be back in New York, with her friends. With her comforts. Yet she couldn't get over how soothing a single breeze was. It made her look at her struggles differently.

She had a few choices. Staying here to die was no longer one of them. Moving had proved she wasn't as weak as she thought. She was hurt, but only superficially. She had been parking the motorcycle when it flipped. She had the helmet on. She would be okay, she told herself. She stressed it to herself. Again and again, like a chant with healing power.

Kayda could go back to the reservation. Recover.

Although the idea pleased her body, she shuddered at the thought. The last thing she wanted was to face her people empty-handed. She had meant to show them she was strong. Was she to return a few hours later with nothing to show for it but a wrecked motorcycle?

Then again, what else could she do? Maybe it displayed true strength to thrust away the worries about her reputation. She would prove her strength. Prove her worth. But first, she needed to recover.

Kayda waited huddled against the drain pipe while the dust storm slowly subsided. The entire time, her eyes watched the dirty cat. He didn't clean himself or sleep or do any of the usual things cats did. He just sat upright, staring right back at her, incessantly out of reach.

Something absorbing resided in those eyes. A wariness, but a confidence, as if the cat didn't trust the world, but trusted that he could navigate it. Kayda thought about that, and what it meant, and found it inspiring.

Once the wind abated, Kayda smiled at her little friend. She didn't try to speak, not again, but she gave the animal a nod of thanks. She pulled her head out of the pipe and shut her eyes at the assault of the bright sun. Working with determination, and unwilling to let it evaporate in the heat, Kayda slid her tennis shoes beneath her and hauled herself up.

Her entire right torso twisted with electricity. It shot straight one way, and then threw her the other. The painful reaction emphasized how physically hurt Kayda really was. One of her ribs was likely broken.

As her body bent away from the pain, Kayda thrust a foot out to counter the momentum. She found herself leaning towards the steep slope of the hill. Her heel drove into the dirt. The rocks crumbled away underneath. Her foot slipped forward and sent her body careening down the decline.

Kayda wouldn't exactly call what happened a fall. It was more of a slide. The slope was steep and peppered with jagged rocks and bunches of grass, but her body ripped along the dirt in a controlled fashion that mostly avoided danger. Panic threatened, but she stuffed it down deep under her stomach. The ground of the canyon came rushing up to meet her, and Kayda simply gritted her teeth and steadied her feet as she skied down the dirt.

She was strong. A hillside didn't scare her. She welcomed the rush.

Her descent picked up speed. Her body hopped a couple of times, momentarily losing purchase with the dirt. Nearer the bottom, her body wiggled, and she felt her control slip away.

When the bottom did come, Kayda was unprepared for it. Her feet were not far enough ahead of her and she toppled forward, rolling into the ground and feeling more beaten up than ever. But she didn't let herself think. She didn't let herself despair. Kayda Garnett propped herself on her elbows and knees, and rose to meet the sun.

Above her, high in the sky, was State Route 89. At the bottom of the hill, she was lost among the dirt and rocks. Beside her was her brother's dented motorcycle.

Chapter 23

For someone so green, Maxim had to admit that Damian was on top of things. Not only did he have a quiet and studious attitude about the crime scene, but he moved through it quickly, checking off all the boxes. He got photographs of the approach and room, close-ups of any damage, and of course, the body. He marked the slugs embedded around the room as Maxim found them. He was on top of the log, recording the comings and goings of all visitors. The kids from school these days came to the job much more prepared than he ever had.

Of course, the real school was the trial by fire. Officers were handed a badge and a gun and kicked out into the streets. Say what you would about classes, but the Field Training Officer program was the best education any cop could get. Three months learning the ropes, riding with a veteran officer, doing real police work. There wasn't a replacement for that kind of experience.

"So let's talk it out," said Maxim to the crime scene technician. It helped his process to bounce theories off others, if only to hear them out loud. He also wanted Diego to be aware of his thoughts. If anyone here could make a slight correction to set him on the right track, it was the biker. "The vic was already in the clubhouse. His bike was parked outside, stood up properly." The detective walked over to the open front door, stepping over the plastic markers for the slugs and blood on the scene.

"The driveway is too wrecked to get any good tracks, but I'm thinking several suspects came straight to the front door." Maxim pointed to the splintered wood. "Forced entry was probably due to a kick from outside. The suspects may have been unfamiliar with the clubhouse, as the door was unlocked and they could have entered easily. That's why I think they came in force, guns ready."

The foyer led to a hallway and a staircase to the second floor of the clubhouse. There was also the living room to the left and the dining room to the right, but Omar's position didn't make sense for those. "I'm thinking the vic was in the back of the house, or upstairs, and heard the visitors before they were inside. Maybe a loud vehicle. He had a gun ready, knowing the rest of the club was still in New Mexico."

Maxim crouched and leaned over and moved his head to various positions in the doorway. He was visualizing angles from various guns, through Omar, to the back wall, which was ripped apart by bullets. "Okay, one shooter has a shotgun. We have the spread on the wall of the hallway, just past the archway. This angle is not possible from the front door." Maxim walked inside the foyer, stepping to the right wall. "I'm thinking this was the first shooter through. He ran to this end of the room to let the others in, and fired."

"He?" asked Damian.

Maxim shrugged. "Just going with the percentages. The important thing is the position here."

The lab tech nodded. "If that's the case, then the blood spatter on the wall behind you is his. The victim may have hit him first."

Maxim nodded. "And we know the vic only got hit with a partial spread of buckshot. I'd say our shooter only got one round off before he went down."

Diego watched them from the edge of the room, leaning under the archway leading to the living room. "Omar was a good shot and he liked heavy guns."

The lab tech pointed to the pistol in Omar's hand. "This isn't a heavy gun, but I'll give you the good shot."

Maxim studied the pistol. It was an old revolver. A .22. It was an odd choice for defense. "Has that weapon been fired?"

"We'll run the work up, but it looks like it," answered Damian. He handled the weapon carefully. "Look at this. The serial number on the bottom of the gun butt is scratched out."

The biker jumped at that. "Gaston doesn't like illegal weapons." The other two turned to him questioningly, so Diego expounded. "Like I said, the New Mexico State Police cleared everybody's handguns."

"But you said Omar wasn't detained."

"He wasn't. He wasn't with us then. But he couldn't have known that he wouldn't be pulled over. What I'm telling you is he shouldn't have had a throwaway on him."

Maxim ran his eyes over the weapon that Damian had set aside. He was hoping something would come to him, but it was just a gun. "You think Omar was up to something that maybe you or Gaston wouldn't have known about?"

Diego narrowed his eyes. "Not a chance. Don't blame him for this."

"I'm just saying the gun—"

"And I'm just saying this wasn't his fault!" Diego dropped his head to the floor and struggled to control his temper. Maxim knew the kid had been under the man's wing. His guilt was apparent, but there was something else. Diego cleared his throat and put his hands up in resignation. "Look, Omar liked revolvers—collectibles—especially from old westerns. He had a few but usually liked them with more kick. Maybe this six-shooter is special somehow. It was just bad luck that he was cornered with it."

Maxim couldn't argue the last point. He made a mental note to come back to it. "So we have, I think, two more guys breaching the door. We have pistol fire from here and here, all centered on the vic. He was hit at least ten times. He didn't have a chance."

"Twelve times, so far," corrected Damian. "It's hard to say before moving him more."

"But we know that some of the bullets came after—when he was grounded." The detective approached the body and stood over it, holding his hand down with a pointed finger as if it were a gun. "The shooters were wild. Erratic. Whether or not they were good shots at the range, they weren't trained for these close quarters. The vic went down but was still alive. They came in close to finish the job. All these center-mass shots, and the head shot, I think, look to be from this position."

"I got four slugs in the floorboards directly underneath the body. Center mass, like you said. This was one tough son of a bitch."

Maxim turned his eyes to Diego. They were the only two at the scene who knew just how tough, assuming Teresa Banks didn't know she represented werewolves.

"And lucky," finished Damian. "The slug in the head embedded into the cranium. It never breached it."

Luck had nothing to do with it. Wolves were people. Their bones could break, but they were stronger than normal bones. The Coconino deputies especially weren't privy to all that went on in Sycamore. Maxim would need to keep them, and Damian, in the dark. Especially about the next part.

Maxim's eyes moved to Omar's chest. "Then the lethal wounds were here. The heart was punctured."

"The blood pattern suggests arterial spray," said Damian. "That was it for him."

Wolves had great constitutions. They couldn't heal immediately—rather, they needed to wait until the next moon phase, their next transformation, and then they would become instantly better. But that didn't mean they were killed easily. Silver was needed, a solid in the bloodstream, to weaken their defenses, to allow them to die. It was a good bet that the ME would pull silver rounds from the body.

Which in itself was an enigma. Maxim patted the magazine at his belt. He always kept silver rounds close, but who else did? Even Hitchens and Cole didn't, in the off chance that they lost control of their firearm.

The killers either needed to be wolves or came in overwhelming force and with a knowledge of the beasts. Yavapai payback for Doka made sense.

"Did anyone know that Omar was in the clubhouse alone?" asked Maxim.

Diego shrugged. "I didn't even know he was here. Maybe whoever it was just got lucky."

Maxim cocked his head from side to side as he considered that. He didn't like relying on such proclamations. Criminals did sometimes get lucky, but usually there were clues in the how and why crimes were planned.

Maxim spun around casually and glanced out the open door. "Why would they smash the bike?" Damian watched him with a puzzled expression. "Outside. After the job was done, they left and knocked over the vic's bike. Why would they do that?"

Diego started. "You don't think the Yavapai did this."

What had Diego said about the Pistolas? A California gang that sent the club to New Mexico. Could they have been involved? "It's just..."

Diego nodded. "The Yavapai aren't bikers. Besides

Doka, I don't even know if any of the others ride. Doka was the one who came up to Sycamore Lodge and associated with Deborah and the others."

"Wait," said Damian. "What does any of that have to do with the bike outside?"

"It's the ultimate disrespect for bikers to mess with another person's ride," said Diego. "Knocking it down, smashing it—men have been killed for less."

The seed of the idea began to sprout in Maxim's mind. "So bikers did this."

Damian pulled his head back. "You think the Sons executed their own guy?"

"No." The detective turned to Diego. "Do the Pistolas ride?"

The biker nodded and his expression soured. "They're an outlaw club all the way. And they would have known that the MC was in a New Mexico police station."

Okay, so Maxim had two groups of suspects. One of them gave him a way to keep this war from starting, if it hadn't already. Maxim still hadn't found proof that the Seventh Sons had anything to do with Doka's murder. If it was possible the Yavapai weren't involved with this, then something much deeper was going on.

"Let's look at the inconsistencies," stated the detective with renewed vigor. He pushed the front door so it was almost closed and moved over to Omar's position. "We have a six-shooter in the vic's hand. Three empty shells in the cylinder. Three slugs in the entryway."

"Three shots fired. Three misses," said Damian.

"Except somebody's blood is on the wall behind me."

"Could he have reloaded?"

"As fast as this went down, not likely. Not a revolver." Maxim crouched over the body and aimed his finger at the front door. "Then there's the fact that one of these defensive shots hit the front door."

Damian didn't say anything. He was still thinking over what Maxim said. He didn't get it.

"Two of the shots hit the wall, but the third hit the backside of the front door. Look at the angle of that thing. The door was closed."

"Ah," said the lab tech, finally catching on. "If the shooters just charged through the door, why would it be closed?"

"Right."

Diego shook his head as if he wasn't confident about the theory. "I don't know. That door slams shut all the time in the wind.

"It's not a whole lot to go on," said Damian, apparently agreeing with Diego. "The door could have bounced open and closed. It does look like the victim fired the revolver, for what it's worth; there are powder burns on his hand." Maxim shot Damian a harsh look as if he had been betrayed. Evidence like that was unreliable. Now he was starting to think the crime scene tech had a bit too much initiative.

Maxim grew annoyed. He liked getting more conclusive results directly from the scene. At least this one was sloppier than the high school—more evidence that it was done by a separate hand—but this was two murders in a row that weren't open and shut. That was the last thing the marshal wanted to hear. And now, the Yavapai and the Sons both had a dog in this fight. How long could Maxim keep them away from each other's throats?

The detective sighed. He dropped his head and spotted a boot print in the blood. "You get a picture of this?" he asked, changing the subject.

"Yeah, but your friend said he accidentally did that when he first arrived on the scene." Maxim glared at Diego, then kneeled beside Damian.

"Do me a favor, along with making sure you have fingerprints of everyone who was inside, make sure you get boot prints too. Me, Diego, even the deputies outside. Make sure you get Diaz. He was rummaging around in here."

"S—sure," answered the tech, standing up. "The prints are on file but I'll do the boots now before they leave." Damian wordlessly went outside, careful not to disturb the doorknob. He had already dusted it for prints but didn't get anything promising. The outside handle had been wiped down, or brushed with a glove.

Maxim sighed. He needed more. Something that would point to the Yavapai or the Pistolas or someone else. Something that would give him a nudge in a specific direction while waiting on the autopsy results. It was already getting late in the day and Dr. Medina might not be able to get to the body until the morning.

His eyes swept the room, past the doorway, Diego, the hallway and the stairs, trying to see all the angles. This poor kid had maybe dug his own grave, but that didn't mean he deserved it. And anyone who pulled off a slaughter like this was only going to continue. Maxim spun his body around to scan the rest of the room, balanced on his toes with his elbows over his knees.

Something was here. There had to be. He was just missing it.

Then he remembered Crime Scene 101. Maxim laughed as he saw it, not sure if it meant anything but funny all the same.

"What is it?" asked Diego.

Maxim stared at the ceiling and the small hole in the wooden beam.

"Don't forget to look up," said the detective. "You said your man liked big guns, right?"

"Yeah."

That had to be it. Above his head, a single large bullet was lodged in the ceiling.

Chapter 24

Kayda found a rhythm to her stride that didn't strain her rib. It was definitely broken, she thought, but stiffness was the key. Any twist of her torso would send the wrath of God through her senses, almost strong enough to knock her off her feet. To avoid that, she settled into a sort of shuffling motion—keeping her upper body straight, dragging her right foot so as to keep the impact on her twisted ankle low, and trying not to bend her left elbow.

She knew she was a pathetic sight. Bits of her flesh were scraped and skinned and her clothes were covered in dirt. With a chuckle, Kayda imagined that she resembled a zombie. She had the walk and the costume—all she needed was the pallor of death. That reminded her of Halloween in New York. She had gone out with friends, all dressed as the undead. The makeup color for their skin was called "dead-guy gray."

The thought made her smile. But then she thought of

her brother's skin flapping in the night wind and her mirth disappeared. A nauseous feeling rose and her throat constricted. Kayda tried to swallow but her tongue was too dry.

She was so thirsty. So tired.

Kayda pressed on, ignoring the sand in her tennis shoes. She realized she still had her motorcycle helmet on. With a tug on the strap around her chin, she let it fall to the dirt.

The sun was no longer at its high point. Perhaps it would disappear behind the peaks and leave her in the dark. It would be better that way. Cooler.

As Kayda Garnett examined the horizon, she saw a bird circling high above. She stopped and thought of her grandfather's story.

"I won't eat you, Crow."

Another smile formed on her lips, and Kayda thought she must have been delirious. What did she have to smile about? She was lost down here. Her plan to find the access road instead of scaling the sheer edge to the highway sounded like a solid one. Now she was beginning to doubt her decision. Her scabbed skin, unaccustomed to the sun the last few years, started to burn. She was dying of thirst. All she needed to do was find a road, find a person, but the only one in sight was the crow in the sky.

It would have to do, she decided. She trudged toward the bird. It flew around and backtracked and landed on trees in such a way as to never disappear from Kayda's sight for more than a moment. Her trek became easier as she pushed herself, loosening her muscles. The bird helped keep her mind off her predicament, but again she second-guessed herself. Perhaps she was mad. There was no bird. It was just a hallucination.

The more Kayda's fears grew, the harder she pushed herself. She even began to twist her stomach and lean forward as she tackled a small slope. The pain shocked her, but it was a welcome feeling. It was real. It proved she was still alive. She fought off the hurt and increased her pace as the crow flew ahead.

She didn't see where the bird landed. As Kayda crested the hill, she couldn't see anything except the rippling stream flowing smoothly over white rocks. She let out an audible whimper and shambled down until her dirt covered shoes touched the cold water. A few paces in, when the water splashed to her knees, Kayda collapsed into the stream.

Her skin burned against the sudden shock. It was painful but pleasant at the same time. Rejuvenating. Kayda imagined she was thrusting off her damaged outer shell. Shedding her skin like a snake. Like her brother. Only she was getting a new one. As the cool water soaked her clothes and washed over her body, she imagined she could breathe underwater. She opened her mouth and welcomed the fluid; her tongue absorbed it like a sponge. Then Kayda emerged, exhilarated. Alive. She saw the bird perched close by on a rock, jumping in and out of the water and shaking its feathers as if to dance.

Kayda thought of her *pahmi's* folktale again. "Thank you, Crow." Then the girl remembered the rest of the story. The coming flood. "Now if you could only fly me out of here."

She sighed as she sat there, dejected but not allowing the thought to spoil her paradise. She would stay there all night if she could, sitting in the stream. Even if she died, she would never be dry or thirsty again. She worked the clear water through her hair. It turned to mud at first, but surrendered and washed out of her long, brown hair, almost straight again. She rubbed her skin, softening the scabs and the burns. Kayda washed out the sand and rocks that had collected in her shoes and wiggled her toes. She felt giddy.

The crow suddenly plunged into the air, its wings wildly scattering drops of water. In seconds, Kayda's friend had left her. And then she heard why. Talking. People talking.

She slipped her soaking shoes back over her feet. Kayda pressed her hands into the submerged ground and lifted herself. She was sore but did it without crying out. When she turned around she saw a couple, a man and a woman, emerge from a thicket of bushes. They were hikers, out for their day's exercise, which meant they had a car close. The couple stopped in their tracks when they saw her, and Kayda managed to stretch her lips into a wide, welcoming smile.

"Are you all right?" the woman asked. Although Kayda had tried to put on a good show, it must have been obvious that she was hurt.

"I'm stranded," she said. "Lost." And then, for absolutely no reason at all, Kayda began to cry.

Chapter 25

Maxim knew something was wrong as soon as he walked into the Sanctuary Marshal's Office. When the young desk clerk saw him, he immediately pretended to be busy. Inside, Cole and Gutierrez sat at their desks, speaking in hushed voices that quieted as soon as they noticed him. The marshal's office door was closed, which was never a good sign.

"Missed you at the crime scene," said Maxim.

Cole just shrugged. "I thought Coconino locked it down."

The detective dropped his hat on his desk and scoped around to make sure no one else was listening. "You know the drill, Cole. If I'm at the clubhouse, I want you or Hitchens to back me up."

Gutierrez chimed in. "What about me, boss?"

"You can go to Starbucks."

The rookie laughed it off and faked a wounded look, but

he wasn't really offended. Maxim's message was clear: if he was going to be surrounded by wolves, he wanted at least one of them to be wearing blue. Hitchens and Cole were the old guys, the veterans, but they were the strongest.

"I thought the Sons wouldn't give you any trouble," protested Cole.

"Hey, man, I would usually think that too, but I won't get extra chances if I'm wrong."

Cole nodded. Motorcycle clubs weren't the most stalwart of friends. Not to cops, anyway.

Boyd's door swung open and slammed into the wall, its fuzzy glass insert shaking within its frame. The young marshal marched out, scanned the room, and faced Maxim.

"Ah, Detective Dwyer," he said, pretending to be surprised at running into him. "I'm glad you've returned. What's your assessment?"

Maxim noticed Cole and Gutierrez sit up straighter. "It was a shootout. Ballistics should tell us a lot."

"I'd rather not wait for all that. The autopsy may confirm or deny anything we have, but we need to take action before that if we mean to prevent a gang war." Marshal Boyd approached Maxim. "Do you think it was the Seventh Sons?"

"Killing their own? That doesn't make any sense. Besides, they're locked up in New Mexico."

"They were released several hours ago. NMSP notified me of the incident."

"Which was?"

"They were just held under suspicious circumstances and

questioned. They were released without charges."

Maxim snorted. Diego had been right when he said that nothing would come of it. "Well, get me the timeline for that so I can rule them out. I don't think it was them. Diego was the first one back and found the body."

A voice came from inside the private office. "Why wasn't that club member brought in for questioning?" A man in a light-blue Oxford shirt and white tie emerged from within. He was a Mexican man, almost forty judging by the gray on the side of his head and peppering his mustache. His hair was shorn short and clean, except for the top of his head where it was a little longer and spiked up. The man had a big nose and a strong brow line, with deep, dark eyes. They stared at him accusatorily.

Maxim turned to the marshal. "Who's this guy?"

Boyd didn't answer. The man did. "I'm your new best friend, Detective. I'll be assisting you in this investigation."

Maxim refused to face him. He searched Boyd's blue eyes for the answer. With a resigned breath, the marshal said, "This is Special Agent Raymond Garcia, of the FBI."

Raymond put a hand out and Maxim shook it with the minimum required cordiality. "Maxim Dwyer."

"I know you," he said. "Small-town detective takes down the Paradise Killers. That was impressive work."

Maxim nodded plainly. He didn't tell the man that he had also outed a rogue CDC agent. Sanctuary had been exploited by the feds before. Maxim knew it was a cliche, but he didn't trust the FBI.

"No offense to either of you," said Raymond Garcia,

"but I'm surprised you've stayed at this small station. You could have leveraged that case into a career anywhere."

That was something else the FBI agent didn't know. Maxim had killed a werewolf, an associate of Carlos Doka. Sanctuary was a special case that needed to be handled delicately. Sycamore's affairs needed to stay in Sycamore. Maxim was plenty happy taking on that challenge.

"Well no offense," countered Maxim, "but what the hell are you doing here?"

The marshal winced, no doubt hoping Maxim wouldn't have introduced his gruff side so early. Garcia took it in stride.

"I want you to know, straight away, Detective, that I'm not here to take over your case. The FBI is very adept at complementing local law enforcement. It's one of my primary jobs in the Civil Rights Program."

Maxim turned to the marshal again. Either way, one of them was going to answer his question.

"It's common for the FBI to investigate violent hate crimes," said Boyd.

Maxim scoffed. "Not this again."

"I know what you're thinking," said Garcia. "This is a gang war, not a hate crime. I understand that. But our resources are often applied to gangs that commit crimes of bias. No matter which way you look at it, a Native American being strung up and skinned alive took our notice. As soon as that skin was hung on tribal soil last night, I was dispatched."

"He wasn't skinned alive," shot back Maxim.

"Regardless—"

"And you don't know what I'm thinking. The Seventh Sons didn't do Doka."

Garcia eyed the marshal. He was skeptical of Maxim's statement but didn't attack the theory. "Whether the motorcycle club was involved with the first death or not, they are clearly implicated. The Yavapai tribe may not require your burden of proof to retaliate."

Both points were sound, thought Maxim. They were again, however, surface observations. "I don't think Omar was killed as Yavapai payback. There's a gang beef with a California club called the Pistolas. I want to check them out."

Garcia's eyes widened at the mention of the club's name. He knew them. "Then you should welcome FBI cooperation, shouldn't you?" Maxim kept a neutral face, unsure of Garcia's meaning. He explained. "I understand that Sycamore is largely unincorporated and the county office allows you to police some of their jurisdiction, but surely you understand that California is out of your scope. Federal leverage will come in handy for that."

The detective nodded reluctantly. "And what about the Pistolas? Have you heard of them?"

Raymond Garcia smiled. "Of course I have. I have a background in undercover gang work. Hey, I'm the right skin color, right?"

Boyd smiled, thinking the two men had found some common ground, but Maxim was still wary.

"I've worked in some of the surrounding areas," said

Garcia. "I know about the Mexican pipeline and the role of the Seventh Sons. That's one of the reasons I jumped at this case. I'm intimately familiar with the gang world. I know some things that would blow your mind. Trust me, I'll be of assistance."

Maxim smirked at the agent's words. In all likelihood, Garcia was ignorant of the wolves. He may have been an expert on gangs, but he had no idea what made the Seventh Sons tick.

"Now I have to come clean," said the FBI agent, to both the marshal and Maxim. "There is speculation of impropriety between this department and the Seventh Sons. Some critics think the Paradise Killings could have been prevented if this office had been doing its job."

Boyd's face reddened. "Now wait just a minute—"

Garcia put his hands up in apology. "That's not coming from me. I'm on your side, Marshal. But if my assistance can provide a sense of impartiality to the proceedings, then all the better. First and foremost, I recommend that we give absolutely no special treatment to the Seventh Sons. This Diego should have been brought into the station for questioning. Given the current events, we need more than his word that he wasn't involved."

Maxim felt defensive at the mention of justice not being served equally under his watch. "Hey, I was the one who arrested Clint James."

"And you released him."

That was news to Maxim. He checked with the marshal, who nodded.

"He cooperated," said Boyd. "We didn't have enough to hold him and he had a good lawyer. He was released after Diego called in Omar's murder, so he's clear there."

The detective sighed. Usually the marshal making that move would have angered him, but they needed a united front against the FBI. "He'll be easy to scrounge up again if we need him. Trust me."

"Detective," chided Raymond, "I just don't want a situation to arise where you rely on the motorcycle club to solve this case. The Seventh Sons are tight. We had a man try to infiltrate their ranks once but they wouldn't take him. We don't know why."

Of course, Maxim thought, the answer was simple: the Bureau's man wasn't a wolf.

"They aren't just a bunch of drunken outlaws," continued Garcia. "They're smart and well connected. Believe me, they have a network of interests that we must consider before clearing them of any wrongdoing. And that includes law enforcement."

"I'm not in anybody's pocket," asserted Maxim.

The marshal cut between the two men. "He's not accusing anyone specifically, Detective. But I do believe his presence can give this investigation legitimacy."

"Well that's bullshit, Marshal. I go where the evidence goes. You should know that about me by now." But Maxim did allow a sputtering of doubt to creep into his ironclad resolve. It was true that the Seventh Sons were criminals. The Pistolas angle was a new one. Who knew what business deals they were up to or what obligations they had? It was possible that the club was tangentially responsible for Doka's death at least, was it not?

Raymond Garcia was an outsider, an FBI agent from the Civil Rights Program here on a bullshit hate crime investigation. But he did have gang expertise. And he did want to stop a war from breaking out. Shit, it was even likely that Marshal Boyd had requested the agency's help, for the very same reason.

Maxim decided that he would give the guy a chance. It wasn't going to be easy to tread around the wolf angle; the detective needed to hide some details because of that, but he could make it work.

"Great," said Maxim. "I imagine you both will want to read my report as soon as possible. If there's nothing else, I'll have it on your desk before I leave tonight."

Boyd and Garcia both nodded at the same time, eager to receive cooperation. The FBI agent turned to the marshal with an almost embarrassed expression. "I hope it doesn't put you out, Marshal, but I'm going to need your office."

Boyd just laughed. "There's an extra desk in the main room. You can have that." The marshal pointed it out and the three of them turned to see Gutierrez pouring himself a coffee at said desk.

"Marshal," stuttered Raymond, watching the rookie spill a packet of sugar, probably on purpose. "I have the authority to assume a command post."

"Take it up with the mayor," he shot back. Cole rose from his seat and approached with an intimidating posture.

"I am accustomed to better accommodations," protested

Garcia.

"Welcome to Sanctuary," Boyd answered, and then stepped into his private office and slammed the door shut.

"Well," said the FBI agent, recovering, "maybe it *is* better for me to sit out here. Keep an eye on you guys."

Raymond Garcia attempted a chuckle to lighten the mood. Maxim and Cole watched him retreat timidly to his desk.

"Sometimes the machine shuts off by itself," said Gutierrez, pointing to the coffeemaker. "Since you're sitting here now, can you make sure to re-flip the switch if that happens?"

Chapter 26

Sycamore Lodge often served as a rendezvous point for the motorcycle club. Now, more than ever, since they were homeless. The Seventh Sons each had a place to call home, of course, but the clubhouse was their communal sanctuary. It being a crime scene prevented their access, so they needed to settle for a town called Sanctuary instead.

Diego had gotten the news to them before they returned from New Mexico. The Sons had immediately regrouped, as any supportive pack did, but besides promises of vengeance and other shows of testosterone, there wasn't much to say. The MC simply spread across one half of the bar area and stared in silence, inebriation dulling their pain. Coarse laughter filled the room but it was the ominous red light and sway of the alcohol that really set the scene.

It was too bad Melody wasn't working tonight to see this, because even Diego was drinking, but after the events of last year, with her mother dying, she probably needed to be as far away from death as possible.

Diego had originally come to Sanctuary looking for his sister, Angelica. Being the older brother nurtured his protective nature, but his little sister had felt claustrophobic under his cloak. She'd moved on, finding her own adventures, calling him every few months with an update. It wasn't until now that Diego realized it, but in Angelica's absence he had watched over Omar like family.

The blood of his brother still stained the knee of his leather pants.

The bottle of Heineken felt both foreign and familiar in Diego's hand. The last time he had a beer, he thought, was at his father's grave. It seemed apt to afford Omar the same honor. More than any other force in a person's life, family had the power to derail.

They heard the V-Twin engine outside that announced their president's return. The MC sat in expectant silence as Gaston entered.

"The police just cleared out," he said. "We got our home back." Gaston turned and saw Clint in attendance. "Holy shit, when did they let this jailbird out?"

Clint James stood and grabbed Gaston in a brotherly bear hug. "Sounds like you all preferred the accommodations in my home state." Diego grimaced at the thought. It had been a bad couple of days for the club. "I think I won out," continued Clint, stroking his mane of a beard. "I've been there before. It ain't fun."

Gaston nodded in agreement and patted the man's bright red jacket. Diego supposed it was a small victory to be reunited again. He wouldn't spoil that for the others. But his dark mood was shared by his brothers, and the levity of the moment dissipated when Clint took his seat.

"I want every single one of you staying over tonight," commanded Gaston. "No exceptions. We stick together to see this through. Understand?"

Curtis and Trent nodded. Clint whooped. Diego's icy resolve was his only answer, and he noticed the same in West's stare.

Gaston paused. "The blood hasn't been cleaned up yet. We'll call someone tomorrow." He was a tough man, but it was obvious he was unsettled at the thought.

"We've all seen a little blood," said the Apache. It wasn't to make light of what had happened to Omar. It was more a statement that they wouldn't be shaken by what needed to be done. The others nodded grimly.

"Gaston!" came a shrill voice from the crowd behind them. A young blonde girl who wore a tight shirt without a bra and jean shorts cut so high that the pocket linings were visible scampered towards the club. West took to his feet quickly and moved beside Gaston. He put his hand up to stop the hot girl in her tracks.

She twirled her hair in her fingers and looked quizzically at the president, but he just set his jaw, not even bothering to turn around. As a fallback tactic, she winked at West.

"Club business," he stated. Then the intimidating man nodded her away. She smartly followed his suggestion.

West Wind faced his brothers again. "The Yavapai have taken the fight to us. We must take it to them."

Curtis glanced at his friends nervously and rubbed his bald head. "The reservation?"

The Apache nodded. "Five of us. Only two of them."

Diego's face darkened. "You're only counting wolves. There's six of us." The two men locked eyes for a moment, but West relented with a nod. "And there are more Yavapai mercenaries. We don't even know for sure that only two of them are wolves."

"I think we'd know," said Gaston.

"Maybe." Diego took a long swig of beer and emptied his bottle. "Maxim told me that Doka's brother nearly started a riot. It would be dangerous for us to go down there. Stupid."

West didn't blink. "I never claimed to be smart."

Diego bounced to his feet. He couldn't sit still anymore. He was too tense. "Look, I'm pissed about Omar. Believe me, I'm gonna find the pricks who did this. But I'm not even sure it was the Yavapai."

"That doesn't track," said Clint. "Back at the station, your cop friend thought I was set up. Guess who came around the Lodge a couple nights ago and started a fight with me? Hotah Shaw. He's Kelan's right hand."

West grumbled. "That guy needs a good ass kicking."

"Me and him had us a three-minute bell. I got mine."

Gaston slammed his fists onto a table. The beer in the half-filled pitcher sloshed from side to side. "You scrapped with one of Kelan's men when you came into town? You didn't think to mention that to me?"

Clint threw his hands up defensively. "Listen, I was just

helping Melody out. Hotah was taking a piss on everybody in here so I set him straight. It was clean and controlled. I wasn't gonna say nothing, but..."

"But you figured after everything that went down, you'd better come clean."

Clint raised his eyebrows as a dog who just chewed up the curtains might. "Well, sure. And I didn't say nothing to Maxim, but he figured it out on his own. He knows I fought with a Yavapai, but he doesn't know who."

Gaston wasn't appeased. "You do understand there's a reason why I gave the hands-off order? The Yavapai are not to be touched. Now one of them is dead and your knife was used to take his skin off."

The hillbilly shrugged his shoulders weakly. "Like I said, the cop thinks I was set up."

"That doesn't make sense," cut in Diego, annoyed at how easily the club got off topic. "Doka was one of them. What if they're being set up too?"

"Or Hotah is going behind Kelan's back," offered Curtis.

Gaston entertained the possibility. Diego decided to give them all he had learned from Maxim.

"Omar was attacked by three or four guys. He was taken down by gunfire. Shot up when he was on the ground. It was sloppy." The rest of the club morosely listened to the details. "We have to consider that wolves didn't do this."

West snorted. Clint spit some beer on the wood floor in disgust. Werewolves didn't like the thought that they were mortal, that they could be taken down by someone weaker than them, but it was a truth they would be wise to admit.

Diego used to be a ranger in the Commissioned Corps, especially trained for the grim task. He knew it could be done, and the others had to acknowledge his expertise.

"Omar wasn't very strong," muttered Gaston. "Diego could be right." Some of the others, upon hearing their president accept the possibility, began to consider it. Diego noticed that Gaston was past that, though, working on the next piece of the puzzle. He turned to Diego. "You think the Pistolas did this."

The statement escaped the president's lips as little more than a whisper, but the fortitude that the words carried made them crystal clear in the loud bar.

"They kicked over his bike," pressed Diego. "That run was a setup. We were meant to get arrested out of state, where we had less influence."

"But the state police are our friends," protested Gaston. "We're tight with Cortez."

"Big help that connection was. The troopers back us only as long as we're the highest bidder. If the Pistolas got to them it would explain a lot: We fuck up a run for El Paso and most of our club gets tied up with the law. If it wasn't for Omar scoping the police, things could be a lot worse right now."

"Fat lot of good that did him," said Clint.

"And if it wasn't for you realizing something was wrong..." said Gaston, trailing off. Diego saw appreciation on the faces of his brothers. They hadn't known how he would fare in their business but he had protected them in the end.

West strode over to Diego and extended his hand. Diego eyed the big man. He was stoic. Not a word or hint on his face as to his meaning, but Diego thought he understood. He moved to shake West's hand. The Apache shot forward with a quick movement and grabbed Diego's wrist instead. Diego tried to move but the clasp was strong. West stood firm and held the wrist as they stared at each other.

"Bygones, and all that," said West. "We put our shit behind us." Diego bit down and clasped the man's wrist in return. "We need to all watch out for each other. Got it?" Diego nodded.

West retreated to the head. Strategies would come later. For now, absorbing the realization of their new enemy was enough. As the group sat in silence, Diego leaned into the bar and waved his empty bottle in the air. He needed an excuse to turn away from the MC. He hadn't told them everything yet.

The biker stood there, with the larger group but alone, as he listened to the wolves make small talk. They needed distractions. They needed confidence. And Gaston impressed them with those things. Diego never would have guessed that the biker brute who stole his sister away from Detroit could be a good leader, but he was. But as long as they had a foot in illegitimate trade, what happened to Omar wouldn't be an isolated incident. Diego couldn't live like that. It was too senseless.

Halfway into his new bottle, he heard heavy boots approach from behind. It was Gaston, still wearing the same shirt from the day before, the gel in his spiked hair flaking away in dried disarray. It had been a long night for all of them. Given their safety, a little downtime was just what the doctor ordered.

"I know he was your friend," said the president. Diego stared at the label of his beer and thought about playing pool with the kid the previous morning.

"He was smart," said Diego.

"He came through for us. And so did you."

It didn't protect him, in the end, thought Diego. Another sip of the cold beer convinced him to come clean. "I thought I wanted this, Gaston, but I don't. The brotherhood is solid—the MC, the riding—but the drugs are just stupid, man. Chasing money like this will always lead to death."

Gaston scoffed. "People will always take what someone else has. You can't avoid it by standing on the sidelines."

"That's bullshit, Gaston, and you know it. Sure, shit could happen to anyone at any time, but don't dismiss your part in this. Drugs, guns, the cartel—you're pushing the limits. You're inviting this kind of thing. You might be okay with that. I'm not."

"You're good at it."

"Yeah, well I was good at my last job too." Diego thought about the Commissioned Corps. A paid government assassin. He had to quit to save his soul.

The president wore a disappointed look. He leaned his back on the bar and glanced at the rest of the guys. "So you're out?"

"If you'll let me. I figure that's an easy call since I'm not a wolf."

"The other guys don't care about that anymore. You've proved yourself."

"It won't change my mind."

The big man sighed heavily and searched for a drink. "I won't give you any trouble, Diego. As long as you take some time to think about it first."

"That won't be a problem. I'm seeing this through until Omar gets avenged. I told you I was getting those pricks."

Gaston smiled and nodded softly. "That's one thing we can agree on."

The two men stood wordless while they took in the scene at the roadhouse. A live band began playing in the other room. They were some kind of rockabilly group, the fifties meets distortion. A thickening crowd wildly hopped beside the small stage. Up on the wooden level of the main bar, the tables had all filled out. Plates of burgers and ribs passed around. The outside patio was no different, although perhaps cooler. Friends stood around fire pits and laughed, unaware what Sanctuary really was.

Diego always liked Sycamore Lodge. It was the unofficial turf of the MC, maybe more official now that Melody owned it. It didn't feel the same, though. Not without Omar.

The front door swung open and Maxim Dwyer entered. He wore his black suit and white panama hat, and Diego noticed that his gun was holstered on his belt. The detective's eyes scanned the interior and landed on Diego and the Sons. He moved through the room, taking in all the customers like he was looking for somebody, and knocked his hand twice on the wood of the bar. Without a word, the bartender poured him a bourbon, neat.

Diego pushed away from that same bar, a feat that was more difficult than it should have been. His tolerance wasn't what it used to be. Gaston, however, patted him on the shoulder.

"Let me take this one."

The biker read the urgency on Gaston's face and acquiesced with a welcome slump onto a barstool.

"Also," said Gaston, before he turned away, "keep what we talked about to yourself. No sense distracting the other guys with your news yet."

The president of the Seventh Sons went to have a few words with Maxim, and the two filed down the back hallway and outside into the yard.

Chapter 27

The smoking pit, as some called it, was just a stretch of dirt in the backyard of Sycamore Lodge. There was no place to sit except for the small stoop immediately next to the door, so patrons wandered in the empty space whenever they needed a moment of downtime. The smoking pit was a graveyard of customer complaints and underhanded plots, scattered cigarette butts, like headstones, the only evidence of the past.

It was out here that Maxim had fought for his life against Deborah, one of the Paradise Killers and ex-president of the Seventh Sons. Now, he had words with her successor.

"What the fuck do you have me involved with?" demanded Maxim, his mask of complacency torn away. Gaston and the detective stood against the back wall at a distance from the few smokers who might overhear. "Am I protecting a bunch of murderers here?"

Gaston worked his jaw, unused to this sort of antagonism, but he took Maxim seriously enough. "It wasn't us. I swear."

"You don't know who could've done Doka?"

"No way. Hell, everyone thought Diego killed him last year."

Maxim moved his face closer to the bigger man's and affixed him with his best glare. He looked Gaston in the eye, trying to glimpse any sign of deception. The Seventh Sons president showed nothing but weariness.

"Diego said you backed us. You released Clint. That says something, right?"

"I don't think he's involved," admitted Maxim. "But he's being an asshole with that fancy lawyer. You too, getting in my way at the clubhouse."

"That's a sensitive area," said Gaston. "It's in both our interests for some things to stay hidden."

Maxim winced at his inclusion in the motorcycle club's inner circle. Partners in crime, partners in time. Gaston was a fool if he thought the detective would be a partner in anything illegal.

"Look, I'm trying to protect you guys. I can't do that if the Seventh Sons keep turning up as subjects of an investigation. And stop getting arrested by other departments."

"We weren't charged."

"Yeah, well, you might be next time."

Gaston sucked his teeth. His patience with the lecture was wearing thin. "I'm telling you. Someone is gunning for us. Setting us up in all this. Those cops in the state police were working off federal guidelines. It didn't come from in-house. They're building a case."

"I don't want to hear that," fumed Maxim. "That means you're fucked. The mayor or the judge or whoever's in your pocket can't help you with the feds."

The president smiled slightly. Maxim thought it was defiance. He'd hit close to home with the line about the judge or the mayor, but Gaston didn't reveal anything more.

"We're clean," affirmed Gaston. "We don't hold product."

"I know," said the detective with callous bitterness. "You're just escorts. Charging a tax. That doesn't make it legal. I can't watch out for you with those charges." Maxim turned away from the man who wielded so much power in this town. "I won't."

Gaston looked away too. The tough guy facade came back. "No one has clean hands in this town. Not the Seventh Sons or the CDC. Not the mayor. Not Sergeant Hitchens, for all his righteousness. And certainly not you after you took that briefcase full of money."

Maxim's eyes were lasers, turned to burn holes right through the man's skull. Even Gaston, the wolf, knew not to look directly at the detective after that accusation. Maxim hated that Gaston was able to say that. He hated that he had given the president cause to say that.

The briefcase had been Deborah's "go" money. When she had commandeered Sycamore Lodge with a handful of hostages, the briefcase was the only thing that stood between her and a free ticket out of town. Gaston had given it to Maxim as a bargaining chip: the money brought her to the table. But with her death, and the ensuing chaos, the briefcase had all too easily disappeared.

Clint James had mentioned the missing money to Maxim in the interrogation room. Now Gaston was showing the detective that the Seventh Sons meant to hold it over his head. Just another insurance policy.

Gaston moved as if he was ready to go inside. He took a few steps away and paused, waiting for Maxim's next move. The detective remained silent, staring at the rough wood texture of the wall. He felt the heat radiating from his face, his anger evident.

"Is this the Pistolas?" asked Gaston, breaking the air.

Maxim didn't look at him. "I don't know."

They allowed the silence to linger as they considered the possibility. Then Gaston scoffed. "They don't have the balls. Let me know if the Seventh Sons can help with anything on your end. But don't worry about us. We can handle ourselves."

Gaston started to leave, but Maxim's gravelly voice had the final say. "That's what I'm afraid of. I don't want any more incidents. I'm serious."

The detective was left alone in the smoking pit except for a drunk sleeping on the steps. Even though he was in an open field, he felt the walls closing in, constricting his breath. It wouldn't do to get worked up, he thought. He just needed to focus on following the evidence and keeping the peace. But somehow, between the FBI and the motorcycle club and the dirty mayor, his career felt like a house of cards.

Chapter 28

Kayda nodded thanks to Officer Gutierrez as he pulled away in his cruiser. She'd run into him at the police station when she asked after Maxim. Since she didn't have a ride anymore, he offered to give her one.

She had initially thought he just wanted to get laid. While he had played it suave and showed off about being a cop, to his credit he didn't make any moves. A cool gentleman throughout their encounter. That was nice in a way, and disappointing—he could at least have asked for her number.

Kayda sighed and rubbed her right side. The hikers that had picked her up lived in Flagstaff. They'd kindly dropped her off in Sanctuary on the way back. In the second-floor clinic, Kayda had completely downplayed the extent of her injuries. She'd told them that she fell down a hill and scratched herself up. Somehow that was less embarrassing than crashing her motorcycle on the side of the road.

The doctor had reported what her body already screamed to her: her rib was cracked. That was good news. Better than a break. After her injuries had been wrapped and treated for infection, she was free to leave. Her first thought, since she was at the police station, had been to talk to the police. So here she was, at Sycamore Lodge, under orders not to drink or be active.

The first one she could control. She had a feeling she'd be breaking the second.

Kayda had never seen the roadhouse before. She'd heard about it, of course. Carlos had taken to it, said it matched his rough exterior. In a way, the venue was what she imagined.

Bars used to intimidate her. This place and the ones back on the reservation were not what she would call classy. Or safe. It wasn't until New York when, for the first time, she'd actually had fun going out. Those establishments were upscale and trendy, of course. She could get dressed up in a little skirt and sip drinks with blackberries in them. Sycamore Lodge? It wasn't that type of bar. The patio was full of brash locals spilling beer on each other. Through the open front door, all she saw was a red haze signaling danger to any cautious enough to pay attention.

Unsettled by her sudden shift of confidence, Kayda almost decided to stay outside and wait for the detective. Then she noticed the row of Harleys lining the side of the building and remembered her primary mission: to make peace with the Seventh Sons.

Without a doubt, she knew she was in the right place—

where she was meant to be. If the sky hadn't been blanketed in darkness, she was confident the crow would be visible above.

The first thing Kayda felt as she entered the lodge was that she didn't belong. She was an intruder and would be spotted as one immediately. And true to her thinking, several patrons did turn their heads and regard her with amusement. But, it turned out the world didn't revolve around her. Everyone forgot about her grand entrance within seconds.

The police detective was nowhere in sight but Kayda immediately recognized the group of bold men to her left. They occupied the entire side of the bar, more space than they needed, yet remained unchallenged for the seating. The men each had attitude; they steamed with residual anger. These were the bikers, the Seventh Sons. She could simply talk to them and see what they knew. In this bar, this public space, she would be safe.

Kayda approached and noticed the biggest man was an Indian, sitting alone at a table. He was gruff, wearing his hair in a topknot and shaved on both sides. His ripped up jean jacket was cut to reveal lean but rippled arms. He was a scary guy, but Kayda thought she could soften him.

"Are you the Seventh Sons?" she asked timidly.

A few of the men glanced her way, but the Indian didn't even raise his eyes from his drink. "Not today," he grumbled.

The response surprised her. She suddenly felt self-conscious. A couple of the bikers, one at the bar and another along the wall, eyed her, waiting for her next move. At first, she decided to run away. Get back outside. Then she realized she was being tested. Maybe, rather than appearing meek, it would be better to double her efforts.

The girl cleared her throat a little too loudly and shot her hand out to the big man, looking to gain his trust, or at least his attention. "I'm from the Yavapai-Prescott Tribe," she announced.

Two wooden chairs scraped the floor as their occupants rose. The Indian man remained seated but darted his head in her direction, rage fueling a rumbling in his throat. "What the fuck did you just say?"

Crap, thought Kayda. She had finally gotten his attention.

The big man stood, his full height several heads above the young girl. Kayda panicked and took a step back. She said the first thing that came to her.

"I'm looking for Detective Maxim Dwyer!" she cried out. Then she realized that name-dropping a police officer might only enrage the gang more.

The biker at the bar, with wavy black hair and a goatee, sprang between them. "West Wind," he cautioned as he pulled her away. "We don't need this tonight."

"We don't like people asking after us, girl," he said, not advancing but not backing down either. "Especially not Yavapai."

"I'll handle this," assured the other biker. He dragged her, not too gently, to the other side of the room, where the bar ended, next to a hallway.

Kayda noticed the men staring at her. Then she took in her savior. He was a cute guy, thin but well built, tanned. His eyes struck her as being pure black. The midnight sky was nothing compared to them.

"My knight in shining armor," she said.

The man smiled cordially and bowed his head with a ridiculous sense of confidence. "Diego de la Torre, miss." He rolled his Rs in an exaggerated fashion when he pronounced his name. It seemed to be a regular part of his repertoire.

"Kayda," she returned. Short and simple was best, she thought.

"Kayda," said Diego a few times, familiarizing his lips to the sound. "That's a nice name. Kayda."

"Thank y—"

"How many kinds of stupid are you, Kayda?"

The girl was aghast at his sudden one-eighty in attitude. "We're past the flirting, are we?"

He laughed a little and shook his head, peering deeply into her eyes, looking for something. She was about to say something, but he relaxed. "I thought you were here looking for a fight. Don't you know the Yavapai aren't welcome in Sanctuary?"

"Oh," she murmured, mostly to herself. She glanced back to the other Seventh Sons find was glad to see them ignoring her. "I've never been here before. I—my brother used to come here a lot."

Diego nodded and asked the bartender for two beers. "Times have changed. I bet that was a long time ago."

Kayda allowed a wistful look to crack her playful front. "It was. He's dead now."

"Sorry," Diego said, biting his lip. He grabbed the beers and handed her a bottle. They both filled the silence by taking a sip.

Kayda felt stupid. She knew she didn't have a plan. In a way, she thought that was the beauty of it. Screw trying to coordinate a series of carefully implemented ideas. The motorcycle accident had taught her that nothing went as planned, anyway. She figured, as long as she ignored any semblance of strategy and had no expectations, nothing could disappoint her.

But then she recalled her brother Kelan speaking to the tribe. She could see his soul bared to them, wounded, writhing in agony. There was no love lost between the Yavapai and the Seventh Sons. In retrospect, walking right up and introducing herself to them was the most insulting thing she could have done.

Diego's voice was softer now. He spoke less like an instructor and more like a friend. "So what are you doing here?"

The girl shrugged. She decided to throw caution to the wind. Ignore the politics. Forget the flirting. She knew it would make her sound like a naive little girl but it had to be said anyway. "The violence needs to stop. I don't want my people getting hurt anymore."

"And why would they get hurt?"

"Don't treat me like a kid," she admonished. "It's already started." Kayda stomped her foot onto the wood floor. "I want it to stop."

The biker smiled at her. At first, Kayda thought he wasn't taking her seriously, but it was something else. She had trouble reading him. "Are you some kind of respected leader on the reservation?"

A sharp laugh escaped her lips before she could kill it. "Just the opposite."

He thought a moment before he spoke, but she never got to hear his answer. The police detective, Maxim, stomped by them, from the back hallway. He saw her and passed, then did a double take and backed up.

"Kayda Garnett."

"I was looking for you, Detective. And the Seventh Sons."

He raised a single eyebrow. "Call me Maxim. And why would you do that?"

"Look for you?"

"Look for the Seventh Sons."

Kayda took a swig of beer and set the bottle down on the bar with some force. "To make peace with my people."

Maxim turned his head to Diego and they shared a patronizing look. Kayda pursed her lips, ready to object, then felt cool liquid on her hand. Her bottle was bubbling over. She snatched back her hand and wiped it on her jeans.

She could tell they fought off smiles.

"What's *this* about?" asked Maxim, pointing to Diego's bottle.

"It's how I grieve," he answered. "You two know each other?"

"We do. But do you? You know who she is?"

Diego turned to her. "Should I?"

"This is Carlos Doka's younger sister."

Diego coughed up some beer mid-drink and it was his turn to wipe his hands clean. Kayda wanted to laugh except she didn't know what the problem was. She hated not knowing. Suddenly she grew tired of feeling embarrassed. She was tired of being treated like an outsider, even if it was true in this case. She thought she could trust the cop, but why had she been flirting with Diego?

"Did you kill my brother?" she blurted out.

Diego's expression turned inward. Was it guilt? It was Maxim who finally answered.

"I need to ask that you be patient with the investigation, Kayda. So far I haven't turned up anything to implicate the motorcycle club."

"And if you did?"

She noticed a line crease the detective's forehead. His voice became tense. "I would tell you."

"Sorry, I didn't mean—"

Maxim waved off her apology. "You need to let me do my job," he said firmly. "I'm trying to prevent violence from exploding between the two gangs. Your presence here is bound to light that match."

"It's me that should be upset, if anybody. It was my brother hanging from that tree. It was his skin on the statue. Instead, I came over with my hand extended."

"What can you do that I can't?"

Kayda crossed her arms at the question. "Keep my

brother from doing something stupid, for one."

She must have said something wrong because both men stiffened.

"Doka's brother is here?" asked Diego with urgency. "In Sanctuary?"

The words stuck in Kayda's throat. Apparently she wasn't supposed to reveal that. They waited for an answer but she didn't know how to explain. "Why? What happened?"

Maxim put his hand on Diego's shoulder to pause the conversation. "You do realize there's been another murder, right?"

"What? Who?"

"One of the Seventh Sons," said Maxim. "A kid about your age."

"I'm not a kid," she said. "I'm twenty-two." But her feeble objection was meaningless in the face of the new development. Suddenly Kayda understood the lingering anger that hung over the bikers like an overcast cloud.

But why take out that anger on her?

"Is Kelan Doka in Sanctuary?" asked Maxim sternly. "Who else is with him?"

Kayda's eyes went from one man to the other. It wasn't what they thought. "He came up this morning with Hotah. I thought—" But she stopped speaking. Kayda was scared, but Kelan... She didn't want to implicate her brother.

"Are they the ones who did this?" asked Diego.

"No!" she protested. "The Yavapai didn't do this. My brother didn't do this!" Kayda felt herself shaking. "He's not like that."

"Kelan Doka did a stint for armed robbery," said the detective. "You must know your brothers aren't saints."

"Not Kelan," she said weakly. "Carlos was into bad things. He set a bad example, but Kelan can be good."

Why wouldn't they listen to her?

"Regardless," said Maxim. "It's in their best interests to come to me immediately. Call them up. Tell them I'm gonna need to talk to them. We can meet at the station."

Kayda didn't want to tell Maxim that neither had answered their phones. That they had left them behind at the reservation to avoid being tracked.

Oh God, she thought. They were up to something. She couldn't deny it. The question wasn't if they would retaliate, it was when and where and, more importantly, how far they would go.

Chapter 29

The cool breeze on the patio felt good, but Gaston Delacroix wouldn't feel a hundred percent until he jumped in the shower back at the clubhouse. For most of the last two days, if the MC wasn't riding, they had been locked up. Their release had finally come on what was maybe the hottest day of the year. That wasn't what spoiled the ride back, of course. It was the call they'd gotten about Omar.

To add insult to injury, their clubhouse had been a crime scene. Gaston had only been allowed entrance to check his possessions, but Teresa Banks had done her job: the club's private effects remained untouched. Gaston's safe hadn't been broken into. Nothing had appeared ransacked, by the police or otherwise.

The president of the club leaned his back against a column next to a wooden booth set into a stone alcove on the patio. Two more booths were in the area but they were empty. Most of the patio crowd huddled by the fire pits as it got later.

It was just about that time, he thought. Time to call it a night. To lick wounds. To recover.

Clint came back outside holding four bottles of Miller, two to a hand. "Keg's busted."

Gaston downed the last of his glass and set it on the table. Clint handed him a bottle, put the others down, and slid into the booth. Gaston remained standing, peering through the open door. He was keeping an eye on the girl.

"She don't look to be incitin' trouble," said Clint through his thick beard, offering his opinion even though it wasn't asked for.

"That doesn't tell us what she *is* here for," he stated matter-of-factly. Gaston took a sip of the beer. It was good, much colder than what came out of the keg. The big man sighed and closed his eyes for a second. No, he thought, he couldn't rest yet. Tonight. At the clubhouse.

Gaston opened his eyes and swept the bar again. His guys were scattered. Curtis and Trent played quarters. West moped alone at a table. Diego hung with Maxim and the bitch. It was bad enough she was here, but the cop was giving him a hard time too. And now Diego wanted out of the MC.

Gaston had put up with West's complaints for six months about the man. Not only was he not a wolf, but he had been a wolf hunter. But Curtis and Trent were cool with him. He'd been tight with Omar. With recent events, Diego actually stepped up. Proved himself. West was finally coming around. All that, just so Diego could quit?

Fuck it. Maybe it was for the best. Melody had been half out like Diego was; her mother had tried to shield her from the mud. Things had been much smoother since. Maybe it would be a good thing for Diego to leave.

But Gaston's pack kept getting smaller. The whole reason he usurped Deborah was to prevent that from happening. To protect the MC. With the Pistolas and the problems sure to come from El Paso, keeping together was more important than ever.

The Pistolas. Gaston still didn't think they were involved. They didn't know shit about wolves. There was no way one of those Mexicans killed Omar. No way.

Hotah Shaw was here the other night. Kayda Garnett tonight. The Yavapai were working something, and Gaston would need to prove it to everybody else somehow.

"Well, fuck me," said Clint, rising from the table. Gaston shook away his troubles to address the newest one: a lone man hiked up the road, straight for Sycamore Lodge. A Yavapai with short, buzzed hair.

"That's Kelan," said the president, narrowing his eyes. Without hesitation, Clint rushed towards the patio steps. "Wait!" called Gaston, gripping the man's arm. "This is too public."

The bearded man stewed in his boots. "That boy knows better than to come here. *Especially* now."

"Maybe he's picking up his sister."

"Fuck that." Clint James brushed the bigger man away and marched out to meet the Yavapai in the dirt.

Gaston took a step after him but stopped and checked

the bar. The others were inside. So was Maxim. Gaston couldn't just run to the police—no self-respecting biker would ever do that—but he couldn't let this happen.

The big man's indecision was only momentary. He decided to keep the peace himself. Leaving Clint alone would be a mistake. Gaston hopped over the alcove wall and landed in the dirt with a thud.

The two men bore down on each other, neither slowing their pace.

"So I see the police in this town are bought and paid for," said Kelan with a sneer. His hatred for Clint seemed ready to tip him into a rage. "You kill my brother and you're out drinking the next night. All in a day's work, huh?"

"You son of a bitch," shot back Clint after a long chug of his beer. "They didn't lock me up because I didn't kill nobody." The biker swung his arm down fiercely and the brown bottle exploded into the gravel next to him, unenjoyed beer soaking the shards.

"Calm down, Clint," urged Gaston. He arrived behind his friend just as the two stopped in front of each other. Kelan's face was smeared unevenly with black makeup, calling to mind war paint. "And you," he said, two firm fingers pointed at the Yavapai, "you shouldn't be here." Gaston almost spit in the dirt at the man's feet.

What was Kelan thinking? This wasn't Yavapai turf. They weren't welcome in Sanctuary.

The intruder paid no attention to the president. He eyed Clint with cold regard, enjoying his hate. "We all know you played a part in it," said the Yavapai. "We know about your knife."

Shit. Gaston wondered how the tribe had gotten that information. Had the skinning knife been mentioned in the media reports already? Did they have someone inside the marshal's office? Fucking Maxim said he would contain this.

"It was your boy," said Clint, looking to the gathering crowd. "The one who I whupped for three minutes that night. He must have stole my gear after he ran off, licking his wounds." Clint spoke loudly and proudly and drew some applause. Gaston thought maybe some of the men here had witnessed the fight.

Kelan spat. "The cops believed that bullshit, huh? Hotah's twice the wolf you are. It would take more than you to beat him."

That rang true to Gaston. Clint was an aging biker who carried most of his mass around his waist. Hotah was a tough guy. Squat. Solid. Built. As much as Gaston hated to admit it, he couldn't see Hotah losing a fistfight to Clint.

"Fuck you," said the hillbilly. "If you were any smarter, you'd realize I was locked up when your brother's skin showed up at your fancy casino."

Kelan's eyes danced over the crowd wildly, sizing everybody up, gearing for a fight.

Gaston felt the thrumming of his heart in his chest. It was beginning. The adrenaline. He could feel the wolf screaming to break free. None of them could change now, of course—it wasn't the right moon tonight—but their strength was deep in their blood. It was a part of them, no matter their form.

"You obviously didn't do it by yourself," accused Kelan. "My brother was too strong for that. Somebody helped you."

"Help?" asked Clint. "Is that why you killed Omar?"

Gaston's people were usually easier to control, but Clint had always been the wild card. The laundromat was an embarrassing case in point. This time, with the kid dead, there was no way to arrest the boiling blood.

The other night, when Clint was here by himself, he'd confronted one of the Yavapai mercenaries. It had been orderly and disciplined, as much as a brawl could be, but it was against club policy, and Clint had tried to hide his involvement. But Gaston knew his men. He was keeping more to himself. Clint's extra bout of defensiveness was a cover for something.

"You sack of shit," shrieked Clint. "Omar was my brother!" He lunged forward at the Yavapai. Gaston hugged him from behind and tore him away.

"Not here," said the president. "Not like this. The last thing we need is more police."

Kelan smiled. "No problem. You want a three-minute bell? I'll only need one."

"That's what your best friend said," replied Clint gruffly. He pulled off his red leather jacket.

Gaston had seen the three-minute bells before. He'd taken part in his share of them. But times were different. Even under equitable terms, Maxim wouldn't appreciate the street justice. Besides, a fight like this, with the current stakes—somebody was bound to go too far.

"Kelan," growled Gaston, stepping authoritatively between the two men. "You've caught me in a very understanding moment." Gaston swallowed quickly. He hated what he was saying to this motherfucker. He hated looking weak. He hated that his club was vulnerable now. "I'm not gonna put you down this time," he continued, putting on a show for the others. "Just get your sister and get the fuck out of here!"

For the first time since he'd arrived, Kelan was taken off guard. He'd never been fully in control of himself, of his rage, but his twisted smile and face paint proved his intentions. He was looking for trouble and came to the most perfectly unfortunate place. Now, however, there was a chink in his armor.

"Kayda's here?"

Gaston saw the opening. He saw the answer to the delicate situation. Shit, it was getting rid of two birds with one stone. "I'll get her," he said. "You can talk some sense into her. Don't start anything."

The big man spun on his heels, watching the two wolves puffing out their chests and refusing to back down. Seeing the momentary lapse in action, Gaston raced to the patio.

It didn't matter. Once he was away, the yelling and the pounding of fists began. The fight was on.

Gaston stopped at the threshold and saw the three standing at the bar. "Hey bitch," he yelled. His voice was so strong that it overpowered the guitar piping through the speakers. Kayda turned to him. The entire bar did. "Control your brother. Outside." Maxim and Diego and the other

Sons immediately rose to full alert. The cop pulled out his cell phone, and Gaston already dreaded their next conversation.

He turned around and saw Clint and Kelan squaring off, a brief lull between punches. Gaston turned on his boot and leaped at the men. His muscles tensed and swelled in his skin. The president was pissed off now.

"This is Seventh Sons turf!" he yelled, stomping towards Kelan.

So much for Mr. Nice Guy.

The next moment was a blur, but Gaston's senses, already primed by the adrenaline, took them all in with ease.

A dark van passing on the street suddenly pulled closer. It skidded to a stop, sending a cloud of dirt over the crowd. The side door slid open with a heavy thunk and two men wearing latex wolf masks lunged out. They had Adaptive Combat Rifles in their hands—the same illegal rifles Doka and the Yavapai had used, the same ones the Sons had purchased from them.

"Gun!" yelled Gaston. He immediately darted to the side and squeezed behind a car, reaching for the pistol in the small of his back. The masked gunmen were faster. A battery of muzzle flashes teased his eyes.

Kelan ducked away. Clint spun around but the gunfire ripped through his back. His feet still carried him from the fray. For a moment, his escape seemed likely but, inevitably, his legs gave out. He collapsed twenty feet away.

The sparse crowd broke into a wild frenzy, some running inside, some to their cars, some even crossing the firing lines. Gaston held off so he wouldn't shoot a bystander. Frustrated, he fired into the air.

The two gunmen flinched at the sound of opposing reports. The wolf masks darted from side to side and quickly located him. The ACRs swung around and Gaston hit the dirt as they pelted the car with bullets, each a resounding metal clunk.

The rest of the MC took cover in the Lodge. Most of them were armed as well. Maxim, holding his pistol, stood by the door and screamed into his phone.

Behind the shredded car, the president took a few hurried breaths and peeked above the trunk. One of the gunmen stood in the middle of the clearing, scanning the crowd. The other let his assault rifle swing down on its strap as he pulled a long knife from a sheath on his leg and advanced on Clint.

The silver light of the moon was weak tonight, barely there, but the glint on the blade was unmistakable. Gaston felt his heart tremble again, but this time it was fear that threatened to overtake him.

Werewolves had little concern for long-term injuries. The wolfskin healed all maladies, removed all pain. But silver retarded that change. It inhibited whatever in the blood made the body strong. Because of Gaston's accustomed immunity, it was quite possible that he was more afraid of that knife than the regular patrons of the roadhouse.

But the gunman was closing in on Clint, and he had to do something.

"No!"

With agility normally impossible for a large frame, Gaston leaped over the vehicle, boots firmly catching the dirt and pushing him forward. Gaston's pistol discharged so fast that he couldn't count the bullets. He charged the midpoint between the gunman and his downed brother, hoping to intercept him. The blitzkrieg was so vicious that the other men, who had heavier firearms, retreated several paces.

As Gaston barreled forward, rifles rose to meet him. More reports, this time from behind Gaston, cut through the air.

"Police," screamed Maxim. "Put your weapons down!"

Nobody listened. Gaston pressed ahead to defend his man, and the two attackers fell back and jumped in the van.

"Everybody get down!"

Gaston's gun emptied uselessly into the vehicle. As its wheels screeched, Gaston's boots skidded in the dirt to stop his wild charge. The van sped away and he moved to Clint.

Maxim barreled past the president as if he were a dog chasing a truck. Gaston could only assume that he was trying to catch the plate number in the low light. The detective was on his phone again, requesting backup that would arrive too late.

The president kneeled over his downed brother. Clint moaned on the floor. He was shot up badly, his backside matted with wet blood. It looked painful, but survivable—at least for them. Curtis and Trent joined him.

"Stay with him," Gaston commanded. The president

marched to the middle of the clearing and stood tall, boldly daring anyone to make another move. He watched Maxim clearing the scene, taking control. For once, Gaston was glad the cop was here.

Then he picked up movement closer to the street and noticed Kelan slumped in the dirt. The Yavapai cautiously rose to his feet.

Gaston's anger took control. His adrenaline surged as he stomped towards the Yavapai. "You did this!"

"What? No!" said Kelan, the fire gone from his eyes.

"Leave him alone," cried Kayda, somewhere behind him, but Gaston wasn't listening anymore. Seeing his friend on the ground like that was game-changing. Politics was best suited for influence and debate. This? This was wartime. And that required soldiers.

The president took a menacing step toward the smaller wolf.

Another gunshot rang through the air, clearer than the others, stronger because it stood alone.

"Goddamn it, Gaston," spat the detective. "Enough!"

The big man's breathing was coarse. He didn't want to comply. He didn't want to behave. The sound of sirens in the distance was perhaps the only thing that swayed him. His grave eyes focused on Maxim as he approached Kelan with his gun drawn.

Once Gaston had decided to let go, backing down was easy. That's when the world softened, when exhaustion from the last two days' events began to set in.

The Yavapai girl brushed past him as Maxim produced

handcuffs. "What did he do?" she cried.

"At the very least," said Maxim, "it's for his own safety." For the first time, Gaston noticed that West was standing right behind him, Diego in tow. Curtis and Trent glared from their post across the yard.

Kelan, while shaken, seemed oblivious or callous to the danger. After his initial surprise, he ignored his sister and spat at Maxim's feet.

"You're the one who killed Skah."

"My reputation precedes me," said Maxim in a mocking voice. "That's right. I killed him. With silver bullets. You wanna guess what I'm packing now?" Maxim casually waved his Glock in the air.

Kayda contemplated the detective with horror. Apparently she hadn't been privy to the events surrounding the Paradise Killings. "I thought you came out to help us," she said.

"I am."

"You're with them," she spat, pointing at Gaston.

Maxim twisted his face, but all Gaston could think about was the presence of the Yavapai. Inside Sycamore Lodge. Outside. The men in the van had retreated in the face of inferior firepower. It wasn't simply Maxim's celebrity that did that. Gaston recalled the fear the silver knife had instilled in him. Then he imagined what a magazine of silver bullets would do.

"The men in the van," hissed Gaston. "They were Yavapai."

Kelan's eyes narrowed and he denied the charge. He was

a wolf, but he saw that he was surrounded by another pack. He put his hands behind his back and accepted the cuffs.

An unquenchable rage built within Gaston's head. This man, Kelan, was the architect of this. Was Gaston just gonna let the cops take him away?

But a cruiser parked on the side of the road. Cole and the rookie jumped out.

Gaston gritted his teeth. One more wolf not on his team.

He turned at the whimpering of the girl. The bitch.

Kelan's sister stood shaking next to them wearing her false surprise like a mask. She was a part of this. This entire thing was a scheme to kill a second MC member.

The big man regarded his men. They all realized the gravity of what he had said. Of what accusing the tribe meant. The Seventh Sons were at war with the Yavapai.

The two officers converged on their detective.

"Better late than never," said Cole. Maxim nodded gratefully.

"Holy shit," exclaimed Gutierrez.

They turned and followed the rookie's gaze. An elderly woman silently sobbed around the side of the building. Her husband was slumped over the hood of the car where he had been sitting, his head still leaking from the hole torn open by the bullet.

Day Three

Chapter 30

The day started with a hangover.

Maxim often had hangovers. But this time, alcohol was absent from the equation. His headache was due to sleep deprivation and pounding his head on a rapidly accumulating caseload. Before he could make headway in one, another would present itself. Three dead bodies in as many days. And even though Roger Gladwell had been an old man, in many ways his death was the worst—because he was the only one who hadn't asked for it.

Maxim made sure to get to the station nice and early, before Marshal Boyd or Agent Garcia were around. Dr. Medina had thankfully shown up but it would be hours before the autopsy was complete. Since the man didn't appreciate being rushed, Maxim decided to pick on the new kid.

Damian answered the phone with his usual chipper attitude. Although he was awake early, Maxim guessed that he had gotten a full night's sleep.

"You didn't tell me you had FBI backing," said the kid. "The Flagstaff RA called and put a rush on the ballistics."

The resident agency was a local field office for the Bureau. No doubt Garcia had checked in with them. Maxim had to admit that jumping the Coconino forensic queue might be worth putting up with the agent. "Are the tests done then?"

"The basics. The agency wanted the victim's revolver run down. I emailed them the preliminaries, but I figured you'd appreciate a call."

"You figured right. This is still my case. Tell me what you have."

"The three .22 slugs in the entryway are a match to the gun. The spent metal jackets left in the revolver were the same used by the three unfired bullets so we could get a perfect test with those."

Maxim nodded. "Get to the good stuff."

"I'm building up to that. Okay, so you know how the serial number was scratched off? Well, we can do microscopic analysis of the underlying metal after applying a chemical reagent. Because the metal under the number stamp is more compressed than the surrounding metal, we can effectively raise the serial number."

"You got it?"

"Yup. Ran it through the system. Goes back to the registered owner of a pawn shop in Bernalillo, New Mexico. A Joseph Chapman, I think. I'll send it your way."

Maxim winced. He had no idea who Joseph Chapman

was, but Clint James lived in Bernalillo. That wasn't a coincidence. More likely than not, Clint was the source of the weapon found in the hands of a fellow Seventh Son. That's why he had been so uncooperative at the start.

"That's not all," said Damian. "You're gonna love this next part."

Not if it was anything like the first, thought Maxim. It wasn't that the kid wasn't helping. It was that Maxim didn't like what the evidence was saying. "Go ahead."

"Okay. I missed it at the scene with all the fresh blood, but there was back spatter on the revolver we recovered."

"Blood?"

"Yes. Of course it was dry by the time I discovered it. And some of the fresh blood had pooled onto the bottom of the weapon. But it got me thinking: Why would a pistol that didn't hit anyone have back spatter on it? Three shots, three misses, remember? So I talked to Brody, the Coconino ME. He's your friend, right? We were comparing notes since he had analyzed evidence from your last homicide."

"Doka," whispered Maxim.

"You're good. It was a double match. The blood on the revolver was his, and all four bullets in evidence have the same striations. That revolver fired the bullet that killed your first victim."

"Son of a bitch," exclaimed Maxim. "That's impossible."

"Wha—I thought you'd be happy."

Damian probably thought he was handing Maxim the keys to the Doka case. Maybe he was, but for Maxim, his headache was just growing stronger.

"You sent this to the FBI?"

The kid stuttered on the other line for a moment. "Yes. It's conclusive. The science doesn't lie. But I'm waiting on GSR tests. I'll have more to tell you soon. In the meantime, I have a bit of bad news."

"You're making my day, kid."

"Hey, I can only solve one case at a time. We hit a snag on the victim at the clubhouse. You know the stray patent boot prints you asked me to check out?"

"Yeah." The few scuffs and prints in Omar's blood had been photographed. It wasn't uncommon in crime scenes with heavy traffic.

"One of them displays similarities to Diego de la Torre. It lines up with his statement about accidentally stepping in the blood. The other one is a mystery. It was imprinted in the blood pool at a wide diameter, away from the body, just like Diego's. That means the blood was undisturbed for a while when it happened."

Maxim nodded. He'd figured as much. "That means someone at the crime scene was sloppy."

"Not exactly. Blood dries from the outside in. If you look at the pictures, you'll see what I'm talking about. The edges of the pool began to dry and contract. They cracked a little bit. You can see that Diego's boot crushed the dried blood."

"What's the significance?"

"This mystery boot print didn't crack that edge."

Maxim furrowed his brow. "The boot stepped in the blood before Diego's did, when it was still partially wet."

"Mostly wet, yes," said Damian. "Tacky. Definitely not

dry. And then you asked me to catalog all the boots at the scene, like I normally do for fingerprints. There were no matches."

"You made sure to get the police officers as well? What was his name... Diaz was wandering around inside there."

"I got their boots as well. They were all negative."

Maxim processed the information. "You're saying that this boot print came from the killer?"

"No," said Damian impatiently. "Remember that the blood had pooled before this patent print occurred. This boot print was impressed a significant time after the victim had been killed but before he was found by Diego."

Maxim leaned forward and put his face into his open hand. He didn't know what the boot print meant except that Omar Rivera's death was more complicated than it appeared. Maybe the autopsy would yield more information. For now, they were lucky to have a usable patent print to test against.

"Detective? Are you there?"

"Yeah, Damian. I'm trying to figure my next move with this print. I'm assuming it's a dead end for now?"

"Correct. I haven't been able to identify the make or size of the boot yet."

"That's okay," said Maxim, suddenly realizing his opportunity. "I'm gonna scan and email you one more boot print. Let me know if it's a match?"

"That's what I'm here for," said Damian. "Anything you want. I'm in this for the long haul."

Maxim thanked the eager forensic tech and hung up the

phone. Just in time too, because his early morning peace was over.

Marshal Boyd and Agent Garcia burst into the office locked in debate. While they had some minor quibbles between them, they were united in their anger at the detective. Really, it was the situation that was upsetting, not Maxim specifically, but they couldn't easily yell at obscure concepts like "gang war" and "civilian death." It turned out that having a living, breathing punching bag was much more effective for venting stress, and for the moment, as the three of them crowded into Boyd's small office, Maxim Dwyer was that punching bag.

"I'm here in response to an anti-Native American hate crime," started Raymond Garcia, "and the only person you take into custody last night is a Yavapai who was witnessed as not being part of the attack? The brother of the original victim?"

Maxim stared at Boyd in a useless appeal. "Oh come on, Marshal. Are you more worried about the PR nightmare or stopping a gang war?"

Boyd tagged himself in. "It looks like I need to be worried about both."

"Look, that's fine, but dragging Kelan Doka in here prevented more violence."

Boyd drew his head back and turned to Garcia. Maxim knew his boss didn't mind the fact that Kelan had been detained. Boyd had a nasty habit of always playing devil's advocate. Always trying to play both sides of an issue. It was the politician in him. And when the feds came around,

Maxim was sure to feel some opposing pressure.

Although he had already made his point, Maxim decided to add on. "If I left Kelan out there to be ripped apart by the Sons, the FBI would only keep spreading rumors of us being in their pocket."

Garcia furrowed his brow. "And are you? Because nothing else could explain your complete confidence that they aren't involved in either of these deaths. You're willing to accuse a California gang that you know nothing about without looking in your own backyard."

Maxim didn't want to dignify that with a response, but things would be so much easier if the FBI was on his side. On top of that, Maxim feared he was starting to lose the marshal. The detective validated Garcia's concern with a nod. "I still like the Pistolas for Omar, but—"

"You know the MO of those guys?" he interrupted, crossing his arms. "They don't go to war. They cozy up to their vics. Get them close. Then shoot them in the back. It's a sign of disrespect."

"The Pistolas were making deals with the Sons. Besides, they can change their MO to disguise their involvement. What if this was a planned hit? What if they knew Omar was alone in that house? Or what if Omar was just a side effect of a bigger play?"

"Let me tell you something," said Raymond Garcia. "Nine times out of ten, when something like this goes down, it's exactly what it looks like. The Seventh Sons killed a Yavapai rival, and the mercenary outfit struck back. Now that's a solid theory. There's no deep conspiracy with an elaborate timetable. No ancillary gang involvement. The Pistolas are an outfit out of the Imperial Valley—California's dust bowl. You're giving them too much credit."

"You just told me they weren't the type to shoot first," reasoned the detective. "That means they're not entirely stupid. Look, you're federal. You've worked with gangs before. I could use your authority to augment my case in California."

Both men looked away from Maxim awkwardly after his request. They traded a glance. An understanding. He was missing something.

Garcia lowered his arms to his hips. "Marshal?"

Boyd squared his small shoulders. He was preparing for a fight. "Detective Dwyer, in light of last night's events, we simply must do everything in our power to end this war. Our department doesn't have the resources—"

"Boyd," warned Maxim. He was getting a really bad feeling.

The marshal swallowed and continued his prepared speech. "Our department doesn't have the resources to handle something of this scope. I've decided to allow the FBI to take the lead on this matter."

Maxim swiped at the air as if this exchange of power was something he could beat down. He felt like ripping the little marshal's head off. This boy who was younger than him but happened to have a mayor for a father was taking his case away. The little prick.

"This is uncalled for," he protested.

"Is it?" asked Garcia. "I'm sure you've gotten the ballistics from Omar Rivera's gun too. The weapon was traced to Joseph Chapman from Bernalillo, a childhood friend of Clint James, who you just released from custody yesterday."

"I didn't..."

"I'm aware Marshal Boyd was the one who kicked him. And I'm aware that he was in this building when Rivera was killed. But we can't ignore that two Seventh Sons are already involved, and if we consider that the only other club member not in custody at the time was your friend, Diego de la Torre, I have a hard time not seeing a conflict of interests here. The FBI has made its case to the marshal and it is clear that this investigation must be driven from the outside. You're too close to it."

While Garcia spouted out the rationale for taking over, Maxim balled his fists again until his knuckles were white. The mention of Diego had almost set him off, but he stopped himself before doing something that couldn't be taken back. He spun around and stared at the door, half considering just storming out and continuing the case on his own.

Going rogue.

But once again, Maxim controlled himself. Over the years as an officer, and especially as a detective, he'd learned to be as deliberate as possible. His outburst had already exposed too much; pushing any further would reek of teenage angst.

"You may have your theories," said Raymond Garcia

softly, respecting the detective's anguish, "but I came down to stop the fighting between the Yavapai and the Seventh Sons. I'm ordering you to stop with this Pistolas nonsense. If it's any comfort to you, I will look into them, but I doubt they're involved."

Maxim tried to peer through the blurred glass of the door's window pane. His back was all these men deserved, but he needed to allow the case to proceed. Whether the Seventh Sons were guilty was still an open question in his mind. He had different feelings about the tribe.

"I admit that I don't think the Pistolas were responsible for the attack on Sycamore Lodge."

"The Yavapai," stated the marshal plainly. Even without proof, it made the most sense.

"They're a small paramilitary pack," agreed Maxim. "Very dogmatic. The appearance of structure more than actual structure, but they have commonalities, like all armies. Those ACRs are their standard issue—the same ones Carlos and Skah used last year. The wolf masks, camo pants—it's like they were uniformed."

"Good," said Garcia, his voice taking a firm tone. "Then that's the next place this investigation will go. Believe me, just because I'm with the Civil Rights Program doesn't mean I'll let the Yavapai commit blatant crimes. As for Clint James, he is currently hospitalized in Flagstaff under a twenty-four hour watch. I've supplemented the Coconino deputies with a special agent."

"You gotta keep the locals honest," said Maxim sarcastically.

"That is exactly right, so you shouldn't feel persecuted by my oversight either. But Clint and the Seventh Sons are going to be investigated here, and you need to be okay with that." Garcia was affirming his rank, but it was clear he wanted cooperation. "By your own admission, the war has already begun. Whether it was the bullet in Carlos Doka's head or the one in Roger Gladwell's, the first shots have been fired. Now it's up to us to disarm and divide. We need order in the streets."

Chapter 31

Kelan had a black eye. It was the only discoloration that remained once the face paint was cleaned off. The injury wasn't really enough to warrant a visit to the clinic, of course—Kayda figured keeping him here was just a way of stalling his release. Her brother wasn't under arrest and was supposedly free to go, but this hospital room wasn't anything like the one Kayda had been in. As she spoke to her brother, her eyes kept wandering to the metal bars over the window. Strangely, they were on the inside, making sure nothing got out.

"I only came up with Hotah," Kelan insisted. If he was in any pain worse than the shiner, he didn't let it show. "When I told him I wanted to go to Sycamore Lodge to confront the Sons, he tried to convince me not to go. He went back to the reservation."

Kayda studied her brother's face. She saw weariness,

anger, annoyance, but she couldn't tell if he was telling her the truth. She never could. She should've known better, but all her life both of her brothers had told her all manner of tall tales. To impress her. To protect her. To mess with her. Like the innocent little sister who aimed to please, she had always taken everything they said at face value.

The Yavapai girl sighed. Kelan claimed not to know the gunmen. The obvious suspicion was that they were from their tribe, but Kayda didn't get a good look at them. Diego had been holding her back, inside the bar and behind him, to keep her from the danger. It was the sort of macho display that her friends in New York looked down on. Kayda didn't see the harm. Actually, she thought it was pretty sweet. But it did make her feel like she was on the sidelines, that she wasn't a part of the proceedings.

So much for her noble quest to save her family.

For a moment, Kayda wondered if she was the problem. She only entertained the thought as long as it took her to clamp onto the next culprit: men. Not all men. Not some kind of feminist outlook under the guise of empowerment. Just the men *in her life*. Her brothers, one dead and one heading that way. Her grandfather, pushing her to earn the respect of her tribe and stay in Arizona. Even Maxim and Diego.

Kayda had taken a shine to the biker, but there was something he wasn't telling her. Some bond that he shared with the detective. And when she had found out that Maxim was the one who'd killed Skah, she didn't think she could trust either of them anymore.

Now, for the first time, Kayda felt herself aiming that mistrust at her brother. She had grown up a lot in the last few days. The shock of seeing her mutilated brother. The ordeal in the desert. Now she was admitting that many of the men she knew weren't what they seemed. It was unavoidable, she thought, to not become colder as a result of her experiences. At the same time, it told her that she needed to open her eyes to the world. To stop seeing what she wanted to see.

What was it her *pahmi* had said? See more than everyone else sees. Then understand more as well.

Kelan grumbled as he sat on the edge of the bed, searching the floor. "Nurse!" he screamed, patience waning. A woman with a deadpan expression peeked in. "Where are my boots?"

"Sorry," said the nurse. "There was a mix-up. I'm looking for them." The woman eyed Kayda and Kelan together and pouted. "You're not planning on leaving already, are you? The detective was pretty clear—"

"My boots."

The nurse sighed loudly, dramatically, and left the room.

"I swear," said Kelan. "They'll do anything to keep me here."

Kayda was privately relieved at the delay. Maxim had told them that Kelan was here for his protection. Whether that was true or not, there was no telling what her brother would do once he was back on Main Street.

"Do you even know what you hope to accomplish here, Keekee?"

"Do you? Don't forget that you're in Sanctuary too. What? You can start shit but I can't? And I told you not to call me that."

Kayda didn't say anything. In a way, it was hypocritical of her to be scolding her brother. She couldn't say one thing and do another. She didn't want to be that type of person. If respect was what she sought, she had to be above that.

Kayda took an unusually deep breath. Her ribs strained against the tight wrappings and she flinched at the sudden pain in her side. She imagined compassion in Kelan's brown eyes.

"Just go back home before you get even more hurt," said her brother.

"I can't return to *Pahmi* empty-handed."

"I said 'home,'" reiterated Kelan. "The reservation isn't that for you. It never was. Go find your white father."

The girl was speechless. Here she was being cast aside again. Being marginalized. Disrespected. Why was it that she fought so hard for those that didn't want her?

The nurse finally returned holding a pair of sand-colored boots. She dropped them unceremoniously beside the bed and disappeared again. Kelan snorted and began lacing them.

Kayda watched, entranced by the banal motion, stewing in her thoughts while her brother prepared to leave her. All the mercenaries—Hotah, Yas—they all wore the same boots. Kayda tried to remember if any of the gunmen last night had them on.

"Who are you to tell me what to do?" she shot back

finally, a little heated. "All my life you've told me I wasn't one of you. You ignored me while you chased your big brother around, trying to fill his boots. Wear your uniform like a good mercenary. Put on your war paint. Puff out your chest. Are you so determined to follow your brother to the grave?"

Kelan pounced to his feet with a suddenness that startled Kayda. He grabbed her arms and pulled her toward him. The jerking motion evoked images of her cracked rib snapping completely, but she bit her lip and the pain subsided.

"The Seventh Sons have done nothing but shit on us! Use us! My brother tried to work with them. Economics, he said. But it was the wrong tactic. I'm not going to follow his path."

Kayda withstood her brother's ire. He seethed just inches from her face, but she didn't look away. "Let go of me," she said calmly.

"I told you not to follow me," he said, ignoring her request. "You should have stayed in New York. The desert is not the place for you. I thought you would have learned that on your ride up here."

Kayda dropped her jaw. "How do you know about that?" She hadn't told her brother about the motorcycle accident. She hadn't told anyone.

He released her. "You were always so stubborn. You should have cried your way back to the airport and hopped on a plane out of Arizona. Instead, you go and talk to the police. To our enemies."

Kayda could barely focus on her brother's words anymore. She kept thinking that Kelan knew. He knew about her spill on the 89. He couldn't have caused it. Kayda didn't know much about motorcycles but she was pretty sure the accident was her fault. So how was it possible that her brother found out about what happened?

Chuck Winston. He was there. He was the one who had nearly run her off the road. He had seen her, Kayda thought. He had looked right at her and walked away.

"Is Chuck working for you now?" she asked. "You had him run me off the road and leave me there to die?"

"What?" exclaimed her brother. "You're crazy. He called us when he found your bike at the bottom of the hill. It had me and grandfather worried."

Tears came to Kayda's eyes. She was suddenly very unsure what her brother was capable of. She thought she could finally see it. A hint that the boy she had grown up with was not telling the truth. A hint that Kelan was lying.

"What's happening to you?" she asked, half sobbing. She didn't want to cry. She didn't want to panic. But the weight of years of naivety was heavy.

Her brother stood coldly in front of her. He was a statue. His physique was never as impressive as his older brother's —Kelan was shorter, more wiry—but it was obvious they were of the same stock. Kin.

His iron stance wavered ever so slightly. Kayda stared at him through blurred eyes. Oh my God, she thought. Bright red contrasted against his dark features.

Kayda didn't know how she hadn't noticed before, but

her brother had an open wound below his chin. A cut across his neck. Blood welled from the stripe and it grew longer, like a line of paint being brushed across a canvas. It must have been a wound from the fight. It must have been treated and stitched and was just opening up now. It bled profusely.

"Kelan, you're bleeding!"

Kayda lunged forward to steady her brother's faltering posture. She pushed him back to sit on the bed. Even as he fought her away in confusion, she applied pressure to the wound, to stem the tide of red.

"What are you doing?" Kelan gurgled. "Get off me!"

Kelan threw his little sister away from him. His temper flared and he wasn't gentle about it: Kayda flew backwards and slammed into the wall. Her cracked rib reminded her of her failing strength—the pain nearly caused her to pass out. It was a great feat of strength that she managed to merely collapse on the floor. Kayda cried out loudly this time, not caring to hide her weakness any longer.

Kelan had used his wolf strength. He had thrown her across the room with little regard for her safety. He'd never done that before. Never crossed that line. Kayda didn't know if she was crying from the pain or from the disappointment.

"What's the matter with you?" he demanded.

Kayda hunched on the floor, staring at the linoleum, breathing rapidly. Her brother took a step towards her then stopped, his rage negating any sympathy he may have felt. He was panting like a lunatic and Kayda checked to see if he was okay.

She was startled by what she saw. The smooth skin of Kelan's neck, devoid of stubble, was clear. There was no blood. There was no wound.

Chapter 32

The pathologist led the two men to Omar Rivera's stitched-up corpse. He grabbed a pair of latex gloves and stretched them over his hands, keeping his curious eyes on Maxim. "I don't usually have an audience down here."

The detective shrugged and didn't explain. Raymond thrust his hand out. "I'm Agent Garcia, Federal Bureau of Investigation. I'm helping run this now."

Maxim thought the word "helping" was subjective.

Dr. Medina shook the man's hand while his gloves were still clean. The two men exchanged some banter. Most civilians were enamored with the FBI; Maxim couldn't begrudge the ME the opportunity to schmooze with a fed.

As Maxim waited patiently, he noticed a new tag on one of the freezer doors. The newest body. Gang violence had led to a civilian death, and he was now dealing with the fallout. Maybe all this was what Maxim deserved.

"So Doctor," said Garcia, locking his hands behind his

back expectantly. "We're all ears. Why don't you just give us the full information dump?"

"I'll give you what I can. Detective Dwyer already had a good handle on the situation, based on his notes."

Maxim shot a competitive glare at the FBI agent. Someone backing him up was validating, but also disappointing. The detective knew how to read crime scenes. He was able to drive investigations deeper without needing to wait on the ME, but all detectives wanted information handed to them. A lucky break. It wouldn't be so bad for a case to be easy once in a while. From Dr. Medina's initial tone, it didn't sound like there would be any leaps in progress.

"We've discussed his notes," said Garcia, "but we don't want to treat them as fact just yet. I expect your conclusions to be independent."

"I understand the scientific method," answered the doctor. There was a hint of anger in his voice. Maxim smirked as the agent continued to burn his bridges in Sanctuary. The ME then corrected his tone, speaking as a doctor would to a patient who disagreed with a diagnosis. "The crime scene and the detective's impressions are often invaluable. This isn't a full-service morgue but I'm able to give our victims some personal attention. Furthermore, we have a county technician running the blood work, ballistics, and DNA. I can assure you that, while our resources might not match the Bureau's, we know how to investigate homicides in Sanctuary."

"Of course. I didn't mean any offense, Doctor."

Maxim ground his teeth. He should be enjoying this more but all he could think about was the level of distraction already caused by the federal intervention. He wanted to get right down to the cause of death. The *real* cause of death. Of course, Maxim couldn't make his concerns known. The apparent cause of death was obvious to anybody without knowledge of wolves or silver. So, ignoring the posturing of the two men, Maxim asked the next best question.

"What can you tell us about the bullet types?"

Garcia furrowed his brow. Dr. Medina paused, but welcomed the interruption.

"Three or four bullet types in the body. The shotgun was easy to isolate. So was the two-two. The other bullets, whether from one shooter or two, are all 9 mm."

"So why the speculation about an extra shooter?"

"Firsthand, based on your notes," answered the doctor, glancing hesitantly at Garcia. "But there's more than that. The majority of the bullets in the body are 9 mm, with separate groupings."

Garcia cut in. "So there were three or four gunmen using light arms and a shotgun."

"Which doesn't match the gunmen who attacked Sycamore Lodge," reminded Maxim.

The FBI agent rubbed the stubble on his chin. "You said there were two trigger men last night. The driver makes three. It could be the same crowd."

"Possibly the right numbers, but definitely the wrong guns. If Omar Rivera was a hit by the same guys, why wouldn't they roll up with assault rifles?"

"Maybe it wasn't a hit. Maybe Rivera surprised them."

Maxim cocked his head. It was a possibility. Something about it sounded right, but it was still too disorganized. Sloppy. Maxim wasn't sure what to think yet.

"The victim put up a fight," continued Dr. Medina. "Most of the blood at the scene was his. That lab tech from Coconino sent me some samples and early conclusions. I'm sure you got a copy, but the short version is that two others left blood traces at the scene. One of them was wall spatter and the other was found on the victim's knuckles, fingernails, and teeth."

Garcia raised his eyebrows. "He bit someone in the middle of a gunfight?"

Maxim smiled. It seemed an odd action without factoring in the wolf angle, but it wouldn't have shocked him anyway. People did desperate things in their last moments.

"One of the 9 mm slugs lodged into the victim's skull without penetrating it. Luckiest thing I've ever seen, like he was wearing a helmet. Regardless, this man had no chance. I pulled sixteen rounds from his body. Twenty-five more were found at the scene, not counting the three he fired from his weapon. Punctured his lungs, femoral artery, intestines. He had several defensive wounds on his arms and hand. Can you imagine that? Trying to stop a bullet with your hand? The only thing more surprising is that it happens all the time."

Maxim nodded. Desperate actions. Anything and everything for one more chance at life. He watched the pathologist point a pen at each of the bullet holes. Sixteen rounds besides the buckshot. What a way to go. Maxim's mind sharpened when the ME pointed out the bullet wound on Omar's right hand.

"Wait a minute. How did Rivera fire his weapon if he got shot in the hand?"

Dr. Medina paused to consider the question. "There's no way this man pulled a trigger with this hand after sustaining this injury. I think it's clear that his shots came first, then he dropped the gun.

Maxim snorted. That explanation didn't work for him.

"What are you thinking, Detective?" asked Agent Garcia.

"For one, Rivera never dropped the pistol. It was still in his hand when we found him."

"You think the crime scene was tampered with?"

"I don't know, but a lot of people were on the scene before I was. The boot print proves that."

"What boot print?" asked Garcia.

"I have the Coconino tech looking into it. It wasn't in the report he forwarded you?"

Garcia scratched his cheek again. "I don't know. I was mainly concerned with ballistics and solving your first case."

Maxim shook off the obvious bait. He leaned in and examined Omar's corpse. "Which hands had traces of an attacker's blood?"

Dr. Medina pressed his lips together, realizing what Maxim was inferring. "Both of them."

The detective nodded. "So how does our vic get shot in

the hand and scratch someone at close quarters, then end up on the ground with a gun in that hand?"

"The three bullets he fired came first," offered Garcia.

The three shots were aimed at the door, which made sense in the obvious way—that's where the attackers had come from—but the gunman's blood was past the doorway, by the right wall. That's where Omar had fired at—and struck—his attacker.

"This bothered me at the scene. We have a vic holding a revolver that fired three shots. We recovered the slugs from the wall, which we confirmed. But a fourth shot was fired that hit one of the attackers." Maxim went over the inconsistencies at the scene. "You didn't find any .44 caliber rounds in the body?"

The ME shook his head.

"What is this about?" asked Garcia.

"I pulled one from the ceiling above the vic."

"But none in the victim or the line of fire either way. How is this round relevant? We're talking about an outlaw motorcycle clubhouse. Who knows how long that bullet could have been there?"

"I don't think we should dismiss it," countered Maxim. "I think it was the kid's single miss. It could have been a warning shot, fired before the shootout, or it could have been a wild shot during a physical struggle, proof of which does exist. With the other bullet, he hit one of the men. The gunshot wound he sustained to the hand would have come after those two shots."

This meant several things. First, they were looking for a

badly injured shooter. A .44 caliber round was not easy to shrug off. Second, the pistol in Omar's hand wasn't his gun. Perhaps it was switched with the Magnum, but for what purpose? Maxim made a mental note to search the computers for crimes committed with .44 Magnums. If the weapon was being hidden, there had to be a reason.

"I think we're making assumptions here," said the FBI agent. "Aside from Clint Eastwood admitting to being in Arizona, until we find a gang member with that bullet inside him, the presence of a .44 Magnum firearm in this crime is just speculation."

"Maybe," said the detective.

They moved on. The doctor neared the end of the description of Omar's injuries. "There was a lot of blood loss at the scene, Detective. The victim was alive for a while after getting shot, which is probably more miraculous than the slug lodged in his head. As you observed, several of his wounds occurred after he was lying on the floor. This grouping in the midsection. He was there for a long time, leaking, and more importantly, staying alive."

"Poor son of a bitch," said Garcia.

The doctor backed away from the body. "You know, there is a similarity to your last victim, Carlos Doka. This man was stabbed in the chest. The heart was torn apart, bullets and blade. Because of the condition of the body, it's impossible to tell, but a knife was the probable cause of death."

Maxim almost stumbled at the revelation. Stabbed in the heart with a silver knife? That solved the mystery of the wolf's death, but it opened up other questions. And doubts. Anybody with a knowledge of Diego's history, for one, would immediately look at him as the prime suspect. Maxim shot a sideways glance at Garcia, hoping he wouldn't suspect the man, but of course his federal connections didn't extend to secret CDC programs.

Maxim whistled softly. He couldn't think of a scenario where Diego would have committed this crime. And then to be so bold as to call it in? The thought made the detective shudder.

"The wounds are the same?"

"No," said the doctor emphatically. "There's only a superficial resemblance. For one, the first victim's heart was not stabbed, and it occurred during an incident separate from the homicide. Doka's wound had already started to heal. The reality is, there's little way of knowing if the same weapon was used. But two victims in a row got me thinking. With the damage to the torso, I might not have noticed it if not for the memory of Carlos Doka."

Maxim nodded and turned his attention inward. He had been in the train yard the day Diego stabbed Doka with the silver knife. The biker had almost died from the wolf's attack. Instead, Doka had run off with the weapon lodged between his ribs, inches away from a kill shot.

Maxim then studied Omar's corpse, his chest roughly stitched together like a baseball. The rib cage had an unnatural lean to it, a signal that it had been removed and replaced, the final result almost matching the human form but still slightly off, an approximation that threw off the human eye. The skin over the chest was squeezed over more than usual to account for the massive hole that had been over the heart.

It was a small coincidence. And other things didn't fit.

Whether Omar had seen anything coming or not, the attackers had shock-and-awed him to get him down. Maxim had considered that the killers were wolves, but there wasn't evidence of that yet. It was just an assumption: to kill a wolf you needed to be one. Or have special knowledge of them.

And that was the disconnect. Here was a dead man, a powerful man, who had been taken down by force, yes, but with small arms. Sure, there was a shotgun, but there were no silver bullets. The center mass shooting when Omar was on the floor suggested that the gunmen were trying to kill the kid, or at least subdue him. But the stab wound was a question mark.

Maxim's theory was that the attackers didn't know Omar was a werewolf. It would explain the light weapons. As it was, two of them had gotten hurt anyway. But if that was the case, where did the silver knife fit in?

"Dwyer!"

Maxim refocused his view. He realized he had been staring blankly at the body, ignoring everything else. Maxim blinked at the doctor, then saw him staring past him.

Hitchens was in the doorway, which was a bad sign because the man didn't like morgues.

"You two had better get upstairs," said the sergeant. "The Seventh Sons are on Main Street."

Chapter 33

Gaston's Harley was backed up to the curb of the Sanctuary town square. He sat sideways on the V-Rod, leaning on the seat but with his boots on the pavement. Half a toothpick twisted between his teeth, his jaws working overtime, mirroring his thoughts. It was a new day, but everything wasn't bright and peachy. The hangover was just beginning.

It took a lot of drinks to give a wolf a headache. Getting drunk was easy enough—the alcohol still diluted the blood—but the craving that the body felt after the binge, the signs of addiction, generally didn't occur. Sure, he always felt dehydrated when he woke up, but it didn't sap his strength as much. This time, Gaston felt like he was dragging.

It didn't matter. The Seventh Sons at half strength were more than enough to send a message.

West and Curtis straddled their hogs on either side of him. Diego chose to park his pretty-boy bike laterally. Unlike the dusty motorcycles of the rest of the club, Diego kept his nice and shiny. With everything that had happened, Gaston wondered where the man had found the time.

"This isn't our smartest idea," said Diego, the only one not resting against his bike. He paced up and down the sidewalk, staring at the Sanctuary Marshal's Office with apprehension. "I mean, getting in their face and all."

"I'm sick of smart ideas," replied West. Curtis chuckled and kept his eyes on the floor as if to conserve energy.

Across the cement plaza, past the light posts and potted trees, Kelan Doka was inside the police station. He hadn't been arrested, which meant he'd be walking out the front door eventually. Gaston assumed the presence of the MC would cause a stir, get the cops worried, and that someone would come out to talk to them. So far, it was as if they hadn't even been noticed.

But they had. Without a doubt, Maxim and that pompous asshole Hitchens were inside rolling their eyes. And if they were really lucky, Kelan Doka had seen them as well and had already shit his pants.

"Tonight's the new moon," said Gaston. His words had a patient dullness to them, but the anticipation was there, underneath. "No way they keep Kelan in the station for that."

Diego shrugged and walked back towards his bike with his hands in his pockets. He caught a glare of something in the sun, licked his finger, and wiped the gas tank of his Scrambler. That's when Gaston finally understood why Diego bothered to clean his bike. It was just about keeping busy when nothing else could be done. It was the same as chewing on a toothpick.

"Any word on Clint?" asked Gaston, thinking along the same lines. Transformed wolves and hospitals didn't mix. He turned his head slightly to peek behind him, expecting Curtis to answer. Curtis was tight with Trent, and Trent was at the hospital making sure Clint was under guard.

"He's straight. Same as before," replied the biker. "He's gonna be hurting like hell when we move him tonight."

"That won't last long," said the president with a smile. The turn was coming very late tonight. The hospital would be quiet. The Sons should have an easy go of sneaking Clint out before the wolfskin healed him.

Gaston Delacroix had been in the same situation the year before. When he'd helped Maxim take down Deborah, she'd stuck him with two bullets—one in the neck. Clint got it worse with rifle fire, but Gaston had been sidelined longer. He had been stuck in the hospital for over a week, waiting on the full moon. He essentially went through the worst of the recovery on his own before being transferred to the Sanctuary clinic. This town, it protected its own. It was a haven for wolves living in a world that wasn't meant for them. Officer and outlaw alike could respect that.

But the Yavapai were no longer welcome in Sanctuary. Gaston had no idea who'd killed Carlos Doka, but Omar was dead and Clint had gotten close. Werewolf or not, they had crossed the line.

Chapter 34

Maxim shook his head in annoyance as he stood by the greeting desk, watching the show outside the front window. Four motorcycles and four tough guys, sweating more and more as the day came on. It wasn't a very interesting performance. Not yet, anyway. This part was more like watching the roadies assemble the drum set. It was the precursor. But something was coming. The second the marshal's office allowed Kelan to go outside, the lights would spin wildly and the music would blare.

"Let me go out there and tell them my mind," complained Hitchens, hands on his wide hips.

"That's what they want, Barney."

"So you're saying they're asking for it." In the sergeant's mind, that was even more reason to go out.

"They're not doing anything illegal," reasoned Maxim. "There's no reason to ask them to disperse. Kelan will have a police escort."

"He'll have an FBI escort," came a voice from behind them. Raymond Garcia had been tailing Maxim around the station all morning, and it was getting annoying.

The detective took a breath and decided not to argue with the FBI agent about the club. "You want to come with us to the reservation?" he asked.

"I don't want you to come at all, Detective. Your history with the Seventh Sons and killing one of the Yavapai will only enrage the tribe."

Maxim stared at Garcia, first dumbfounded but quickly feeling the anger creep in. "This is my case, Agent, even if you're taking charge of it."

The man put his hand up. "Don't work yourself up over this. I've already spoken to Marshal Boyd about it. It's nothing personal. You can continue your homicide investigation from here."

Maxim traded a glare with Hitchens. "The Yavapai are part of that investigation."

"You've taken your shot on the reservation. I know we have new information now, but let me take mine."

This was a vindictive move by Garcia. He was asserting his power. He was saying that the job Maxim was doing wasn't good enough. But even though the detective didn't like the man right now, he couldn't let him go down to the reservation by himself.

"Fine, but you don't know what you're getting into down there. Sergeant Hitchens is going with you. He knows the area." Since Cole had the day off, Hitchens was the only wolf on staff, but Maxim didn't mention that part.

Hitchens stepped forward and nodded. "It's true. I know my way around."

The FBI agent was about to deny the request, but shrugged it off. "You want to keep eyes on me, keep one of your men close? Okay then. But you'll be in a follow car, Sergeant, and you'll answer to me."

Hitchens nodded carelessly. "I wouldn't have it any other way."

Raymond Garcia neared the glass and crossed his arms over his chest. "Look at them out there, making themselves known. It can't be denied—their presence is proof of their involvement."

"One of their own did get shot," offered Maxim.

"Sure. The innocent motorcycle club. I'm sure they're just bringing flowers to the dead man's kids."

Hitchens stuck his chin in the air and took a territorial tone. "Roger didn't have any kids. It was just him and his wife, Emma."

"So what? You're displaying your knowledge of the locals?"

"No, Agent Garcia. I'm establishing that this is a tight-knit community and we'll do whatever we can to protect them. We're not gonna protect a guilty motorcycle club while innocents die, and I'm offended by the attitude." Hitchens threw his hands in the air. "The hell with this. I'm telling them to disperse and don't you try to stop me."

Maxim didn't this time. They watched him saunter outside toward the bikers.

"He's right, you know," said Garcia. "The Seventh Sons

have targets on their backs. They shouldn't be anywhere near Sanctuary."

"What happened to protect and serve?"

"I save it for the people who deserve it." Agent Garcia turned and headed back into the office. The detective followed. He wasn't done yet.

"That joke you made? About the flowers? It's more true than you know."

"Yeah?"

"When I talked to the coroner's office, they told me the Sons had already contacted them. They're paying for the funeral."

"That's because they know they're responsible."

Maxim grunted in frustration. He couldn't completely discount Garcia's point. Maxim had lectured Diego about the same thing: Evil begot evil. Club business was bound to follow them home. But he needed to make sure that Garcia understood the other side too.

"The point is that they're more than they appear. Most of them live outside Sanctuary, but the club has damn near adopted it as a home. They know everyone. Take care of them. Emma? She's gonna be seen to. What's the FBI gonna do for her?" Garcia didn't answer as he sat down at his desk. "These guys, they care about the town more than you think. You accuse us of protecting them, and that's true to the extent that it's legal, but they want to protect the town as well. They're here as a show of force, to make Kelan think twice about returning."

"Or maybe he'll just bring more guns next time."

"I'm not saying they're perfect, or even ideal. They're fuck ups. Flawed just as much as any of us. Probably more."

The FBI agent sat with a blank expression, bored with the debate. "So what are you saying? They're like family? No matter how bad they are, you're stuck with them?"

Maxim smiled sarcastically. "Not quite, but things go more smoothly when the law acts like the responsible older brother sometimes."

"Brothers," repeated Garcia, shaking his head dismissively. "As long as they're not blood brothers."

There was a loud click beside him. Garcia jumped before realizing the switch on the coffeemaker had flipped off. Garcia sighed and turned it back on. The distraction punctuated the end of the conversation.

The detective strolled a few more steps to his desk and collapsed in the swivel chair. He'd made his point, he decided. There was a fine line between keeping the peace and being a dick, but it was possible to walk it. Maxim couldn't expect Garcia to understand Sanctuary immediately. It would be a start, at least, if the agent would stop exercising his authority over everybody every chance he got. He wasn't the only one with answers.

Maxim's desk phone got half a ring off before his quick hand snatched it off the receiver.

"Detective Dwyer."

"Yo, this is Damian. From Coconino."

"I know who you are, kid. What's up?"

"I got your victim's GSR results back. The gunshot residue on his hand mostly matches the revolver we found, but there's an anomaly with the primer elements."

Maxim leaned forward. "With the powder?"

"Yeah. The casings are made out of brass, which is pretty common. But here's the thing. The GSR showed traces of nickel. We couldn't reproduce that in the tests."

Maxim glanced at Agent Garcia as the man leaned back in his chair and crossed his black boots on his desk. Maxim swiveled his chair the other direction and lowered his voice.

"What does that mean?"

"Well, it likely means that the victim fired a weapon with nickel-coated jackets. Now, being shot with a gun can sometimes give a false positive for having fired one—the residue goes both ways—but nickel coating isn't very common. In this case, none of the bullets at the scene had matching residue except for one. Can you guess what the exception was?"

Maxim pounded his fist on his desk. "The .44 slug in the ceiling?"

"Exactly."

The detective's anticipation became obvious. Garcia turned his head to watch Maxim's reaction to the phone call.

"How did you get that without a .44 casing?"

"Easy," said Damian. "The slug has residue from the explosion. It didn't hit anything else before embedding in the wood so the evidence was preserved nicely. You see what this means?"

"Sure. It means the gun is a plant." Maxim raised his voice for the last part, since Garcia was listening in anyway.

"Yup," said Damian, beaming. "You know, a lot of what

I do is just textbook stuff, but seeing you read the scene like that without any science was pretty amazing. You immediately suspected something."

"Don't sweat it, kid. Most of what you do is impressive to me."

Garcia's black boots swept to the floor. "What is it?" he asked.

Maxim stuck one finger in the air as he missed something Damian had said. "What's that? Did you find anything else?"

"No," said the kid. "I was just asking about that extra boot print you wanted me to run. You haven't sent it over yet."

"Oh that." Maxim turned back to his desk and saw the paper imprint he'd created. With a sideways glance at Garcia, he shuffled some other reports on top of it to disguise the subject. "Yeah. I'll get that to you. Thanks."

By the time Maxim hung up the receiver, Raymond Garcia was on his feet looming over the detective.

"What was that about?"

"The revolver is a plant," repeated Maxim. "GSR proves that the vic fired a .44 Magnum. Combined with the other inconsistencies at the scene, I think it's safe to say that the revolver we found was placed in Rivera's hand and fired three times after he was dead."

The FBI agent crossed his arms. "Maybe there's something there," he admitted. "But we can still trace the gun to Clint James as a probable source. Whether Omar Rivera was involved in Doka's homicide or not, Clint is still in the middle of this."

"Not necessarily."

"Listen to me, Detective. Your troubled little brothers, the guys outside, the ones who are actually here—who we can see and touch—they're the ones neck-deep in this. Their presence is proof of their involvement."

Maxim shook his head. "They check out. Most of the Sons were out of town when Omar Rivera was killed. Clint was still in custody."

"So he had a helper. And don't think I didn't discover that Diego de la Torre was attacked by Carlos Doka last year. If anybody helped Clint, it was him."

Maxim calmly took to his feet and leaned on his desk. "I don't see it, Garcia. You don't know Diego like I do."

"In point of fact," he exclaimed, "your association is exactly what concerns me. And we still have Clint's skinning knife and revolver tied to the first body."

"Clint claims his saddlebag was stolen. He was being his usual evasive self but eventually admitted it. He said the knife was in there. He didn't mention the firearm, but I'd bet it was in the bag as well." Maxim snapped his fingers as if it had been so obvious. "That's it. That's the reason Clint was lying his ass off in the interview. Besides getting into an unsanctioned brawl with one of the Yavapai, he was holding an illegal weapon. A throwaway. Gaston would have had his ass for either of those infractions."

The FBI agent appeared incredulous. "You're saying your innocent motorcycle club is being set up?"

"It's worse than that. The killers stole Clint's saddlebag,

left the knife at the first scene, killed a club member and planted the revolver on him. Now it looks like Omar killed Doka."

"With Clint's help."

"Right. And what does all this do?"

"Besides defy plausibility?"

Maxim narrowed his eyes. "It starts a gang war." Garcia scoffed, but Maxim wasn't done. "It also gives us some new information."

"What's that?"

"Think about it. Whoever killed Omar Rivera also killed Carlos Doka. Since we know the kid didn't have the gun, the revolver is a link to both murders."

Both men became silent as Hitchens stuck his head in the office, Kelan Doka in tow. The Yavapai wore a black T-shirt and cargo pants tucked into his desert boots. "The MC is still outside," said the sergeant. "I figure nothing's gonna change until we get this one outta here. Better now than never."

Garcia nodded. "Give me a minute." He turned to Maxim and leaned in conspiratorially. "I understand the importance of keeping the knowledge of Clint's weapon from the Yavapai. Let's not discuss the matter with anyone else except the marshal for the time being. I understand your theory, but we can't ignore the fact that Clint and Omar could have been involved in something together on the side. Weren't the Paradise Killings the result of extra-curricular club activity as well?"

Maxim forced himself to take a breath. "Tangentially."

"I'll take that as a 'yes.' Just don't make any assumptions about the Seventh Sons. That's all I'm asking."

"Ditto," said Maxim as the FBI agent turned to go. He kind of smiled and shot Maxim a parting glance before heading out.

"Fair enough."

Raymond Garcia was a tough read for the detective. He seemed like a decent cop. His head was a little too far up his ass, but that wasn't the worse he'd seen.

Maxim took a few steps from his desk, stretching his legs. He eyed the three men in the front room. Hitchens instructed Kelan and Garcia on the procedure for the escort. The FBI agent, of course, made changes to the plan. Maxim chuckled and studied the men's boots. Garcia had a black pair of steel-toes. Kelan wore sand-colored desert boots. All the mercenaries wore similar clothes, Maxim knew. They thought of themselves as their own private militia force. He applauded his foresight in asking Renee, the clinic nurse, to spirit away Kelan's boots so he could steal a quick impression.

And now they had to let the Yavapai man go. It was a shame, but it had to be done. Too many uncertainties still surrounded the homicides.

Just then, as if to bring clarity, the audible rumble of motorcycles grew louder. Maxim quickly realized that the racket was caused by more than four engines. He hurried to the front door of the marshal's office and joined the others in gaping out the window.

A line of beat-up motorcycles rode down Main Street.

Eight, ten riders wearing black jackets with a skull and crossed pistols. Most of the Mexicans lined the block at an even spacing and remained on their bikes. Two of the men parked across the street and approached the huddled Seventh Sons.

Maxim snickered. "What was it you said about presence being proof of involvement?"

Agent Garcia didn't answer.

The Pistolas were in Sanctuary.

Chapter 35

The smoldering expression on Gaston's face was almost enough to counter the bravado of the ten Mexican gang members surrounding them.

All the Seventh Sons were on their feet, facing the street. The road had essentially been closed off by the parade of motorcycles. Their choppers were old and of varying makes: Harley, Buell, Indian, Yamaha. Most of the riders stayed on their bikes, killing the engines and sitting with arms crossed, bandannas over their mouths. If they had weapons, none were visible.

Sergio Lima flipped up the collar of his jacket as he approached. It hid most of his neck tattoos, making him look clean-cut with his bald head and thin mustache, except for the teardrop next to his left eye. Hector Cruz trailed behind like a loyal dog. The older man was sweaty and looked the worse for wear after their ride.

"What is this?" demanded Gaston. He would have

normally felt safe in front of the marshal's office, but this move by the Pistolas was a bold one. If they had wanted to make a statement, it was a success.

"Just passing through," said Sergio. "Heading back to Cali. Figured we'd say hi."

"How'd you know we were here?"

The Pistolas president shrugged. "Figured you'd be at the bar or the clubhouse. We were coming from out east so we checked the town first. Our type tends to stand out." Sergio's eyes ran up and down Main Street. He briefly checked out the post office and fire department, but it was all in anticipation of commenting on the building they were parked in front of. "You filing a police report?"

"We got business with someone inside," said Gaston gruffly. He was pissed off and didn't mind showing it, but he wouldn't give the Pistolas the satisfaction of acting like their entering Sanctuary was a big deal. He wasn't going to ask twice.

"Business, you say? That's funny, because that's why I'm here." Gaston narrowed his eyes but Sergio replied with a smile. "You see, the way I do business is, I receive money and perform a service, or I pay money and receive a service. And since I'm not speaking in hypotheticals, I was wondering what the fuck I paid you for two days ago?"

"That wasn't on us."

"What good are escorts if they can't protect a shipment?"

"It was state PD. They knew something was up." Gaston felt like an idiot explaining something to Sergio that he had probably set up. "They were waiting for us."

"Don't care. Your job is to avoid that."

"El Paso has people in New Mexico that are supposed to have a handle on that. We know those cops but we can't buy the whole state. Something came down on them from above, and don't think I don't suspect you."

A few paces away, Hector Cruz grumbled. Sergio tilted his head dismissively. He didn't bother defending his club or denying anything. He just spoke as if the point was inconsequential and moved on. "Reparations must be made."

"That's not a problem," said Gaston. "I've already got a plan for the next load."

"It's too late," snapped the Pistolas president. "You already missed another shipment." Gaston was taken aback by the news. "That's right. We sent a truck yesterday."

"Why didn't you tell us about that?"

"From what I hear, you guys were locked up. Besides, this trouble with the police, these murders—El Paso doesn't like that kind of attention."

Gaston stepped into the little punk's face. West blocked Hector from moving in, but no scuffle took place. This was the wrong place and time for anything to happen, and both clubs knew it.

"Fuck this," said Gaston. "You can't just roll into my town and tell me things are changing. Business was fine for a long time before you came into the picture. You don't run things. You're not even old enough to buy a drink."

"I haven't yet found the bartender who won't pour me a

cerveza." Sergio Lima turned to the side, disengaging from Gaston's face-off. "I may be young, but I'm used to getting what I want. It's all I know."

The bigger man scoffed. "Well, I'll give you a crash course in business. I'll go to El Paso myself. Get you shut out for this."

"You're too late there, too. I already talked to them. That's where we came from. You're done."

"Bullshit."

"This is just a courtesy visit on our way back home. The Seventh Sons are out. The highway is ours. Stay out of our way and we'll leave you be." Hector Cruz laughed heartily. Sergio watched him, proud to give the man his moment, then continued. "In the interest of not letting things get ugly, El Paso forgives the debt you owe them. As long as you stay away."

That was all bullshit. Nothing this skinny kid said could be real. Even if he had worked something out with the Mexicans in Texas, it could be undone. The Seventh Sons had a strong claim on the Interstate. No matter what happened, Gaston would dare them to ride through Arizona.

"Oh. One more thing," said Sergio. "We want that Albuquerque leverage you have. It will be useful to El Paso." Gaston felt his eyes go wide.

"What's that?" asked Diego, approaching. "What is it you want?"

"Nothing," said Gaston.

"It's not nothing if—"

"Diego!" barked Gaston, throwing his hand up. Now wasn't the time to explain. Fucking Diego was being a pain in the ass lately. Gaston was trying to give him some leeway, but questioning his leadership in front of another gang was not gonna fly. Already, Hector and Sergio traded a glance at the exchange.

It didn't surprise Gaston that the Pistolas knew about his leverage. The blackmail threat allowed the Sons to put the squeeze on the Albuquerque city council, and thus, El Paso. It helped solidify their Interstate pipeline. Without it, the MC could be more easily cut out.

"Not a chance," stated Gaston flatly.

Sergio's dark eyes tensed. His show of force wasn't having the intended effect. Gaston made sure the little punk knew that. Sergio recovered, and the two Pistolas backed up, gloating.

"Think about it," he urged. "Come up with a number that's reasonable. You might need the cash to go into another line of work."

Gaston laughed in their faces. "Nothing changes," he said firmly. "Anyone you send through Arizona is going to be accountable to me."

Sergio frowned, passing looks to the other Seventh Sons present. "Your MC looks smaller than usual." His gaze rested on Diego, and he smiled. "Guess there's one less *chicano* in the club now, huh?"

Chapter 36

"This is it," said Maxim.

The police were staring out the window, tentatively watching events. The Pistolas were about to be on their way without any violence—then something sparked an argument. The Mexicans cleared off their bikes and converged on the pack of wolves.

Maxim turned around and pointed at Kelan. "Stay inside," he commanded. He drew his Glock from his waist, locked eyes with Hitchens, and nodded towards the door. Maxim was the first out; the sergeant and Garcia trailed close behind. They sprinted across the wide plaza as the crowd of bikers readied for a fight, which at the moment still looked to be in the shouting stage.

"Police!" he screamed. "Stand back!"

Both clubs quickly parted for the authorities. Maxim scanned everyone for weapons. Nobody was armed with anything other than fists.

"Back up!" he ordered, waving the Pistolas across the street to kill the last vestiges of a scuffle. That's when he noticed a muscled man with sunglasses lying on his curbed motorcycle. He had prison tattoos on his bare chest and stomach. Likely more all over his arms under his jacket. The man grimaced while he clutched his chest. One of the Pistolas helped him up. The skinny kid who had started the argument glowered at Gaston, eyes wide.

By the smirk on Gaston's face, Maxim could easily guess what had happened. Somebody just pissed off the wrong werewolf.

Hitchens and Garcia spread out, weapons still drawn. They helped line up the Pistolas across the street. Two of the bikers moved to pick up the toppled motorcycle.

"Leave it for now," ordered Maxim. "What happened here?"

The Seventh Sons and the Pistolas alike said nothing. Tight lips, all of them. It didn't matter. Maxim wasn't going to arrest somebody for two seconds of tussling, especially when the visitors had asked for it.

"You," said Maxim, considering the skinny kid. "Come here."

"Sergio Lima," said Agent Garcia, behind him. Maxim turned as Raymond approached them. "A fresh face in the Pistolas. Their new president. An up and comer."

Maxim couldn't hide his surprise. Their president was nothing more than a kid. He had his own gang?

"Who are you?" asked Sergio.

"*El federal*," answered the shirtless Mexican.

Garcia waved the other man over. "Hector Cruz. *El Mecánico*. The Mechanic. He's a fixer, not only of bikes." The man in question approached. Hitchens put his hands up to stop the other Pistolas from getting closer.

Maxim studied the two men, or the kid and the man, and immediately knew he had a problem. Hector had a life of prison advertised all over him. If it wasn't obvious from his tats, his dead expression told the story. In some ways, Sergio appeared the opposite. The ink on his neck was crisp, more professional. Even the teardrop was done with skill. He could have passed for a nice kid. He even had a cool attitude. But his eyebrows outlined ruthless eyes that had seen more than his years should've allowed.

"We haven't met yet," said Sergio, extending his hand to Garcia. The FBI agent only returned a snort. Sergio shrugged. "That's okay. Maybe next time you're at *La Cascada* we can talk."

Maxim shifted glances between the two. He couldn't believe what he was hearing. Garcia knew about the Pistolas, but how did they know about him? The detective looked at the agent inquisitively, but Garcia just shook his head. It wasn't something they could talk about right now.

Hitchens was busy patting down the line of Pistolas and asking them questions. So far, he hadn't turned up anything. Maxim knew he wasn't going to. The motorcycle club wouldn't have rolled into Sanctuary and camped out in front of the marshal's office if they were carrying. But it was good he had them here just the same.

He inspected the line of bikers. None of them resembled

the gunmen in wolf masks, but it was hard to be sure. Automatic weapons didn't afford a lot of time to notice details. He decided that failure to make a positive ID couldn't rule them out.

"What are you doing here?" asked Agent Garcia.

Sergio shrugged again. "It's a free country."

"Yeah? Who told you that?"

Sergio let out a slight chuckle.

"Where were you last night?" asked Maxim.

"What, that thing at the bar? You got us wrong, homie. We were in Las Cruces last night."

"Where's that?"

"New Mexico," answered Garcia. "Just outside of El Paso, Texas. But the more important side of that border is Ciudad Juarez in Mexico. Las Cruces is just where these guys congregate."

Sergio nodded with a smile. "That's right. At the bike show. At least a hundred people must have seen us."

Maxim swallowed. That would have meant the Pistolas had been riding for the better part of the day. It also meant that Sergio Lima had better connections than Garcia thought. Texas was the border crossing for the Mexican Mafia. If a ratty California gang was doing business that far east, they must be important to someone.

"Do you know anything about the murder of Omar Rivera?" Maxim asked.

The kid looked bored already. "Who?"

"You know anyone in the New Mexico State Police?"

"Nah. I don't like pigs."

Maxim scowled. The kid had said it with complete abandon, daring the detective to do something about it. If the FBI wasn't around, he might have.

Hitchens returned. "They're clean. No guns, no drugs." Maxim nodded. He was still deciding how much shit to give the Pistolas for their little stunt. He could book them, impound their bikes, give them something to think about. If they were known gang members, their fingerprints would already be on file. That reminded Maxim to check their boots. To a man, they each wore cowboy boots, some leather, some scaled, but all with flat, pointed soles. Nothing like the prints he was looking for.

"You got nothing on us," said Sergio.

"No? What's this?" Maxim grabbed the president's leather jacket and pulled, spinning him like a child till he was facing the other way. A large patch was stitched into the back of the black leather. Two crossed pistols behind a skull. The Pistolas were regular old Mexican cowboys. "Colors are illegal in Sanctuary. I could cite you for wearing these alone."

"That's some bullshit," said Hector. Sergio just stared at Maxim stubbornly.

"Lucky for you," interjected Garcia, "we're gonna let you go with a warning." Maxim shot the agent a fiery look but was ignored. "Why don't you and your guys stay in California? Out of Arizona and out of trouble."

Sergio raised his arms in surrender. "Whatever you say, *federal*."

As the Pistolas hesitantly moved to their bikes, Maxim

exchanged looks with Garcia and Hitchens. The sergeant had seen his rank pulled but didn't appear upset about it. Hitchens was just happy to have the outlaws leaving.

Sergio Lima passed Gaston sitting on his bike. The bigger man wore a silent smirk. "Pathetic," said the Mexican. "You can't even control the local police."

Maxim glared at the cocky kid, but the gangster didn't turn back to him. He signaled his boys to leave. The motorcycles blared to life in unison, a heavy sound that filled the street, and buffeted the onlookers with vibrations as they passed.

As soon as it became quiet enough to speak, Maxim's features transformed. "What the fuck was that about?" he asked pointedly, but when he turned, Garcia was already marching back inside.

Hitchens let a hiss escape his lips. "A catastrophe avoided, at least." Then he followed the FBI agent.

The Seventh Sons relaxed on their bikes again, lounging as they had been the entire morning, as if nothing had happened at all. Gaston innocently chewed on a stub of a toothpick. Diego moved to his Scrambler.

"Good to see the police are still in charge," he said, donning his gold helmet.

The detective scowled and left them at the side of the street. The Pistolas were just one of his problems today. Another one was still inside. Two, if he counted Garcia, which he was beginning to.

As Maxim entered the marshal's office, he saw Kayda limping awkwardly down the stairs. "Are you okay?" He moved to support her. "What happened?"

The young girl shrugged him off coldly. "It's nothing. I just tweaked my rib." After another rigid step and another wince, she finally leaned on his shoulder for support. The second she hit the bottom floor, she pushed him away. She was a stubborn one.

"I saw those guys before," she said, pointing out the window. "They were the same ones who were headed south yesterday morning. They rode right past me."

Maxim pondered that. That was right after Omar had been killed. Their alibi for last night may be solid, but the early hours of the morning could have found them miles from Texas. But if the Pistolas had been at the clubhouse, why would they have headed south towards the reservation?

Agent Garcia returned with Hitchens and Kelan Doka in tow. Kayda's eyes lit up at the sight of them. "Wait up," she said.

Kelan's dark expression revealed his ill humor. "I got nothing else to say to you."

"Fine," she said stubbornly. "I wasn't gonna talk to you anyway. Just wanted to ask if I could get a ride back to the reservation."

"Find another way," said her brother.

"Nah," cut in Agent Garcia. "Jump in with us. It'll give us a chance to talk."

Maxim thought it was interesting that there was animosity between the girl and her half brother. He wondered what that was about. Maybe she knew something. Maybe he could corner her and get her to turn against

Kelan.

The detective waited by the door as the escort crew headed out and disappeared around the corner. The Seventh Sons were watching, but they were also in the middle of some kind of argument. Big surprise with them.

It had been a shitty morning. Tensions in Sanctuary were high, and Maxim didn't know how much longer the police could contain the situation. After last night, he didn't even know if it was fair to call it contained.

One thing was sure. He was damned happy that the Pistolas and the Yavapai were clearing out of his town.

Chapter 37

Diego de la Torre zipped up his leather jacket and pulled his riding gloves taut over his hands. The heat was becoming oppressive again. It had made the bikers lethargic. Relaxed. But something about being decked out in riding gear had reversed the effect. The extra layers and metal armor didn't slow him down; Diego was amped to move.

"Heads up," said Gaston, nodding towards the police station.

Diego's cone of vision through the full helmet was narrow. He liked to think it made him more focused. Sergeant Hitchens stepped into the sunlight with Kelan, Kayda, and the other man the Pistolas had called a fed. He wore the light blue collared shirt and tie that he had on before, but now had added a blue jacket with a logo for the —"

"FBI," scowled West. The other bikers paused as they straddled their bikes.

Diego allowed himself to be distracted by the new development, too. He wondered what the FBI was doing in town. He couldn't imagine any scenario that was good.

"Police escort," said West.

Gaston snickered. "We still ride that punk out. Warn him not to come back."

Diego shrugged and started his bike before the others. The engine hummed beneath him. "I got better things to do."

Gaston was annoyed with him. "Like what?"

"He's going after the Pistolas," said Curtis.

The president shook his head. "Hell no. The Yavapai are in-house. We need to deal with that threat first. Then we can look outside the state."

Diego was ready to shoot out of there but paused to state his case. "Not sure if you noticed, but the Pistolas are in Arizona too."

"Are you forgetting that Clint is in intensive care right now?"

"Are you forgetting that Omar is stashed in a freezer? We can't let these assholes come right to our clubhouse and kill one of our own."

Gaston growled as he watched Kelan escorted to a white sport utility vehicle. The Yavapai man had a thin smile as he flaunted his bodyguards.

"What was Sergio talking about?" asked Diego.

"What?"

"The leverage he wanted."

Gaston shook his head. "Don't worry about it."

Diego sneered. "Worry about club business, just don't worry about club business, right?"

Gaston shook his head instead of answering.

"What if it got Omar killed?"

The president winced as he considered it for the first time. "You still think those stupid bastards knew how to take him out?"

"No way," asserted West.

The Sons watched as the SUV loaded up. Hitchens broke off to his own squad car, shooting the MC a look of warning. "That bastard in that truck set all of this up. Kelan always thought he was smarter than everybody else. We need to stay on him. And we can't afford to split up." Gaston took on a more aggressive tone. "We won't. We move as a pack and deal with the threats one at a time."

Diego gritted his teeth and revved his engine. "I told you why I was staying, Gaston, and it's not for club business. Fuck the drug pipeline. I'm doing what needs to be done for Omar."

West Wind perked up at Diego's mention of staying. Diego hadn't told anybody about his choice yet. Maybe they knew now. It didn't matter. He couldn't concern himself with the politics of brotherhood anymore.

Gaston opened his mouth to respond, but Diego slapped the shaded visor over his face. With a twist of his hand, his Scrambler launched into the street. Diego picked his boot up off the asphalt and leaned forward, not even giving the Seventh Sons a glance back.

The biker didn't know exactly what had happened to

Omar yet, but he knew the Pistolas were involved. That snide comment Sergio had made about there being one less Mexican in the club was all he needed to hear. That asshole was guilty. It didn't matter if he was surrounded by nine of his best men—Diego had been trained to hunt individuals within a pack.

Diego de la Torre raced towards the highway, settling in for the long trip to California.

Chapter 38

Maxim watched the bikers through the office window. The Seventh Sons were ready to roll out but Gaston held them up to make a call. The detective sighed and slipped his cell phone into his hand. There was a better than good chance that Maxim was the recipient of that call. On cue, his phone buzzed. Maxim answered and walked away from the glass.

"Where's Kelan being transferred?" demanded Gaston.

"He's not a prisoner. He's free to go."

"Go where?"

"He's on his way back to the reservation. That's where he'll stay if he's smart."

Gaston grumbled at the news. "You got that right. Why don't you call your men off?"

Maxim almost laughed out loud. "Because they're not *my* men, first of all. These are the marshal's orders. And besides, I'd give the same command."

The voice on the line did not sound pleased. "You forget

about our unspoken deal?"

"It's unspoken because it never happened, Gaston."

"Keep telling yourself that. We both know who you are."

Maxim spun around in anger. "Who I am? What's that supposed to mean? Who am I, Gaston?"

The president was taken aback by the detective's anger and didn't respond.

Maxim wiped his brow and slumped into his desk chair. He scanned the empty office to make sure he could talk in private and sighed. "Listen, the only privilege I confer on the Sons is my legal responsibility to deflect any attention to lycanthropy."

"That's the CDC's job."

"And the CDC isn't in Flagstaff anymore." Maxim thought about Nithya Rao, the former CDC liaison with the marshal's office. She was the one who first told Maxim about the werewolves. She'd been in charge of Sycamore. She'd also been a primary player in the Paradise Killings.

With Nithya's disappearance and the lack of a replacement thus far, Maxim now carried the torch. "This is what Sanctuary is for you, Gaston. A place to hide, a place to blend in. It's not my fault if you choose to jump out of the shadows."

The president scoffed. "In case you didn't notice, Kelan came after us. I've got one man dead and another close call."

"And I'm working on it," insisted the detective. "But harassing a police escort is gonna give you a whole lot more trouble than you want."

Gaston shouted obscenities. The detective heard the

Harleys revving in the background. Maxim knew that no matter what he said, the Seventh Sons would follow Kelan. Making sure they didn't cross the line was his main concern.

"Leave them alone Gaston. It's not just Hitchens in there."

There was a moment of silence while Gaston debated. "What's the FBI involved for?"

"I don't know. Hate crime bullshit. But I think he wants to take you down."

"For what?"

"For breaking the law, asshole. Trust me. You don't want to be anywhere near that kind of heat."

"He doesn't have anything on us."

"Then keep it that way." Maxim ended the call without waiting for an answer.

The bikers were hardheaded. When it came down to taking advice from a cop or doing something stupid, stupid always won. Sure enough, he heard the engines of the motorcycles speed away like dogs on the chase.

The detective's frustration nearly boiled over then and there. He had multiple homicides with multiple suspects, a renegade group of bikers who had their own idea of justice, and an FBI agent with a stick up his ass. In three days his town had been flipped on its head.

And Gaston Delacroix had the gall to say he knew who Maxim was.

As the rumble of Harleys faded out, Maxim took several deep breaths. Honestly, he didn't care to babysit the bikers anymore. Even Diego, who he considered a good friend, was an outlaw now. Maxim wasn't responsible for them. He was only responsible for the law. He would only try to save the men as far as they deserved.

Suddenly, he found the marshal's office eerily quiet. Gutierrez was out on patrol. Hitchens was following Garcia to the reservation. Maxim didn't know where the marshal was but his office door was shut. Main Street was empty. The detective was alone with his thoughts and he wasn't sure if he liked it. The peace that he so desperately wanted felt out of place.

"Time to think," said Maxim aloud to the spacious room.

Then it hit him. Garcia was shoving him to the side. He didn't want him on the reservation. He didn't want him anywhere near the case. But the FBI agent had just tied himself up for the day. While Garcia busied himself coordinating with the tribal police, Maxim had time alone to investigate.

Imagine that. Time to actually do his job.

He started with the freshest questions in his head. Maxim woke his computer and pulled up the National Crime Information Center. The NCIC database was managed by the FBI. That thought made Maxim smirk. It had an entire file of gang listings. It would be a lot more useful than Raymond Garcia.

Hector Cruz was the man Gaston had mixed it up with. His rap sheet was impressive, both in length and breadth. In his forty-six years, Cruz had managed to serve twenty-one of them in various institutions. Juvie and small-time jail stints early on, but his crimes became more serious. His importance obviously rose as well because he stopped doing small-time jobs. Bigger and better things led to bigger and better busts, and even the best lawyers couldn't keep him out of prison.

Garcia had called him the Mechanic. As far as Maxim could tell, it was because he liked to get his hands dirty. He had run with a street gang in Mexico while a US fugitive. Eventually, he landed with the Pistolas. No matter where he was, though, he was always involved in the bad stuff. Drug trafficking, aggravated battery, armed robbery, sexual assault. He was a suspect in two murders: one was pled down to manslaughter, the other case didn't have enough evidence to get through the District Attorney's office. Ironically, his longest stretch in prison was spent for the drug charges because of mandatory minimum sentencing. Luckily for him, California prisons were overcrowded. Drug offenders were regularly released early. Since Cruz's most recent violence occurred in Mexico, he'd been set free after serving six years in Lompoc.

Sergio Lima was the next name Maxim ran. As opposed to Cruz, there wasn't a whole lot on the kid. He was only nineteen years old and wasn't on anyone's radar until he was voted in as club president. Known associations with the Pistolas and various Mexicali factions. Nothing big. No Mexican Mafia. No known family ties that would have explained that. It just happened. That was a red flag for the detective. Something wasn't right with Lima. The most likely explanation was that he was a lot more connected than he appeared.

Maxim looked up the number for the New Mexico State Police and gave them a call. He recited his name and badge number and asked to speak to the patrol sergeant. He waited a minute before being connected.

"Cortez."

"Hi, this is Detective Maxim Dwyer of the Sanctuary Marshal's Office."

"That's what I was told. How can I help you?"

"I'm calling regarding the bust your department made two nights ago. Do you recall your guys detaining an Arizona motorcycle club, the Seventh Sons?"

Cortez sighed and seemed slightly put off, but Maxim couldn't be sure over the phone. "I led the takedown. The suspects were observed in the proximity of a drug shipment, but we didn't find any contraband on them. They were questioned and released."

"Overnight?" asked Maxim.

"Yes, well, it was a little busy that night. They all had personal firearms and we wanted to run everything before we cut them loose. What's this about?"

"I was mainly interested in why the motorcycle club was detained in the first place."

"I told you. They were in close proximity—"

"I know that, Cortez. I'm asking how was two nights ago any different from any other visit the Sons make to your state?"

More silence. Then, "Look, don't give me a hard time on this. You know how these guys are."

Maxim wasn't sure what the patrol sergeant meant. He

thought he was talking about the Sons. Did Cortez have some sort of relationship with them? Maxim decided to go with a generic answer that wouldn't give his ignorance away. "They're always pissing somebody off."

"You're telling me," answered Cortez. "Look, this kind of thing normally wouldn't have happened. It came through from above. I don't know how things work in Sanctuary, but we've got so much brass up here we could start our own horn section. It's like the tubas have no idea what the trombones are doing."

The man had abandoned caution and launched into a series of complaints. It sounded like the Seventh Sons were regular visitors to New Mexico and the state police usually let them slide. "So someone up top—"

"It was a new mandate. I just do what I'm told. Tell Gaston his problem's not with us."

Maxim almost snapped at him. From what he could tell, the sergeant thought Maxim was on the take, bought out by the club as Cortez himself probably had been. Was Sanctuary's reputation that bad? No wonder Garcia had an axe to grind.

Instead of outing the patrol sergeant, Maxim decided it was best to keep the information in his back pocket. He thanked the officer after another minute of friendly commiseration and hung up.

So Diego was right. The Seventh Sons hadn't been arrested randomly. It wasn't a tip that had come in. Somebody with connections had convinced the department to switch allegiances, at least for that one delivery. If Sergio was connected to the Mexican Mafia, and that's who the Sons were undoubtedly working with, then that shined a new light on the events of the last three days.

Maxim leaned back in his chair and ran the facts through his head. This was a lot bigger than Sanctuary and even Arizona. The potential players on this board were from California and New Mexico, Texas and old Mexico. Shit, it was even federal.

That last thought reminded Maxim of the familiarity the Pistolas had with Agent Garcia. With everything that was going on, Maxim had forgotten to ask him about their association. The Mechanic, Hector Cruz, had personally known him. Sergio Lima knew *of* him, but they hadn't met yet. That meant that Agent Garcia's history with them went back a ways.

Maxim figured, if he was going to do some digging, he had to explore all avenues equally.

He scrolled through his phone and found the next number. It was his sole connection in the Bureau, and calling Lawrence Hendricks a connection was a very tenuous stretch. He was an intelligence analyst—but most of the time that was a fancy way of saying copy clerk. The man was only twenty-seven, just three years out of grad school, and was already jaded with his career. Maxim always thought his combination of debt and lack of job satisfaction might come in handy one day.

Unfortunately, the number was disconnected.

Maxim sighed and went back to his computer. He would do this the old-fashioned way. He picked up his desk phone and dialed the number to the Flagstaff resident agency. A woman answered and the detective identified himself and asked to speak to Lawrence Hendricks.

"I'm sorry, he's back at headquarters."

"DC?"

"No, Phoenix."

Of course, he thought. Hendricks was assigned to the Phoenix Division. They had satellite offices throughout the state, and he only moved to Flagstaff while he was studying a rabies outbreak. Now that there was nothing there—no terrorism involved—he'd resumed his usual coffee-fetching duties further south.

"I see," said Maxim, partially dejected. He decided to attempt his line of questioning anyway. "Raymond Garcia is working out of your office now, isn't he?"

"That's right, Detective."

"Well, he's currently conducting interviews at the Yavapai-Prescott reservation and I didn't want to bother him, but something's come up in relation to his possible undercover work."

"Yes?"

"Would you mind confirming for me if he's worked with the Pistolas before? They're a Mexi gang out of Southern California that has been encroaching into Coconino and Yavapai counties."

Dead silence for a time. "Detective," she finally said, "I'd be happy to instruct you on the proper procedures for information requests, but it might just be easier for you to ask Agent Garcia directly." The suggestion was made snidely so as not to disguise the sarcasm.

"No, no. That's okay. I'll just wait and ask him, I suppose."

Maxim hung up the phone and shook his head. Pressing them for any kind of information was dumb. He didn't get anything, and there was a good chance they'd give Garcia a heads-up.

Next Maxim dialed the Phoenix headquarters and asked to be directed. After a couple of strikeouts he was surprised when the man answered so quickly.

"Lawrence Hendricks."

"What's up Law?"

"Um, who's this?"

"Detective Dwyer, over in Sanctuary."

"Oh, Maxim. You didn't find another lake full of rabies, did you?"

"Tanks are more like watering holes than lakes. But no, it's nothing like that. I was just on with the Flagstaff office about an Agent Raymond Garcia. You know him?"

"Not really. I haven't been in Flagstaff for months. What's he do?"

Maxim was immediately deflated. "He's out of Civil Rights."

"That skinned body at the high school?"

"That's the one. Things are pretty crazy up here. Anyway, Agent Garcia is tied up at the reservation and something came up. He told me he'd done some undercover work before and I was wondering which gangs, you know? Do you have a moment?"

"You mean in between computer solitaire and manning telephone calls for these pompous assholes? Sure. Let me look it up."

Maxim waited silently. He figured any small talk would just distract Hendricks from the request. If the man was already helping him out, there was no need to butter the bread any further.

Asking the analyst for a favor was weird. They had met after a rabies outbreak the prior year. Hendricks mostly focused on bio-terrorism. As such, his personal expertise was not especially useful to Maxim. Still, he had clearance that the detective didn't.

"Okay, yeah," he said, coming back to the line. "It looks like it's been a while since he's done undercover work. He did a lot of vice stuff, you know—posing as a fence, money deals. Anything particular you're looking for?"

"Has he been undercover with a biker club in California? They go by the Pistolas."

"Hmm. I don't see anything like that here. He doesn't look like he's been embedded on the West Coast."

"Damn." Maxim was sure that Garcia had ties to Cruz. He was about to assume he'd just struck out and thank Lawrence, but then he remembered something Sergio Lima had said. His alibi for the attack last night. He was in Texas. "What about Texas? Any mafia ties with Mexico?"

"Oh, well sure. That's all over the place. It looks like Garcia split his time between the Midwest and Texas, the latter all dealing with border smuggling."

That was it. Sergio was a new West Coast player with

contacts in Mexico, and the two sides were trying to squeeze the Sons out of the middle of the sandwich: Interstate 40 in Arizona.

"When was the last time Agent Garcia dealt with the gangs down there?"

Hendricks muttered to himself as he looked. Maxim figured he wasn't especially happy doing this for him, but it beat whatever else he had scheduled for the workday. "Let me see. It's been a while. Agent Garcia transferred—"

Maxim waited a moment. "What?"

"Uh... Hold on."

"What is it?"

"Um, I shouldn't really be divulging this stuff, Maxim."

"Come on, Law. It'll just take another second."

"No. I could get in trouble for this. I gotta go."

"Law!"

It wasn't a strong appeal and it didn't work. Lawrence Hendricks hung up the phone.

So Maxim had stumbled onto something sensitive. Something Raymond Garcia hadn't told him. Maxim glanced at the closed door of the marshal's office and wondered if Boyd knew what was going on.

It didn't matter. Either he did and he wouldn't say anything, or he didn't and would warn Maxim not to poke into the matter. Besides, if Maxim was right, then Garcia had more going on with the Pistolas than even the FBI knew about. If that was the case, Marshal Boyd was surely in the dark.

Maxim thought about the baseball metaphor as he

depressed the switch hook with the telephone receiver and got the dial tone back. His third swing wasn't a strike but it wasn't a hit either. It was more like a foul: not quite good, not quite bad. Just a precursor to his next attempt.

Maxim Dwyer cleared his throat and hit redial.

Chapter 39

It didn't take too long to catch up to the Pistolas. Ten of them were side by side, riding high and tight. They weren't running from the Sons. They were taking their time. Enjoying the road trip.

What cocky bastards.

Diego figured he would give them a large cushion. The Interstate was a long road and the Pistolas didn't have many route options. It was a straight shot to California. Just as the biker considered how easy tailing the club would be, their silhouettes on the horizon turned off. They must have been stopping.

That was odd. They'd been heading west, about to leave the confines of Sycamore and enter the desert flatland. Instead the Pistolas were exiting.

The Scrambler accelerated ahead. Soon, Diego realized the Pistolas had transferred south onto State Route 89. That was trouble.

Diego generally avoided the 89. It was Yavapai territory. Besides, Interstate 40 led right to Joshua Tree, and Diego had used it before heading south to Palm Springs in the past. There was no need to cut south in Arizona.

But the Pistolas were an Imperial Valley outfit. The south of the south of California, and beyond. Their stomping grounds extended to Calexico and Mexicali. Without a beef with the Indians, they could ride home this way without trouble.

Satisfied that the mystery was solved, Diego followed the bikers onto the state road. A nervous flutter filled his stomach as he broke club protocol. Ironically, the rest of the Sons might be doing the same thing, minutes behind him. Kelan's police escort was sure to come this way. Would the Seventh Sons follow?

Diego decided that it was unlikely. Even if they did move south on the state road, they would stop once the confines of Sycamore forest ended. Past that, they would be riding into Chino Valley and the Quad-City area, and that was looking for a fight.

Good thing that's what Diego was in the mood for.

In his haste to make the detour, Diego rode a little too close to the Pistolas. He relaxed his grip on the throttle and eased the bike down. Ten was too many.

It wasn't long before they left the trees behind. The hilly terrain smoothed into a valley as the sand commandeered the landscape. Visibility suddenly exploded and Diego felt like a fish out of water, and there were no fish in the desert. He slowed down even more to compensate, but was disconcerted when the Pistolas pulled over to the side of the highway and huddled together.

They must have spotted him.

The biker slowed to a rolling crawl, sizing up the Mexicans. It was still ten against one, no matter how many times he counted. But Diego's shotgun was a pretty slick plus one. He patted the Benelli M4 in the holster and remembered that the Sanctuary police had searched the Pistolas. The pack didn't have a single gun. Still. Diego figured he only had ten or twelve shells total. The numbers weren't favorable.

Diego parked on the shoulder. He was still far enough to hope he hadn't been seen, although the dust he now kicked up was likely to attract attention. Were they talking about him? He lifted his visor to get a clear view of the group but the sun was too bright. Diego could only open his eyes to slits. He gave up and shut the visor again.

The Pistolas, interestingly enough, split off into two groups. Six of them waved and continued south. The remaining four rode into a rest stop ahead. No. That wasn't right. Diego squinted. They moved slowly along an access road before the rest stop. From this distance, Diego hadn't even seen the street there. And no wonder: the small dirt path led to a nondescript building surrounded by a chain-link fence on one side and a crumbling wall of concrete, which lined a dried-up creek, on the other. Diego couldn't make anything of the place but he imagined it was condemned, proof that the desert sucked even stone and metal dry.

And for some reason, the four Pistolas pulled into the property.

Immediately, Diego considered that this could be a trick. A decoy, a ploy to protect Sergio. All the bikers had helmets and bandannas covering their features. It wasn't easy to make out which group Sergio was with. But one of the four men wore his jacket open, exposing a bare chest. That was Hector Cruz—the Mechanic, and Sergio's right-hand man. If he was staying behind, no doubt the club president was as well.

If not a decoy, then was this a trap? Were the other six men *really* leaving? It was possible they only pretended to start back to the Imperial Valley. They could wait for Diego to sneak after the smaller group and come at his back. He would be cornered.

What were the other possibilities? This building could be a safe house. The Sons kept them. They were a California MC, but they might be moving into Arizona. Was that possible without Gaston knowing? It would be a ballsy move, being sandwiched between the Yavapai and the Seventh Sons. Then again, so was riding into Sanctuary.

The biker decided to wait. Hector and the others disappeared around the side of the building. The larger group faded into the horizon. Diego sat there, and not a whole lot happened until a white Ford Explorer raced by him. Diego turned away as soon as he pegged it as the FBI vehicle carrying Kelan. With a smile, the biker realized his helmet covered his face anyway, and it didn't matter which way he faced. Diego's entire outfit was matte black except for his metallic gold racing helmet. It was a distinctive look. If anyone glanced his way and knew what to look for, they would've spotted him.

The Explorer didn't stop or even slow down. Diego twisted his body while straddling his bike and checked north. Sergeant Hitchens drove by in his brand-new police cruiser. This time Diego looked straight at the vehicle, but the glare on the windshield blocked his sight of the officer.

Diego waited some more, this time for a different set of bikers. The Seventh Sons never came into view. As he'd predicted, they didn't follow the escort past Sycamore's border. They would not be encroaching on Indian territory.

Good, thought Diego, they weren't doing anything stupid. As for himself, well... Diego wasn't one to look inward. He relied on other people to tell him when he was fucking up. That's why he never carried his cell phone and usually did things alone.

After a time, Diego was satisfied that things were quiet. He killed his Triumph's engine and walked his bike ahead on the shoulder. As the little dirt road came into view, he noticed the highway bridged over the tiny creek. A little stone wall marked the overpass, but he could pull off the road on either side and lead his bike down into the ditch. This, he decided, would keep his actions out of view. Instead of following the Pistolas the same way in, he could hike up the desolate creek bed in silence until it met up with the property's stone wall. It was perfect.

Diego eased his helmet off. Hot air blasted his face and it felt like heaven. The dust didn't matter. It was movement, breeze against his scalp. Diego removed his gloves and ran his fingers through his tattered, wet hair. He unzipped his jacket before deciding to pull it off altogether. He would have considered going shirtless like Hector, but Diego decided that he wasn't a douche bag. The biker slid his shotgun into his grip and headed up the creek.

It was quiet as he approached the wall. It was made out of cinder blocks, and not all of them had agreed to stick together anymore. The mortar was worn down. The paint chipped along with the cement. It was as if everything in the desert was trying to propagate more desert; dust to dust.

As Diego advanced, he almost plodded right into a rattlesnake. It coiled away from him then froze. The biker gave it a wide birth, wondering if his armored boots would have protected him. Weren't rattlesnakes supposed to, you know, rattle? Diego chuckled. He pictured chasing the Pistolas, shotgun in hand, on the border of enemy wolf territory, only to be taken out by a snake.

He reminded himself that he was in the desert now; everything was trying to kill him.

Diego trudged up the creek bank and pressed himself flush against the cinder blocks. It wasn't a high wall to begin with, and it was shorter where the top row of blocks had been stripped. A quick peek over revealed the side of an old administration building. Simple architecture, flat roof, scant window placement—whatever purpose the building served, it wasn't a house.

The yard was empty. Diego moved along the wall to get a better view. Sand and dirt, cracked step stones, a couple of smaller buildings in the back, all lined with a metal fence except for the wall along the creek bed. Diego didn't see the motorcycles. His gaze swept past the property but there was nothing but hills and trees. He was sure the Pistolas were here. The bikes must be on the other side of the building.

Well, he thought, no time like the present. He laid the M4 on its side along the top of the wall and boosted himself up and over. He landed in a crouch, acutely aware of the lack of brush to camouflage him. He retrieved his shotgun and scampered against the building, keeping out of sight of the windows.

Diego slipped around the corner of the building. The back wall had two windows and a door between them. The biker tried to peek inside but the dimpled jalousie panes were closed. One of the glass sheets was missing, but cardboard or something closed it off. In fact, the entire window was covered from the inside. No visibility in or out. Diego ducked below it anyway and tried the doorknob. It was locked.

As he leaned his head in to listen, the door shook and he heard a slam in the distance. Diego froze. It was just a vibration. Someone had closed the front door on the other side of the building. Diego pulled up the ghost ring sight of his shotty and checked both sides of the property again. He was stuck out in the open here. He could either run back to the wall or try to make it to one of the smaller buildings farther into the yard.

While he debated his options, an engine came to life. A motorcycle. It came from the side of the building, where he assumed the bikers had parked. Shit. They were taking off already.

Diego quickly slid along the wall toward them, ducking the next window. He raised the shotgun vertically to keep it from poking around the corner and giving away his position. He listened. It only sounded like one bike, and it hadn't moved yet. The rider was waiting for something.

"Don't move, holmes," said a guttural voice behind him.

Diego's instinct was to spin around or dash past the corner, but he knew better. Guns were on him. He turned his head slowly and saw Hector Cruz and a man with a bandanna over his face holding pistols to his back.

"Drop that 12-gauge real slow," said the older man.

"Good eye." Diego decided he still had a chance to escape around the corner. Without fully turning around, he lowered the M4 to his side, holding it harmlessly by the barrel, and stepped away from the corner. As he moved, he glanced to the side of the building. It was a dirt driveway with four parked choppers. A lone rider cut the engine of his motorcycle and raised a pistol.

Diego dropped his shotgun to the dirt.

"You a real stupid *ése* for rolling up to us with that," said the guy standing next to Hector. Diego couldn't make out his face, but it wasn't the president. Neither was the other one behind him.

"Where's Sergio?" he asked nonchalantly.

"Who's asking?" shot back Hector.

The biker bowed with a smile. "Diego de la Torre, at your service. You guys buying property in Arizona now?"

Hector grunted. The old man was permanently in a non-shit-taking mood. Too hardened to give a fuck. If Diego was gonna get out of here, he would need to do it by appealing to somebody else.

"I need to talk to Sergio Lima," he stated again.

"*Chupame.*"

"If you don't mind, maybe one of your boys would rather take you up on that."

Somebody rapped Diego on the back of the head. He started to fall forward but caught himself. The banger behind him wiped off the bottom of his pistol and told Diego to shut up. The man picked up the shotgun and checked Diego's belt for other weapons. "What's a *mierda* like you following us for?"

Diego's hand went to the back of his head to soothe the pain. The blow had slightly dazed him. Luckily, he didn't feel any blood. "I'll only talk to Sergio."

"Sergio's not here," said Hector.

There were four bikes and three of them. He knew one person was missing. Still inside, probably. It made sense that it was *el presidente*. "Too bad for you then."

"Why's that?"

"I want out of the Sons."

The three men stared at him suspiciously. Of course it wasn't going to be that easy, but it was an opening.

"*Que come mierda.*"

Diego shook his head. "*Es verdad.* It's true. I don't want to end up like Omar. I know who you guys got backing you."

Again, the three men eyed him. This time they didn't have anything to say.

The back door clicked and opened, and out strutted Sergio Lima. He smiled magnanimously and approached Diego. He was a skinny kid, especially up close, but his face was cold, his eyes calculating. He didn't just luck into the head of the MC.

"*Entonces*, you want to move out to Cali?" he asked.

Diego blinked away their disbelief. "Or stay in Arizona. Help you expand."

Sergio scoffed. "That's bullshit."

"The Seventh Sons are bullshit," Diego replied. "Besides, I'm not really one of them."

"I could've told you that. What'd you think would happen hanging around a bunch of *gringos*?"

Sergio and, in turn, the others relaxed. They were casual, in control of the situation and knew it. "*Compruebe el frente*," barked Sergio to one of the guys wearing a bandanna. He nodded and went around to check the front of the property. The president turned back to Diego. "Where are the others?"

"They're not here," answered Diego. "I swear. It's just me."

"Why?"

"'Cause you killed Omar, right?" Diego clenched his jaw and tried to hide his distaste. He wanted them to admit to killing the kid. He needed to know. Maxim and the police would take forever with the evidence. The biker didn't even know if the Sanctuary detective had any power over a

California gang.

Sergio nodded slightly, an implicit acknowledgment of the deed. "Can't say that you're stupid to wanna ride with us. But I can't just take your word for it."

"Let me help you," persuaded Diego. "I can do things you can't." Hector sneered but Sergio just raised his eyebrows expectantly. "I know the Sanctuary police."

Sergio nodded. "*Sí.* But if I'm to believe you, I need more than your word. I need proof."

"What do you want?"

"*Fotos.* Blackmail documents. There's a councilman in Albuquerque who works with *La Eme*. He has... unfortunate habits. The Seventh Sons have proof of this. Photos of him with crack whores, high out of his mind. It would destroy him."

Diego realized this was the leverage the Pistolas had mentioned to Gaston. They were trying to free the squeeze Gaston had on the Albuquerque councilman. Remove the Seventh Sons from the equation.

"That's why you were at the clubhouse," posited Diego. "It was supposed to be empty. You set up the drug run to be intercepted, to get us in jail. You probably even did it with help from the councilman, promising to relieve him of his burden. He co-opted Gaston's police support." Sergio smiled as Diego retraced the plan. "But you didn't expect Omar to be there. He was supposed to be in jail with the rest of us. You wanted to search the clubhouse for the blackmail photos, but instead you walked into a gunfight, then you had to hit the road."

"I just wanted what was mine," declared Sergio.

Diego's face darkened. So it was club business that had killed Omar. Drugs. Money. A play for power. Was he even surprised?

The fourth banger came back to the yard. He nodded to Hector and Sergio. No one else had followed Diego there.

"What about Doka?" asked Diego. "Did you kill him too? Start all this shit with the Yavapai?"

The three men glanced at each other. Sergio laughed. "Relax, homie," he said, patting Diego on the cheek. "You're starting to sound like a cop."

The kid annoyed Diego. It was his smugness. His attitude of superiority. Diego just wanted to grab him by the shoulders and shake him, like the adults in his life should have. Instead, he simply smiled.

"Tell you what," continued the president. "You get us these photographs, that's an automatic in. I won't make you kill anybody to prove you're loyal. No blood in. The Seventh Sons get brushed aside without violence."

Diego nodded. "How will I contact you?"

Sergio snapped his fingers at one of his boys. "*Cabron?*" The kid pulled out a burner phone and tossed it to Diego. "I'm on speed dial."

"Okay."

Sergio motioned with his head for him to leave. Diego extended his hand to retrieve his shotgun.

"No," said Hector, intercepting the weapon. He hefted the silver Benelli in his hands. "You get this when you come back."

"I want an update tonight," said Sergio, walking back into the building.

Diego nodded again. As he walked away, he remembered what Gaston had said about the Pistolas. They pretended to play nice, then shot people in the back. Diego made sure to step away with an eye on the others. Once he was back in the creek and on his way to his Scrambler, he took a deep breath. He preferred close calls with rattlesnakes.

Chapter 40

Kayda noticed Agent Garcia keeping his eyes on the rearview mirror. The Seventh Sons had stopped tailing the rented Explorer a while back, but it didn't hurt to be sure. Kayda figured the FBI agent was keeping tabs on her brother in the back seat as well.

Now that they were safe, Kelan was grumpy about being escorted by the police. He had planned on being picked up by Hotah but something fell through. Kelan had been left without a ride. A bit ungracious, she thought. Kayda turned around and saw her brother staring at her. His expression was accusatory. It was clear he didn't want her around either.

She averted her eyes to the rear windshield and the Sanctuary police officer driving behind them in the follow car. Chances were, their transfer to tribal police would be uneventful.

The young girl faced forward again. She didn't want to

acknowledge her brother anymore. He'd sold her out. The tribal police—Chuck Winston—had left her for dead. Was this another hard lesson that her betters were teaching her? Kayda felt pain in her mouth and realized her grinding teeth had bitten her tongue. The warm taste of salty blood filled her mouth.

Raymond Garcia casually held the wheel with one hand. He smiled at her. "You know," he said, "you both are very lucky to be getting this escort. That motorcycle club back there is dangerous."

No one said anything for a few seconds, but Kayda appreciated the attempt at conversation. Anything to fill the void.

"What's the FBI doing in town?"

"Your brother's murder might have been racially motivated. It's my job to make sure your family is protected. I'm here to help you."

"How can you help us?" she asked.

Kelan grumbled again in the back seat. "Kayda, we don't talk to cops."

She spun around on a dime. "If you really want to wash your hands of me, you should stop bossing me around."

Her brother didn't respond. He just focused on the distance, on something else. As Kayda resumed facing the road, she noticed the hint of a smile on Raymond's lips.

"It's okay," he said. "I understand how your tribe might not like the federal government too much. I'm not trying to change your mind about them, but you should consider me a man who wants to get to the bottom of your brother's death."

The car was silent again. If the FBI agent thought he could appeal to Kelan's emotions, he was dead wrong. Kayda knew he would never give in, never betray his renegade code. Even if there was a way to help their brother's memory, Kelan would refuse to take part if it involved police assistance.

Death affected everybody differently. Seeing her older brother hanging from the statue like that had been horrifying. Her immediate response was shock. Pain. But the next morning she had just wanted answers. There was no doubt that Carlos being killed had elicited an entirely different response from Kelan.

"The best thing we can do," said Raymond, another attempt at his plea, "is talk to the police on your reservation. Hook up with your friends. Make sure everybody is safe and accounted for."

Kelan scoffed. "Yeah, so you can lock them up."

"Mr. Doka, if anyone was involved with that shooting at Sycamore Lodge last night, then yes, I'll lock them up. But my primary concern is keeping anything like this from happening again. I can protect you if you know anything that might help."

Kayda's brother simply laughed at the offer. She wondered if Raymond had a point. Did she need protection too? She had just an ancillary involvement in this. But what about her family? What about her *pahmi*?

"You don't think anyone will come to the reservation, do you?"

"They already did," said Raymond. "To string your brother up for all to see. If they did it once, they could do it again. Who knows what they have planned next?" Kayda thought it over. The FBI agent noticed her opening up and pressed on. "Are either of you two aware of the Seventh Sons riding into Prescott or the reservation recently?"

Kayda shook her head. She'd already mentioned that she had just arrived in town. Her absence meant that she didn't know anything about the activities of the motorcycle club or her brother. She wondered if all the troubles of the recent years could have been avoided if she'd stayed. Carlos being involved with the Paradise Killings, dirty deals with the Seventh Sons, his murder and Kelan's juvenile instincts for revenge—it was all just boys killing each other. It was bad for both their families.

"Fine," said the FBI agent. "You don't know anything. Right? You don't like the police. I wonder if there's a reason for that."

"There's always a reason," said Kelan.

Raymond nodded. "Let me ask you this, Mr. Doka. Are you aware of any side dealings, perhaps not above board, in regards to the Sanctuary Marshal's Office? Maybe with Detective Dwyer, specifically?"

Kayda turned to the man and studied his features. It was strange for the FBI to be asking about the local police. Wasn't it? What was he asking Kelan about?

"You mean that he killed Skah?" answered her brother. "He's a murderer."

"I'm aware of that, but I was hoping you knew of

something that didn't occur in the line of duty. Something extracurricular."

Kayda turned back to her brother. He was tense but leaning back, just waiting out the ride. He surprised Kayda by answering.

"Everybody knows the Seventh Sons pay off the cops. We'd be blind to hope for justice through the police."

Kayda recalled Maxim's familiarity with Diego. He was at ease in Sycamore Lodge, the MC's bar. If he was in their pocket, then she had been a fool to think going to him could have helped her family. Diego, too, darkened her thoughts. The biker's involvement with the club was undeniable.

"Dirty cops... Do you have proof of that?" asked the FBI agent.

Kelan just shrugged. "Proof's a burden for the police. I don't need it to act."

Kayda narrowed her eyes. Her brother had come awfully close to confessing involvement in an attempt to show up a federal agent. That was always his way, appearances first.

"Sometimes you can be right and wrong at the same time, Keekee."

"Stop calling me that."

Raymond Garcia turned to Kayda with a puzzled expression. "What do you mean by that?" He glanced into the mirror to gauge Kelan's reaction, but her brother just laughed.

"You wanna be a leader?" Kayda asked. "You wanna be a man? Playing to people's fears only works in the short term."

Kelan laughed some more before responding. When he did, his voice was curt. "The police can't protect us. Like it or not, little sister, I'm all you've got."

She scowled. Raymond shot them both puzzled looks. Kayda decided that she would ride the rest of the way in silence.

Chapter 41

Maxim leaned back in his parked TT so he could stretch his legs. The engine hummed as the air conditioner created a private oasis from the heat. The workday was nearing an end but the summer sun was still high in the sky, a lone torch in a plain of blue. It was strange for the detective. He wasn't used to the flat terrain of Phoenix. It made everything more expansive. The massive sky encircled the world, making everything feel a bit smaller by comparison.

The Federal Bureau of Investigation's Phoenix Division was a brand new building that didn't help the feeling. Sharp lines cut across the sky forming giant blocks. The windows protruded from the walls and looked more like rows of mirrors hanging on a wall. The alternating glass colors of blue and white reminded Maxim of the ocean and the clouds, but it reflected the sun harshly. It wasn't a beautiful building but it was instilled with a sense of design, a far cry from the utilitarian monstrosities of the eighties.

Maxim had made the drive to the Phoenix headquarters because he needed to see Lawrence Hendricks in person. The workday—for office workers—was coming to an end. Already Maxim could see the dripping faucet of employees exiting the building. It was only a matter of time before Law was one of them.

As he waited, he privately worried that this was an awful waste of time. Two hours each way. But with Garcia pushing him away from the Yavapai and the Pistolas, Maxim didn't have anything else to do. The truth was he didn't have much to go on.

A thin, black man in a tailored suit passed in front of Maxim's view. The detective chuckled. Lawrence Hendricks was a young man who didn't look like an FBI employee. Of course, he wasn't a special agent, only an analyst, but he still looked way off the mark. He had very short black hair, perfectly trimmed. His sideburns, mustache, and goatee were all barely there, just enough to hint at the style while still remaining clean-cut. In contrast to this, he had large, pointed eyebrows that enhanced the expressiveness of his face. His fashion sense didn't stop at personal grooming, either. His suit was slim-cut, hugging his waist; his button-up shirt was smartly striped; and his tie and gray jacket had a shiny metallic sheen to them.

He kind of looked like a movie star version of a hip Wall Street up-and-comer.

The TT shifted into gear and followed the man down an aisle of cars. As he reached his luxury SUV, he noticed the slow car tagging along and turned. Maxim rolled down his passenger window.

"How's it going, Law?"

The man narrowed his eyes and turned back to the building as if he were having second thoughts. "Pull out to the street. Let me pass and get behind me."

Maxim nodded and drove out of the parking lot, making sure that Hendricks didn't attempt to leave another way. He did what he said he would, and when the black SUV drove past the detective into the street, Maxim followed.

The Sanctuary detective wasn't too familiar with Phoenix. He'd driven through it several times but that was about it. What always impressed him was the modern, clean downtown. It wasn't as aged as New York or Los Angeles. Even Downtown Flagstaff had an antique quality about it. But Phoenix was all crisp metal and glass. Maxim wondered if the city had an old town where it was otherwise.

After several minutes, Hendricks pulled into a small diner that was still in the lull between lunch and dinner. The man hurried inside without waiting for his friend. Maxim parked, tapped his jacket pocket, and followed him inside. Hendricks sat at a table in the back, away from the only other occupants at the bar.

"This is some real spy shit," said Law when he neared.

Maxim shrugged and slid into the booth. "It's just coffee," he replied. As he said that, the aging waitress approached. Maxim ordered a coffee with lots of sugar and Hendricks got a latte.

"So how's the FBI been treating you, Law?"

Maxim figured it was best to start with small talk.

Hendricks looked a little nervous and the two hadn't seen each other in a while. Plus, getting the analyst worked up about his employer wouldn't hurt.

"Sheeit," said the man, stretching out the word so it was almost a sigh. "We're just administrators to those suits. They need us for intelligence but steal all the credit. If I was smart I'd go private."

"There a big commercial market in bio-terrorism?"

Law shrugged off the joke. "Nah, man. That's just one of my specialties. But I feel like my education is going to waste, you know? Pushing papers isn't what I signed up for. I feel like I'm getting stupider every month."

Maxim nodded. He wasn't sure what to say.

"Hey, you got a degree?" asked Hendricks.

"Yeah. Criminology. What else?"

Hendricks chuckled. "I bet you always wanted to be a cop?"

"I guess I watched too much TV as a kid."

"Shit, we all did."

"What about you?" asked Maxim. "Why don't you apply to be a special agent?"

Law raised a single eyebrow and smirked. "Carry a gun? Why? So I could get shot at? Besides, it would mess up my suit." Maxim glanced at his gun belt. It wreaked havoc on his jacket lining.

The waitress returned and placed their mugs on the table. Maxim tasted his coffee. It was a little too hot but old and bitter. He supposed he had to put the sugar in himself. Only one packet was at their table so he leaned across to the other booth and grabbed all the sugar there. After he finished with it, he slid the caddy over to Hendricks.

"So look, Law. I got this Special Agent breathing down my neck for looking into a California gang. He's making it hard for me to do my job, you know? All I want is to solve these homicides."

"Garcia take over your case?"

Maxim sipped his coffee instead of admitting the embarrassing fact. But here, talking about it worked for him. "Something like that."

Hendricks nodded. This was something he understood. Being marginalized. "I get it, but I could lose my job for this."

The detective glanced around the diner and confirmed that no one was paying them any attention. Then he pulled an envelope from his jacket pocket and slid it to the other side of the table. Maxim knew that Law was in debt. Student loans, snazzy clothes, an expensive car—it didn't get paid by FBI wages. On their last phone call, there had been a sort of implicit agreement that Hendricks would only take the risk if he could benefit from it. While neither of them had outright said the word money, Maxim had a feeling it would do the job. Still, as the analyst peeked inside the envelope, Maxim felt anxious. What did Hendricks think of him?

What did Maxim think of himself?

"I don't even wanna know where you got that," said Law, slipping the money into his pocket.

"Just a slush fund. Nothing like you think."

Hendricks nodded and put his coffee cup to his lips. He

was delaying the inevitable. Maxim tried to be patient but the wait became excruciating. Besides, Law had already accepted the money. Just as Maxim was about to tell him to speed it up, Hendricks spoke.

"You were right about the hate crime stuff being bullshit. That's just a pretense."

"So what does he have working with the Mexicans?"

"I told you. He doesn't do the undercover work anymore. He got transferred to another division. And it's not Civil Rights. Garcia's been moved to Public Corruption."

Maxim furrowed his brow. "What is that? Politics?"

"A lot of it, yeah. But any city or state officials."

"You're saying he can put the screw to high-ranking government leaders?"

"If that's what you call arresting them."

Maxim grumbled. "But blackmail, coercion. Is there any evidence of that stuff?"

Hendricks narrowed his eyes. Either he was being purposely obtuse or Maxim was missing something. "What are you talking about?"

"Straight up. I'm investigating links between Agent Garcia and the Mexican Mafia. He did a lot of undercover work around them in Texas. A lot of border work. Maybe at some point he was turned. Now that he's in Public Corruption, is there anything to indicate that he's working the political angle for the Mexicans?"

"No, man. What I'm saying is that Raymond Garcia's been busting city officials for working with the gangs.

Mexican, American, Salvadoran—it don't matter. His history of working on the street gives him amazing insight into the life. Now he's taking them down from the top. Chopping off heads. He's been a thorn in all their sides."

Maxim almost choked on his last sip of coffee. "Wait, what? I thought I was gonna find out he was corrupt. That there was some sort of internal investigation on him."

"Nope," said Hendricks. "He's squeaky clean. He'd be all over us if he saw this little meeting."

The detective finished his coffee, letting the sludge of sugar at the bottom of his mug slide down his throat. It still tasted bitter. This whole situation was as bad as the coffee.

"We were just talking," said Maxim, sliding out of the booth.

"Yeah. About a high-ranking investigation. With an envelope of cash."

Maxim checked the windows. The streets beyond the blinds were clear. The diner was still mostly empty, and the few patrons inside were definitely not FBI.

"What's the matter?" asked Hendricks. "Relax." Maxim backed away from the table. "I could get in trouble for this too, you know."

"Thanks, Law."

Maxim rushed out of the diner, completely aware that he was acting erratically. Still, he wasn't worried about appearances. Amped by the shitty coffee, the detective didn't feel better until he was in his air-conditioned car and speeding north along the highway.

When he calmed down, he realized Lawrence Hendricks

wasn't setting him up. It was just intel. A straight trade. Otherwise, why would he bother telling Maxim that Garcia was in Public Corruption? Thinking back, Maxim felt a little silly for his behavior.

What he couldn't get past was the anger. He was sick of being called dirty, whether or not he bent the rules once in a while. He pulled out his cell phone and paused, staring at it.

Was it tapped?

He didn't care. If they were listening then he wanted them to hear. He wanted them to know that he knew. He sent the call.

"Sanctuary Marshal's Office. This is Marshal Boyd."

Maxim didn't even introduce himself. "Marshal. Agent Garcia's not who he says he is. He's not here with Civil Rights. He's in Public Corruption." The detective flicked his blinker on and passed a car one-handed.

"What are you talking about, Detective?"

"He's here to shut the Seventh Sons down—and the Sanctuary Marshal's Office with them."

Chapter 42

"I'm a failure," asserted Kayda, unable to look into the kind eyes of her grandfather. She leaned against his kitchen counter and stared at the floor until she heard his heavy sigh, then he turned back to his rabbit.

It was a fresh kill, skinned hours earlier. Her *pahmi* was preparing it for a stew. Greens, carrots, and roots simmered in a large pot. The blood of the animal was already included in the broth along with the bulk of the meat; the preparation was only waiting on the scraps and the bones. They were important but only as the finishing touch— according to her grandfather, the blood was the most important ingredient.

Pop.

Kayda watched with gruesome curiosity as her grandfather handled the rabbit on the counter, just a husk of what it once was, now in a state that wasn't quite animal or food. It was a sobering sight, but also comforting. This was something she had missed in New York. Wicasa's gnarled fingers broke the small joints apart deftly.

Pop.

It was disgusting. It wasn't civilized. Yet her nose could already detect the enticing scent of the blood stew. Like all things, she knew the result was more pleasant than the process.

"Failure is a strong word," said Wicasa, minding his preparation. "The rabbit is a terrified beast. Its entire life it hops from bush to bush, always fearful of the sky and the ground, always running to the safety of its warren at the slightest turn of breeze."

Pop.

Kayda almost rolled her eyes. She loved her *pahmi* but this wasn't the best time for one of his parables. She readjusted her stance and rubbed her sore side. Her rib hadn't improved over the course of the day.

"I don't want to hear about the hard life of the rabbit, *Pahmi*. I could've died out there."

Her grandfather nodded matter-of-factly. He understood her, took it in stride as if he expected it.

Pop.

Kayda considered telling him her suspicions, that Kelan had put Chuck Winston up to it, but she couldn't bear to impose any more on her family. She was sure it would break them apart for good, like so many bones of a rabbit.

"Unlike the rabbit, Wiha, you found your strength. It carried you, with help from the crow, did it not?"

"So I'm alive and the rabbit's dead. Is that your moral?"

The old man turned to her and smiled. "Of course there is a lesson in that. But this," he said, holding up the twisted leg of a rabbit, bone and meat ripped asunder, "this is not a failure. Even in death, the rabbit provides."

Kayda cocked her head as her *pahmi* casually tossed the leg into the pot. "Death serves a purpose." She frowned as she said the words. They were too vague to be meaningful, useless as a guide and easily misinterpreted. Her frustration became evident. "What purpose killed Carlos?"

Wicasa shot her a sideways glare, but instead of chiding her, the man remained silent.

"You're wrong, *Pahmi*. Death is meaningless. Crime, greed, ambition—they're everywhere. In New York, people die in accidents all the time. Or just from being in the wrong place. A girl in my class drowned in a diving pool. Death comes without reason. It's random."

Pop.

Her grandfather worked a little more in silence. Kayda soon regretted trampling his point. It felt as though she had bullied the old man. As if she was an imposition. A part of her screamed that she didn't belong, but she knew that was wrong. Everything was wrong. And she didn't know how to fix it.

"I saw his blood, *Pahmi*. I saw it across Keekee's neck. A neat slice flooding with blood. Then nothing."

Wicasa stopped fidgeting with the carcass. He dropped the remaining scraps into the stew and covered the lid. Then he moved gently to the dinette table. As he readied himself to sit, the old man's strength gave out and he collapsed into the chair. Kayda lurched ahead to catch him, but he was already safely in his seat.

"*Pahmi!* You must be careful."

The old man held her hand on his shoulder and smiled at her. Kayda allowed her worry to ease under her grandfather's beaming eyes. They were wet with emotion, but they were proud.

Of her.

"My Wiha," he said gently.

"Am I crazy?"

"You see what no one else can, but you do it without understanding."

Kayda sat down next to her *pahmi*. Something was wrong.

"What is it you most want?" he asked her.

The answer seemed obvious. "The truth."

The old man smiled patiently and shook his head. "No. That is not all. You want justice. You want a better way. Like the moon, you want to be a guide."

The girl knew her scrunched up face revealed her hesitance. "What could I do?" she asked, not expecting an answer. Not wanting one. "How could I help?"

For a minute, the only sound in the cozy kitchen was the simmering of the stew. That was just fine with Wihakayda. It reminded her of being a girl again. Sitting in the kitchen, playing with her hair, waiting for dinner. Except in those memories, her brothers were around, if not playing *with* her, then at least playing *around* her.

"The moon dies every month," said her grandfather.

"Her role in the night sky waxes and wanes until she is no more. But she also comes back to life every month. You can't see her immediately. You think she is lost. But she is stronger than ever. Stronger than she thinks."

Kayda studied her *pahmi*. She felt both stirred and foolish at the same time. How was it that this old man could instill such emotion in her?

"Tonight is a new moon," he continued. "A night for new beginnings. Changes. Not just for you, but for the whole tribe."

She looked into her elder's eyes, begging for answers. Pleading for comfort. "How can I help?" she asked. This time, she wanted to hear. To see. To understand.

"You can be more than you've ever dreamed, Wiha. You can mean more to the tribe than you've ever imagined." The old man's face took on a bold aspect, blood rushing to his cheeks. "In the desert, you discovered your strength. Now, you must find your will."

Chapter 43

Maxim sped up Interstate 17 towards Flagstaff. He was making good time but it would still be an hour before he reached the marshal's office. He was so busy worrying about what to say to Garcia and the marshal that he'd forgotten how late it was. It wasn't until the sun dipped behind the mountains that he realized his rant might need to wait until the next day.

Suddenly his car chimed as a call came through the Bluetooth connection. Maxim pressed the button on his steering wheel.

"What's up?"

"Maxim, it's Damian again. You asked me to look at that new boot print."

Maxim flicked his headlights on. "Is it a match?"

"Yes and no. The boot you made an impression of is by a company called US Patriot Tactical. They're a full service military retailer. It's an army boot."

"I know that, Damian," he answered gruffly. "I had the boot in my hands." Maxim knew his impatience was unfair. He hadn't bothered to look up the company. The army boot lined up. As he had told the marshal: the Yavapai see themselves as a military outfit.

"Of course," answered the tech meekly. "But that was important news to me, since the boot print in the blood wasn't complete enough to ID the make."

Maxim decided to ease off his aggravation. He took a moment and asked as nicely as he could. "So is it the same boot or not?"

"No, but it's the same exact *type* of boot. The imprint in the blood had an identifying scuff where one of the treads had been sheared in half. Your boot print did not indicate this damage. Additionally, your boot was a size eight. The print in the blood was much larger. Comparing the two, I think we're looking for an eleven."

Maxim slammed his hand on the edge of the steering wheel. "Perfect!" he said.

"I didn't think you'd be so excited about narrowing down the size and make of the boot."

"It's more than that, Damian. These suspects all run together. They all wear the same uniforms. It's just a matter of checking his known associates' boots. We'll tie one of them to the crime scene."

"But maybe not the murder."

Maxim shook his head. "One step at a time. Standing above the body is good enough, anyway. Look, I gotta call this in. Is that all?"

"For now. Anything else is just a matter of sitting in the queue. Unless you got something else for me?"

"Nope. Call it a day. Thanks for the extra effort."

"No problem."

He disconnected the call and immediately scrolled through his contacts to make another one. The operation was a little clunky through the Audi interface, but he much preferred that over the voice commands. Half the time they did the wrong thing.

Hitchens picked up after two rings. "If this is about Garcia, the marshal already gave me a heads-up."

"Oh, good. That'll save some time."

"How'd you dig that up, anyway?"

Maxim swerved into another lane. "I went down to Phoenix, but keep that to yourself." The sergeant laughed and Maxim realized that Hitchens wasn't with Garcia, otherwise he wouldn't be speaking so freely about him. "Where's Agent Garcia now?"

"He's FBI, Dwyer. He punches out before the sun sets. He's on his way back home."

"Really? How long ago?"

Hitchens calculated. "Fifteen minutes, tops. He left me here to follow up another lead."

"He has a hotel room in Flagstaff, right? Maybe I could beat him there."

"What in the hell do you want to do that for?"

Maxim smiled. The sergeant's cantankerous attitude always hid the best intentions. "Never mind. How did you guys do at the reservation?"

"I'm still down here. After we talked to Kelan and his sister and his grandfather, we've mostly been looking for some of the other troublemakers. We coordinated with Tribal PD, but if you ask me, they were dicking us around. The best way for them to help is to get out of the way. Know what I mean?"

"That's a given. Listen, Hitchens. I got a hit on the boot print in the clubhouse. It's a US Patriot Tactical boot. Same as the one Kelan wears, but not his. What we need to do is round up the mercenaries and find out who wears a size eleven."

"Shit," said the sergeant, suddenly realizing that his busy work on the reservation wasn't a waste of time. "Well that's easier said than done. It looks like three of Kelan's men have gone off the grid. Three. That number sound familiar?"

"The wolf masks. Two shooters and one driver."

"Exactly. I've been knocking on doors for the last two hours but haven't gotten eyes on them. Still have a few bars to check before I'm outta here, although from what you're saying, these guys aren't going to turn up."

"Yeah," agreed the detective.

"You got a warrant out on anybody?"

"I can advise but we don't have enough for a warrant. I'm not even positive that the others wear the same army boots. I'm just pretty sure."

"It sounds like the best lead we have to me."

"Yeah. What are the names of the associates?"

Hitchens took a second to gather his notes. "Okay, we've got a Hotah Shaw. He's Kelan's best friend."

"I know him."

"Okay. The other two are a younger generation. Small-time. Yas Harjo and Jim Bullard. All missing. You know, there's a new moon tonight. That means the MC and the Yavapai are gonna be MIA."

"I know. I don't ever lose track of the moon phases anymore."

Hitchens laughed. "I bet not. That also means I need to get outta here and go underground with Cole."

Maxim nodded to the speakers. The two officers usually aligned their days off with the moon phases, but many of the shifts were workable anyway. Even if Hitchens stayed on a little late tonight, he had several hours before he turned.

"Okay, Sergeant. I'll let you go. Watch your back and notify me if you get any word on them."

"Will do."

The call disconnected and the music came back on. It was a radio station that was losing its signal. Maxim sighed and reminded himself once again to download some music onto his phone. He listened to Johnny Cash between bouts of static until the dissonance grated on him and he shut it off altogether.

The silence wasn't any better. All Maxim could think about were the three Yavapai men on the run. Two of them he hadn't heard of before. New kids joining an old group with legacy baggage. It wasn't right for the sins of the fathers to be passed on like that.

For some reason, Maxim's thoughts turned to Diego. Here was a guy who was sensible, a little rash, but smart. He had been in government service. Like the Yavapai kids, he had also fallen in with the criminal element. Just two nights ago he'd been detained by NMPD. He'd trailed after the Pistolas when they cleared out of Sanctuary. Just like all the others, he was getting sucked under the wheels of brotherhood, an old steam engine, chugging along headstrong until the tracks ran out.

Maxim wondered if the same could be said of the marshal's office.

A foreboding sense of unease crept over Maxim. Diego had gone after the Pistolas. He was mad about Omar's death but new evidence pointed to the Yavapai. Maxim had to stop the man before he did something... rash.

He didn't know why, but he tried Diego's cell phone first. The biker never had it on him and Maxim was accustomed to leaving messages. Diego didn't much like computer technology or the thought of being tied down. The bike was a way to escape that. So was leaving his cell phone in his apartment. For somebody on the run from an old life, the sentiment made sense, but Maxim couldn't understand why he wouldn't keep a cheap phone in his pocket. Screw the data. Screw Facebook or the app of the day. But stay connected.

It was evident that Maxim and Diego had very different senses of responsibility.

Right as Maxim was about to end the call and try a different number, he was startled by Diego answering.

"What are you doing with your phone?" asked Maxim.

Diego chuckled. "The MC's closing ranks. We're safer

together so everybody's staying at the clubhouse. Figured I should at least keep my phone where I sleep."

"Oh good," said the detective, relief washing over him. "I thought you were going after the Pistolas. Listen. Sitting tight would be the best thing for you guys. I just got word from Hitchens down on the reservation. Three of Kelan's associates are missing."

"Hotah?"

"Yeah, and two others. They're the ones who shot up Clint. I have evidence that ties one of their boots to Omar. Get what I'm saying?"

"The Yavapai killed Omar?"

"Everything has been them. It always has been."

Diego didn't reply immediately, but the stunned silence didn't last very long. "That doesn't make sense. I *did* tail the Pistolas. I talked to their president. He as much as admitted they killed Omar."

"What?" Maxim thought about the scene, the small arms fire, about what he had already known. The Yavapai would have used their ACRs.

"The Pistolas were in the clubhouse looking for something."

"Looking for what?"

"It's not important," said Diego.

"The fuck it isn't."

"It's not, Maxim. It's just some leverage they need to displace the MC in the pipeline. Something they can hold over an Albuquerque city councilman. What's important is that they're the ones who were at the clubhouse. They shot up Omar."

Neither of the men said anything while they thought the puzzle over. Maxim had figured that Garcia had used the FBI to get NMPD to arrest the Sons. Now he realized it was the Pistolas. El Paso. Maxim's car hummed over the barren highway, speeding through the night. He knew he could beat Garcia to Flagstaff, but he needed to have the crimes sorted out before he knew how to approach the agent.

"Wait," said the detective. "This can still make sense. The boot print that the Yavapai mercenary left was after the blood had begun to dry. Our timeline works. Kayda saw the Pistolas riding south back to Cali that morning. That means four men were up there. They broke into the clubhouse and were surprised by Omar. They shot it out, got what they came for, and left Omar for dead."

"Except they don't know about wolves," finished Diego. "They've heard the rumors, but they don't believe. It's the only reason they would have entered the clubhouse so unprepared."

"Two of them got hurt as it was." Maxim still hadn't gotten hits on any hospitals. He'd only recently expanded the search to southern California. Somehow, he doubted they would find anything.

"So the Yavapai came later," concluded Diego, "looking for payback. The morning after they found Doka's skin on the reservation. Maybe they're working with the Pistolas or maybe it's coincidence. Either way, they were at the clubhouse and they know what silver bullets do to werewolves."

"It was a knife," said Maxim. "Someone stepped next to Omar's body after he'd been on the floor for a while. They stepped right in the pool of blood and stabbed him in the chest with silver. I'm sure of it. In fact, it has similarities to Doka's wound."

"You think it was my knife?"

Maxim thought about the year before. The biker had been attacked by a vicious wolf. It pounced on him, thinking he was unarmed, and had gotten stabbed in the lung for it. Doka scampered away and had been a ghost ever since, until two days ago when he'd been discovered hanging outside Sanctuary High.

"The Yavapai's fingerprints are all over Doka's homicide as well. They distracted Clint at Sycamore Lodge that night. Had the best chance to steal his skinning knife. I'm pretty sure Clint had an illegal firearm in his bag as well that was used to kill Doka. That's the revolver that was planted on Omar. It was all to make it look like the Seventh Sons were involved. But the silver knife works against them. Only people who had access to Doka would have had the knife. Only they would have been able to finish off Omar."

"You think the tribe killed their own man?" asked Diego. His voice was torn, as if the possibility of such a despicable act would never have occurred to him. "That's impossible. Kelan was his younger brother."

The detective remembered the fire in the young man's eyes the night at the casino. Kelan burned with helpless rage.

"Maybe Kelan doesn't know about it," offered Diego. "You didn't charge him for Clint, right? He's not on the run right now—the other three are. Maybe it's a coup."

Maxim paused as he took in Diego's words. "You're saying the Yavapai killed Carlos Doka without Kelan's knowledge?"

"Think about it. With Doka dead, Kelan becomes the de facto head of the mercenaries. What if they're gunning for him next? What if he was supposed to get shot up alongside Clint?"

Maxim did remember that Kelan had ducked away from the gunmen when the shooting started. "It sounds plausible," he finally admitted. "But there's something we're missing. Why now? After nine months, why is Doka killed now? Why tie it to the Seventh Sons?"

It didn't take Diego long to come up with the answer. "They're working with the Pistolas."

All things being equal, Maxim wouldn't have considered an agreement between the Pistolas and the Yavapai. The mercenary outfit was too small to rely on. More likely the Pistolas would just steamroll them along with the Sons. But the Yavapai did give them leverage. Perhaps the Pistolas didn't want to move into Arizona and needed small players to support them. Perhaps the Mexicans didn't care about Chino Valley and Prescott—nobody else did. Or maybe the Pistolas needed some deniability. The Yavapai and the Seventh Sons had a very public feud. Perhaps all this was a way to keep the cartel out of the news.

"That might explain the coincidence of the Yavapai

showing up at the clubhouse after Omar was left for dead," said Maxim. "Once the Pistolas told them what happened, Hotah and his guys had to clean up the mess."

"It also explains the safe house."

Maxim cocked his head as he lost Diego's train of thought. "What safe house?"

The biker sighed as he considered how much to say. "There's a building off the 89, between Paulden and Chino Valley. I followed the Pistolas there after they left Sanctuary. I wondered about them having a property in Arizona. It's on the edge of Indian territory—maybe the Yavapai own it."

"You got an address?"

"No. It's just out of Sycamore, sandwiched between a dry creek and a truck stop." Diego almost said something and then took on an excited tone. "I think it should be empty soon. The Pistolas will be preoccupied. If the Yavapai who killed Omar are hiding somewhere, it's a good start."

"Slow down," urged Maxim. "You said you were at this building. Did you see the Yavapai? Any sign of them?"

"No..."

"Don't go over there. Let me get a warrant. Backup."

"Do you have enough for a warrant?"

Maxim suddenly felt very aware that the new moon was tonight. With Hitchens and Cole gone, the marshal's office wouldn't be properly staffed. The FBI might be able to help with manpower, but things would take longer.

"We need to observe the location," Maxim finally said. "See what's going on there. Establish a pattern of business."

"Fuck that. They killed Omar."

"Goddamnit, Diego. I'm telling you to stay away from that property. This is a police investigation. You can't just run around with guns like an outlaw."

"Once these guys find out they're wanted, they'll be in the wind. That's if the police didn't stir up the reservation enough already."

"Just wait Diego. I'll be there tonight. Your whole club should be hiding out while they turn anyway. Don't try to do anything alone. Don't be reckless. Think about your sister, man."

Diego considered the appeal. He sounded subdued; he was so close to what he wanted but had to give it up. "Fine," was all he said. Then he hung up.

Maxim shook his head slowly and checked the time on the dashboard. Still a half hour to Flagstaff. There was plenty of time.

The detective wondered what Diego had meant about the building being empty soon, that the Pistolas would be preoccupied. There was likely some club business going down that Maxim wasn't privy to. Hopefully that business would keep them clear of the Yavapai.

But then Maxim thought about Diego's nature. He was a lone wolf, ironically the only member of the club who wasn't a wolf. He'd been mentoring Omar, helping the kid out. Maybe Diego had needed to feel like a big brother again after his sister had left town. With the kid dead, Diego was bound to be desperate. He had his brother's blood on his hands.

At that moment, Maxim realized that he and Diego didn't only differ in their senses of responsibility. They also had opposing ideas of duty. Of justice.

Diego de la Torre would kill a man for revenge.

The biker's hesitant agreement to stay away from the safe house didn't instill confidence in Maxim. Unfortunately, the detective was too far away to do anything about it personally. If Diego wanted to head to Yavapai territory, he could be there very soon.

Maxim made one last call.

"Hitchens, buddy, you driving north on the 89 now?"

"Sure am. The reservation was a bust. The boys are in hiding."

"Forget about that. There's a property I want to get eyes on. The Yavapai might show up there."

"Right now?" The sergeant became exasperated. "Maxim, you know I need to go 10-7. I can't be on the job anymore tonight. The moon's not gonna stop for this."

"It's not that. I'm afraid Diego's gonna ride south to do something stupid. You might cross paths on the highway. If you do, pull him over, take him into custody—whatever you can to protect him."

Hitchens sighed as a form of complaint. "If I do detain him, I'll need to transfer him to you."

"Yeah," said Maxim, beginning to relax. "I can do that."

"Okay, Detective. What if I don't see him?"

Maxim considered it. There was no way Diego would actually stay put. "Then head for the clubhouse. Pick him up if he's there."

"Fine, Dwyer, but that's about the limit of what I can do. Take my advice: sit on any leads you have. You know as well as I do that the best time to take these criminals down is in the early morning. In light of the new moon, they'll be sleeping it off extra late tomorrow."

It sounded sensible. "What about you, Barney?"

"Well, you're fucking with my beauty sleep, but Cole and I will be at the station first thing. 6 a.m. Call me if you need us sooner."

Maxim nodded. "Sounds like a plan."

Chapter 44

Several eight-by-ten photographs were arrayed across the pool table. They were images of Albuquerque City Councilman Eduardo Chavez. Despite the high quality of the physical prints, the source material didn't hold up. The pictures were grainy. The lighting varied from decent to horrible. They wouldn't win any photography awards, but they were still worth a lot, especially to Councilman Chavez —the pictures unambiguously presented the politician in a moment of weakness. Two prostitutes had alternated snapping photos of the councilman in various compromising positions, half naked and ignorant of their actions. This was in no small part made simple because of his inebriated state: the man was clearly smoking crack cocaine in two of the shots.

While the pictures would normally be humorous to the Seventh Sons, they stared at the pool table in a somber mood. Gaston knew it couldn't go unsaid, even if they all knew it.

"These are the reason Omar's dead. The Pistolas lured us away from the clubhouse so they could break in and steal our blackmail evidence. The kid fought back and the Mexicans panicked. They left the clubhouse without getting a chance to search it. Without getting these."

West Wind, Curtis, and Diego remained silent. They hadn't known the details of the MC's leverage until now. Gaston figured he owed them the explanation.

"Diego says Maxim has proof that the Yavapai finished Omar off. They're the ones who killed him, even though the Pistolas started it."

"Started, ended," said West coldly. "They both need to go down for their part."

Diego nodded, but Curtis remained deep in thought. Gaston knew he was the voice of reason. He usually didn't like it, but he wanted his input now.

"Curtis?"

The man kept his head down and rubbed his chin for a moment before answering. "It's not just the Yavapai and the Pistolas. What if El Paso's involved too?"

"So what?" asked Diego. "They're over there. We're here."

Curtis shook his head. "The point is, the Pistolas aren't just a bunch of Mexicali rejects. They're stronger than they look."

"So are we," said West.

"I'm just saying that we can't fight them both at once."

Gaston stopped them before it devolved into a pissing

match. "He's right. The Pistolas are pompous and will push around whoever they can, but they have connections we want to keep happy."

"They need to pay," said Diego.

"And they will. With their wallets. But the Pistolas are too important to El Paso now. If we attack the hand, the head will get angry."

Curtis nodded his support. "We don't need a third enemy."

"But El Paso is probably behind all of this," protested Diego.

Gaston nodded. It was a possibility. "But they haven't made a move against us yet. My guess is they know what the Pistolas are doing—maybe are even encouraging it—but they want to be kept isolated. They need us cooperative if this doesn't work out."

West grumbled. Diego's eyes shot to the floor. It wasn't a popular decision, but it needed to be made. Gaston was not about to take on the Mexican Mafia.

"And how can we work it out?" asked Curtis, apparently on board.

"That's the best part. When Diego talked to them, they gave us a way out. I'm gonna give them the leverage they want." Gaston began stacking the pictures together into a manila folder. "Sergio wanted to meet him solo in the closed diner off the 66. They said the bloodshed ends if they get these."

Curtis was cautious—he liked to play the percentages—and this point irked him. "No offense, Diego," he said, "but you walking into something like that alone isn't gonna work."

Diego didn't respond. Everybody knew that Diego wasn't as strong as the rest of them. "That's why Diego isn't doing the job," said Gaston. "I am."

"I'll get your back," said West.

"No. Sergio's supposed to make the meet personally. If he sees more than one person, he won't show."

"He might not show anyway," said Curtis, "since you're not Diego."

"That's true," admitted Gaston, "but he'll see I have this." He waved the manila folder in his hand. "Sergio wants this whether it's from me or Diego. He'll come inside."

"And if it's a trap?" asked West.

Gaston smiled back. He welcomed the challenge. "They won't be able to beat me during the moon phase. Those punks have no idea what we're capable of."

Now the Apache smiled too. If it came to blood, the MC couldn't lose tonight. It was clear West hoped they would start a fight.

"But what about Omar?" asked Diego with a scalding tone.

"You said it yourself. Hotah and his men killed him."

"But the Pistolas tried."

"And failed. Listen, Diego. I get the rage. I want to tear their heads off too, but I need to think about the future of the MC."

"You mean the bottom line, don't you? That's why you didn't want me going after the Pistolas back in Sanctuary.

They're your golden ticket."

"It's not like that," said Gaston, hackles rising. "What I said before still stands. The Yavapai are the enemy. They're the ones we need to take out. And we'd be able to look into it if you didn't tell your cop friend about that safe house."

Gaston was heated. The emotions that he'd been trying to hold in were coming out. He understood that Omar's death shook everybody up, especially Diego, but lately the man was questioning every one of his decisions. He'd been a solid member so far, but maybe it would be better if he did leave the club.

The president collected his temper and put his hands up to quell the protests. "I don't want any arguing about this. You did a great job finding the safe house, Diego, but the cops will be on top of it tonight. As we all know, the new moon means we need to lie low. The marshal's office has worked with the CDC before. They can do it again. Any major wolf activity will get us hunted. We can't afford that."

Everyone traded glances. It was frustrating for the club to have their power but not be able to use it. But staying alive was the priority. The CDC was the most dangerous to them.

"Now," continued Gaston, "we've got a few hours till we turn. We need to handle things perfectly. I'll meet Sergio by myself and get him to agree to terms with the peace offering. Curtis, Trent is still watching over Clint at the Flagstaff hospital. You need to go down and get him out of there. We can't have him turning in public. And we especially can't have any injured deputies or civilians, so be stealthy about it. Get back to the clubhouse if you can. Otherwise, just wait the night out in the wild."

Curtis nodded.

"What do you want me to do?" asked West.

"You and Diego should stay here. Hotah and his guys are MIA. Who knows? They might try to come at us right here. You should be ready for that. With any luck, Curtis will get back here with the others."

"The Yavapai are not going to come at us here," said Diego. "They never have, except when they knew Omar was alone and hurt. You just want us locked down."

"And is that a bad thing? I just explained why we need to stay hidden tonight."

"I'm not a wolf," Diego shot back. "I'm free to go out tonight. I told Maxim about the safe house because he's trying to catch killers. If I have a chance of getting to them before he does, then I'm going to take it."

"Don't be an idiot. It's dangerous out there."

West Wind shook his head. "Your balls drop all of a sudden?"

"You guys don't get it," said Diego. "It was never about the danger, it was about the reason. Omar's a pretty good one. I'm going out there."

Gaston just laughed. He couldn't believe what a pain in the ass Diego had become.

West's face darkened. "Diego, the cops are gonna be out there. I can't back you up."

The biker turned his back to them. "I never asked you to."

"You tied our hands with this," said Gaston. "The Sanctuary police have silver bullets."

"You're worried about getting shot?" he asked. "Welcome to my world."

The president clenched his jaw. "I don't want you getting shot either. Sitting it out is the smartest play."

"No way," said Diego. "I'm not selling Omar out for fatter pockets."

Gaston slammed his fists on the pool table. "You're full of shit, Diego!"

"No!" he yelled back. "This club is."

Diego moved to leave. Gaston stomped after him into the living room and spun him around.

"You son of a bitch. I'm the head of this MC and you're gonna listen to me."

Diego scoffed and peered at the others. "You call this a pack? I don't want any part of the Seventh Sons, then. You hear me? I'm out. The police aren't gonna stop me. This club's not going to stop me. Nothing can stop me until I get my hands on Omar's killer."

They watched as Diego stormed out of the clubhouse. The Triumph's engine came to life and Diego rode away. Gaston kicked over the coffee table.

Diego was going to get himself killed.

Chapter 45

Maxim Dwyer leaned against the dirty stucco of the second-floor breezeway. The motel wasn't fancy, but it wasn't one of those run-down pay-by-the-hour dives. It serviced Flagstaff tourists—campers and others who required short-term accommodations. A fireplace, a full kitchen, even a guest bathroom, if the detective's guess was correct. It wasn't so bad, really; Maxim had just figured that the FBI put up their people in nicer digs.

Between an alcove wall and a soda machine, the night shadows hid him pretty well, and he had a perfect view of Raymond Garcia's doorway. The rest was just waiting. A part of Maxim felt that he was wasting time with this confrontation. Another part of him didn't think the case could advance without it.

None of the speculation mattered anymore. Maxim watched the agent's white Ford Explorer park just below, its headlights briefly sweeping over him. The detective shied away from the night like a stalker.

Raymond Garcia exited his vehicle. He was alone. And just on time. As Hitchens had reported, the agent had clocked out and headed home. Maxim watched the man zip up his blue FBI jacket then reach into the SUV and grab a bag of Mexican fast food. He slammed the door with a sigh and headed up the outdoor staircase, walking and stopping at his door, just yards from the detective. Maxim waited until he heard the lock click open.

"You know, a bottle of red wine and a couple of wood logs would make this more romantic."

Garcia tensed but recognized the voice. When he turned around, he was slightly annoyed. "What are you doing here, Detective?"

"I'm working a case. What are you doing?"

Garcia stretched his neck and scanned the hallway and the parking lot. "Your car's not parked here and you're sneaking around the shadows. Not a recommended move with a federal agent."

"Relax, Garcia. I have some new information."

"You could have called."

"I put BOLOs out for your three missing Yavapai."

"You did what?" Garcia had taken his familiar authoritative tone. "You were ordered not to take action against those men. It's why I had you stay behind today."

"Why don't we go inside and talk about it."

"I don't think so, Detective. It's a nice night." Garcia let his room door partly close and stood against it, blocking entry. Again, he glanced around the area. They were alone.

"Say what you have to say."

Maxim nodded dismissively. Inside, outside—it didn't matter. Although he had already decided what he was going to say, something at the last second convinced him to soften the blow. Seeing Garcia alone in a motel room with his cheap tacos made him more relatable somehow.

"I appreciate the Bureau's interest in this case."

"Do you?" asked Garcia with scorn. "Because when I arrived yesterday you dismissed my presence as a joke. As interference."

"Let's just say that what little experience I've had with the feds hasn't been great. Sanctuary's a small town. Sycamore's mostly wild. There's usually no call for feds around here."

"This is *your* town, huh?"

Maxim bit his tongue. This wasn't going the way he'd expected. "Listen, last year, the Paradise Killings were orchestrated by a CDC agent. That part wasn't in the news —nobody needed the bad publicity—but it was true. So excuse me if I don't bend over backward for you."

Raymond Garcia studied the detective with a curious expression. Maxim could tell that he didn't want to believe the statement, but that he did. "What authority did the CDC have here?"

"It's a government secret." Maxim didn't elaborate. The last thing he needed was to be laughed at when he mentioned the wolves. Besides, it was sort of fun to play that card on an FBI agent.

Garcia's doubt returned, less adamant than before, but

he dropped the issue. "Whatever criminal actions may have occurred in the past, the FBI's a different agency. I'm a different agent."

Maxim narrowed his eyes. "You should have disclosed your relationship with the Pistolas."

Raymond Garcia opened his mouth, then paused and thought better of it. He was dumbstruck for a second, but the seasoned agent recovered well. "One moment," was all he said, then pushed inside his room.

That got him, thought Maxim. The detective moved to follow Garcia in. As he reached the door, however, the agent returned to the threshold, arms crossed over his chest. He had put his fast food away.

"I was undercover," said Garcia. "I know how Sergio's comments earlier could have appeared as proof of misconduct, but I was undercover."

"Were you? They knew you better than that."

"Sure," said the agent. "When you go that deep, you can't just bullshit your way in. You have to live it. Believe it. You need to relate to these guys to get them on your side."

"How is that different from my relationship with the Seventh Sons?"

Again, Garcia moved to answer immediately, then stopped himself. He didn't want to misspeak. Not now, when everything would be coming out. They both knew they would understand each other perfectly after tonight.

Maxim filled the silence. "It didn't bother them that you were a fed."

Garcia's strong brow furrowed. "Wait." He rubbed the

gray stubble along his chin as he thought another moment. "You think *I'm* dirty?"

The detective smiled. "It was my first thought."

The FBI agent laughed. "That's ridiculous. If anything..."

"What? If anything, I'm the dirty one? What exactly have I done that gives you that impression? I mean, fuck the rumors and the high school commentary in the *Noise*."

"The Bureau doesn't run operations based on local tabloids, Dwyer."

Maxim laughed and shook his head at the ridiculousness of the situation. "If you think I'm dirty then come right out and say it. Tell me why. This whole 'they say' and 'I'm on your side' shtick isn't winning me over. I've been straight with you. I'm trying to solve three murders. Whoever's responsible, whether white, Indian, or Mexican, is going down. I promise you that. The question is, are you gonna help me or get in my way?"

Garcia winced slightly. He took offense at being called an obstacle. That much was clear, but there was something else. Was it doubt?

"Detective," he said, "I'm here to assist the marshal's office due to the sensitivity of the crime. Any hindrance you believe I'm creating is imaginary."

Maxim Dwyer chuckled some more. It was sad. The man was going to make him come out and say it. "You know, while you were down at the reservation, I had some time to do some digging. You want me to trust you, believe you, but that's never gonna happen if you keep lying to me."

"Detective, what are you—"

"Public Corruption," Maxim asserted. "That's what you're working. The entire and only reason you're in Sycamore is to burn the marshal's office."

Agent Garcia stared at the detective in disbelief. There was a momentary panic before he decided what to do. An agent used to undercover work might've died before revealing the truth. But Garcia also knew that Maxim's information was specific and solid. Raymond's eyes softened.

"How'd you get that information?"

"It's my job," said Maxim coldly. "And I'm good at it."

Garcia shook his head. The man rubbed his eyes. It had been a long day and his face assumed a resigned expression. "Well that puts a crimp in this operation."

"No shit. But I'll make it easy for you. You want full disclosure? You've got it. I can tell you about anything you want except for CDC business. You'll need to request that from them."

"Okay, Detective. I'll bite. Let's start with the Seventh Sons. It's no secret that they bribe law enforcement throughout Arizona and the Southwest. The Sanctuary Marshal's Office is the closest department to them. Explain to me how you'd be uninvolved."

"I get it," said Maxim, smiling. "Cut off the head, watch the rest of the body squirm. The FBI wants to make an example out of Sanctuary. A warning to the others." Garcia nodded. "It's simple. The Sons don't conduct their illegal business within Sanctuary town limits. Our official jurisdiction is tiny. Coconino allows us to work in the Sycamore wild where it makes sense, but catching cases is different from making them. Stings need to be coordinated through them."

"So you're saying Coconino is dirty?"

"Not that I've discovered. It's a large county. Sycamore is mostly just campgrounds. The area is quiet. Largely ignored."

"Sycamore Lodge is in Sanctuary," he said, still doubting.

"It is, and operated by a former Seventh Son, but Gaston doesn't drive illicit goods through there. I've made that clear to him. We have an understanding that protects my town. And as far as drug trafficking is concerned, the marshal's office has standing orders from the CDC to leave the case to the feds."

"They don't have that authority."

"You'd be surprised. Besides, the DEA is following their recommendation. Any interstate commerce, and that's what it is, is out of my hands. I'd be surprised if County and Highway Patrol didn't have similar restrictions."

Again, the lines on Garcia's forehead deepened. This was much more than he'd expected to hear. Maxim wondered how the agent had been out of the loop regarding the standing orders, but it wasn't anything that was broadcast. If his operation wasn't clearly targeting the motorcycle club's drug trade, it might have been allowed to continue unnoticed.

"The truth is," finished Maxim, "all that is above my pay

grade. When it comes time for the Sons to go down, and it *will* happen, if the agency in control wants my assistance, I'll provide it. But I'm a sworn officer of Sanctuary. Protecting its citizens is my priority. And clocking out at the end of the day isn't an option if I have a possible lead that ties to two bodies."

That information, of course, took Garcia by surprise. "What do you have?"

"A boot print in Omar's blood matches the mercenary outfit. It's not Kelan's, but I'm guessing it belongs to one of our three missing associates."

A light breeze passed over the men. It energized the FBI agent. His eyes were suddenly electric. "I left your sergeant down there to follow up some leads."

"He didn't find them." Maxim paused and took another look at Garcia. They each had assumed the other was the bad guy, but maybe now they both had cause for second thoughts. "Then you'll help me?"

"Of course," said Raymond Garcia, shutting his motel door and checking the handle to make sure it was locked.

"What about your dinner?"

The agent shrugged. "Fast food's my guilty pleasure. It gives me heartburn anyway. You have a location?"

"One of the Sons followed the Pistolas to an old building between Sycamore and Chino Valley. He didn't see any Yavapai activity, but if they're on the run it stands to reason that they're there."

Garcia started marching to his car, all business. Maxim fell in line. "The Pistolas and the Yavapai," said Garcia with a tinge of disbelief. "What do they have in common?"

"An enemy," answered Maxim. "The theory is that they're working together. I don't know how deep it goes, but I've got a feeling that the mercenary outfit is making moves without Kelan's knowledge. They killed his brother. He may be in danger next."

"I'll put in a call to Tribal PD. Put a unit on him. He likely won't agree to be detained in protective custody again so it'll have to do." Garcia turned and looked up the steps at the detective before continuing. "What's your plan?"

Now it was Maxim's turn to be taken off guard. He didn't expect this much cooperation. "We'll need a warrant on the building. It's outside my jurisdiction, and not exactly friendly territory, so I could use your federal muscle."

Garcia smirked. "The Bureau's not gonna approve that without solid surveillance first. We don't operate like a small-town police force."

"I know the drill," said Maxim. "Manpower is going to be light tonight anyway. We need to ride and observe the location. Get the comings and goings on record. See what we're dealing with and hopefully set up a raid for the morning."

Raymond Garcia paused as he opened the door to his Explorer. Maxim swore he saw a smile on the man's face. "You're talking about pulling an all-nighter."

Something about the man's demeanor inspired Maxim with the confidence that he could be trusted. "I just wanna make sure nobody gets hurt."

Chapter 46

The Sycamore moon was hidden tonight. Diego knew exactly where it was, though. It had set with the sun, but it would be hours before the alignment was complete.

The biker had hunted wolves once, in a past life. The moon meant life and death to the wolves, as well as to him, the hunter. It was rife with paradoxes and dual meanings. The argent orb in the sky was both frightening and beautiful, massive and inconsequential. And tonight, as it began a new lunar cycle, the moon was both invisible yet ever present, like a god.

This occasion was anything but an official wolf hunt, however. This was for Omar. This was personal. Diego was here under no orders but his own obligation to a kid he had called a friend.

Another point that made Diego acutely aware that this wasn't an official operation was his complete lack of preparation. He didn't realize until he parked his Scrambler that his shotgun holster was empty, his beautiful M4 unfired and in the hands of a Mexi gangbanger. And unlike the old days, Diego even lacked his silver knife. If his guess was true, it would be in Hotah's possession, taken from a Carlos Doka too injured to fight back. Diego expected nothing less from Hotah; all the rumors he'd heard painted a portrait of a vicious criminal. It would be a trick to take the knife from him and kill him with it, but that was the biker's only play.

This time, quite alone, Diego needed no one else to tell him he was an idiot.

He scampered along the dry creek bed silently. It would have been ideal to do a full circle around the property, to survey who was inside, but the vegetation here was too sparse to make any other approach realistic.

Diego wasn't sure who he would find inside. He guessed that the Pistolas had only been planning to make a pit stop. Did the meet at the diner change that? Did a couple of the Mexicans head to Route 66 while the other two headed back to Cali? And the biggest question: Were the Yavapai hiding out here?

In truth, Diego was betting on a long shot. A last roll of the dice with all his money on the line. He tried to ignore the fact that he had always left Indian casinos with a hole in his pocket, but that was exactly the lure of gambling.

This time would be different.

This moment felt right.

If there was one thing Diego was an expert of, it was wolf behavior. Tonight, before the new moon, Hotah would look to seclude himself or make a move. With all the heat—the police, the FBI—the biker was banking on the mercenaries keeping a low profile. Something in his hunter instinct told him he was right.

Diego crept up to the wall and checked the yard. The scene of his close call today was empty. The biker vaulted the fence, as before, and set himself against the wall of the building. This time he wouldn't expose himself without knowing where the outlaws were.

The wilderness was silent tonight. There were no birds, no crickets, and thankfully no rattlesnakes. There wasn't any sign of people either. Diego wondered whether the Pistolas had gone through with the meet or seen through his lies and skipped town. But Diego had to have been at least moderately convincing. Otherwise, the president would have killed him. But maybe once Diego had discovered this place, they decided to clear out. It certainly appeared to be abandoned.

Diego decided to skirt the wall to the front. Just as he ducked a window, a light went on inside. He froze and glanced above his head. The window was covered with a shade on the inside. Thin paper had been taped over the opening—opaque, but translucent against the light.

Then he heard the muffled sounds of conversation. The words were too faint to make out, but there were at least two men inside. It sounded like they were hanging out in the back room. Diego decided to attempt entry from the front so he could sneak up on them.

Luckily, there was no foliage to crunch under his boots. The sand silenced his approach and Diego reached the cement porch without incident. A quick peek showed all clear, so he snuck around to the door. The lights in the front of the building weren't on, and his ear on the door didn't reveal any sounds within. Then another thought came to him. Diego moved to the other end of the porch and checked the dirt driveway that ran alongside the building. This was where the Pistolas had parked their bikes before. Now, it was all clear.

Diego began to have second thoughts as he returned to the door. At least two men were inside; it would have been nice if he wasn't alone. West might have been right next to him if Diego hadn't turned Maxim on to the safe house. Maybe that had been a mistake, but Diego was freely sharing information just as it was given to him. Second guessing himself wasn't a common thing for the biker to do. Besides, he trusted the detective completely.

The realization didn't make a one-man assault any easier.

Time to shit or get off the pot, thought Diego.

The biker slid his gloved hand over the doorknob and turned it. The door inched open silently and Diego slipped into the empty room. He was in a short hallway that led to a small lobby. An old couch with worn fabric rested against one wall. A small wooden table that was missing a leg lay toppled next to it. Flyers with the title "Chino Valley Visitor Center" were scattered on the floor, outdated and underappreciated. It looked like this had been a welcoming center at some point, but now he was only greeted with cobwebs and whatever furnishings weren't worth selling. Beer bottles, old and new, were strewn about the floor, evidence that this building was never fully abandoned.

Diego walked cautiously towards the back, stepping lightly over the cracked tiles. A room broke off the main hallway and led to another in the back, where the light came from. Once Diego turned the corner, the voices became clear.

"Hotah said to stay here, Yas."

Then back, complaining: "He treats us like we're useless."

Diego took a quick inventory of the room he was in. Cardboard boxes, empty cans of spray paint, and more beer bottles. He picked up an empty Budweiser and figured it would have to do.

"That's not true. You know we're not like them."

"'Cause they don't think we're tough enough to survive the disease."

Diego positioned himself against the opening to the adjoining room and allowed his eyes to adjust to the light. He saw the shadow of the one he figured was Yas, the one complaining, pacing the room.

"We don't even know what he's doing." Diego heard the sound of duct tape being pulled off the wall.

"Don't do that. We're supposed to keep the windows covered."

"This is the backyard, Jim. I just want to check."

Diego listened as the other man paced to the far wall. The biker figured it was worth a peek.

Two men, both Yavapai, peered through the back window, dressed in camouflage cargo pants and desert boots. They were the gunmen from the night before, without the wolf masks. Yas held a beer. Jim crossed his arms behind him. The men appeared a bit nervous, perhaps, but didn't have the anxious mannerisms that Diego would have expected. Wolves should be feeling the effects of the moon, but there was another hour yet—maybe they were still in control.

But what was it Jim had said? They weren't like Hotah?

It would make sense. After the deaths of Carlos and Skah the year before, the Seventh Sons were only aware of two living werewolves among the Yavapai ranks: Kelan Doka and Hotah Shaw. What if these two weren't infected yet?

As Diego studied them a little more, trying to come to a decision, Jim suddenly turned his head.

"Shit," said the Indian.

Yas turned to see what the alarm was. Diego burst forward into the room and lifted the beer bottle over his head. If neither of these men were wolves, then he was confident he could take them. As he prepared for the two men to charge him, he locked eyes with Jim—then the Yavapai glanced to his side. Diego noticed two black Remington assault rifles in the corner nearest him, the ACRs resting casually against the wall.

Everybody lunged at once. Diego flung the bottle of Budweiser at Yas and reached for the nearest gun. Jim leapt ahead to stop him. With a deft move, Diego scooped up the rifle and spun out of the way, shoving Jim into the wall. In a fraction of a second Jim recovered, turned, and rammed his skull straight into the butt of Diego's weapon.

Jim crumpled to the floor.

Yas was now halfway across the room making a beeline for the biker—he slid on his heels as the automatic weapon blasted several rounds over his head. Yas fell back and landed, sitting, on the floor.

All action ceased. Diego stood triumphant over Jim's unconscious body and held the rifle up, dead set on Yas.

"I know you were the ones that killed Omar," said the biker.

"Hey man, I just do what I'm told."

"Where's Hotah?" he demanded.

"I... I don't know. He said he was going out. It's almost the new moon."

"I know that, you piece of shit." Diego hadn't had a chance to look into Jim's eyes, but he had Yas' undivided attention. There was no eyeshine. No sign of the wolf.

"And the Pistolas?"

Yas squirmed uncomfortably. "Who?"

"I know you're working together." Diego raised the butt of his rifle threateningly and Yas put his hands up.

"Okay! Okay! They're not here. They don't need a place to hide. We just use this place to meet with them. It's lower key than the reservation."

"And where are they now?"

"I don't know. Cali, man. We don't want them here seeing the turn, and they don't want to hide out with fugitives."

Diego nodded. That made things much easier for him. "Where's my knife?"

No answer.

"Where's my silver knife?"

"It's in the portable," said Yas, relenting. "Out back."

The biker glanced out the small rip in the window covering. He'd remembered seeing the smaller buildings earlier. They were technically portables—trailer-like structures set on blocks—but they were full size with high ceilings, like a garage or workshop. He would need to check them out.

Diego was lucky Hotah wasn't here, too. If the biker could get the knife back, then he wouldn't be afraid even if the wolf did return. "Let's go get it then."

"Sure."

Yas got up slowly and started moving for the door. Diego checked Jim. He still appeared to be asleep.

"Wait," he commanded.

Diego grabbed the other Remington ACR and slung it over his shoulder. Then he paced to a vacant corner of the room and trained his sights on Yas. "Pull down the duct tape from the window. Tie him up. Legs at the knees and ankles. Wrists behind his back."

The Yavapai nodded and did as he was told. Diego hurried him along as much as he could, but it still took some time. The peace of mind was worth it. Finally, the biker shoved Yas out the back door.

"Slowly," said Diego, keeping a few steps behind the man. The night was silent, the yard abandoned. "Wait," he ordered again. Yas stopped and Diego hurried to check both sides of the main building again. No one there. No vehicles either. "Okay," he said, urging the man to keep going.

Across the backyard, past the scattered succulents that grew wild, the two additions looked like extended sheds. Diego had a hard time coming up with ideas for their use, but like the flyers inside, it was clear Chino Valley hadn't needed a visitor center for at least twenty years. Diego put the thought out of his mind and kept an eye out for trouble.

Boots in the sand, trudging slowly ahead.

"You know," said Diego, "the Pistolas aren't your friends. If they move in on Arizona, they'll strong-arm your tribe too."

Yas scoffed. "Not likely. That's the beauty of the Quad-City. Nobody wants it."

"So what, everybody wins except the Sons?"

"Sounds good to me."

"And what does Kelan think of your grand plans?"

No answer.

For some reason, Diego thought about Kayda. She had been genuinely concerned for her people, but how much did she really know them? The Sons did some bad things, but the Yavapai lent themselves out to the highest bidder. Thinking of it that way made it clear why the Pistolas didn't see the Indians as competition.

Diego felt he could see the whole picture, but parts of it were still blurry.

The two men passed the first portable on the left. It was built at the end of the driveway, along the yard's chain-link fence. Diego hopped up onto one of the concrete blocks supporting it and checked the dark window. He couldn't see anything inside. The lack of movement was a good thing.

"You know the chances of surviving rabies?" Diego asked, returning to the ground. "If you get bitten?"

Yas scoffed again. "I could fight it off. The resistance runs strong in the blood of our tribe."

Diego kept his rifle high. "Maybe, but I bet you know more Yavapai that have died than have made it through."

Yas didn't answer again. He continued walking to the second portable on the right, set against the back of the yard. He stopped when he reached the door and turned around. "We left your knife in here."

Diego nodded. He took another encompassing view of his surroundings. He glanced back at the main building. He climbed up and looked inside this portable. Everything was dead quiet.

"Okay," said the biker. "You walk in first."

Yas took both steps at once and opened the door.

"Slowly."

The man stepped ahead into the darkness. Diego filed in behind him. The ambient light didn't reveal much of the interior, but the smell hit him. The combination of rusted pennies and cleaning fluids. The smell of death and the ensuing cleanup job.

Diego scanned for his knife on a table and a counter but didn't see it. Then he ran his eyes over the contraption. Near the back of the small building was a heavy metal bar braced to the ceiling. Chains hung from it.

Yas, in the middle of the room, reached for a hanging light bulb.

"Stop."

It flicked on. Diego squinted against the light and instinctively backed up. His night vision was blown but he wasn't blinded. Yas was just standing there, watching him. Behind, under the metal chains, was a section of ripped away carpet, a large stain darkened the floor beneath.

This was where Carlos Doka had been killed.

As Diego went to move forward, he felt resistance. The strap of the ACR around his shoulder held him back like a seat belt during a collision. But then it ripped him backwards and off his feet. Diego flew out of the portable and landed hard on the cold ground.

He kept his grip on the assault rifle. As the biker raised his body to face the man that had flung him outside, he only had time to see Hotah's fist bearing down on his face.

A finger went for the trigger.

Diego was no match for the wolf strength, and he entered the blackness.

Chapter 47

Gaston paced back and forth in an unlit, defunct roadside diner that hadn't been used in years. It was a remnant from a different time, a quaint era when the world was made up of smaller roads and congenial people. Now it was just a lonely husk that did nothing more than announce the neighboring town to those who still drove on Route 66.

The big man had arrived early and alone. His bike was parked to the side, visible but out of the way. The Pistolas had curbed Omar's bike in a show of disrespect. Gaston hoped they would leave his alone. It shouldn't come to that, though. There wouldn't be trouble.

The sun was long gone. The Sycamore moon as well. The absence of the watching sentinels made for a dark night. Perfect for shady dealings.

Gaston kept telling himself that a deal was necessary, that he was doing the right thing.

He tried not to think about Omar. He tried to shut out

Diego's objections. Shit. The fool wouldn't even be a member of the club soon. Gaston needed to look out for those who wanted to stay. For those who still lived. A deal with the Pistolas was the only way he saw to make it work.

Gaston winced as he heard the single motorcycle pull up outside. All the rationalizing in the world didn't make him feel good about it, but there was no turning back now.

The big man quit his pacing and jumped up to sit on the bar, each of his black boots resting on a high chair, elbows on knees, fingers clasped together. He would get the Sons through this. Just as he did with the Paradise Killings. They were survivors. All wolves had to be.

As the door swung open, Gaston offered a measured smile.

Sergio Lima entered the dark restaurant. His crisp, bald head caught a distant streetlight and framed his face in darkness. He stood still for a moment until he placed his opponent, then approached.

"I guess ordering a *cerveza* is out of the question."

Gaston shook his head in response. Sergio was playing it cool. Trying to come off as a man in full control of the moment. "With the power shut off, the beer would be hot anyway."

Sergio Lima searched the alcoves of the diner warily, trying to peer into the shadows that surrounded him. "Good place for an ambush, *ése*." He smiled wide, white teeth dominating his face. The expression wasn't comforting. With the line of tattoos down his neck and shoulders, it reminded Gaston of the Day of the Dead festival. Sergio's was the never-ending grin of a skeleton, an affectation placed on what was already dead.

"Don't worry. This is about business. I'm here to deal."

Sergio raised his eyebrows. "Where's Diego?"

"He won't be going with you." The Pistolas president was not surprised. He was a kid who was street-smart beyond his years. "To be honest, he's not mine to give."

Gaston wasn't sure why he added that last part. He regretted mentioning it even more when it caught Sergio's attention. Disorder amongst his ranks wasn't something best advertised. This was a meeting of presidents. Of equals. Both were maneuvering. Both had to display power and cleverness, to one-up the other without offending. It was a delicate game.

"Where's my evidence?" asked Sergio.

The wolf smiled.

Gaston patted the manila folder that rested next to him. He swept it off the countertop and held it out to the kid. Sergio glanced behind him, still checking the place out. Gaston turned and saw the kitchen door on a swivel, a small window framing a decrepit workspace, already scavenged of anything of worth. Sergio eyed Gaston for a second longer before getting closer. When he grabbed the folder, he took a few steps back and opened it.

The Pistolas president flipped through the large color prints of Councilman Chavez. "Not a good resume for a mayor," he said. "But what's this paper shit? I want the digital copies."

"Keep going," said Gaston calmly.

Sergio paused as he felt a trap about to spring, but he eventually flipped to the last document. It was a photocopy of a driver's license. Sergio narrowed his eyes as he saw who the owner was. "What's this?"

"Armando Jimenez," answered the big man.

Sergio closed the folder slowly and lifted the back of his jacket. Gaston tensed, and Sergio showed him that there was no gun. He slid the folder into the back of his jeans for safekeeping. "Who the fuck is he?"

"Don't play stupid, Sergio. Not with me. He was one of your boys that shot up Omar."

The Pistolas president considered Gaston carefully, his cold eyes a mask yet all too easy to read.

"You underestimated us, Sergio. You were wrong thinking I don't have anyone in the Sanctuary Marshal's Office. Sure, he pretends he's not bought, but he is. And I know the details of the crime scene. They suggest Omar shot Armando. He was the one with the shotgun. Am I right?" Sergio Lima crossed his arms and lifted his chin. Gaston had his attention now. "I'm guessing you set us up to get arrested and planned on stealing those pictures from an empty clubhouse. But Omar was there, and he gave you more trouble than you expected. It was a mistake. A kid like you shouldn't have underestimated someone your age. He bit and scratched up one of your guys, but he tagged Armando real good, didn't he?

"You retreated south on your way back to the Imperial Valley. Almost made it home, but Armando was dying. You had to stop in Yuma, figuring that was close enough to

California. Shit, Yuma is practically Mexico. I'm sure you know it like the back of your hand. So you took Armando to a doctor with a business on the side and got him stitched up. The problem is, the Sons hear about everything that goes on in Arizona, even along the border."

Sergio had been listening intently, trying to gauge just how exposed he was. When Gaston was finished, he chuckled. "So what? You have a dirty doctor who stitched up a Mexican."

"His blood was at the crime scene, Sergio. The police have his DNA. One tip from me and he'll be arrested for Omar's murder, and who knows who he takes down with him."

Sergio's stiff posture became lax. He dropped his arms to his side but didn't say anything. Gaston leaned forward on his perch, taking on a friendly note.

"Those pictures in that folder are all copies," continued Gaston. "There's no such thing as originals anymore. Those digital files have been copied so many times it's impossible to undo. You'll never take away our leverage on Albuquerque."

The Pistolas president narrowed his eyes. "So what's all this for then?"

"It's a gesture of goodwill. The Seventh Sons are reasonable. We'll share Albuquerque with the Pistolas. You'll never get our leverage, but now you have it too. On top of that, we'll never tell the police about Armando Jimenez. You can let him recover in peace. It was the Yavapai that killed Omar anyway."

"That's bullshit, *ése*. They're taking credit for that?"

Gaston gritted his teeth. He blocked his dead brother from his mind. He hated doing this. It was betraying a friend, but it needed to be done. "I'm giving you an out, Sergio. The Pistolas didn't kill my man."

Wisely, the president didn't respond.

"That's what I'm offering you, Sergio. A partnership. Better terms. A piece of control of Albuquerque. And nothing ugly to upset El Paso. But we keep Arizona. The Seventh Sons stay in business."

Sergio nodded slowly. "And if anything happens to you..."

Gaston smiled. "It goes without saying that Armando will get picked up."

Sergio chuckled again. "I'm a lot of things, Gaston, but I'm no sucker. I never really thought this was as simple as Diego coming to our side. But I knew I had to hear you out. Now you expect me to believe that bygones will be bygones? That we'll just shake hands and put everything behind us?"

"I do," replied Gaston confidently. "But there's one more condition. You're right that my guys will only settle for blood, but it doesn't have to be yours."

"You want me to betray the Indians."

"I know you made a deal with them. But they're too weak. They can't help you in Arizona. Only the Sons can. You deliver them to us, give us justice, and then we can shake hands."

Chapter 48

Hollowside Way was on the western edge of the reservation. The last of the winding streets that braved the wild territory, it extended into the forested hills. The end of the street looped in on itself, sending drivers back the way they came, but there was a short offshoot for those who wanted to stay.

The taxi dropped Kayda Garnett off as soon as she saw her brother's red pickup truck. He often came here to turn. It was a place where one could be alone with the stars, away from the shine of civilization. It was a place where one could roam wild. Kelan knew it was a place where he wouldn't be bothered.

Kayda smirked. Apparently, Kelan had underestimated his pestering sister.

She approached the parked truck, wondering if he was still inside. He wouldn't be in his wolfskin yet. There was still plenty of time. When she reached the truck, however, it was empty. The windows were down. Kelan had left his cell phone and a pistol on the driver's seat.

She sighed. Boys and their toys that caused more trouble than they solved, especially given Kelan's short temper. At least he was smart enough to stay out of trouble tonight. And the phone explained why he hadn't answered her call.

The girl took in her surroundings, past the street, out into the rolling hills. The leaves of a thousand trees rustled in waves. She heard a faint car horn blare. It was muffled. The sounds of the city seemed so distant, even just ten minutes away. Kayda looked up at the stars and marveled at how bright they were. In that moment, she was a world away from New York.

Where was the girl that had gotten that Health Administration degree?

What would happen to her?

Wihakayda, the person she was right now, had to admit that she didn't know what she wanted. She could only say that the pull of family was much stronger than she had expected.

An alarm sounded behind her. No. A phone call. Kelan's phone rang and buzzed, crawling along the car seat and rubbing against the gun. Her brother was in demand tonight. But he was all hers.

Kayda was going to find him. Tell him to straighten up. Tell him that she could see the pain in Wicasa's eyes, the hurt he was causing his family. She could help him. She could help them both. Kayda could stay, if only her tribe would let her. If only her brother would accept her.

The sound of a car interrupted her search. The glow of the headlights was obvious before it turned the corner. She pressed against the pickup truck reflexively, not sure who else would know to come here. Then a blip, a flash of red and blue along with a half second of a siren, announced the police officer's arrival.

It was Chuck Winston.

Kayda ran to the front of Kelan's truck, keeping it between her and the cop. She hadn't confronted him yet for being left on the side of the highway. She wasn't sure what to tell him. She didn't know what to do about it.

Chuck parked his car in the middle of the asphalt loop and left his lights on.

"Kelan!" he called.

Kayda ducked.

Chuck muttered something under his breath and exited his cruiser, leaving the door open and the car running. He marched hurriedly to the truck, which Kayda hid behind. The officer saw the vehicle was empty, called out again, then made off into the wild.

He was only ten steps in when her brother answered.

"I'm here," he said, trudging up the hill. His somber face was especially calm tonight.

"I've been calling you."

The two men met halfway. Chuck began explaining something. It sounded urgent, but there was no need to yell anymore. Kayda couldn't make out the specifics of the conversation until her brother raised his voice.

"What? Right now?"

Chuck nodded and continued conveying his message. Kayda slid along the edge of the truck and stuck her head out as far as she dared, hoping to overhear them.

"I gotta go then," said her brother.

Chuck spoke more measuredly now. He said something about it not being smart. Kayda heard the word warrant. But her brother shook his head. She knew that stubborn look.

Kelan climbed the hill and headed for his car. He was pissed off, and his eyes shone red against the headlights of the police car.

Between his expression and the arrival of Chuck Winston, all of Kayda's previous confidence made a run for it.

She wanted to hide as Kelan jumped into his truck. Then she realized, if Kelan pulled away, she would be left alone with Chuck. That was the last thing she wanted. Not now. Not yet.

With Kelan's back turned, she sprang into the bed of his pickup. He hit reverse and pulled alongside the police car, then shot around the loop of Hollowside Way. The breeze battered coldly against Kayda. She squeezed beneath a tarp that was tied down. It flapped loudly in the wind, but she was out of sight.

Safe for now, she thought. Kayda gazed up at the dark sky and thought she could see a raven flying overhead. Lies. Truth. Kayda knew that bad things were ahead.

Despite his best attempts, Kelan was going to do something stupid tonight after all.

Chapter 49

"How'd you know we were working with the Yavapai?" asked Sergio. It wasn't meaningless banter anymore. Like a man who didn't want to make the same mistake twice, he truly wanted to know.

Gaston jumped down from the bar and smiled. He hadn't known—not for sure. The series of coordinated strikes between the two factions raised the possibility, and the safe house Diego found on the border of Chino Valley showed their hand, but it was still just a guess. Gaston didn't want to let the kid know that, though.

"Playing them, you mean," he said instead. "It was clever of you, stoking the fire that was between us, pitting us against the other. But it didn't work. There's a manhunt out for your friends as we speak. You picked the losing side. The weaker side."

Sergio Lima scoffed in the face of his failure. He found something funny. The thought aggravated Gaston. The big man was missing something, but he was still in control of this situation. The new moon was close. Right now, Gaston was nearly invincible.

"Strength is overrated, *ése*." The Pistolas president strutted toward Gaston with a sneer. "For instance, your boy, Omar, he was a tough son of a bitch. He knew how to take a bullet."

Gaston clenched his fists. He tried to swallow his anger but the juice was flowing. He could feel it spread through him, invigorating him. "Don't fucking talk about him."

"Or what? You'll sink this deal you're offering us? Don't you get it? El Paso doesn't want to share. *La Eme* is moving in on the Southwest. There's no room for *gringos* in this crowd."

Gaston's neck twitched. Any other time it could've well been the anger, but he knew it was something else. The turn was imminent. It clouded his brain. He worked his jaw open and closed to try to focus. His breath came out as a low rumble.

Sergio put his hands up and smiled. "*Calmate ése*. I'm just fronting." He retreated from the bigger man, towards the door, closer to safety. "But you see," he said, turning slowly, "I didn't finish my point. Omar was tough, but it didn't save him in the end. And your friend, Diego? I never believed that *chingazo* for a second. If he showed up here, I would've killed him. All you've done was trade your life for his."

Gaston began to laugh, a wide smile playing across his face. A part of him had wanted this. Business was one thing, but now, especially as his instincts began to take over, as the wolf came, revenge sounded much sweeter.

"You stupid mother—"

The next events happened quickly. The wolf was coming soon. Its looming arrival brought on a variety of tensions in the body. Tight muscles, tingling, some distortion in the hearing. It served to avert his focus, and too late did Gaston hear the squeak of the kitchen door swinging open behind him. He began to face the noise when he felt a thud against his back. A loud sound, a gunshot, simultaneous but more slowly realized, followed.

Gaston tumbled to his side as he attempted to dodge. His limbs splayed out on the floor, the maneuver nowhere near as graceful as he'd planned. His back opened up. Jagged spikes tugged at his nerves. Gaston tried to stand, but his lower extremities didn't cooperate. A strange numbness overtook him.

He turned and saw Hector Cruz emerge from the kitchen, holding Diego's silver shotgun. The man's mustache, usually obscuring his lips, couldn't hide his monstrous smile. Hector's bare chest looked like it had a new tattoo on it—a welt dead center—until Gaston realized that was where he had punched the gang member earlier.

Hector noticed what he was looking at. "You know how to throw a punch," he said, then held up his weapon. "I decided to bring something with even more punch than you." Hector returned his aim to the downed president.

Gaston growled.

"More strength," said Sergio, chuckling, heading to the door. "See what I mean? What does it give you, really?"

Gaston didn't say anything. He was surprised that the well-placed shot had downed him so easily. But it didn't burn. It hurt like hell but it didn't burn. That meant there wasn't silver in his bloodstream.

"And what about weakness?" continued Sergio gleefully. "You tell me not to partner with the Yavapai because they're weak. Don't you see? That's exactly why I *did* choose them. I don't want strength in Arizona. I want cooperation. Submission. Interstate 40 runs right through Sycamore, and the last thing I need is real competition."

Gaston grimaced at the two men, feeling the pain in his body disappear. Sergio motioned for Hector with his head.

"*Apurate*," he said, and left the diner.

Hector Cruz laughed. Gaston wanted to move, but he couldn't. He thought maybe he was in shock. The shotgun squared to his face, and Gaston turned away. Once again, he felt the blast before he heard it.

Chapter 50

The windows of the Ford Explorer were slightly cracked open. It was a rental car sitting in a highway rest stop; it didn't look suspicious by itself, but there was no sense keeping the engine on and drawing attention to the FBI agent and police detective within.

Both men had taken off their jackets and ties. They stared in silence at the property. The rest stop was a couple hundred yards to the south—not ideal, but it was the only place to park inconspicuously. The position afforded a decent enough view of the side of the building, but some of their visibility was blocked by an errant roadside billboard.

Maxim grabbed Raymond Garcia's binoculars. "Is this the best view we can get?"

"It's good enough," replied the agent. "We can see if anyone comes and goes from the highway. We can see the front and back doors of the main building."

Maxim nodded but wasn't as confident. The windows of the safe house were covered from the inside. The portable in the back blocked the view of the yard and the other building. A truck in the driveway obscured some sight lines too. But with the north wall along the dry creek, their current vantage point was the only one.

"Can't tell what the building is. It's not a residence."

Garcia was on his laptop stealing Wi-Fi from the empty food court. "Maybe a shut-down water treatment plant or something?"

Maxim lowered the binoculars. "That creek has been dry as long as I've lived in Sanctuary."

Garcia shrugged but kept his attention on his computer. His face glowed blue. "How long has that been?"

"Thirteen years."

Garcia raised his eyebrows. "Here it is. I was partially right. The Yavapai don't own this property, and neither do the Pistolas."

"Who does?"

"The city. We should've known by the crap condition it's in." Maxim chuckled and handed Garcia the binoculars. "It says here the building was a visitor center. Chino Valley was the first capital of Arizona Territory, before it was Chino Valley anyway. When the town was founded after Interstate 40 came through, they had the idea that it would be a tourist attraction."

"I'm guessing that didn't really work out."

Garcia shook his head and put the laptop aside to continue the binocular surveillance.

"We can't read the plate number on that truck from here. It might be visible from the road."

"No," said Maxim. "I was watching the property as we passed. That driveway snakes around the building. You'd need to walk right up to the front door to see it. Maybe one of us should hike out there and get a closer look?"

"Not yet. Let's make sure there's no movement before we expose ourselves. Remember, there's no rush. We're not moving tonight."

Maxim nodded in agreement. If that truck belonged to Hotah they would have immediate cause to go inside, but they were gonna wait till the morning regardless. Smarter to play it safe.

"Well, we've only been here a few minutes," said Garcia, "but I don't see any activity at all. Were you expecting something different?"

"I don't know," acknowledged Maxim. "Proof that the Pistolas are working with the Yavapai."

Garcia smirked. "We could get them on trespassing."

"We'll see something. Waiting is the job."

Garcia nodded absently as he watched the property. "Man, I haven't been on a stakeout like this in a long time."

Maxim could imagine. Raymond Garcia had usually been on the other side of busts. He was never the guy waiting in the van with a rifle. He was the one inside the drug nest. Right next to the criminals. One of them.

The detective marveled at how his outlook of the man had changed over the course of the day. He couldn't say he trusted him yet, and he was sure the feeling was mutual, but he seemed to be a straight shooter.

"Tell me," said the agent. "Is this how you usually work?

One of your non-official CIs gives you a tip?"

"It's a small town," answered Maxim. "Knowing people is everything."

Raymond nodded as if he understood. "Thirteen years in Sanctuary, huh? What brought that about?"

Maxim's mood began to drop. "I moved here with my wife. She was born in Sanctuary. We met in school. I wanted to be a cop and they had an opening."

"The perfect storm."

"Yeah."

Garcia didn't notice that Maxim wasn't keen on the subject. "I have a wife. Maybe when this is done the four of us could get together for dinner or something."

The detective grimaced. "She's dead."

"Oh shit," he said, slapping his leg. "I read that somewhere. Sorry about that."

Maxim shook his head to show it wasn't important. The misstep created a lull in the conversation, but Garcia was determined to pass the time.

"So why stay? In Sanctuary, I mean. The Paradise Killings made your career. Go federal. Go to Phoenix or LA. Why stay in a small town with no family? To be completely honest, I figured one of the reasons you didn't move on was because you were getting kickbacks from the motorcycle club." Maxim turned to him with a look of disapproval. "Look, when a small-town detective is driving around in an Audi, a Public Corruption agent needs to take note."

"It's only a TT. I really wanted an R8."

"Shit. If I'd seen you driving that around, you'd already be in jail."

Maxim laughed. It felt good to change the subject at least. "Don't you get tired of busting cops?"

The FBI agent turned to the detective. "You can't just think of me as the federal version of IA. It's not usually the police I go after. Corrupt government officials are destroying this country. Governors, mayors, councilmen—even Congressmen. There are so many hands in so many pockets it's impossible to wipe it out. These guys enable gangs. They perpetuate violence without even thinking about it. Because of their ties to this country's infrastructure, some of them are a bigger threat than the drug lords I used to go after."

Maxim was impressed. "I get it. I'm just giving you a hard time, Garcia."

"Call me Ray, Maxim. Look, you seem like a good guy. You wanna put the right people in prison. But you're close to some of the Seventh Sons. To Diego. Once you let people like that get their hooks into you, you're done. Not immediately, but surely. It's like quicksand. It may take time, but you'll sink."

That little speech drew a longer silence than the mention of Maxim's wife. Part of it was because Maxim knew Garcia —Ray—was right. The agent had lived and breathed corruption. He knew it started small. Even Maxim was pissed about Diego's proximity to the club. Working with them, within the law, was one thing, but when you got so close to something it was in your face, it became hard to see the line.

They stared at the peaceful buildings for a while longer. Nothing moved out there, but Maxim knew Diego wouldn't steer him wrong. He was a man of mixed morals, but he was loyal. Solid. Their friendship wasn't a sign of Maxim's propensity for crime; it was proof that there was still enough in Sanctuary worth saving.

"You asked me why I didn't pick up and go last year," he said suddenly. "Why I'm still a small-town detective. The answer is roots, man. Sometimes they dig deep into you."

Again Garcia nodded, turning over the detective's words in his head. Something resonated with him. It brought a calm to them until Maxim's phone rang.

"Yup."

"I can't find him," said Hitchens.

"Diego? He's not at the clubhouse?"

"No one is. The Sons are all gone."

"Shit." Garcia turned towards his alarm and Maxim waved him off. Vigilante justice, werewolves—he didn't even know how to begin to explain what could be going down.

"Sorry Maxim," said Hitchens, his voice urgent. "My time's up. I've got to disappear for the night. If the MC is smart, they'll do the same. Make sure you don't make a move tonight. Just observe. We'll back you up first thing in the morning."

Maxim ended the call. His nerves were kicking in. He could feel it.

Somehow, he knew the peace wouldn't last the night.

Chapter 51

Lying in the bed of the pickup truck, Kayda felt like an idiot.

She didn't know what had gotten into her. One minute she felt like a complete failure, then a pep talk from her grandfather turned everything around.

Part of it, she told herself, was that she had started feeling better physically. Her scratched skin, her sore ankle, even her rib no longer caused her pain. "Blood fortifies the body," her *pahmi* had told her. "The strength of one becomes the strength of another." She had nodded and humored him, but now she wondered if she had taken his words too lightly.

Was the rabbit blood really that efficacious? It had energized not just her body but her spirit. All of a sudden she had been invincible again. With purpose.

The decision to confront her brother had been straightforward enough. But indecision and second-guessing had caused her to lie hidden, unannounced, for a thirty-minute drive. The exposure to the elements had shaken her resolve. Even after Kelan had parked, Kayda remained under the tarp. Waiting.

For what, she didn't know.

Now the time ticked away and she had no clue where she was or what Kelan was doing. At one point she'd heard some voices but everything had gone quiet.

How long had it been? Ten minutes? Twenty? And somehow, the longer she stayed still, the harder it was to move.

A small sound, a pitter, perked her ears. It was as if a single raindrop hit the tarp, not loud but magnified by its proximity. There weren't any clouds in the sky. It was a dry summer. It couldn't be raining now.

Another drop. Then another. The mystery distracted Kayda just enough for her to pull the covering away.

She saw a large raven sitting on the wall of the pickup bed. Its beak pecked urgently at the plastic tarp.

"Oh my God," she said. The bird was huge up close. Its black feathers shimmered in the starlight. Its feet and beak were rugged and dull, each ending in pronounced edges. The raven blinked, and Kayda looked deep into its ball of an eye, a black hole caught inside a marble, and she saw herself.

Without warning, the raven took to the sky. Kayda could feel the waves of air against her face with each flap, and she understood. Truth and lies came from within. It was up to her to choose. It was up to her to see.

Kayda Garnett lifted her head and surveyed her

surroundings. The pickup was parked next to a few structures, but she had never been here before. It was quiet, but she knew the highway was close. She could hear the occasional car speed past.

She lay back down and gazed into the sky. The bird was gone, but a single black feather fluttered down, reminding her of her conviction.

Chapter 52

Drip.

There wasn't any light. Not yet. Diego didn't dare open his eyes.

The first step was simply to be aware.

It wasn't a conscious decision. It had just happened. One minute, the biker was blissfully asleep. The next: awareness and pain.

Consciousness was overrated.

His neck was stiff. There was a throbbing in his head, a build-up of pressure. Something wasn't right. Something was out of balance. Diego felt like he was floating, but not the kind of blissful, weightless floating of space. This was hard on his body, as if he were deep underwater and reacting to the pressure.

He tried to breathe slowly and regain his faculties. He remembered marching Yas to the back of the property. Getting ambushed by Hotah. He had been captured, but not killed.

Drip.

There it was again. That sound. So close to him.

Diego de la Torre opened his eyes.

The brightness hurt. For a moment, it was blinding, but then he realized it just enhanced the pulsing in his brain. He had been knocked out, by a wolf, no less. A direct strike to the skull. He probably had a concussion, or worse.

The strain on his head intensified. Diego tried to move, to ease the tension with his hands, but he was stuck. Bound, somehow, but free. A wiggle of his arms set his whole body in motion, a sickening swim that made him nauseous.

Stop moving, he thought. Stop.

Drip.

The sound. Above him. Diego's eyes refocused. On the ceiling above his head, he saw a swath of red. He thought of Omar. The boot print. He was looking at a pool of blood, only this time, it was his.

Flaunting the physical order of the universe, a drop of blood escaped Diego's head and flew straight up into the air, towards the ceiling. Towards the slowly building pool.

Drip.

The biker jerked away from the unnatural sight. His entire body swayed again.

The room wasn't that dark, actually. He'd just been disoriented. And the laws of physics were working just fine.

Diego de la Torre was upside down.

He was in the portable. Yas and Jim stood by the other wall, just noticing he was awake.

Shit, thought Diego, I shouldn't have moved.

He looked to his feet. He was hanging from the chains on the ceiling, each foot attached to a horizontal iron bar. His hands were tied behind his back with something. Not metal. Not plastic.

Below him, a square was cut out of the carpet, presumably to make his collecting blood easier to clean.

"Nice of you to join us," said Hotah. Upside down and lit by a single incandescent bulb, the man was terrifying. He wasn't tall but he was squat and built of muscle. He wasn't wearing a shirt; the only decoration over his hard muscles were two necklaces of bone that hung around his neck. His hair was wild, dirt-stained and uneven, and fell over his cheeks. Gray eyes stared passively behind a mask of black and gray face paint. He was a wolf, and he was dressed for war.

Diego tried wiggling his hands behind his back. There was some give in his bindings.

"You know," Hotah said, "the Pistolas tried to push us around first. We're closer to the Imperial Valley. To them. But they don't want Chino Valley. The reservation isn't as easy for them to maneuver in. So we told them that we would help take out the Sons. A good deal for both of us."

Drip.

Diego winced at the sound. It must have been a small cut. Head wounds bled a lot, especially when upside down.

"How long do you think that's gonna last, asshole? You're a bunch of mercenaries, selling yourselves to the highest bidder."

Hotah smiled. Diego's orientation started to spin Hotah out of sight, but the Yavapai placed a solid arm on the biker's leg to steady him. Diego stopped with the three men ahead of him.

"They can't take on the whole reservation. The tribe follows us. The casino supports the entire town of Prescott. We're too much of an institution to displace. We may not control the most fruitful land, but we're kings of our desert. Can the Seventh Sons say the same? Sure, your MC has contacts—governments, police, gangs—but you're just a leech on everyone else. You take. You don't create prosperity. Nobody will mourn the passing of the Seventh Sons."

"The police are on to you," said Diego. "They know you were the gunmen that attacked Clint. They know you killed Omar."

Hotah narrowed his eyes and shot a glance behind Diego. The biker twisted his head, trying to see the other side of the room. The angle was bad.

"There's no evidence of that," asserted Hotah. "What they know and what they can prove are two different things."

"Says the fugitive hiding in the desert."

Again Hotah glanced behind Diego. "It's just for questioning," he said, but his voice had lost its confidence.

Then Diego heard footsteps. A fourth person was in the room. The man came around into view.

"You."

Chapter 53

The car door opened. Maxim flinched. He lowered the binoculars as the interior light glared. He had been so focused on the stakeout that the sudden movement had caught him off guard. Maxim glanced across the driver's seat and saw Raymond Garcia returning, holding a couple of fast food bags. The agent tossed one his way.

"I hope cheese works for you."

The detective examined the contents. A burger wrapped loosely in paper rested on top of a box of fries. Something yellow dripped from the sandwich, but Maxim doubted it was cheese. As Garcia sat down, he placed two sodas in the cupholders.

"Anything?" he asked.

Maxim shook his head and took a bite of the burger. It was greasy. Too much mayo. The bun was soggy. For some reason, it was delicious.

"You know, this stuff will kill you," mumbled Maxim

through a mouthful of food.

"That's what guilty pleasures do. Don't tell me you never eat fast food?"

"Hey, I may live alone but that doesn't mean I can't cook." Maxim shoveled some fries into his mouth. They were good but a little too salty.

"How's a homicide detective find time for that?"

"Benefits of a small town, I guess." Maxim wasn't really just a homicide detective. He investigated all of Sanctuary's big cases. When he was busy, like the last few days, he would sometimes forget to eat. But that wasn't the usual routine. "Most of my work can wait till the morning, you know?"

Garcia didn't answer while he bit into an onion ring. While half the crust remained in his hand, the entire onion slid out and burned his lip. He doused the pain with soda, checked the binoculars, and then returned them to the dash.

They ate the rest of their meals in silence. After half the burger, Maxim's stomach caught on to the quality of the meal. He crumpled the sandwich in the paper and abandoned it in the bag, settling for the fries instead. Garcia had already scarfed everything down and was back to the stakeout.

"I think you're right about waiting until the morning," he said. "It's almost two. Nothing's gonna happen tonight."

Maxim grunted in agreement. He began to consider the possibility of a nap when, right next to his head, something hit the window.

It was a loud rap. Both men flinched away from the

sound. A large black blur fluttered in their vision and dropped to the ground.

The window was open a crack to let in the cool air, but nothing had come inside. The glass had held. In an instant, Maxim leaned against it and peered down. A raven stood on the asphalt holding its wings spread.

"A bird flew into the window."

"You're kidding me," said Garcia, leaning over the detective to get a look.

The raven didn't appear to be hurt. It eyed them cautiously, showing its feathers.

Raymond moved back to his seat and shook his head. "Looks like some kind of mating display."

Maxim laughed nervously. "Maybe he's hungry." He stuck a french fry through the thin opening in the window and dropped it to the floor. The bird cocked its head a few times, picked up the fry, and bounded with it to the edge of the lot until it was partially hidden in the shadow of a bush. It only took a couple of bites before spitting it out.

"Even he won't eat this stuff."

"What is that?" asked Raymond.

"It's just—" Maxim stopped when he realized Raymond wasn't talking about the raven. He had his binoculars up again, watching the building. "What is what?"

Raymond studied the scene before answering. "I don't know. I thought I saw someone pull something from the back of the truck."

Maxim immediately went to alert. He scanned the yard but it was too far to make anything out. "The bed of the pickup?"

Garcia nodded. "Yep. I thought someone was back there. But I don't see anything now."

The detective furrowed his brow. The thought that they had missed something was unsettling. Maxim glanced at the bush. The raven was gone. Only the french fry remained. He turned around and surveyed the street and the sky. Nothing was amiss.

"What if there's no one in the main building?" asked Raymond. "We're covering the front and back doors. We can see the truck and the yard. But we don't have a good view of those buildings in the rear."

"You think someone's in the back. They came out and got something from the truck and went back in?"

"I don't know that they grabbed anything. Nothing big, anyway. The movement was quick and small."

Maxim took his turn with the binoculars and examined the red truck. It appeared undisturbed. "Could've been a raven," he said with a smirk. He leaned back in his seat, watching. The thought of something developing completely dominated Maxim's attention. No more thoughts of sleep. No more munchies. He was wired. Sharp.

And luckily, it didn't take very long to see something.

The yard, what was visible of it anyway, was lined with a cinder block wall on the far side. A figure scaled it and breached the backyard.

"Someone's there," he said.

The figure ducked against the wall and turned his head both ways. He was a big man. An Indian. It was—

"Shit," said Maxim.

"What is it?" Garcia waved his hands impatiently and Maxim passed the binoculars over.

"It's West Wind," said the detective.

Raymond Garcia turned and stared at the detective. "A Seventh Son."

Maxim's stomach turned, and it wasn't the fast food. He'd sworn to the agent that the Sons weren't involved. That they weren't the enemy. West was the newest member of the club and Maxim didn't know him that well. And here he was, fucking everything up.

"He doesn't appear to be armed, but I can't tell for sure." Garcia opened the car door.

"What are you doing?"

"We need to go in there," asserted Raymond. "Either the Yavapai or the Pistolas are inside. The presence of the Seventh Sons is trouble." The man stood outside the Explorer and checked the binoculars again. "It's a bit of a walk, but it's better than alerting anyone to our presence. I say we just hoof it along the street." Garcia slammed the door.

Maxim exited the vehicle, if only to keep up with the FBI agent. He had second thoughts about what they were doing, but he knew Garcia was right. "Backup will take a while."

Garcia nodded and passed a spare bulletproof vest to Maxim as he donned his own. "Call it in. We've got to move."

The detective peered into the night sky, wondering where the moon was hidden. "It's dangerous, Ray..."

The man pulled his dark blue jacket from the back seat and put it on, yellow FBI lettering leaving no room for compromise. "It can't be helped."

Maxim checked the spare magazine on his belt. The one reserved for special occasions. "These things... They're animals."

"I've seen worse." Garcia took a few steps toward the highway and turned back with a solemn expression. "This is it, Maxim. Time you see who the Seventh Sons really are. Time you find out what you're made of."

As the man stormed towards the old building, Maxim couldn't help but feel some admiration. And guilt.

Chapter 54

Kelan was taller than his best friend but skinnier and less imposing. The three Yavapai men smiled as they listened to him speak calmly.

"Chuck said no arrest warrants have been issued. They're just looking for us. Tribal PD will be involved with whatever case they're building. We can contain whatever evidence they have."

The words only relaxed Hotah on the surface. Diego could see the lingering worry under the skin. The man walked away and peeked out a window, although the view of the street was blocked from there.

"Kelan," exclaimed Diego, confused. "You were supposed to be at the reservation."

He smiled. "That was the plan, but once Hotah captured you, he gave me a call. He knew I couldn't pass this up."

"You don't know what you're doing."

"Don't worry. I made sure I wasn't followed. It's just us,

here."

Diego glanced at the other Yavapai. Hotah moved to the other end of the room to check another window. Diego worked at freeing his wrists.

"No," he whispered. "You don't understand."

Hotah called out. "I'm gonna check outside again."

Kelan turned his head. "Don't go to the front. They'll be looking for you up and down this highway."

"I'm not an idiot," he grumbled, and walked out.

Kelan turned back to his prisoner. Yas and Jim were across the room, behind him, but watching Hotah through the window. Diego took this as his opportunity. "Look, your sister says you're a good guy."

"Don't mention Kayda," he warned.

Drip.

"Fine. But this," said Diego, waving around with his face, "this whole thing—it's not just about getting back at the Sons."

Kelan scoffed suspiciously and kneeled next to the suspended man. "Meaning?"

"Think about it. Your brother, Carlos, led the mercenaries. Now that he's dead, you're the man. You should be in control."

"I am."

"Then stop the bloodshed. Prove your guys aren't running wild."

"My guys follow my lead."

"They're making moves behind your back."

Kelan just laughed. "This is a pretty desperate ploy to

save yourself. You're gonna be my friend now?"

"You need all you can get. You think Hotah's your buddy? What if he wants to lead? If he takes you out next, who's in charge?"

The Yavapai momentarily glanced at Yas and Jim and then looked back at Diego.

"Kelan, the Seventh Sons didn't start this war. We didn't kill Doka, I swear to you. It was Hotah and *his* guys. They murdered your brother. Tried to kill you when they attacked the Lodge. I'm telling you, they're coming for you next."

Kelan didn't know what to say for a minute. They both turned as the door swung open. Hotah returned with a red twinkle in his eye. "Nothing out there, Kel." The Yavapai nodded and waved Hotah over. He kneeled down too, so everybody was on the same level.

"This dumb son of a bitch thinks you want to kill me." Hotah pulled his head back in surprise and Kelan turned away from his friend, back to Diego. "A year ago, our outfit was running well. A new casino was being built, Carlos had managed a deal with Deborah to do the dirty work of your MC. It was stuff Gaston and your guys couldn't know about. They didn't have the stomach for it." The Yavapai shook his head wistfully. "There was a market for our services. We were profiting. And you and that cop shut it all down."

Kelan glanced at his boys. "Detective Dwyer killed Skah. He's gonna pay for that. If we ever find Nithya or your sister, they're getting it too."

Kelan extended an empty palm to his friend. "Give me

the knife." Hotah observed the two men and reached for a sheath on his thigh that the biker hadn't noticed before. He slid out a long silver knife, Diego's knife, and extended it to his friend. He placed it in Kelan's hand.

"But you," continued Kelan, fingering the grip, red eyes burning into Diego, "you stuck this knife into my brother's chest."

He suddenly stood up and stepped away. Kelan brought the knife down hard towards the biker. Diego pulled against his bindings and tried to wiggle away. The blade pierced the floor a few feet from Diego's face. He stared at the knife embedded in the exposed flooring as Kelan watched in glee.

"I want to kill you most of all, Diego de la Torre. You didn't kill my brother. Even worse. You made *me* kill him."

The biker tensed as the man became more frenzied. Saliva spit from his lips. The moon was close.

"Carlos became weak. He was a shell of his former self. He couldn't lead anymore. The mercenaries were fading into oblivion." Kelan shook his head in rage. "With the Pistolas pushing into Arizona, we needed a shot in the arm. We needed to do something. *I* needed to do something."

His words became soft, almost apologetic. Hotah and the others watched their leader with admiration as he spoke of his sacrifice. "After months and months of trying to nurse my dear brother back to health, he still wouldn't recover. He was alive, but the silver had permanently crippled the wolf. He never healed. He never turned. So I did what I had to do for our people.

"I started this war, Diego. I took advantage of the

Pistolas' timing. I shot my brother in the head with Clint's gun to put him out of his misery. I skinned him with Clint's knife. I strung my brother up for the tribe to witness, to give them what they needed to get behind the mercenaries again. I put Clint's gun in the hands of your dead brother, to enrage and implicate your MC. The downfall of the Seventh Sons was entirely orchestrated by the Yavapai, and the next move in this fight is going to be bleeding you dry and skinning you, just like you made me do to my dear brother."

There was a bang as the door slammed. Everybody jumped and spun around, ready for a fight. Kayda Garnett stood in the doorway, watching her brother with tears streaming down her face.

Chapter 55

"What the fuck did you just say?" demanded Kayda.

A look of shock plastered Kelan's face. Her brother turned away from her. Hotah put his arms around her and pulled her away from Kelan.

"He gave your brother harbor for the last year," said Hotah in explanation. "Kept him hidden from the cops."

Kayda's breaths came quickly. "Carlos was with family the whole time?"

Kelan couldn't meet her gaze. She turned to Hotah. "He was in a bad way, Kayda. He wasn't recovering like he should have. Kel thought he needed a shock to the system. That maybe the gunshot would trigger something. Bring him back."

Still her brother wouldn't look at her. He stared down at the floor. At a knife. She saw Diego hanging upside down, the right side of his hair matted with drying blood. His eyes pleaded with her for help.

"What's he doing here?"

Kelan finally addressed her. "He was the one who killed Carlos."

Kayda pushed out of Hotah's arms, marched to her brother, and slapped him across the face. He sneered at her. "*You* killed him," she said.

"He wasn't the same. He wasn't strong enough."

"He was alive." Now it was Kayda who couldn't look at her brother. "He was a person. It didn't matter if he was bedridden for the rest of his life. You took away any hope he had. You took away my chance to see him again."

She felt the tugs of grief overcome her. She didn't look at Diego or Hotah or Kelan. Everyone else dissolved away as she cried, covering her face with her hands. Did she not want them to see?

The raven. The lies. The truth.

Kelan put his arms around his sister and gently pulled her away from Diego. "You shouldn't have come here." She shook her head, wanting to fight against his support. His strength. "Carlos was a great man. He will be remembered well. But our tribe needs someone like me now."

Kayda thought back to the night at the casino. Once again she saw the rage in her brother's eyes. It had all been for show. All to garner the support of their people. Kelan's outfit, *her family's outfit*, was manipulating the tribe.

She pictured the raven once again. The one that had guided her so well. The one that had perched atop her brother's mangled skin.

Kayda threw Kelan off her. She slapped him again.

Punched him. Both arms swiped at his face. "You ripped our brother apart like an animal!" she screamed.

Kelan backed away from her but she pursued. She clawed at him with her nails. She wanted to inflict any small amount of pain that she could. Her brother's face, at first surprised, twisted into rage. Insolence. His irises reflected red, and he growled.

The slap was fast and brutal. It was like back in the Sanctuary clinic, except this time she had deserved it. Kayda tripped on the edge of the ripped carpet and fell to the floor. When she looked up, she saw for the first time how much her brother truly detested her. The other Yavapai did nothing but watch silently. Yas even enjoyed what he saw.

Drip.

Kayda studied Diego. Suspended. Helpless. A victim of his own doing. He had seemed so nice at Sycamore Lodge. Cute even. But was he a killer just like her brother? Would he ever accept a world where the Yavapai tribe found success?

She stifled her sobs and cleared her mind. Kayda didn't know if she cared anymore. If she couldn't believe her own brother, why did Diego or Maxim deserve her trust?

Diego's knife stood in the floor close to his face. It was a specialty blade. A weapon meant to kill wolves. The weapon of a hunter.

Kayda returned her scorn to her brother. "I'm gonna tell *Pahmi* what you did." She rose to her feet defiantly. "We'll let the people choose their leader when they know the truth."

The sneer on Kelan's face eased. He lowered his gaze and looked like a man who'd had a burden removed from his shoulders. It wasn't surrender: it was acceptance.

Kayda Garnett brushed carelessly past her brother. He didn't deserve another word. Her judgmental eyes swept over the others on her way out. Hotah was the only one who appeared ashamed. He clenched his jaw and shook his head ever so slightly, struggling with a decision.

"You shouldn't have come here, little sister," said her brother. She ignored him and reached for the door.

Suddenly, Hotah's eyes widened. "Kelan, No!"

Kayda spun around and saw her brother raise a pistol. She threw her hands in front of her face and backed away, but the shot came hard and fast. Her aching ribs were nothing compared to the shock of her exploded collarbone.

Kayda felt bubbles in her chest.

She raised her eyebrows, stunned. She couldn't tell if it was curiosity or disbelief. Kayda had finally gotten the truth about everything.

As her knees gave out, she felt Hotah catch her.

Chapter 56

Diego squirmed against his bindings. "She's your sister, man!"

Kelan stood as still as a statue, refusing to react to his horrible crime. Jim and Yas were spooked. Even Hotah contemplated their leader in disbelief.

He cradled Kayda on the floor. She was rasping heavily, broken up only by the occasional choked breath. Blood was in her lungs. With every drip that slowly bled Diego dry, Kayda would find it harder and harder to breathe. She would eventually drown in her own blood.

Diego worked his hands behind his back. His wrists were loose now. He peeled something away. It was old duct tape, probably the same that had been applied to Jim earlier.

"You started all of this," said Diego through gritted teeth.

Kelan's head cocked slightly, the only movement that broke the illusion of stone.

"You're gonna be the downfall of your tribe."

Diego could tell that had struck a nerve. Kelan turned to Hotah and the others. Doubt of their loyalty crept into his face. "Just the opposite, Diego. The Yavapai have been meek, walking underfoot with our tails between our legs. Only strong leadership can shake us out of that pathetic state." He turned to Diego. "A call to action. A fire to stir our hearts. Revenge to quench our souls."

The other three men watched dubiously as Kelan justified his actions.

"How much longer are we willing to be pushed around?" he asked, challenging them. "How much more should we grin and bear? No. We will bite down on those that starve us. We will devour those that attempt to destroy us."

Red shone in the man's eyes. His head twitched. The pistol trembled in his hand. It was almost time.

"And you, my loyal friends," said Kelan to Jim and Yas. "It will soon be your time to join the pack. Hotah and I will guide you. Make you strong." The words encouraged them. Their doubt faded.

"You're gonna bite more people?" asked Diego. "Attract more attention? After last year, that's the last thing your tribe needs."

Kelan scoffed. "The CDC isn't here anymore. They've stayed clear of our reservation since the Paradise Killings. There's no more oversight."

"That's not true," said Diego. He didn't know what was going on, but he did know the government wouldn't let werewolves roam free. They were just keeping a low profile until their presence was needed.

Kelan laughed, and Diego pulled the last of the duct tape off his hands. He held the balled-up tape in his fist so the others wouldn't see it fall away, and hung upside down, strangely confident.

"I'm not gonna lie to you," said Kelan, stepping closer to the suspended man. "You're gonna die horribly. My brother, you know, was killed before he was skinned. I don't think I'm going to afford you the same courtesy."

Diego focused on the silver knife embedded in the floor. It was only a few feet away. Now that his hands were untied, he could probably reach it. Kelan noticed Diego's gaze, and smiled.

"You wish you had the knife, don't you?" He moved towards it and Diego tensed. The biker needed to strike a fine balance between grabbing it as soon as he could and not giving away that he was untied. Diego waited as Kelan kept talking. "How many wolves did you assassinate with this knife in service to the CDC? How many innocent people died by your hands?"

Diego studied the other Yavapai. He could see the hatred in their eyes. Hotah laid Kayda on the floor and rose to his feet. His eyes were glowing too. The wolf was feeling the surge of power that was coming.

It was just Diego and the silver knife.

"You know the problem with werewolves?" he asked, meeting Kelan's scowl. "They underestimate everyone else."

Hotah approached them. Diego dropped the ball of duct tape. Kelan narrowed his eyes.

The door of the building slammed open. A blur darted in and took Hotah off his feet. It was West. Both men crashed into the counter on the far wall.

Kelan turned to face the new threat, and Diego reached for the knife. He could barely touch it.

West Wind pounded on Hotah with bare fists. The two men snarled at each other. Jim and Yas backed up in fear, then picked up their rifles.

Diego swung forward, then backward, trying to pick up momentum. Kelan crouched on all fours, about to pounce on Hotah's attacker, but the two men were moving fast.

Hotah swept West off his feet. The Yavapai tried to slam his leg into the Apache's stomach, but West rolled away. Suddenly, he pushed off the floor and caught Hotah in an uppercut.

The moment West Wind stood apart, rifle fire cut through the air. The Apache ducked away from the sound. Bullets ripped past Diego's head. Jim held his ACR up, pointed away from the group, but Yas fired wildly. Kelan dove away from the burst. Diego swung uncontrollably in the air, shying away from the fire as best he could.

West was too smart to stay put. He left Diego with a momentary glance, his face fierce and without fear, then shot out the door through which he had come.

"Stop shooting!" yelled Kelan.

Hotah jumped to his feet and growled—a low, guttural rumble that was inhuman. He darted outside in pursuit of the Apache.

Diego swung forward, then backward.

"See what's going on," Kelan commanded. Jim and Yas nodded and left the building. Kayda coughed on the floor and rose to her elbows. Then Kelan turned back to biker.

Diego's motion brought him closer to the knife, and he reached out for it.

Kelan saw the threat. His wild eyes widened for only a fraction of a second before his lightning-quick reflexes took over. He lunged at the knife.

But it was too late.

Diego wrapped his hand around the familiar grip, its cold metal bringing with it a sense of calm. The biker tugged and the knife came free just as Kelan grasped for it.

Without a moment of hesitation, Diego slashed at the throat of the wolf.

Kelan pitched back. Diego's momentum began to pull him away, and he stretched his reach. Kelan raised his hands to protect his neck, but the very tip of the silver sliced horizontally across his Adam's apple.

The wolf sprang to his feet and then fell backwards as if the entire building had rocked. He clutched his throat, covered it as if his hands were bandages.

Blood began to seep from between his fingers.

A cry that was something between desperation and disbelief rang coarsely through Kelan, but it was obvious the effort caused him pain and he shut up. He stood again, without the use of his arms. His face wore an absent expression.

Without purpose, Kelan Doka wandered out into the open air.

The steady sounds of the creaking chains as Diego swung back and forth were broken only by Kayda coughing blood and phlegm. The world slowed its swinging.

"Are you okay?" asked Diego.

Just a gagging sound in response. Kayda drew her hands in front of her face and marveled at the blood. She was in shock.

Diego, hanging upside down, did a sit up and reached for his ankles. The knife wouldn't help to cut the chains, but maybe he could untie himself. The fit was tight, however. He needed both hands, but his instincts wouldn't let him release the knife.

Kayda Garnett stumbled to her feet, her weakened frame leaning against a wall for support.

"Help me," said Diego, pointing to his feet.

The girl gazed at him with a strange expression. She was confused. Was she dying?

She turned away and bumbled out the door after her brother, leaving Diego de la Torre alone.

"Well fuck me."

Chapter 57

Maxim and Ray pressed against the wall of the building, gripping their guns tightly. The rifle fire had stopped but its message was clear: the police were outgunned. Gutierrez and Kent were on the way, along with the local police, and a part of Maxim wanted to hang back and wait.

The two men listened intently, their senses likely the difference between life and death. Garcia, in the lead, glanced back and shook his head. The detective hadn't heard anything else either.

Moving into the backyard of the complex would be risky, but that's where the activity was. There wasn't much choice but to hug the building.

Ahead, parked along the side driveway, sat the lone pickup truck with the tarp in the back that they had watched. It was as good a cover as any.

Maxim patted Garcia on the shoulder and pointed to the truck. The detective separated himself from the wall and carefully snuck ahead. Stepping into the center of the driveway afforded him a better angle of the backyard. The truck would be a perfect flanking position.

From here, Maxim could make out both portables in the back. They were large, permanent structures, despite the cheap construction. The closer one on the left had blocked their view from the Explorer. Now Maxim could see the second one, further back, with a light on.

That's where everybody was hiding out. Away from the street.

The sound came as a hiss. It was muffled and almost faded into the landscape, but Maxim recognized it as man-made. Somewhere between a whisper and a call to attention. Someone was close.

Maxim raised his hand to warn Garcia of the danger. Then a Yavapai turned the corner, from the backyard to the side driveway, facing the two cops.

Maxim was exposed. He hadn't reached the truck yet and was standing in the open.

"FBI! Don't move!" ordered Garcia, gun raised.

The Yavapai answered with his assault rifle.

Maxim backpedaled and fired a shot at the same time. Automatic fire erupted in the driveway. Garcia retreated as he laid down covering fire, but Maxim's heel slipped in the sand. He lost his balance and landed hard on his side.

"Yas!" called out the Indian.

Garcia ran out to Maxim, firing a burst as he did. The Yavapai shied away from the ricochets against the wall. As he ducked around the corner, the FBI agent helped Maxim to his feet and they both retreated to the front porch.

"There's at least two of them," shouted Maxim, realizing the man had called a friend. The detective checked his magazine—he wasn't sure how much he had fired—and patted the silver rounds at his waist. Were these men wolves?

"The Seventh Son?" asked Garcia.

"No sign of West. The third building at the end was lit up. They're in there."

He nodded. "We need to cover these corners until our backup arrives." Raymond hurried to the right side of the property. A wall and a small path along it led to the back. As he peeked around the corner, Maxim checked the driveway side again.

Bullets shredded the wall beside him. Before Maxim pulled away, he saw one of the men, the one firing, take up position behind the truck. That had been Maxim's idea. The other was along the wall, inching closer.

Without exposing his head again, the detective blind-fired around the corner, keeping his aim along the wall to stymie the closer man's advance. He could hear the Yavapai scrambling away.

"I've got silver!" Maxim called out. Although he wasn't empty, he decided to switch to his alternate mag.

"What?" asked Garcia. Maxim turned to him and shook his head.

"Two over here," he said instead.

"Clear on this side."

Maxim's face clouded over. Something was wrong.

"Hotah's not here," he said in a low voice. "Keep an eye out."

Garcia understood. It only looked like they were in a shootout with only two Yavapai, but there had to be more. And where was West Wind?

The FBI agent waved silently to catch Maxim's attention. Raymond made a motion with his hand pointing down his side of the building, then pointed to his eyes. He wanted to check it out, try to flank them.

Maxim didn't think it was a good idea. He glanced up the driveway and saw the Yavapai advancing again. He ducked away before they had a chance to shoot him, but they fired some rounds his way anyway, just to get the point across. Maxim turned to Garcia and nodded. His plan was better than waiting for them to come.

The FBI agent disappeared around the building while Maxim blind-fired again. Just two shots. He didn't want to waste the silver. Hell, he didn't want to waste the lead either. He wasn't armed for a raid. This was supposed to be a stakeout.

Maxim scanned his surroundings. He couldn't keep poking his head out from the same place. It was only a matter of time before Yas, set behind the truck, would take him out. The other one was sneaking up, ready to turn the corner any second and unload on Maxim with an automatic weapon.

The detective glanced to where Garcia had stood. Nothing.

Get out of here, thought Maxim.

He could've just followed Ray, but that would be giving up their position. Maxim felt that he had to distract the Yavapai, to keep them busy. That would allow Ray to get the drop on them. So Maxim did the next best thing. He abandoned his corner, hustled to the front door, and barged in.

The building was dark. Maxim was left in a hallway, but he immediately found a room bordering the south wall, along the driveway. A single small window was covered in paper, the pale light from outside washing him in a soft glow.

This was it.

Maxim raised his Glock, ready to strike with silver, and waited.

For a moment Maxim thought he had miscalculated. That maybe the man had already passed the window and was coming around behind him. But the self-doubt vanished as the perfect silhouette slid across the window.

Maxim fired three shots in a tight burst. The window made a horrible cracking sound but the paper only showed three bright holes. The shadow behind the window danced and flew backward.

Then hell rained inside.

Maxim leaped out of the room as the paper tore away in threads. Shards of glass flew inside and a cacophony of sound ricocheted off the floor and ceiling. Back in the hallway, Maxim rested against the wall as the noise died down. Then he heard pistol reports in the back.

Garcia had flanked them.

Maxim flew to his feet and charged towards the back of the building, kicking empty beer bottles out of the way. He was looking for a similar overlook on the Yavapai position, this time in the back corner.

The Indians retaliated. First one rifle, then the other. The detective heard two more pistol shots as he rushed into the back room.

Damn it. No windows. The back corner room had no windows.

There was a lull in the combat. Maybe the Yavapai were reloading. Maybe they were licking their wounds. Maybe Garcia was dead. Maxim followed the wall until he was at the back door. A window had a portion of paper removed, allowing a view of the outside. The detective peeked.

Someone retreated back to the truck. That meant the Yavapai had not followed Ray. Hopefully the agent was making his way back to the front.

Before Maxim pulled away from the window, he saw another figure in the dark, supporting himself against the wall of the second building.

Kelan?

What was he doing here? Garcia and Hitchens had dropped him off at the reservation. The local police were supposed to keep eyes on him. Was he a part of this?

Maxim shook off the thought as he heard a rumbling sound. It came from the front of the property. A motorcycle.

Garcia. Maxim's priority was finding Garcia. He raced through the hallway to the front. The door was still wide open, and Maxim saw the scene without revealing himself.

Sergio Lima stood next to his bike, holding his hands in the air, facing someone.

Maxim rushed towards the door.

"I said get on the fucking ground, Sergio!"

Garcia had his firearm trained on the Pistolas president from ten feet away.

Maxim grimaced. The two of them were surrounded—Yavapai on one side, Pistolas on the other. It didn't give them a lot of options, but effecting an arrest like this was risky. Sergio begrudgingly cooperated.

Another rumble grew louder. Another biker approached from the street. Garcia spun to cover the new threat. It was Hector Cruz, of course. Career criminal. Lima's right hand. Maxim knew he wouldn't go down as easily as the kid.

Maxim Dwyer switched his magazine back to lead rounds.

"Stop right there!" ordered Garcia frantically. "Get off the bike!"

Cruz stopped his advance but remained straddling his motorcycle. He revved the engine in defiance.

"Do what he says, asshole!" called out Maxim, stepping onto the front porch. Sergio, halfway crouched, widened his eyes at his appearance. Hector sat still, his thick mustache masking his expression.

"We're not breaking the law," said Sergio.

"Shut up!" commanded Garcia.

Maxim took a breath. Backup could not arrive too soon. "He's right, Garcia," he said, keeping his pistol raised. "We arrest them now, we don't have anything on them except criminal trespass. Let them go. Our hands are full here."

Sergio cocked his head. He knew he had stumbled into the middle of something. He didn't know what but he was smart enough not to care. He turned to Garcia. "What do you say, *federal*?"

Garcia sneered. He took a step backwards, but stopped. He was exposed where he was. Slowly, he shook his head.

"I can't do it, Maxim," he said gravely. "You showed me that you could be trusted. You came to me with information, regardless of whether it implicated the Seventh Sons. Now I need to show you that you can trust me." Garcia reached for his handcuffs.

"It's not necessary, Ray. We could pick them up another day."

"We just need to hold them until backup arrives."

Maxim saw Hector's face contort at the news of impending police. This was a man who wasn't going back to prison.

The detective wanted to impress on Garcia that it was too dangerous. That he already trusted him. He wanted to tell him that Kelan was in the back and had probably been a part of these crimes all along. He wanted to tell him the Yavapai outfit was the real danger. He wanted to tell him about the new moon, and the coming wolves.

Instead, Ray flashed Maxim a confident smile. It was the kind of expression that assured the innocents that the police were the good guys. That the authorities were in control.

The moment didn't even last long enough to be

considered a moment. Garcia's eyebrows shot up, and his posture tightened.

"Look out!"

He raised his weapon towards the corner of the building and fired. Maxim spun around and saw Yas Harjo in the driveway. They both fired at the same time.

Everybody went to the floor. Even Hector. But the Indian wasn't fast enough.

Maxim hit the man in the shoulder, then the elbow as he recoiled. It was only lead but it hurt him. The Yavapai retreated out of sight. Garcia kept firing after him. Then Maxim heard the shotgun blast.

He turned, still on his side, as Garcia crumpled to the ground. Hector was behind him, aiming the weapon for another go as Maxim opened fire.

The wild shots missed, a couple hitting the motorcycle as Hector ducked. Sergio stood up and reached for his bike. Hector fired a blast towards the detective, who took cover inside the doorway.

Maxim laid out some covering fire to keep the Pistolas ducking behind their bikes. He tried to give Garcia time to get up, but he didn't move.

"Ray! You okay?"

He heard a groan as Sergio drew a pistol. A glance to Hector revealed that he was having trouble with the weapon. It was an autoloader—it could've jammed.

It was a pretty shitty opening, but it was all he had.

Maxim burst out of the doorway and bolted towards the downed FBI agent. He fired a shot to make Sergio duck again and hooked his hand into the shoulder of Garcia's vest. He heaved.

Garcia had his eyes open, and he was conscious enough to understand what to do. While being dragged on his back, he lifted himself awkwardly to his feet. It was like dragging a wheelbarrow without wheels. They stumbled, but they covered ground quickly. Ray raised his gun and pulled off a few shots. Maxim trained his Glock on the driveway, keeping it clear, then dragged Garcia up the porch. The threshold of the building was cloaked in darkness, somehow a deeper shadow than the moonless sky. At that moment, it was the most inviting thing Maxim could imagine, like the safety of hiding under a thick blanket.

As the detective crossed the threshold, a single thud rapped against his back.

Maxim burst into the dark hallway and ducked into a lobby, placing Garcia out of the line of fire. This was a good room. Central. No windows. A view of the front door down the hall but a corner to take cover behind.

The FBI agent slid strangely against the wall. He didn't have enough strength to sit up. Maxim crouched and stretched his shoulder. It smarted, but the pain wasn't especially nefarious. He'd played paintball a lot in the past, and that's what it felt like—that he had been tagged.

He was out of the game.

The detective put his gun down and patted his bulletproof vest. The Kevlar had stopped Sergio's slug. In this game, the rules were different. He wouldn't gladly walk away, congratulating his opponents. If he went down, it would be kicking and screaming, to the last.

Garcia groaned again. Maxim eyed the door and then bent over him, pulling away his blue FBI jacket. A large swatch of blood stained Garcia's torso, just under the vest.

"Holy shit," said Maxim.

"That motherfucker," said Garcia, still clutching his gun. "That motherfucker."

Maxim kneeled closer to his friend. "He got you below the vest."

Garcia stared past the detective, as if the darkness could reveal its secrets to him. "That motherfucker."

Maxim got on his phone. He called 911 and asked for an ambulance. He gave his badge number and told them an officer was down. It was a slower process than he would have thought. All the people that had called for him—had they gone through the same desperation?

Then he called Gutierrez and Kent and updated them on the situation. The rookie said they were en route, flashing reds and blues.

All the while, Maxim glanced nervously at the front doorway.

Where was their backup?

"It doesn't work," said Garcia, finally turning to the detective.

"What's that, Ray?"

"It doesn't work if we're dirty too."

Maxim stared hard at the man. He was controlling his breathing. It took effort to speak.

"You were looking at me and I was looking at you," said

Maxim. "I thought you had a relationship with them."

Garcia laughed. "No. I never did."

Maxim shook his head sadly. "I don't have one with the Sons either."

The FBI agent nodded, slowly, with measure. "Maybe you don't. Not yet. But you're heading down that path, Maxim. You need to cut it off before that happens."

Maxim checked up and down the hallway and sighed. He turned to Agent Garcia, watching the blood pool on the floor. "I know, Ray. I know."

Chapter 58

Diego emerged through the door and practically fell down the two steps to the dirt. He didn't think about how stupid it was to call attention to himself—he just coughed up the vile stench of death and bleach that permeated the portable. It felt good to be right-side up again. He breathed quickly, almost hyperventilating, and couldn't get enough of the fresh air.

He had thought he was going to die in that hellhole.

Automatic gunfire brought Diego back to his senses. At first the biker guessed the men were after Kayda. Then the thought of West and the Seventh Sons came to mind. But he knew his brothers were tied up tonight. No. The gunfire was Maxim. The police. He knew they would show.

Diego scanned the courtyard. No signs of Kayda at all. Where could a hurt girl have run off to?

The property's back fence was easy to scale. Fifty yards west was an open desert. Escape was easy. As the biker tried to cut through the darkness, his eyes caught a red reflection. At first, he was afraid it was a wolf. The thought of Hotah sneaking up on him again made him wary. Diego squeezed the silver knife until his knuckles were white.

Hotah had chased West. The two wolves would likely keep each other busy for a while. Real wolf fights, not backyard brawls with a bell, were vicious, extended affairs. At this time, with the new moon, both men would be at peak strength, and any wear and tear would immediately be repaired as soon as they transformed, ready to fight anew.

It wasn't going to be a pretty night for the two wolves. Hotah was tough, but Diego would put his money on West any day. That was one cold Apache.

Confident that the yard was quiet, Diego continued surveying the area. Staring at the reflection in the distance longer revealed that it didn't move. It was the brake light reflector of a vehicle. Diego squinted as his night vision returned. It was a black van, the one the Yavapai had used to gun down Clint. It wasn't visible from the highway—it was just barely visible from here. An abandoned property seemed as good a place as any to dump it.

Closer to him, there was the smaller portable. It was still closed up, lights off. Diego trudged over to it and checked the door. It was locked.

The next most obvious spot was the main building. The light was still on in the back room where he had gotten the jump on the Yavapai.

"They're inside the house," said Jim.

Diego ducked against the smaller building. Jim and Yas

circled the visitor center, moving from the driveway to the back door. They passed a pickup truck that hadn't been there when Diego first crossed the yard. Diego assumed it belonged to Kelan. Hotah had called him up after the biker was captured so that Kelan could enjoy skinning him alive.

What a friend.

"I know that," snapped Yas. He favored his left arm, not supporting his ACR properly. He'd been wounded. "Go around through the front. Flush them out towards me."

Jim nodded and disappeared down the driveway again.

Two Yavapai taking on the police? What were they thinking? Maybe Kayda was inside after all. Maybe they were so wound up about tonight's events that they were willing to die to get her.

As Diego watched them split up, he knew they'd made a mistake. Yas stood alone, his gun trained past the open back door.

At first, the biker crept silently towards the unsuspecting Yavapai. When his foot crunched on a dried plant, he abandoned all sense of stealth and charged.

Yas heard the sound and started to turn. Diego swung his knife down as he raced forward. Yas threw his forearm up to counter. Their arms cracked against each other without the knife connecting, but Diego bowled ahead into the Yavapai at full speed. He lifted Yas up off his feet and pushed him through the open doorway, where they both slid along the floor. A silver knife rolled across the tile.

Diego immediately reached for the ACR. It was strapped around his opponent's neck but he twisted it away from the wounded arm easily enough.

Yas cried out in pain but tugged on the Remington with his good hand. He kneed Diego in the stomach and scrambled to his feet.

The biker didn't release his hands from the weapon.

Both men forced their weight against each other, vying for control of the rifle. Diego slammed Yas into a wall. Yas spun Diego around and they fell deeper into another room. At one point Diego thought he'd gotten the weapon loose, but Yas head butted the biker and slipped away again.

Momentarily dragged by his grip, Diego twisted and bore all his weight over his shoulder. The strap of the ACR closed around the Yavapai's neck. The two men were back to back, and when Diego bent forward, Yas lost his footing. His body lifted onto Diego's, all his weight constricting his throat. Diego stood firm, unmoving, holding the assault rifle in front of his face with a death grip while he felt Yas kick his feet, searching for ground.

In a moment, it was over.

Diego squatted lower, sliding the dead man to the floor. The biker's thighs burned. He was dizzy. He wasn't fully recovered from the ordeal in the portable, and he had lost a lot of blood. But at least he had his knife back. And a rifle to boot.

Behind him, a loose tile cracked. The biker spun around and tried to pull the weapon into a firing position, but it was still attached to Yas. The maneuver was clumsy and slow. By the time he faced his six, a gun squared at his head.

"Diego."

The biker let out a heavy sigh of relief and slumped to his ass. Yas clumped down like a rag doll. Maxim Dwyer lowered his gun.

"Detective."

"The Pistolas are out front. Sergio and Hector. Ray's hurt."

Diego blinked away his sluggishness and saw the blood on Maxim's hands. He turned and untwisted the rifle strap. The corpse rotated unnaturally, like an alligator clamped to its prey, until the biker shook it off without regard.

Maxim, however, circled Yas with interest.

"I don't think this homicide needs solving," said Diego.

"US Patriot Tactical."

Diego checked the magazine of the rifle and only partially made out what Maxim had said. "What?"

The detective crouched and pointed at Yas. "The boots. There's a mark on the right sole. This is the man that stabbed Omar in the heart."

Something washed over Diego's face, then his whole body. It took a second to realize it was relief. "Then it's done. I'm done."

"What's that?"

"I'm out," said Diego, picking up his silver knife. "Of the Seventh Sons. I'm free."

Maxim's face tightened. "We haven't made it out of this yet."

Chapter 59

Kayda pressed her eyes closed in a panicked grimace. That was how dreams were supposed to end, right? Dying. Choking on her own blood. Shot by her own brother. The aftermath had carried on far too long already, but certainly she couldn't actually die in her dream.

The girl opened her eyes. She rested her head against the wall of the portable. It was no good. She wasn't waking up.

Kayda coughed and red spittle dotted the stucco. Her breathing was labored. She knew the liquid was in her lungs. That was the worst part. The fear that her body wasn't working the way it should. That her organs were failing her. The easiest things, like drawing breath, couldn't be taken for granted anymore.

As Kayda swallowed a gulp of blood, she again recalled the rabbit blood. What kind of strength did her essence provide?

She had exited the other portable and stumbled to this

one, towards the truck. The gunfire had caused her to circle around the back of it, on the edge of the yard, hugging the fence. It was as good a place to hide as any, but it wasn't a good place to die.

Was there such a place?

The night was still now. Peaceful. The shooting had stopped.

She pulled away from the wall to take in the surroundings. The sheer amount of blood that was on the side of the building struck her. How was that possible?

Then she realized some of the marks were shaped like handprints, leading toward the driveway.

It was Kelan's blood.

Kayda's brow hardened.

The steps came easier to her now. Before she had been wayward, but purpose drove her spirit and her body.

Death served a purpose.

She leaned against the wall for support, just as her brother had done, and followed in his footsteps.

Chapter 60

"Aren't you supposed to have a whole team or something?" insisted Diego.

Maxim grunted and headed back to Garcia. "Ray was my team. We were just staking out the place, keeping eyes on it to build a case for a search warrant. We weren't supposed to move tonight, remember?"

The detective would have been annoyed if he had the time. Diego was here for the Yavapai. West showed up to rescue him. If the Seventh Sons had stayed out of this, he and Ray would be watching safely from a distance as the Pistolas and the Yavapai, and *Kelan*, all connected the dots for his case.

"Coming here during the new moon was stupid," he added.

"Sorry," said Diego in earnest, "but I always told you that's the best time to hunt."

Maxim didn't answer back. This wasn't about blame.

The three of them were trapped inside, surrounded, until backup arrived. "What was Kelan doing here?"

"It was all him. He killed his brother. He strung him up so his people would see it and fall in behind him."

Maxim stopped. He tried to fight the shudder that rumbled in his stomach. The things people did for power didn't usually shock him anymore. Not after the Paradise Killings. Not after his wife succumbed to rabies from a self-inflicted injection. But Kelan killing Carlos gave him pause.

The detective shook it off. As he advanced into the spacious lobby, he exposed himself to the open hallway—to the front door. He reacted to the blur of movement and dove forward before he heard the shots. Three, four reports rang out. Maxim slid forward to safety without getting hit. He rolled on the tile floor and saw that Diego was still behind cover.

That had been a pistol. Inside the building.

"Drop the weapon, Lima," shouted Maxim, scooting up against the corner. "We have you surrounded."

He heard scathing laughter. Maxim smiled and looked to Raymond, right next to him. He was still breathing, holding his side, blinking slowly. Maxim's smile vanished.

"Are you serious, *ése*? That's not what it looks like to me."

"It's because you don't realize it yet, asshole. In two minutes you're gonna have ten units blocking the exit."

More laughing. "You hear that, Hector? *El cabrón* thinks the Chino Valley police are his friends." Maxim's face scrunched up. There was no way the Pistolas had that kind of juice. But this was government property. Maybe the Yavapai had some kind of deal with the locals. Maxim had assumed that they only had Tribal PD in their pocket, but why not Prescott and Chino Valley too? They might as well own the entire Quad-City area.

Still, there was no way they could have the police dispatchers throw away an emergency call. From another officer needing assistance, no less. But maybe it did mean the local department would drag their heels getting here.

Maxim blind-fired around the corner and peeked out, just catching Sergio jumping out of the hallway. His last pull of the trigger clicked empty.

Sergio was inside somewhere. Suddenly, Hector swung around from the front porch. Maxim pulled back as a well-aimed shotgun blast threw up shards of ceramic.

Diego peeled himself away from cover and aimed the Remington ACR down the hallway. Its automatic burst took Hector off guard. Maxim heard a cry as he went to reload. Diego shouted, "That's my Benelli you bastard," then fired another burst. He swept his aim from side to side, tearing the hallway apart.

Maxim checked the damage as the silver magazine clicked satisfyingly into place. Sergio darted outside. The detective fired one shot their way, but they were too far already. He couldn't afford losing the ammo, to be honest. It didn't matter that the rounds were silver; it mattered that they were all he had left.

He heard their motorcycles start. The Pistolas were running. At one time Maxim had offered them that chance.

Now, Ray was bleeding to death next to him. Sergio and Hector weren't allowed to leave anymore.

Maxim admired the weapon in Diego's hands and decided he needed to get one of those.

"Wait!" he heard out front.

"Jim," said Diego. It was the other Yavapai. Diego pulled out his empty magazine and looked around, as if he should have had more with him. "I need more ammo." The biker disappeared towards the back of the building before Maxim could tell him to stop.

Whatever. Maxim clambered to his feet and rushed the door. He had at least a few silver bullets. And Jim, werewolf or not, wouldn't like them.

The Yavapai fired the ACR in the rough direction of the retreating Pistolas. They circled away from the Indian and sped north on the highway.

The bad news was that they got away. The good news was that Jim had turned his back on the detective.

Maxim jogged lightly forward with his Glock raised. "Jim Bullard! Put the gun down!"

The man froze, then turned only his head. Maxim slowed to a stop. They were still twenty yards apart. Maxim would have preferred to be closer but a steady hand was more important.

"I've got silver in here, Jim."

The Yavapai smiled. "I'm not a wolf, you dumbass."

"And if you don't drop the rifle, you never will be."

Maxim slowed his breathing, steadied his firearm, and waited for the man to make his move. Jim finally surrendered his hands and turned around cautiously.

"Don't shoot me, okay?"

"Just put the weapon down!"

Jim pulled the strap over his head.

"Slowly."

The Yavapai did as he was told. He dropped the rifle on the ground.

"Walk backwards. Ten steps."

As Jim complied, Maxim approached. He secured the weapon and had the man go to the ground. He cuffed his hands behind his back and saw Diego emerge from the building, shaking his head. Maxim smiled.

With his knee on Jim's neck, his cell phone was immediately in his hand. He called Gutierrez and told him they had two Pistolas northbound on State Route 89, armed and dangerous. They were to blockade the street and take them out, no matter what.

Chapter 61

Gaston's Harley V-Rod Muscle wobbled as he shifted his weight. It took a few seconds, but he regained his balance and continued south on the 89, on the trail of Sergio and Hector.

It was a simple highway, just a single lane in each direction, split only by dotted diagonal whites. Gaston took special care to focus on the paint, doing everything he could to stay on the road.

It wasn't easy to see with only one eye.

The blast from Hector's shotty had taken a few fingers off Gaston's left hand. The rest of the shot mangled his face and ear. It was all gone, but his right eye still worked. A skeletal grin played across the big man's face, no small feat through ripped muscle and blood.

The pain was unbearable. It continually threatened to shut the man down. He fought against it. Gaston would not rest. He wouldn't let the Pistolas get away from him that easily, no matter how much of a head start they'd gotten.

Not tonight.

The air was buzzing, a live wire of energy. Crisp. Cold against his open flesh. When he felt the tug of sleep, Gaston sped even faster, countering nature with adrenaline.

Gaston didn't know where he was going, but the building was close. North of Chino Valley. Ahead, he saw two motorcycles circle into the empty highway. The two individual headlights turned towards him, north, and raced closer.

It was a dark night, lacking the illumination of the moon. He couldn't see details, just headlights, but somehow Gaston knew it was them. Sergio and Hector. He was surprised. The Pistolas should have been heading south, back to the Imperial Valley. They should have been running.

The moon may not have been visible but it would guide Gaston well on this hunt.

The screaming engines neared and Gaston felt himself laugh. There was no sound against the coarse wind, just a guttural vibration.

Two headlights, coming up to meet him. He might as well pick one of them.

With last second abandon, the Seventh Son swerved into the opposite lane and charged the Pistolas. It wasn't a game of chicken as much as it was a sudden collision. Both bikes attempted to avoid him, but he met one of them head on.

Gaston's body launched off his V-Rod and slammed into another. Then he tumbled, first on asphalt, then dirt.

The world spun and stabilized. Gaston's knees and elbows raked against the street, unprotected by his simple muscle shirt and jeans. As the friction of pebbles and dirt scraped his skin, his body came to a stop. Gaston smiled. Better to match his face, he thought.

In the distance, a single brake light sped away.

Gaston heard a cry of pain. He turned and saw Hector Cruz stumbling across the street. Although he wore no shirt, his thick jacket and helmet had cushioned much of his injuries. He was frantic, flipping back and forth, searching for his bike.

That's right, thought Gaston. He didn't want him giving up yet.

The grounded motorcycles seemed a mile away. More importantly, Hector's shotgun was lost. Gaston rose to his feet and growled.

His ankle was hurt. Broken. Gaston couldn't put weight on it. He glanced at the injury like it was an annoyance, then gritted his teeth and put his weight on it anyway. A sharp groan escaped his lips as loose bone cracked, but the pain subsided with each step.

Hector slowed his movement when he noticed the other man. He watched in horror as the mangled form of Gaston Delacroix approached.

"You know," said Gaston, his skull showing, "I was hoping to hit Sergio, but I'm almost happier it worked out this way."

Hector Cruz dropped his jaw. His thick eyebrows and mustache stretched to their limits in disbelief. Then he bolted into the desert, slightly limping.

Gaston plodded patiently across the highway, unconcerned with the possibility of traffic, and began his hunt.

481

Chapter 62

Kayda stumbled to the red pickup truck. It was so cold and lonely out here.

Where was everybody?

The driver's door was still partially open. Kayda leaned on it and drew it wider.

Kelan Doka sat in front of her, both elbows on the steering wheel for support. He was a mess. His buzzed hair was matted with blood, and his arms and face were covered in sweat. His breathing was sharp and ragged and rapid.

Kayda laughed. It was an odd reaction, she knew, but the weight of everything that had happened to their family over the last week threatened to crush her otherwise. It was their perfect dramatic tragedy, Shakespeare, played out to a tee. But Kelan was the cause of all of it. It felt right that she would see him like this before she passed.

In the distance a wolf howled, long and menacing. Kelan stirred and noticed his sister for the first time, but he didn't turn to her.

"I don't think I'm going to turn," he said. "The silver..."

Lost was the arrogance in his voice. No longer was he the over-confident brother she knew. Kayda suspected he must have been frightened. She didn't know what to tell him.

"Keekee..."

"You need to drive me," he said, picking his head up. "Take me to the old woman."

Her brother was ordering her around again. Kayda snorted, but it turned into a hacking cough and she spit out more red fluid. "Twice now, you've left me to die. Now, when it's your time, you ask to be saved?"

Kelan turned to her. His eyes were wide. She could see the wolf in his retina, a weak tint of red where the light caught it. But no strength remained in his gaze. He trembled like a child. Just as Kayda had seen at the police station, a sharp cut tore across Kelan's neck. Only this time, the line was jagged where his flesh folded outward. "I can't die," he gurgled.

Kayda Garnett put her palm on her half brother's chest. It was a gentle action, but there was no comfort in it. The bond of family was absent. Kelan struggled to feign a smile; all it did was reinforce the lie.

All those years growing up as a little girl—being picked on, hounded, pushed astray, and blamed for all their problems. Carlos, the hardened criminal. Kelan, the jealous trickster. It took her entire life to realize it, but her brothers had been right. She wasn't one of them. She never had been.

Kayda thought about her grandfather's words. "Death serves a purpose," she told her brother, and pulled him toward her.

Kelan was puzzled by the statement. He threw his arm against her shoulder to counter the pull. His elbow jarred against her bullet wound. It hurt, but Kayda bit down hard on her lip. More blood filled her mouth. She refused to open it else she might scream. Instead, she choked it down and forced him into an embrace.

"Is that not what you told our dear brother?" she asked. "That he would be sacrificed for the good of the tribe?"

Kelan pushed away with all his might but it did little. It amazed Kayda, her strength and his weakness. He had always been able to overpower her. Now he was of little concern.

Brother and sister exchanged another look before his will gave out. Kayda coughed again and blood spattered against Kelan's face, intermingling with his tears. Her lungs felt torn apart and she tasted a fresh mouthful of blood.

In a moment, free of shock or panic or confusion, she decided, if she was going to choke on someone's blood, it would be the blood of her enemy. The blood of her brother.

Kayda Garnett leaned in and gave her brother a gentle kiss on the cheek. Then she lowered her head and clamped her mouth around Kelan's throat. He tensed as she pressed close. She could feel his heart beating, not at his chest, but by the pumping of blood that leaked from his neck. It washed into her mouth: warm, salty, strong. It wasn't for Kelan anymore. The Doka brothers had bled their last drops. It was time for a change.

The girl jerked away, excited and horrified by the feeling surging within her. This time, when her lungs took in air, there was less pain. Her breath didn't wheeze out of her chest the way it had moments before.

Without pausing to consider her condition any further, Kayda tugged her brother out of the truck. He fell sideways and crumpled to the ground. She stood over him, looking down at the pathetic man, almost feeling sorry for everything he'd been through.

"How?" he cried weakly. "You're no wolf. How are you still alive?"

She stepped over Kelan and climbed into the truck.

"Witch," he rasped, before she slammed the door.

Chapter 63

"Where's the ambulance?" screamed Maxim to the air. He knew he should have been clearing the rest of the buildings, but Garcia was close to losing consciousness. Besides, Diego had told him the back was empty.

Jim sat by the porch, dejected. Maxim and Diego had helped Garcia outside, but there were still no sirens. Maxim paced the front yard, holding the ACR, swearing that he would look into the possibility of a 911 blackout. He would burn any officers involved in that.

"Hold on, Ray," he said again. Each time he repeated the phrase, it had less power. He thought about the last thing the man had said, about Maxim's relationship with the Sons. Would those be his final words?

Before Maxim could yell again, his phone rang. It was Gutierrez.

"Sir, we're in pursuit of Sergio Lima, heading south on 89. He saw the roadblock and made a U-turn."

"Shit. Hector too?"

"We only saw Lima. Kent and I are in pursuit, but his bike's fast. He's losing us and I'm having trouble raising the local PD."

Maxim ground his teeth tighter. "Just get over here. Don't worry about police. Just make sure you get paramedics over here."

"I heard it over the radio. They're en route."

"Good."

Maxim ended the call and shook his head violently. If Sergio was on his way back here, that gave the detective another chance at him. He moved closer to the highway and scouted north. It was late and dead.

He glanced south to the rest stop where Garcia's Explorer was parked and began to return to the porch to recover the keys but stopped. Sergio was moving fast. Maxim didn't have time to run to the truck.

He heard a car start. The pickup truck in the yard spun around. It drove onto the rough sand before climbing back onto the packed dirt of the driveway. Headlights blinded Maxim and came closer.

Instinctually, he raised the assault rifle. The glare of the headlights kept him from seeing who was behind the wheel. He considered that it could be Kelan, and that he should fire, but then he noticed the man lying on the ground.

The split-second indecision cost Maxim his chance. The red pickup bore down on him. He dove to the side. He wasn't sure, but he thought the truck swerved away from him. Within moments, it was on the highway and headed south.

"Damn it! I thought you said it was clear!"

Maxim turned to Diego, who just shook his head and shrugged. He looked at the man lying beside him, eyes half open, breathing slowly.

Everything seemed hopeless. Everything had gone wrong. The dominoes were falling but the plays were haphazard, made out of desperation instead of calculated planning. And Garcia was too heavy a casualty.

Maxim wasn't going to let Sergio walk on that.

He flipped the ACR into his grip and stomped out to the street. He stood in the middle of the highway, in between both lanes, and saw the single light of a motorcycle.

Maxim braced the assault rifle against his shoulder, fully aware that it had been a while since he'd fired anything like this. He switched the firing mode to semi-automatic and aimed along the sights, waiting for the biker to get closer.

Sergio's speed on the flat street was impressive. He bore down on Maxim yet the police lights weren't in sight yet. He decided not to risk it. The detective stepped to the edge of the road to make sure his line of fire would not travel along the highway.

He could see him now. The skinny kid on his chopper. Arms high, head lowered. The ACR lined up perfectly with his center mass.

No. Maxim didn't want to let this motherfucker go that easily.

He lowered the rifle a nudge, targeting the motorcycle, and fired a single round.

The bike flipped. The headlight formed a circle on the street as Sergio tumbled from the machine. Both masses hopped and rolled and careened down the street, and Maxim had to get out of the way.

Sergio cried out in pain. Past him, the night sky turned red and blue in a manic frenzy.

Maxim turned as he heard more sirens coming from Chino Valley to the south. It was a paramedic truck.

He rushed to wave it down. It skidded to a halt and two men leapt out carrying a foldable stretcher and some equipment. They heard Sergio and headed for him.

"No. Fuck that guy. Agent Garcia is on the front porch. He needs a hospital right now. Call another van for the rest."

They nodded under his cold glare and wordlessly followed directions. Maxim heard Sergio calling out to him, insulting him or offering him a bribe. The detective didn't care. He didn't hear it. He just watched silently as the paramedics attended to the FBI agent.

Unfortunately, Raymond looked worse off than Sergio.

Chapter 64

Gaston answered his brother. A deep howl that resonated in his chest and left the muzzle of his mouth. The animal felt the draw of the moon, invisible to most but not to his kind.

It reinvigorated him. Snapped his bones apart and back into place. His scraped skin gave way to a thick coat of brown fur. His torn muscles tightened and mended. Gaston Delacroix was whole again, and this time he felt better than ever.

The other wolf's call had come from West. He was far away, on his own hunt. Hotah yelped. It was a short cry followed by a long call. West was giving him all he could handle, and Kelan didn't answer.

Gaston wouldn't be joining them. Not yet. The president would enjoy his own blood tonight.

He sniffed the ground and quickly caught the scent. Sweat and gunpowder. Machine oil. Fear. Hector Cruz was known as the Mechanic, but he'd fixed his last engine.

Gaston's powerful paws bounded towards his prey, moving faster than the poor man could hope to outrun. It was unfair, really. But this wasn't about an even contest. Revenge wasn't supposed to be sporting. It was supposed to be one-sided and ruthless.

The feeble man hopped away ahead of him. He turned back and whimpered. The pathetic gangbanger stunk of beer and sweat and the soil in his pants.

Gaston went for the belly. He sidestepped a half-hearted swipe and dug his teeth deep. The blood in his mouth electrified him, and Gaston shook his head from side to side, savoring the feel of ripping flesh.

Within minutes, another howl overtook the plains. It resounded over all of Chino Valley, and Prescott, and the reservation. It was a message proclaiming, to anyone listening, who ruled Arizona.

Epilogue

Chapter 65

"There are a lot of loose ends," said Marshal Boyd, scrolling through the report on his monitor.

"A few," agreed Maxim. "I just heard from Gaston. He tipped me off about a doctor in Yuma. Apparently he treated one of the Pistolas after the shooting of Omar Rivera. With any luck we can follow that lead to more arrests."

Boyd nodded, leaning back in his high leather chair behind his desk. The grand furnishings made him a small man by comparison. Perhaps that was why his actions were forceful and measured. The marshal was the son of the mayor. He was bred for politics. A little thing like biology wouldn't get in his way.

"More than likely we'll have a manhunt leading into Mexicali. We'll need to coordinate with the local authorities and prepare extradition. I think we can tap the FBI. They're all hands on deck with this. They need answers."

"Well, Sergio's not giving them."

"He's conscious?" asked the marshal.

"According to the FBI. They have him in custody and he came to. He broke his legs and injured his spine but his prognosis is good. Physically, anyway. As far as the law goes, he doesn't have a lot of options. No point in talking because they're not giving him a deal."

Boyd raised his eyebrows. He mentioned that Sergio might have strategic value against the Mexican Mafia. He said they were following up with the blackmail photos found in his possession. Maxim nodded but tuned the marshal out. Raymond Garcia was in the OR as they spoke. It had taken all night to stabilize him. The blood loss was a problem. After the doctors had handled the initial triage, they allowed his body some much needed rest before they operated again.

The detective had been allowed to see him. Briefly. He was anesthetized and unconscious. Covered with tubes. Maxim had tried to tell him that they'd taken down Sergio. That Hector's mangled body had been found near the highway. It was just one last thing he'd wanted to give the FBI agent. One last reminder that justice prevailed.

It had fallen on deaf ears.

Some people liked to believe the world was a just place. That the good guys would be taken care of. That innocent civilians could just put their heads down and work hard and they'd be okay. Maxim conveyed that message on the outside—it's what the people wanted to hear—but he didn't believe a word of it. So when he'd told Ray about the accomplishments of the night, it rang hollow. He didn't believe the bullshit, and the FBI agent wasn't awake to hear it.

But the man had survived the first hours. There was something to be said about that. Recovery might be slow and it was difficult to gauge long-term damage, but Raymond Garcia would live.

"I want to talk about this first draft of your report," continued Boyd.

Maxim's eyes rose to meet the marshal's. "First draft, sir?"

"Yes. This case will be scrutinized. Your fame and the notoriety of the Seventh Sons compounded with the shooting of an FBI agent—it's the Paradise Killings all over again."

Maxim could tell that Boyd was already managing spin. In truth, this was a win for the marshal's office. No hate crime had occurred. The heads of a violent motorcycle gang from out of state had been taken down. A fringe mercenary outfit had been dismantled. There was justice for the shootings of a civilian and an FBI agent. Sanctuary officers made it out okay without any semblance of impropriety, and the Seventh Sons weren't implicated in any wrongdoing. Aside from minor points, Maxim didn't see a problem with his report. There was no political poison.

"I don't think there'll be any issue with the execution of the busts," said Boyd, "but there are some small corrections I'd like you to make. For instance, you don't mention commanding Sergio Lima to pull over before you fired on him. I'm sure you did and not including it in the report was just an oversight. Likewise, I'd like you to mention that he was riding wildly, with no regard for the safety of others, including yourself."

The marshal was a professional ass-coverer. There was a way to write police reports, a language built from legal maneuvering and prediction of court challenges. Little things like that went a long way. "Of course. Anything else?"

"Jim Bullard is copping to the attempted murder of a police detective and a federal agent, as well as the murders of Roger Gladwell, Omar Rivera, and Carlos Doka. He claims that Kelan Doka was the ringleader, but he makes no mention of Hotah Shaw."

"He was the fourth Yavapai. Jim's protecting him because Hotah got away. He must have left the scene before Ray and I came in."

Boyd twisted his lips as if Maxim wasn't getting the message. "And neither you nor Agent Garcia ever personally witnessed Shaw at the scene?"

"Diego did, sir. And Kayda Garnett was with them."

"Diego." The marshal almost spat out the word. Maxim knew it was because he was a variable the marshal's office couldn't control. Organized outlaws like Gaston made deals with the police. Diego de la Torre followed his own path. "Diego may have been confused about who or what he saw. I've spoken to Ms. Garnett today and she claims Mr. Shaw was never there."

"She said that?"

Boyd's blue eyes were sharp. They remained affixed on Maxim as the marshal nodded his head. "Kelan Doka, Jim

Bullard, and Yas Harjo—those were the last of the mercenaries. Since the other two were found dead at the scene, we are relying on Bullard for reporting the actions of their outfit, which he is happy to do. Additionally, the Yavapai-Prescott Tribal Police Department claims that, under guidelines from our office and the FBI, they detained Mr. Shaw on the reservation last night. He'd been involved in a bar fight. There were witnesses."

"He wasn't there," protested Maxim. "What time did that happen?"

"Shortly after Sergeant Hitchens left the reservation. Well before the events of the bust."

"They're lying." The detective didn't care what the corrupt reservation police claimed. He believed Diego. He trusted Diego.

"This is about what we're able to prove," said the marshal.

"What about the Sycamore Lodge attack? There were three men: two shooters and a driver. Kelan may have orchestrated that plan but he was a bystander."

"Bullard claims to have been the driver. The van allows access between the front seats and the back. Did you actually see a third man behind the wheel?"

Maxim shifted uncomfortably in his chair.

"Detective, there is no room in your report for controversy. We can indict the individuals involved in this incident, not the entire Yavapai tribe. Kayda is being treated as a victim in all this. She is being held up as a hero to her people. She has their support, and in turn, she gives us their unified cooperation."

"So this is about PR," he said incredulously. "We're going to let a murderer go free to play nice with the Yavapai."

Marshal Boyd's face tightened and flushed with color. His next words were firm. Precise. "Yas Harjo's boot is the only physical evidence that ties any of the mercenaries to the scene. Jim's testimony and Ms. Garnett's witness give us solid cases, but we have nothing to arrest Hotah Shaw for. I am sorry, Detective, but dragging this out is the wrong course of action. Jim's public statement about the Yavapai killing their own is vitally important to the health of this and neighboring communities. Ms. Garnett's support of the Sanctuary Marshal's Office will be invaluable in preventing any slanted media coverage claiming we are in league with the Seventh Sons."

The detective continued grinding his teeth. He couldn't believe what he was hearing.

"Besides," said the marshal, showing that he still had more to offer, "this knife cuts both ways."

"Meaning?"

"It means we want a clean resolution to this. We are treating Ms. Garnett as a victim of abduction. Of course, we can't really say for sure what she was doing there, but I don't think she was involved. Neither do you."

"I'm beginning to change my mind."

"Regardless, we have the same problem with your friend, Diego de la Torre. Forgiving his history of being prone to rash actions, the marshal's office is painting his involvement at the scene as purely innocent. Can you honestly tell me you believe that to be the truth?"

The detective bit his lip. Boyd was threatening to arrest Diego for his vigilante actions. He was showing him the good guys benefited from selective prosecution as well.

Boyd continued. "There is also the matter of why you and Agent Garcia moved in to the property in the first place. Your surveillance uncovered a man sneaking onto the property. A West Wind..." The marshal glanced at the monitor again to search for a last name. Maxim knew it wasn't there. He didn't think the Apache had one. Boyd shook his head and dropped the detail. "He was also nowhere to be found during the bust. You can understand the sensitivity of mentioning that a member of the Seventh Sons Motorcycle Club was present. Seeing as how we have no plans to prosecute him, and seeing as how he has an alibi at Sycamore Lodge last night, I'd like you to reevaluate your report. Perhaps it was one of the Yavapai that you saw patrolling the complex instead. That would make for a cleaner package."

Maxim sighed. He didn't mind the politicking sometimes. As long as he wasn't managing it, he understood the need for it. In truth, he was pleased the local tabloid media wouldn't have ammunition to claim he was on the motorcycle club's payroll again. Boyd protected the entire department as well as himself. But letting Hotah get away—even if he was going to anyway—deflated Maxim.

But the detective was done fighting. He had to admit, losing Hotah made the rest of their case bulletproof. Maxim grumbled in half-hearted complaint and nodded to the marshal. "Give me a couple hours," he said.

The marshal was going to say something, but his phone rang. It was the loud, jarring tone of old-school landlines. It cut their conversation off, and Maxim was relieved for that. Most of all, it was someone else's problem. He rose to his feet and headed out the door, glancing back in case the marshal wanted to stop him. Boyd simply nodded and picked up the receiver.

Maxim approached his desk but didn't sit. He took in the view of the large office. Hitchens glanced his way but knew better than to ask. Cole, also, was somewhere around, probably out on patrol. The men had come in first thing in the morning, just as they'd said they would. There was no need for a raid but there was still plenty to do. The station always buzzed after big busts like these.

Gutierrez had worked all night and was refilling a cup of coffee at the empty desk Ray had used. He kept his head down and didn't say anything. Maxim would need to talk to him. Tell him the slow police response wasn't his fault. Nothing bad had come from their failure to detain Sergio on the highway. But the rookie was a good officer. Not really a rookie anymore. He knew this wasn't about blame, just brotherhood. Emotional support for everyone. They were bound by duty, bound by blood, because it could have been any of them that had taken a bullet the night before.

And tomorrow night, it would be the same thing all over again.

"Detective," called the marshal, standing outside his

office. His face was crestfallen. None of the pomp from moments before lingered. "I just heard from the hospital. Maybe you should sit down."

Chapter 66

Kayda Garnett stood in the courtyard of the new casino, just under the Jewel of Prescott. She thought the iconic statue of the hand gripping the moon was the best place to present herself to the tribe. It, like her, was the symbol of something new. It was also the symbol for painful growth. The statue where her brother had been displayed to enrage the tribe would forever have its own legend.

The tribe braved the hot sun to see the young girl, the hero of the Yavapai. They lined up along the walkway and took turns, offering consolation and gifts. It was the way of her people. Death was celebrated when it brought pride. When that failed, it was up to the family to right wrongs. Once again, the reservation found themselves at ground zero for a scandal, and once again they needed someone to protect them.

In one short day, Kayda had guaranteed their future safety.

Kayda had needed the truth about her brother to come

out. It was the only way to address it, like a rot that had set in, placed under the harsh light of a hospital lamp. That was how to cut it out.

Hotah Shaw stood beside her, his muscles glistening in the fine mist that sprayed over the garden to combat the daytime heat. He didn't have a shirt on, to show off his battle scars from the night before. Slashes across his chest and arms, bite marks taken when he was in his wolfskin, had only partially healed. He would need to wait another two weeks to fully recover. It was yet another lesson for him and the people.

He wore the silent vigilance of a bodyguard, but the wolf was much more than that. He was a carryover from the old way—a consistent, if shaky, figure that the people could look to. It was his word, more than anything, that had put Kayda where she was. After Hotah had been led astray by Kelan, he desperately wanted penance.

He also wanted to stay out of prison.

Kayda glanced past the crowd, at one of the police cars set up on the perimeter. Officer Chuck Winston leaned against his cruiser, a look of nervous discomfort on his face. Kayda's first reaction had been to take revenge against the man who had abandoned her in the desert. But like Hotah, Chuck had only been following the leadership of her brother. There was more at stake than the personal affronts between them. The Yavapai were small and dwindling. The police were a valuable asset to her. Without their shared strength, they wouldn't be able to fight the coming future.

The two men were just soldiers. Now they served a

different captain and would do as Kayda wished. That protected them from outsiders—from Maxim, Diego, and the Seventh Sons.

Kayda shook some more hands. She smiled. She nodded. She even managed a laugh here and there. None of it was an act. For the first time, she truly felt the camaraderie of her people. She felt that she had a purpose. A place. It was only too bad that her *pahmi* couldn't see this.

Wicasa hadn't come out. He hadn't been able to. A combination of health and the shame of his two grandsons took their toll on him. Still, when Kayda had been alone with him, he couldn't hide how proud he was of her. His spirit had always propped hers up. This morning he had reminded her that the Yavapai tribe was the first to ever designate a woman chieftess, generations ago. Kayda balked at his high aspirations. But sitting here, looking at the faces of her people, she began to think it wasn't so crazy.

And just as her *pahmi* had been her crutch when she was weakest, she would stand by his side now. She would make him stronger.

Next in line was a grizzled old woman. Even though the wrinkles were more cracked and numerous, Kayda was surprised that she recognized the old hag. Back when Kayda was a child, she'd always been scared of the crone. It surprised her the woman was still alive, but even more so just how small and unimposing she looked now.

The elderly woman was hunched over and brittle. She smelled like she hadn't bathed in weeks, but the odor could have been from the noxious remedies she oft prepared. The woman took measured steps as she approached and held up a small knife.

Hotah stepped forward menacingly.

"No, it's okay," said Kayda, speaking gently but with conviction. Hotah turned to warn her. She nodded her head to the side curtly. Hotah Shaw stiffened. He kept his eyes on the woman, and wordlessly backed away.

The small blade was a tool more than it was a weapon. It was short and sharp, like something her *pahmi* would use for food preparation. It was carved from bone and wrapped with reeds. It was a ceremonial artifact.

Kayda accepted the gift and was startled to see it wet with blood. Rather than let her shock be apparent, she displayed her first fake smile of the day.

"*Wihanmuha*," said the crone.

The young girl furrowed her brow at the archaic dialect. It sounded like their language, but it didn't mean anything. It was gibberish.

"*Wihanmuha*," repeated the woman, taking the hand that held the dagger into both of hers. The old lady squeezed and Kayda felt a pinch in her palm. She tensed and realized her palm was bleeding.

The bone knife had a spur built into the handle. It stabbed those who clutched it. Kayda studied the bone and wondered how much blood it had spilled in its time, then checked the old lady's hand. Countless scars, pock marks, dotted her ragged palm.

The old lady smiled a toothless grin. "Moonwitch."

She had heard that before. An agent of the moon. A

guide to her people, she would light their prey but also shine on the misdeeds of the hunters. Witches were always born with new moons.

Kayda exchanged a glance with Hotah, who wore a darkened expression. Then the old lady kissed Kayda's palm and receded into the crowd.

"Strength in blood," said Kayda, remembering taking Kelan's blood into her mouth.

Her injuries had not healed. They were still very much there, but muffled, in the background. Kayda's gunshot wound had been stitched up at the hospital. She was advised against leaving, but something had given her the strength to tune out the pain, to function despite the hole. The cracked rib, at one time so restrictive, was now only an afterthought.

She searched the crowd, but the old crone was gone. Kayda knew the woman would be around the reservation, on the outskirts. Hard to find, but close at hand.

Then she heard the piercing cry of a raven. The bird landed just above them, perched on the silver orb. The people murmured in hushed tones that took Kayda off guard.

It wasn't fear; it was respect.

Kayda Garnett realized she could never leave her people. She had never truly left them, not even in New York. She would protect Hotah, but the reign of the wolf was over. For their small people to survive, they would need something more subtle. More cunning.

The bird above cocked its head, keeping its black eyes on the people below.

Chapter 67

A wispy breeze blew over the small crowd of bikers. Short blades of grass shuffled slightly as if massaged by the current. The colorful flowers that dotted the well-kept lawn were out of place, too regular and jarring to be natural, yet they comforted the families of the dead who rested there.

Cemeteries were supposed to be lush and beautiful, but it was just a veneer layered over the dirt and the bones.

Diego remained silent as the priest spoke about the tragedy of losing a young life. Omar would never get the chance to live to his potential, but he would still live in the hearts of those who were close to him, of the few who gathered around his grave. Death was often senseless, he said, blindsiding those who were most invested in life.

What a crock of shit, thought Diego. The gunplay of the last few days had been the direct result of criminal activity. The real tragedy was that kids like Omar were easily sucked into the allure of being an outlaw.

It pained Diego to admit it, but he'd gone along for the same ride. His hesitance didn't excuse it. Only now, after he'd finally had a chance to breathe, did he realize just how far he was willing to go for justice. Diego had almost gone to the other side. He was almost another fond memory in a hole in the ground. That probably would have made most men feel lucky.

The priest's words faded into the background, along with the other monotone comforts people bequeathed to the dead. Omar had been a smart kid who fell for the same trap of invincibility that afflicted all youth. There was nothing else to say.

In the distance, a row of motorcycles lined the field. Parked along the outer fence of the cemetery grounds was a shiny Sanctuary Marshal's Office squad car. Sergeant Hitchens sat inside keeping an eye on the proceedings, making sure there wasn't any trouble. It was a wasted effort. Diego had a sense for things like this, and he knew there'd be peace for a little while.

How long would that last? He had no idea. El Paso was probably pissed about Sergio Lima getting caught. He had proof on him that he was blackmailing an Albuquerque city councilman. Maxim had said the FBI would run with that and try to come out with a Public Corruption win for Raymond Garcia. It signified a possible link to El Paso. Egg on their face. It meant the Seventh Sons lost some leverage and potentially garnered the ire of the Mexican Mafia. Gaston was concerned about future dealings with the Mexicans but was confident that it could be salvaged.

Diego wished them the best but it wasn't his problem anymore.

After the words were said and the coffin lowered into the ground, the workers disbanded. There was no family here, no real friends, and before long only the Seventh Sons remained. Clint was back, fully healed after the transformation the night before. He opened a bottle of Jack Daniels and poured it over the fresh grave. Curtis and Trent stayed close, recalling positive memories of the kid.

It was nice enough, Diego figured, but it was still a funeral.

"I'm just glad you're not lying next to him," said West Wind. His tough features and partially shaved head made the sentiment sound mushy by comparison, but Diego didn't give him shit for it. Gaston and the others converged on them.

"I don't think I've thanked you for coming for me last night," said Diego. "If you hadn't shown up when you did..."

West Wind shook his head. "It was nothing. I was just helping out a brother." The man's look bore into Diego. It was the sort of earned camaraderie that he'd shared in the service. The Apache hadn't needed to back Diego up. There was every chance they would have been arrested, but West came and he took on Hotah, the most dangerous of the remaining Yavapai. Wolf fights rarely ended in death because of their superior constitutions, but if the Apache was to be believed, he had kicked Hotah's ass pretty damn good.

Gaston put a hand on each of their shoulders. "We need to move past Omar," he said. "We need to focus on who's left. El Paso's big, and if they intend to take us on, we'll need a unified front."

The other Sons huddled closer, nodding in affirmation. Diego only sighed.

"I'm done."

Diego didn't expect stunned silence. By the looks on their faces, his brothers already knew. They wouldn't try to stop him. Diego had once again proved that he wasn't afraid of the guns. He just wasn't like them, and it wasn't because they were wolves. Diego was a loner, but he wasn't really a rebel. He didn't shun authority for the sake of it. And he didn't want to make a living by stepping on the backs of others.

The Sons were good guys overall, but sometimes they could be real assholes.

The MC talked a little more and split up. Clint proposed plans for the night: a wake at Sycamore Lodge. Eventually, Diego broke off and headed to his Scrambler. As he sat on his bike and pulled on his riding gloves, Gaston caught him.

"You sure about this?" he asked, at a loss for saying anything of substance. Diego nodded, not meeting the man's gaze. "Where will you go?"

"I have a feeling I'll be around Sanctuary for a while. My lease isn't up for a few more months, so there's that."

Gaston chuckled. Diego wondered if the big man thought he'd change his mind and show up at the clubhouse one day. Hell, even Diego didn't know. The last couple of years had seen so many changes in his life already—he wasn't sure where he was supposed to land.

"I'll figure it out," said Diego, talking more to himself. "I've always kind of had to find my own road."

The men shook hands and Diego rode straight for the Interstate. He had a feeling he was going for a long, long ride.

Chapter 68

The bottle wheezed as Maxim squeezed out the last of the lighter fluid. He tossed the empty plastic into the pit with the rest of the sodden content. There wasn't a lot of time left. The sun was going down and the camera on his phone wasn't great in lowlight. Plus, the detective didn't want to give himself a chance to change his mind.

He struck a wooden match and tossed it in, watching the recording video on the screen of his cell phone. Flames shot high into the air, and Maxim backed up during the initial burn.

This would have been a good time to have a cigar, he realized.

Maxim had never really smoked. A few here or there casually. A cigar when someone had a baby. Or when somebody died.

Raymond Garcia had taken a turn for the worse earlier in the day. His blood loss had led to complications, and the agent had a stroke. It was a delicate situation for a while, but the marshal's office had just gotten word that Ray succumbed to his injuries. He had gone into a coma and then, two hours later, went brain-dead.

Maxim didn't have a cigar, but he had a half-full bottle of Makers 46. He took a swig and did his best to hold his camera hand steady.

"Was Ray more right about me than I was about him?"

It was a stupid question because Maxim had been off base about the FBI agent. Garcia had proven to be a reputable guy. A man who had immersed himself in the depths of criminal behavior time and time again yet emerged as a straight shooter. He'd moved up the ranks and genuinely wanted to make this a better country.

It kind of put Maxim's small-town vigil to shame.

Detective Maxim Dwyer watched the stacks of twenty-dollar bills darken and curl in on themselves. The fire had a mesmerizing effect. It was an agent of freedom. A burden reduced to wisps and ashes.

Raymond Garcia was right about the corrupting effects of money and power. Even though Maxim wasn't bought and paid for, he had gotten too close. He had allowed himself a freebie, paid for a down payment on a silver TT, bribed a federal analyst, and stashed the rest of the briefcase full of money away for a rainy day.

Maxim knew he was a good person, but what other people thought mattered. Friends and enemies alike needed to see who he was.

He stopped the recording once the damage was done.

The flames and smoke would linger for a while. Maxim was fine with that. It gave him something to watch as he drank.

Soon, after the scope of what he'd done fully settled in, Maxim Dwyer sent the video to Gaston with a short text message.

"This is who I am."

-Finn

Read Next:
The Green Children
Sycamore Moon Book Three

Continue the Sycamore Moon series
where Domino Finn books are sold.

DominoFinn.com

Be notified when new Domino Finn
stories are released, right to your inbox.
Sign up at the website and never miss another book.

Connect

If you're reading this, it means you demand more from your urban fantasy. Dark forest monsters are good for a scare, but they're nothing without a layered cast of characters and realistic plot drivers. *Sycamore Moon* is my stab at a cut above the rest: driving mystery, true friends banding against impossible odds, and themes that hopefully make you put the book down and ponder, if even for only a minute.

My writing process demands quality control at every step of development. I hope you agree *Sycamore Moon* is the premium product I strive to make it. Unfortunately, doubling down on originality and quality in an on-demand world has drawbacks. It's simply not possible for me to get you a brand-new novel every month or two. The process takes time.

That's where you come in. Together we can build a better book.
All you need to do is connect.

- Join the Outlaw Underground, our private Facebook group. (www.facebook.com/groups/dominofinnfans/)

- Leave an all-too-important review where you bought the book. Each one helps more than you know.

- Recommend this book to your friends. Link it on social media.

- Join my reader group newsletter, get a free story, and hear from me only when I have new releases or important news. You'll never miss another launch sale again. (dominofinn.com/newsletter/)

Simple, right? Five minutes of your time makes a world of difference to me, Maxim, and Diego. Thank you for your heartfelt support. I'll keep writing as long as you keep reading.

- Domino Finn

Preview:

The Green Children
Sycamore Moon Book Three

Ongoing lives, no matter how interesting, trended toward routine.

Diego de la Torre's time in Sanctuary had been anything but ordinary. Fistfights, shootouts, wolves, witches—and a body count larger than the eighteen months he'd lived here.

But lately, things for Diego had been business as usual. The tow business, specifically. He was now a biker-turned-blue-collar. A clock-puncher.

Diego's company truck rumbled along Interstate 40 on the way to another suit with a flat tire. His third job this year wasn't the most glamorous, but it wasn't the crappiest either. It was honest work, dealing only in breakdowns and emergencies. None of the scams the tow companies in Detroit pulled that preyed on hardworking people. Diego didn't do cold tows. The open Arizona land had no demand for them. There was something to be said for that.

The open road appealed to him too, but it wasn't enough.

Driving a rig was simply too low key. Sure, there were errant threats from disgruntled drivers and arguments over distance and money, but those were nothing more than bluster. There was no real danger anymore. That fact never stopped Diego from secretly hoping the next call would be the one where somebody threw a punch or pulled a knife.

Hey, there was nothing wrong with a respectable disagreement once in a while.

But Diego considered the bright side. It was a beautiful spring. It was a legal paycheck. He hadn't been shot at in nine months. Life always offered the hope of something more, with the caveat that the best of times were often the most bland.

The old days he longed for... They weren't bland. An ex-service man, an ex-biker outlaw—Diego had lots of stories. He wanted to regain that source of adrenaline. Changing tires and charging batteries wasn't cutting it.

So when a frantic woman lunged into the highway in front of his speeding truck, Diego once again felt that spark.

He jammed the brake pedal to the rubber floor mat. The six tires smoked and scraped against the asphalt, causing the rig to swerve dangerously. By the time it came to a stop, the tow truck took up both westbound lanes.

Luckily, traffic was light this morning on account of it being Easter Monday, the day after the holiday and the cap of a long weekend. No vehicles rear-ended him. Diego swiveled his head searching for the woman.

A fist pounded his window and made him jump. The woman

had somehow circled his truck.

"You've got to help me!" she screamed. "Help!"

Again Diego scanned the area. The dense forest on either side of the highway cut down visibility, but aside from the crazy woman in the middle of the Interstate, nothing appeared amiss. She yelled again to get his attention.

"All right. All right," he said, shifting his rig into reverse. He backed up over the wide shoulder and didn't stop till his back wheels were in the dirt. It wasn't a graceful parking job, but it wouldn't cause any accidents.

"What the hell do you think you're doing?" he demanded as he kicked open his door. The woman clutched at him like glue.

"My daughter," she rasped. "My eight-year-old daughter is out here."

And then Diego immediately understood the mad look in the woman's eyes, the shimmer of sweat on her skin despite the crisp breeze. She wasn't crazy. She wasn't a tweaker. She was a mother living her worst nightmare.

"Slow down," he said, grabbing the woman by the shoulders. She was slender. Thin nose, narrow lips—everything about her was fragile except for her wide, gaping eyes.

She shook against his grasp. Her long brown hair, almost black, swung wildly as he held her.

"You need to calm down for a second," urged Diego. "Look at me."

"She's out here."

"Look at me."

She turned to him and brushed the hair from her face. Her light-brown eyes met his and relaxed for a moment. He glimpsed them in their normal state, at ease, welcoming. Kind. The woman had a natural beauty that was elegant and soft.

"What happened to your daughter?"

She took a breath. "We were hiking in the woods. Just ten minutes ago."

"Where?"

"Up there," she sputtered, pointing north to the trees. Besides the access road, the area was heavily wooded. The Sycamore forest, they called it.

"She came to the highway?"

The woman became exasperated again. "I don't know."

Diego searched up and down the 40. The only clear sight lines were along the road. He hadn't seen any pedestrians before pulling over. If the little girl was only a few minutes away, she wasn't on the street.

"Okay," he said, grabbing the woman's head to lock into her eyes again. "Don't worry. We'll find her." She returned a slight nod.

The biker climbed into his truck and reached for the CB.

"Hey, Harry. You there?"

It took a second to raise the man, but he answered.

"Diego? What's it look like?"

"Uh, I'm not there yet. I might be a little late."

Harry's voice immediately grew coarse. "You better not be. Not again."

"I'm serious, Harry. Call up Chuck to cover for me."

"I'm not gonna call Chuck 'cause I've got you."

Diego hissed. "There's a missing kid out here. This is an emergency."

"It's always an emergency with you, Diego. Can't you—"

The biker switched off the radio. He didn't have time to deal with his boss.

"Take me to where you last saw her," said Diego with comforting confidence.

The woman smiled at him. There was something alluring about a smile from a stranger. Not a business smile like a cashier might flash, but an earnest one from the heart. Maybe the appeal was in what came next. In the desire to get to know the person better. In the possibilities ahead.

Diego remembered that smile because he realized he might never see it again.

Pick up THE GREEN CHILDREN
where Domino Finn books are sold

Also by Domino Finn

About the Author

Domino Finn is an award-winning game industry veteran, a media rebel, and a werewolf junkie. As a grizzled author of urban fantasy and litRPG, his stories are equal parts spit, beer, and blood, and are notable for treating weighty issues with a supernatural veneer. If Domino has one rallying cry for the world, it's that fantasy is serious business.

Take a stand at DominoFinn.com